COSMIC FEVER

BLISS IS JUST ONE PARTICLE AWAY

A NOVEL

ERIC J. ADAMS

Black Rose Writing | Texas

ISBN: 978-1-68433-330-1
PUBLISHED BY BLACK ROSE WRITING
www.blackrosewriting.com

Printed in the United States of America
Suggested Retail Price (SRP) $19.95

Cosmic Fever is printed in Calluna

Thanks to all the friends and colleagues who helped make this fable a little wiser and richer, among them Nancy Ryan, Peter Hale, Rahul Prasad, Joe Gerardi, Bethany Richardson, Eric Elfman, and David Miller. To my valiant sons Jesse and Gabriel, my jewel of a partner, Kathleen. To my mother, the reigning queen of spun tales. To Julie Mark Cohen for her heroic editing. And to the all the poets, philosophers, scientists, lovers, and dreamers who steadfastly believe that the source is a single well, deep and ample enough for us all.

But leave the wise to wrangle, and with Me,
the quarrel of the universe let be.
And, in some corner of the hubbub couched,
make game of that which makes as much of Thee.

—Omar Khayyam, Rubaiyat 45

COSMIC FEVER

BOOK I

"Something unknown is doing we don't know what."
—Sir Arthur Eddington

ONE

Ethan Weiner-Gluckstein, Ph.D., cleared the dread from his throat and counted less than a dozen reporters and bloggers assembled for what was the most significant scientific announcement in half a century, maybe longer. Certainly since Einstein's Theory of Relativity. Or the discovery of wispy subatomic particles. Or the first hint of cosmic inflation. From his perch behind the lectern in the campus auditorium of the Stanford Linear Accelerator Center, Ethan thanked the Lord above that the University's president wasn't on hand to see how utterly he had failed.

Ethan pressed his quivering lips to the microphone. "Good morning, everyone. Testing one, two. Thanks again for coming. My apologies. We'll get started shortly. Bear with me. We're waiting on MSNBC, ABC, and Fox. Considering the urgent developments in Pakistan…"

Ethan's voice trailed to a mumble. He had hoped for an auditorium packed with scores of journalists jockeying to ask questions, faculty members on hand to cheer the crowning achievement, and over-excited grad students capturing video on their smartphones upon the realization they were witnessing momentous history. Instead, the lecture hall was peppered with a handful of mostly male scientific journal stringers and row upon row of empty red plastic seats. Before today, he could think of nothing more terrifying than speaking before a crowded room. Now he stumbled upon something worse—speaking before a near empty one. Ethan berated himself for not arranging a university film crew beforehand, but he was counting on the major outlets to capture the excitement with their oversized cameras and furry microphones. Once again with more gusto than usual, he muttered the mantra of his life: *What did I do wrong?*

His lips grazed the microphone, and a shock of static electricity zapped

1

away the few molecules of self-confidence that remained. "For those of you kind enough to arrive on time, a big thanks. Soon, I promise."

Whenever he felt this way, Ethan reminded himself that in a universe without edge you're always in the middle but never in the center. Minutes passed, and not a straggler wandered in. Clearly, either developments in Pakistan had escalated to crisis proportions or the major news media had chosen to shun today's press conference.

Ethan spotted his most promising graduate assistant, the raven-haired beauty Shivana Farooq. She stood proudly in the back of the room wearing a perpetual smile of eagerness, though her prodigious greeting talents were wasted on all the journalists and fellow researchers who hadn't bothered to come. He waved her forward for a quick conference. Shivana clicked off her high heel shoes and picked up the pace until she arrived at the podium.

"Shivana, are you sure the press announcements went out?"

"Email, Facebook, Twitter. Even phone calls," she said in a Persian accent that sent Ethan to that nearest of celestial bodies, the moon.

"What happened?" he wondered.

Shivana shrugged her shoulders. "It's beyond me. I may come from a repressive culture but people in my homeland, even the extremist dogs, respond to invitations with sincerity."

Just when Ethan thought the situation could not get worse, the rear doors swung open wide. University President Randall Mahoney barreled in, framed in the otherworldly glow of the hallway backlighting. The moose of a man surveyed the room and dropped his massive jaw at the sea of emptiness. Followed by his Yes-People entourage, he mounted the stage like the stag that he was.

"Where the hell is everybody?" he asked Ethan.

"Who?"

"The important people, that's who."

"Shivana and I called all the media outlets. We worked all day on the release."

Mahoney scanned the auditorium with his trademark derision. "Fooled me."

"Sir, for an event like this we could have used weeks of prep not merely 24 hours."

"You're not thinking strategically, Ethan, that's your problem. If I had given you weeks we couldn't have scooped CERN, now could we? One day is time enough. But this kindergarten bullshit...this is ridiculous."

Ethan tried to conjure what he might have done better to rally the media. He couldn't envision a thing. Oddly, he felt slightly pleased about the disaster. Even though he and scores of Stanford physicists had worked on the project, the majority of the breakthroughs had been made by colleagues toiling away at the European Organization of Nuclear Research, or CERN, as the acronym plays in French. The august organization had scheduled their announcement for tomorrow, and the physics world was abuzz with anticipation.

"The announcement rightfully belongs to the Europeans," said Ethan with a serving of gumption that surprised himself.

"Screw the Europeans. They've been screwing us long enough. They got the Higgs boson, what more do they want? Greedy bastards."

Ethan resisted the urge to flee. "We could cancel," said Ethan.

"Cancel my ass," said Mahoney. "We're not blowing this opportunity. You're going to go out there and sell this like nuclear war. Screw this up, Ethan, and you'll find yourself..." the man searched the dark recesses of his mind for the scariest, meanest threat he could conjure..."you'll find yourself teaching undergrads."

The thought didn't displease Ethan. In fact, he found it quite reassuring. But maybe he was reading the threat incorrectly. He masked it well, but certain social conventions and non-verbal cues eluded him.

Mahoney turned to Shivana. "And what's your name again?"

"Shivana."

"Shivana. Let me guess...post-grad, foreign-born, brilliant, talented, and ambitious beyond belief. And pretty doesn't hurt. Well, let me tell you how things work in these neck of the woods. If this announcement fails to generate heat, I'm sure it wouldn't be difficult to find a few inconsistencies in your visa application. Comprende?"

"Yes, sir."

Mahoney took a seat in the wings. He propped his feet up on the chair in front of him to watch the execution unfold, a bag of popcorn the only missing prop. Ethan endured another bite from the microphone. "Testing, one, two, three."

Ethan straightened his stance, regained his *persona academia* and gathered his wits the best he could to talk about the subject he loved more than anything in the world. The time had come, the moment was now to announce to the world the brilliant theory that would change everything.

Shivana cupped her delicate hand to whisper into Ethan's ear. "You can do it!"

She was right, Ethan thought. What choice did he have but to plunge? Self-defeating mantra be damned. You can change a mantra, right? Destiny belongs to the individual, not the universe. *We are what we choose.* Couldn't that be a new mantra? At least that's how Ethan decided to delude himself for this momentous occasion. He stepped up to the shock of the microphone, but this time it didn't faze him.

"Ladies and gentlemen, colleagues and members of the press, as you know, Albert Einstein spent the last decades of his life searching for a unified field theory – a theory that encapsulates the four incongruous forces that govern both astrophysics and quantum physics —*gravity, electromagnetism,* and the quantum *strong* and *weak* forces. A Theory of Everything. Along with countless scientists, mathematicians, philosophers and prophets before and after him, Einstein envisioned a single, beautiful harmonized equation that describes the universe at the moment of its creation and during its last death throes. An equation that reveals the mysteries of the cosmos from its smallest strings to its largest galaxies – across this universe and all the universes beyond ours, the entire conceivable multiverse represented in one elegant organizing principle, consolidating every conceivable push and pull on the strings of time and space. Einstein's dream, Hawking's mystery, Feynman's conundrum. The mystic's prophecies all folded into one. The DNA of the universe revealed. The very finger of God.

"Well, my colleagues, I am thrilled and honored to tell you...that day has arrived."

TWO

Dr. Omar Farooq pressed his brown eye through the eternally shuttered mini blinds. One cannot flash too much dark visage in this city, in this corner of the world, not with Palestinian blood running through your veins. And in this business one can't be careful enough. With the regular staff off for the day at the Palo Alto clinic and no patients skulking about, Omar felt free to select the satellite transmission of his choice, Al Jazeera and its 24-hour coverage of the conflict in Afghanistan, the send up in Pakistan, the backlash in Iran, and non-stop coverage of the calamity that was Israel.

He removed his Italian leather shoes and, as habit goes, unfurled his *sajada* onto the floor. Omar dropped down to kiss the faded stains of his grandfather's blood. Omar had worn two holes in the prayer rug where his knees pressed the earth to praise God five times daily. He had shed countless tears on each stitch of modest embroidery tracing the rug's edge in its never-ending pattern consecrating God's infinite wisdom and His universe without end. How many times had Omar counted the fringes of this mat, frayed now to the nubs?

As a boy, the carpet had softened for him the hard rock of the Jabalia Refugee Camp, with its attack of green Israeli uniforms and tanks of dust. The sajada traveled with Omar and his growing beard to undergraduate studies at Tehran University where Renaissance domes stood side-by-side with the fanciful minarets of prayer's call. Here he learned to love books of the West and the faith of the East with equal ardor. The floor of God cushioned his loneliness during medical training in Italy at Turin. During his residency in Las Vegas, it provided a shield against the double-edged sword of America's crass materialism and spiritual paucity. And now in the Valley of Silicon, it brought solace to his life in exile. Adherents to other religions may require gilded edifices or graven images, but a proper Muslim needs only a carpet on which to pray and pure intent. Not always in possession of the latter, Omar was thankful for the former as he began the incantation inscribed on his heart.

AshHadu An La Ilaha Il-lallah, Wa Ash hadu Anna Muhammadar Rasul-allah.

I bear witness that there is no deity but Allah and I bear witness that Muhammad is His Messenger.

His calming prostrations were interrupted by an insistent rap on the back door. He rose quickly, pressed an ear to the door and paused for clues.

"Who is it?" he asked.

"It's me," said a female whisperer.

"Password?"

"Foxtrot."

"Two minutes."

Actually two minutes and 38 seconds. Omar returned to the floor and hurried through the remainder of his prayers at a pace not pleasing before the eyes of Allah. He rolled up the sajada and kissed it for the 24,314th time. His wife Shivana, the promising scientist-in-training at Stanford, had taught him well how to count.

"Hurry," said the female voice.

Allah, forgive me my sins. He unbolted the locks and opened the door on a striking blonde with freckled alabaster skin balancing effortlessly on four-inch stiletto heels. Omar's heart double-timed on her Western beauty. "Come in."

She glanced left and right. "No one here, I hope."

"Not a soul," said Omar.

"Because if I get caught, there's hell to pay. And I mean that literally."

"Absolutely certain."

Sandra Lee Spridgen peeked around the corner just to make sure. Then she unhitched the top button of Omar's cotton shirt and fell into his arms.

"Oh, Omar, I can't take him anymore," she lamented.

As if on a chariot with sword drawn, Omar reared to protect his dove. "I am here for you, eternally."

"Do you know what he did today?"

"Tell me, my lamb."

"The gay porn websites, the moisturizer stains on the sheets. I feel violated, and he isn't even touching me."

Sandra Lee buried her nose in Omar's furry chest for a direct channel to the source of his ardor. Omar gladly enveloped her with all the empathy she deserved. "Do not despair, the non-believers wallow in their own excrement."

"Oh, please, cut the Jihad crap. Take me."

Sandra Lee made herself available for his advance, but Omar hesitated, for there were principles higher than love. "Not in this room," he stuttered.

"Why not?"

"I am forbidden from defiling where I pray."

She rolled her eyes. "What's prayer got to do with a thing like this?"

"Everything," he said.

"Well, can I smoke in here at least?"

"It violates health regulations."

"Really? You're just like him. Only straight." Sandra Lee grabbed her handbag and started toward the door.

"Wait, my star! Don't go."

Sandra Lee turned, and Omar saw the little girl disappointment in her face. "What?"

"I beg of you. Anything you desire."

"*Anything?*"

"Anything."

"Then talk to me."

Omar was afraid she might say that. "Talk to you. Right here?"

"Right here."

"As you wish."

Omar shut his eyes and reached deep into his heart for the inspiration of Rumi and Hafiz and all great Sufi poets residing in timeless splendor.

"Your eyes are the translucent gates of heaven open for poor souls like me to glimpse the eternal."

Sandra Lee leaned into him and offered him her neck. "That's more like it."

Omar drank her scent madly and cursed himself for defiling a poetic tradition designed to praise God in ecstasy. But what could he do? "Your lips praise the mysteries of the cosmos in a lyric that pleases the ears of angels."

Sandra twirled toward the waiting room couch. Unzip went the knee-high stiletto boots.

"Your ample breasts are compared to the mountains of Jordan, and the fragrance of your skin is as the August oasis."

"More, more!" she squealed.

"The winds sing your name as they kiss the oceans. Your desire is the breath that wild wolves crave in the desert night."

"Take me on the caravan."

"Your vagina is the first fig of late harvest burst open to pleasure the world with succulence and flavor."

"Oh, God, yes!" Sandra spread her fruit and planted her blood red fingertips deep into Omar's buttock, drawing his loins toward her in a mad race to the mountaintop.

Omar implored Allah—not for intercession, for Muslims are forbidden from requesting divine intervention—but for will power. Try as he might, Omar could not muster the fortitude to resist the weekly rendezvous with Sandra Lee. He knew of no power he might summon to oppose her tanned thighs glistening beneath tendrils of flaxen hair, her eyes the blue of Aqaba, her mound of Venus as smooth as the deserts of Arabia.

He was no more capable of resisting her today than he was four months, 13 days, and four hours ago when the couple first connected on Jdate.com *where tens of thousands of Jewish singles interact every day!* Both were attempting to court the forbidden.

Sandra Lee's self-penned online bio had read thus:

Jew-at-heart blonde seeks relationship to explore our shared spirituality in intimate settings. I love shopping malls, men with hairy chests, non-vegetarians and faraway motels. Ballroom all the way. Mama's boys need not apply.

The listing leapt at Omar like a gazelle. He mistook *Jew-at-heart* as to mean *true believer,* precisely his romantic prey. He ate meat, bristled with hair, and harbored a quaint fondness for faraway motels. And cha-cha-cha? Quite well, thank you, but only within the confines of a very small patch of floor, as when would he ever have the opportunity to practice outside his shuttered bedroom? *Blonde* didn't hurt either. So exotic.

His return salvo:

Semitic lover will transport you on carpets of fire to a paradise where love and God share an embrace and the worlds below twinkle with the lights of righteous lovers everywhere. Tango for two.

Sandra Lee assumed *Semitic* to mean *Jewish*, which, of course, it does. But as Omar explained on the starchy motel sheets after their first shared afternoon, it also describes a wide swath of peoples loosely connected by ancestry dating back to Noah's son Shem and to every civilization in western Asia with linguistic roots in the Afro-Asian family of languages from Maltese to Ethiopian, and naturally to Arabic and Hebrew in all their colorful variations.

The first rendezvous had occurred in an Applebee's in the agricultural town of Gilroy, the garlic capital of the world, an hour's drive from Palo Alto. After the non-Jew disappointment of the initial sighting, each saw in the other something not half bad, fairly nice if truth be told. Over her bacon burger, Sandra smelled the pheromones of a real man, unlike her husband. And Omar couldn't take his eyes off the shapely infidel. They dispensed quickly with the niceties and climbed over the thinning row of Oleander that separated the restaurant's parking lot from the extremely affordable Days Inn next door. It's been the same weekly garlic-immersed routine since then. Until today when Sandra insisted upon coming to the clinic against Omar's wishes.

If it were up to Omar, if he had the moral fortitude for which he pleaded every day, he would never see her again. *Praise Allah, make this the last time, give me the strength to refuse the beguile of this delicacy of a female when again she calls.* But all the prayers from here to Mecca were useless. A dog only knows one way to eat.

Omar snapped off his belt like a horse trainer and tossed it aside. His erection grew ardent as they fell onto the waiting room couch.

"My dark prince!" she squealed.

His pants dropped like a peace talk, and he pulled off his shirt in one violent motion. Omar settled firmly on top of Sandra as prescribed by Sharia law, but what attempt at righteous action could save him now?

Forgive my heart of weakness, Allah. And with these words on his wicked lips, Omar pressed into Sandra Lee's flesh with a passion reserved rightly for the Good Name only. A perpetual sin of commission, that's what this was. With every kiss of her American whiteness and each whiff of her shaved armpit, he ached with untold regret.

"Yes, yes!" she shouted.

Such is the penalty reserved for slaves of lust. Omar consumed Sandra Lee knowing full well that cavorting in such a *haram* manner, each sigh from that woman, every hump and heave further ensured the damnation of his soul. *Flog me until I bleed.*

Since Omar had surely lost any chance of entering heaven, he felt it at least his obligation to fully satisfy her. Worse, he did so with the understanding that manly pride drove his action. Worse still, he knew he was certain to return to wallow again and again in this ungodliness. And what of his lovely wife, Shivana? *Hell is not hellish enough for the likes of me.*

Sandra neared climax. Omar could tell by the high-pitched chirps she emitted from the back of her throat like the wives in the mountain tents of Sinai when their men rode off to battle.

That's when Omar heard the first gerbilish chants outside.

Omar checked his breath. He lifted his head.

Sandra Lee popped open an eye. "What are you doing?"

Omar cocked an ear. "Shh! Listen."

"I'm *this* close."

He whispered, "They're back."

"Who?"

"*Them.*"

Dr. Omar Farooq solemnly re-belted his pants and found his loafers.

"You're kidding?" Sandra Lee protested.

Omar jumped to peek through the mini blinds.

Outside, the protesters packed tightly, as if for warmth. They carried well-worn signs with graphic images of torn-up fetuses.

Sandra Lee waited until she was decent before chancing a blue eye through the slit of the mini blinds. She spied half the Pro-Life Crusade from her husband's church prancing about across the street like it was a Friday night football game with Crosstown High on the field.

The busybody Bev Gilliam held one placard high that read in black and red letters *Stop Hitler's Holocaust.* The sharp-tongued Cindy Zusin, all sad now that her husband found the courage to leave her endless bickering, waved one reading: *Mommy, Why Do They Want To Kill Me?* Holier-than-thou Jill Ponce-Greene, her two seven-year-old twins in tow, obviously had a direct line to the Almighty because her sign proclaimed, *They Say Choice, God Says Murder!* There were more, at least a dozen protesters Sandra Lee recognized from the church and dozens more she didn't. What else should she expect? Her pastor husband, Harlen, fires off an incendiary sermon on Sunday past, and surely as *Christ* follows *Jesus,* a coffee klatch gathers outside the clinic for a feel-good, pro-life protest.

And look, there were Margie and Dathan Lean fired up as usual. There's some unholy shit going on in that house. And in the back, way back, a freaky purple-haired girl with a toddler on her hip.

Sandra Lee turned to Omar. "Looks different from the other side."

Omar cracked open the blinds a hair wider. "See that woman there with the yellow blouse?"

Sandra Lee recognized her. "Tammy Felix."

"I know that name. She came in here several months ago."

"No way!"

"And that buxom redhead, third from the right?"

"Virginia McMann."

"In here twice in the last two years."

"Get out of town."

"Her daughter, too. Truly. I am in violation of HIPAA policies in sharing this information, but I need you to understand the hypocrisy of your society."

Sandra Lee looked at Dr. Omar, really looked at him. "I'm sorry. You don't deserve this."

"Thank you."

"I mean it."

She gave him a peck on the cheek that reminded Omar why he was crazy for this beauty in the first place. Under the cruel and shallow exterior of this queen hid a walnut of compassion and understanding.

Dr. Omar wrapped his arm around Sandra Lee's shoulder. "We have to get you out of here."

He keyed open an interior door that led to an interior hallway that led to a marijuana clinic owned by an ex-hippie transplant from Marin County

11

for whom abortion rights trumped the risk of lending a spare key to an abortion doctor of Palestinian extraction.

Sandra Lee stopped and turned to Omar with a pout. "But we didn't dance."

"No, we didn't. Next time. Let's hurry."

"Go now," he instructed. "And may Allah be with you."

In Tehran, Omar had studied at the foot of the wise Imam Fazouy, blessed be his name, a beneficent man who held no animosity for the West whatsoever. He had taught Omar and the other fervent students that freedom does not set you free. On the contrary, it entraps you, enslaves you. Freedom renders you weak like a woman and cowardly like a small boy. And worse, it leads you down a narrow unavoidable path of sin en route to a destination of ruin. Engaging in sin, manufacturing and marketing it, and worse collaborating in sin only served to amplify the consequences and speed of the calamity sure to follow, which is why the Great Satan America is to be feared and needs to be destroyed. So said the Imam. This was not dogma but moral certitude, proven by the pages of history. Look to the Romans, the Greeks, and the Hindu apostates to the East for proof. These were human truths that reflected the judgment of God, praise be to Allah, written within the Qur'an and without.

Shunning sin is what sets you free. Omar knew this, naturally, and prayed on it daily. Acting on it was another story altogether. Did not al-Nawawi say that *purity is half the faith*? If submission were as easy in body as it were in mind, there would be no need for prayer, thanks be to Allah for his munificent understanding of human frailty.

He watched Sandra Lee, wife of a preacher, screech away in her Mercedes, and then he bolted shut the door.

The chant grew louder in front. Omar knew well the power of the crowd to foment hatred and quash reasonable thought, having seen it with his own eyes in a different land under different circumstances. Through all his desperation and pain, all he ever wanted was to assist humanity. That's why he had become a doctor, to help people. How he ended up an abortion provider in the vapid United States, he never understood. But did not Abraham's handmaiden Hager say *I have settled some of my family in a barren valley.* Such was the curse of his people.

He spread the mini blind to gaze upon the protesters.

A rock shattered the window. Shards of glass sprayed his face. The crowd cheered the direct hit.

Omar felt a sharp pain on his right cheek, and he touched it instinctively. His finger returned with a drop blood.

This was it. This was the end. He would find his wife Shivana immediately, rescue her from Stanford University and return together to the Middle East, to the insufferable Palestinian territories, if need be. A devout man can endure only so much.

A rapping on the back door caused Omar's tongue to swell with adrenalin. Was it Sandra Lee returning, trapped by the vigilante brothers and sisters of her very own tribe? Or was it a crowd of *them* coming to upend his world forever?

THREE

University presidential threats be damned, Shivana Farooq squealed with delight. To be here, at this moment in time, shoulder to shoulder with *this* pronouncement. Does it get any better than this? Shivana measured the scowl on President Mahoney's face, but she would not entertain the notion of banishment from the Physics Department.

She swept the dark waves of hair from her face and glanced again at the golden watch hanging loosely around her delicate wrist. Still no sign of MSNBC, still no CBS, not even the Science Channel. She took a big gulp and scolded herself for not following up with the 407 invited media guests one last time (a number, she couldn't help but remember because it equaled the sum of the cubes of its digits). And she hated to disappoint Ethan, who was brilliant, and correct at all times in matters of significance (actually 98.667 percent of the time, according to her calculations), and she felt lucky to have a doctoral sponsor such as he.

Here at Stanford, released from the shackles of her past, Shivana was free to pursue her deep desire to explore the mathematical fundamentals of the cosmos, the very essence of the nucleus of the atom and the forces that bound all matter and energy together. What is the origin of the universe? It is not some obtuse image of a stern God perverted by the faiths of mankind. It is a simple, pure equation, a *mathematical equation.*

Shivana loved counting. She counted as colleagues 287 of the most brilliant nuclear physicists ever assembled here at Stanford. She measured to an accuracy of 20,000th of an inch the two miles of the linear accelerator buried ten meters below her feet. She loved nothing more than the poetic equations that gave mankind an understanding of the theories of high-energy, gravity, string, stabilization of moduli, the cosmological constant, mechanisms for inflation, terms for singularity resolution, supersymmetry breaking, topology and changing transitions.

She *adored* black hole physics.

The more numbers, the better, for counting required exactitude and precision. Counting shielded Shivana from the half-lies and hypocrisies of the creed that had shaped her, or misshaped her, as the case may be. Shivana recounted with immeasurable pleasure the 218 days since her departure from Tehran. The 1,242 days since she last endured the burqa's sweat of humiliation from the inside, a perspective she wished on nobody, her husband included. She felt so alive in these hallowed halls, this empirical sanctuary free of narrow-minded thinking and the provincial punishments of her family, clan, heritage. All of which added up to the largest and most pleasurable number of all—a hundred million light years removed from that black hole of history from whence she came.

She had to work hard to contain her excitement as Ethan continued from the podium of the Stanford auditorium. The *Stanford auditorium*, imagine that!

Ethan found a rhythm: "After four years of intensive collaboration, the International Mathematical Union has announced that 181 top mathematicians and computer scientists from the U.S. and Europe, including here at Stanford and at CERN, have successfully mapped a complex geometric structure known as E_8, a complex figure portraying 248 dimensions. The E_8 has remained an enigma until recently powerful computer networks unlocked the formation's underlying structure."

Emboldened, Ethan fired up the projector and called up a PowerPoint slide. "Here's a simplified version."

"And a complex version..."

"We care about E_8 because a few years back, astrophysicists realized that its star-like pattern appeared to map a relationship between gravity, electromagnetism and the strong and weak forces. In other words, the spinning E_8 unifies the four fundamental laws of nature.

"There's only one problem with E_8 theory. Its proof depended on the existence of a very special particle, known as the *Higgs boson*, predicted by the Standard Model. The particle is often called *the God particle* because its existence would seal the evidence of the Theory of Everything. Recently, researchers from the 20 European member nations of CERN powered up the world's largest machines – the massive Large Hadron Collider, a 17-mile tube buried securely 300 feet beneath the French-Swiss border. With the help of physicists here at SLAC, including myself, we now can prove the validity of the Theory of Everything."

Shivana triumphantly held up a USB flash drive, crowded Ethan at the microphone, and said, "In your electronic press packets you'll find one of these. It contains all the information from each supporting organization as well as the complete E_8 equation, all 80 gigabytes of it."

The room was silent. Shivana was sure it was with triumphant awe at the announcement. Ethan knew otherwise. He had attended enough of these events to know that silence is deadly.

"Any questions?" he whispered into the microphone.

A journalist's hand popped up. "Hi, I'm wondering if the equation has been verified and certified by the Numerical and Astrophysical Council?"

Ethan was happy to take this softball question. "We've received provisional approval and expect full council acceptance at the next intercessional meeting scheduled in spring of next year."

A representative of the *Journal of Scientific Exploration* asked, "As you know, Gödel's incompleteness theorem states that no matter how many mathematical problems we solve, there will always be other problems, and then more — an infinite number of problems to solve. Doesn't this suggest there can never be a final *deterministic* theory of everything? Something must be beyond the theory or else the inexhaustible realm of physics would cease to be inexhaustible."

Ethan pondered the question as he had many times before. He glanced at Shivana and saw the argument in full swing.

"The short answer is *you are correct*, but Gödel's theorem doesn't presuppose contradiction, just infinity. We knew that already, didn't we? Just as it can be argued that there are an infinite number of problems to solve, it can also be argued that all answers, infinite as they may be, will support and confirm the Theory of Everything, rather than refute it."

A writer stood up to ask, "Dr. Weiner-Gluckstein, why did you preempt the CERN announcement and why is this announcement being made by a failed theoretical physicist and a common post-graduate student, when the honor should rightly fall to others more intimately involved in the findings?"

Ethan stuttered to respond. "I, ah...I think..."

The president rolled his eyes.

Ethan's self-doubt that had so astonishingly disappeared for these past few minutes returned now in a bombardment of woe. Ethan didn't need to dig deeply into his memory banks or seek the services of a psychotherapist to locate the source of his crushing self-doubt. He had been a gangly 13-year-old on the bimah, high above his family and junior high friends at Temple Ner Shalom, his unruly dark hair slicked back with creams, his neck squeezed by a red tie, his shoulders collared by a suit fitted three months earlier for a growing boy.

Flanked by two nurturing rabbis, the young man leaned over an open and sacred Torah scroll. Rabbi Levin gently filled Ethan's hand with a silver pointer and led it to the Hebrew letter *Shin* somewhere near the bottom of the middle column. He had practiced his weekly Torah portion, *Parashat Lekh-L'kha*, time and again, that wasn't the problem. Perhaps he had even over prepared as was his wont even at that age. But in practice sessions, Ethan's fingers had followed Hebrew words in a bound book, printed in a familiar Modern Hebrew font, always with the comfort of vowels below the letters to aid in pronunciation. But here on this parchment of deerskin, the handwritten word of God did not contain vowels or punctuation marks, just an infinite stream of hand-drawn Hebrew letters.

Ethan grew woozy. The Hebrew letters, in all their dignity, wiggled before him like worms spilling from a bucket. Ethan loosened his tie and kicked off his left shoe. He closed his eyes in hopes that upon their reopening the letters might have settled down to rest. No such luck. His father, grandfather and great grandfathers had been rabbis. In the old country, generations of Glucksteins were renowned for their erudition in all things Talmudic and rumored the forbidden Kabbalistic as well. Quite often a whisper of the radically esoteric found its way into the family teachings before being snuffed out by the stern look of a grandmother or distant great uncle. Ethan looked down at his parents in the front row, his grandmother all the way from Miami, his cousins, and the four girls from his seventh-grade class brave or unpopular enough to have accepted his invitation. And there in his bar mitzvah panic, the spirit of his ancestors swirled around Ethan. He felt their presence, but they were powerless to help him remember the very first word of his well-memorized Torah portion on the day that had been selected to prove he was son of the commandments in the eyes of God and his community.

He knew the English. He could recite the biblical portion in English:

Now Abram and Sarah were very distressed for they had no children. God said to Abram, "Look toward heaven and count the stars to see how large your family will be."

Ethan locked onto the horrified gaze of his father, a patient man by nature if a bit distant and preoccupied at times by the more abstruse subtleties of the *Mishna* and *Responsa*. Ethan's mother wore a smile, fake and strained, in the shallow way she did when she found herself no longer in control of the situation. Ethan took a deep breath as his mother had always advised him to do when he was losing it. Rabbi Mignoni leaned in and whispered the first line of Ethan's lines, but the B'nai mitzvot didn't hear the words, couldn't hear. All his senses joined forces in a riot of sensory overload. Time dilated, space compressed.

Shutting down was the only option. And that's what Ethan did.

Then in front of God, his family, and the few classmates kind enough to come, Ethan cried the soft, gentle tears of the boy he feared he always would remain. The congregants were generous in their silence, but Ethan's shame was loud and clear. One of his tears landed on the parchment, on the open lean-to of the letter *Gimmel*. Ethan remembered that much. The Rabbis freaked. They rushed forward to sweep away the Books of The Good Name to prevent further damage, for these scrolls were precious, and this one, in particular, had survived the Holocaust and had landed in a Nazi museum before being rescued and gifted to this community. This precious Torah had survived pogroms, the merciless winters and the cruel neighbors of the Ukrainian steppes unblemished until Ethan's salty tear landed on an innocent Gimmel causing the tiniest of smudges on the sacred letters of God's law. In their haste to remove the scroll from Ethan, the parchment ripped. Just slightly, but visibly. The congregants gasped in unison as if the word of God were no longer eternal.

The rabbi returned the scroll to the closeted safety of the Aron Kodesh and Ethan stood at the bimah, shivering. Nothing to read and nothing to say. He felt ashen and wished he could vanish in a column of smoke. Ethan did what every good Jew does when all is lost, he recited the holiest Haiku in Judaism...

Shema Yisrael Adonai Eloheinu Adonai Echad.

That took all of about eight seconds. And so Ethan repeated in English, *Hear Oh, Israel, the Lord our God the Lord is One.*

One of the rabbis, Ethan couldn't remember which one, promptly began chanting the opening line of the closing prayers.

At the reception afterward, despite a hall decked with blue and white streamers and a DJ imported from Bensonhurst, Ethan melted in a corner hoping never to engage the world again. Ethan's father ignored him the entire evening and emerged only at the very end against the clamor of Greek caterers stacking chairs. Ethan never forgot his father's words. "Not everyone, my son."

What did that mean? Ethan had trouble enough deciphering the subtleties of language. To make it worse, Ethan's father was so thoroughly sloshed, a state Ethan so rarely witnessed, Ethan possessed no point of reference to determine the subtext of the man's comment. Verily, if scores of meanings attended every word of Torah, certainly a son had cause to find folds of meaning in the spurn of a father.

Not everyone *what*? Not everyone successfully completes his bar mitzvah ceremony? Not everyone becomes a man? Succeeds in life? Pleases their fathers? Lives a worthy life? Deserves the skin and bones of an earthly dwelling?

To this day the utterance perplexed Ethan. After this failed announcement, he was sure it always would.

On the stage with the University president growing antsy, Ethan stuttered and mumbled. His self-doubt was the only announcement being broadcast here. One by one, audience members folded up their laptops. The auditorium seats folded up automatically behind as they stood. The place turned into a venue of folds. Grumbling toward the exits they left, bowing down to the text messages awaiting them. How could they miss the significance of the announcement? Or did they know something that Ethan didn't? He glanced at Shivana and saw her gaze of perplexity...or maybe Ethan was misreading a social cue once again because Shivana stepped up to the microphone with her characteristic ferocity.

"Now wait a minute good people," she began. "First of all, Dr. Weiner-Gluckstein is a gifted physicist with 32 peer-reviewed journaled papers. Look them up. Second, though he's too modest to say it, *he* was the inspiring leader of the Stanford team that developed the mathematical equations needed to calibrate the ATLAS detector – the 145-foot long camera that allowed CERN experimental physicists to detect the Higgs boson as it sped by at nearly the speed of light. We feel it is a valuable contribution to explain these findings to the 99.9987 percent of society that doesn't read obscure publications like yours. And, yes, I am a post-graduate student, and I couldn't be prouder than to be up here on this austere podium representing the tens of thousands – hundreds of thousands—of post-graduate students who have invested tens of millions of person-hours on behalf of scientific research in physics and related fields. We are the backbone of the academic world, and every project of importance from astronomy to zoology would come to a roaring halt without us."

Her pronouncements, passionate as they were, did not stem the exodus. Still, Shivana did not for a moment regret her strident position. Enough was enough. This was the Theory of Everything, after all. If she backed off every time someone gave her a bit of holier-than-thou lip or a cold shoulder, she would still be in Iran mending canvas tents, her fingers bloodied and torn like her mother's and sisters'.

She was barely done when President Mahoney mounted the podium in a single bound. Spittle formed at the corners of his mouth. "Ethan, my office tomorrow morning, 8:00 a.m."

He spun around to face Shivana and drove in daggers with his eyes.

"And you, my little pretty, bring your visa."

FOUR

Penny Lean hated her name. Who wouldn't?

Penny as in coin, the cheapest one, the one nobody wants. *Silver, gold, buck, credit card*, any name is better than Penny. You walk all over pennies in the street and don't stop to pick one up. Ten don't buy you nothing. Big honchos talk about outlawing pennies and rounding it all up to nickels like pennies don't count. And if *Penny* didn't suck enough, what about *Lean* to cap it off? Not *fat, rich, strapping, mean,* but *lean.* Her parents adopted her and threw on a tag like *Penny Lean* to boot. Talk about born under a bad sign.

Her protest sign read *Lock Her Up* because it came from a different kind of rally, but she held it high anyway because people who kill babies should be stoned, killed, rotting in hell. Plus the church people usually gave her five or ten bucks after the protest to get something to eat, sometimes twenty. Her piercings and tattoos gave her away in this white-bread crowd, not to mention purple hair. A round peg in a square hole here in front of the abortion clinic, but name a place where Penny Lean does fit in? And no way she was thinking Jesus was gonna swoop down to save her ass just because she stands out front of an abortion clinic chanting slogans. That chance slipped away a long time ago.

She moved to the side of the crowd so her parents wouldn't spot her and shouted: "*One two three four, abort no babies nevermore!*"

On her hip, Emmett Jessup sucked a chocolate Tootsie Pop. He was too young to make out the words on the people's signs, but he ogled them nonetheless—cut up babies with big heads, devil with pitchforks, crying Jesuses.

"Hold this, honey." Penny handed the sign to the boy and fumbled in her bag for a cigarette.

"Mommy loves you like flowers."

She sucked down a drag and felt sick to her stomach. The doctor told her the Lithium might make her nauseous. No shit, it's the same toxic crap they use in laptop batteries. What the hell did he think? Plus, her last Meth kick was like 12 hours ago. Who wouldn't feel sicker than a dog?

She yanked Emmett away. "Let's hurry. Mommy's gotta throw up."

No way she was gonna heave in front of these drips, and she didn't want her parents to spot her, so she hustled around the back of the shopping mall, office park, whatever the fuck it was, to where they dump the garbage and cardboard boxes. Penny prided herself on holding her barf until the right place and time. It's a skill a girl's gotta have.

"You're my little man, ain't ya?"

Emmett's head bobbled *yes,* and he held on tight.

She hightailed it passed the storefronts for the foot doctor, chiropractor, discount pet food store, dry cleaners, yogurt shop, health food taqueria, and around the bend of the marijuana clinic.

"Man, wouldn't it be nice to live inside *there* for a while?" Penny said. "And if your deadbeat dad paid his child support, I could cop an eighth and find someplace to live permanent like. *Dickwadasshole.*"

"Dick wa ass ho," repeated Emmett Jessup, tasting the words in his mouth for the first time.

"Don't be talking bad about your father like that. He loves you."

Penny deposited Emmett on the curb. "You wait right here like a good boy. Mommy is gonna talk to the bushes for a sec."

Emmett smiled and looked at the little curbside puddle of water. What's this? A used hypodermic needle near the sewer drain. *Let's draw Xs and Os in an oily puddle. Left hand or right?*

Penny cut a path through the brush and clawed up the hill. She didn't want her little boy hearing. He heard enough already with the ruckus she regularly drummed up. Penny found a flat clearing. She let it rip.

Damn, barfing feels good. Not while you're doing it, but soon afterward, mighty soon, like the whole world is off your fucking shoulders.

She lit a drag and inhaled deep. The distant horizon looked hazy like a Heroin fog. She peered down the hill for Emmett. Yep, there he was. Same place she left him, playing quiet and nice with a stick. Man, did she get lucky with that little guy.

Penny sleeved her lips and tongued away the vomit chunks. What she'd give for a beer right now to wash away the nasty taste.

She started back down the hill.

A metal door creaked open. A crack of fluorescence lit the scene. From the door/light/crack came a blonde lady in shiny black stiletto boots. Tall and totally expensive.

Penny felt her way down the hill, toward her boy.

She knew the lady, seen her before somewhere. But all those *siliconevalleytrophywives* looked alike.

Penny knew that woman. But from where? Then it registered. *That's it.* From church, always sitting up front, first pew, center right, smiling with all the sincerity of the Fourth of July.

Goddamn preacher's wife.

And the kicker: Behind her stood some *towelhead* rubbing the lady's butt and sucking her down like a tall drink of vodka. *What the hell?*

Penny glanced over at Emmett because she didn't like her son seeing shit like that. He wasn't watching anyway, all interested in his little sticks and boats in the puddle below.

One last repulsive genital rub and the couple separated.

Penny watched the preacher lady click open her dark Mercedes, sleek enough to shuttle some dictator in Africa. She vroomed that thing hard and punched it into reverse.

The dual white backup lights brightened Emmett Jessup's face. A pointy stick or something in his mouth.

"Emmett!"

Penny barreled down the hill, her backpack flying. She flicked her cigarette in the crispy underbrush, hoping it wouldn't catch fire, because she'd been accused of arson a time or two.

Emmett twisted toward his mom.

"Emmy, run! Get outta there," she barked.

The car in reverse picked up speed toward the boy.

Emmett scrunched his face.

"Run!"

Emmett froze under the glare of the white backup lights.

"Run!" Penny tripped. She fell. Her mouth filled with dirt.

Penny righted herself and lunged down the hill. "Ninja! Run!"

The Mercedes flew backward.

Oh, God please, take it all, but let my Emmett live. "Baby!"

Penny never did reach her boy in time.

The distance was too great.

Emmett never did move.

Too young to fear.

Thankfully, the luxury car's all-wheel disk brakes squealed the sedan to a stop barely a witch's tit from the boy's nose. The driver fuckin' oblivious to the near fatality.

Penny damn near fainted.

The asshole lady screeched away, just missing a shopping cart as she flew over the speed bumps like Bat Woman or some shit.

Penny reached Emmett and smothered him with hugs and kisses. "That fucking lady, did you see her?"

Emmett nodded yes.

"I swear, I'll kill her. Let me look at you. You all right? That's all that counts. Come to Mommy, Em, I love you. Do you know that?"

Emmett smiled.

The taillights disappeared around the corner. Penny scooped up Emmett Jessup because he was her everything. "Do you know how much Mommy loves you? Like thorns in thickets."

Penny spied the towelhead slip inside the building, seconds before the thick metal back door rattled shut.

Penny said, "I'm pissed."

"Me pissed."

Penny Lean hoisted Emmett on her hip and marched to the back door.

Pound, pound, pound. Yes, Penny can pound.

Openupmotherfucker. Pound, pound, pound. "Now!"

On the inside, Omar heard the insistent rapping. He pressed his cheek to the door, hoping to assess the urgency. If it were Sandra Lee, she was in peril or driven by a love so ardent she risked a return. Omar hastily conjured new poetics in anticipation. And if it were a group of anti-abortion protesters, well, Omar was never one to hide his tail between his legs.

Omar puffed his chest and opened the door wide. He saw a crazy girl with purple hair and a little boy waving angry fists. He felt relieved at first. A plea for a back-door abortion happens all the time.

"Your little bitch almost ran over my little boy."

"I'm sorry, what?"

"The one you're skankin'? *That bitch* almost ran over my boy."

Omar honestly hadn't seen anything, and frankly, the woman's demeanor frightened him. "But—I—."

"And you know what else? I know who she is. And I saw you humpin' her, so I know what's going on."

"Yeah," Emmett added emphatically.

Omar detested situations. Situations led to complications. And complications led to trouble. And clearly here was a situation. "I have no I idea to what you are referring."

"Yeah? Well, I've been in church with her, and I can tell you her preacher husband is all fire and brimstone and he's gonna be pissed."

"What do you want?" Omar asked.

Penny glanced across the parking lot. What did she want? Good question. "You Arab? Iraqi or something?"

"Palestinian."

"Then I'll tell you what I want." Penny smiled because she was smart. She knew every Arab owned a bomb, maybe two, heck, ten. "I want a bomb."

Omar reeled. "You must be joking."

"I'm not kidding. I want a bomb."

"I'm a doctor, for God's sake."

"Don't you mean for *Allah's* sake? You don't fool me."

"My apologies, but you are totally mistaken."

"Her name is Sandra Lee Spridgen, and she's married to Pastor Harlen Spridgen of the *Calvary Baptist Crusade for Christ the Son Jesus, Savior of the Globe, 1st United Church*. I know 'cause I grew up in that *bullshithole*, so don't make me puke again."

"How old are you?" asked the doctor.

"I've been around, believe me."

"I can see. And how old is the boy? Two, three?"

"None of your business."

"So you know the woman. Many people do."

Penny searched his brown liquid eyes. "Hey, wait a minute. You're *that* doctor, right? The one nobody says they go to. I know you."

"I have nothing to hide."

"You're *fucking* her? Ain't that ironic.

"Please don't use that term."

"And if you ain't fucking her, then I'll be damned if you didn't just slip her a back alley abortion. And I ain't sure which is worse—fucking the preacher's wife or yanking her fetus. *You* tell me. So give me a bomb or me and my son here are going straight to the cops or publicity or whatever, and we're gonna let them know what we seen."

Omar smiled because he had learned it is always wise to smile at an enemy.

"And whom do you presume would believe you?"

"Try me."

"I have money," he said.

"How much?"

"One hundred dollars."

"Bird feed."

"Five hundred."

"Not even."

"Two thousand dollars."

Penny flipped Emmett to the other hip. Not bad. Two grand would pay the first-and-last month's rent, seeing as Emmett's father wasn't ever coming through, she knew that. She stopped to think.

Penny watched Emmett search for his own reflection in the shine of the man's shoes.

Omar opened his wallet and spread out hundreds. "Here, and I have more. Your child looks hungry."

"My child is fine."

Penny peeked into the wallet, flush with green. "You know what? Money ain't gonna do it. Your hottie almost ran over my baby and there ain't no money in the world worth that. Look, I may be nuts, but I'm not a rat, and I want a bomb."

Dr. Omar began shutting the door. "I am sorry, I cannot be of help to you. You are gravely mistaken."

Penny pulled out her cell phone like a pistol. She scrolled through the address book and tapped the entry marked *Church*. "See that? That's a direct line to her husband. And he's got an army of fat-ass Baptists who do whatever he says, believe me, I've seen it, and so have you. Matter of fact right out front there's a shitload of them. A bomb or else."

Long before the Arab Spring had turned the region into the Arab Nightmare, Dr. Omar had seen the game of one-upmanship played by the finest in the Middle East. He had no intention of caving into such demands.

On the other hand, that's the problem with people with little to lose, there's no negotiating precisely because they have nothing left to lose. Anger begets rage, and rage begets courage, and courage begets more anger in an endless loop composed of the dark matter within us all.

Penny hit the *talk* button.

Omar shot out an arm. "Wait!"

Even if they didn't believe her, imagine the scandal, the sensation sure to ensue. Omar had much to lose, as did Sandra Lee.

Penny flipped the lid closed. "I'm listening."

Omar calculated as best he could with an extortion threat on one side and an angry mob on the other.

The bomb wasn't even officially his. Omar's second cousin, Abd Al-Ala Farooq, drove an Uber at night and had the unfortunate habit of speaking his mind far too readily. The world owed Abd Al-Ala big time he believed, and he wasn't afraid to tell his rides. An immigration official, not liking the driver's brand of politics, noted Abd Al-Ala's information and made some discreet inquiries. Abd Al-Ala's papers were not in order, and he was forced into a hasty departure. Before he left for Vancouver, Abd Al-Ala asked Omar to store his possessions, chief among them a homemade bomb. Omar refused at first, but Abd Al-Ala invoked the names of shared relatives and collective grievances. Omar, in yet another moment of weakness, relented to the tearful kisses of his fleeing cousin.

Omar had no plans to *use* the bomb. Perhaps those martyrs who gave their body and souls in sacrifice for Jihad sat in heaven now near the Angel Gabriel at the foot of the all-Merciful. However, God had provided Dr. Omar Farooq neither the guile nor the courage required to blow himself to smithereens. That's the problem with the intellect; it leads you to question. *Blow yourself up for what?* A fleeting headline for a bloody cause that would continue forever? And the virgins awaiting in heaven? Omar was most pious, but he just didn't buy it.

Omar had promised himself to quickly dispose of the bomb. But how? He possessed no expertise with bombs. What if he should hurt someone during disposal? Or worse, get caught? He cursed Abd Al-Ala and hid the bomb away, adding to his daily prayers a plea for a solution to his unholy predicament.

And now this. Handing over a bomb to a purple-haired teenager with obvious emotional issues was problematic, to say the least. Where would she use it and why? Would it be traced to him?

"Please, young lady, be kind to yourself and fair to your son. He so deserves it. Look at him, he shares the face of God. He has his whole life ahead of him as do you."

"You don't know shit."

"Take the money, it will serve you much more wisely. Take advice from one experienced in making many mistakes."

"You're a sweet talker."

"I speak the truth and in your best interest."

"The friggin' bomb and nothing less," she demanded.

"I beg of you. A bomb will bring you only misery."

"No dice."

Omar saw the girl's stubbornness. He thought of his brilliant wife, Shivana, and her dreams of finishing her study at Stanford and embarking on a brilliant career in theoretical physics. But mostly he thought of Sandra Lee and the ungodly mess he might lay on her suburban doorstep if he should misplay this move.

On the other hand, there might be a tidy solution.

"What would you do with a bomb?" he asked.

Penny smiled. "None of your business."

"You won't harm her?"

"Who, that Botox queen? I got bigger fish to fry, believe you me."

"If I give it to you, your lips are surely sealed?"

"My lips kissed more girls than yours ever did. You have my word."

"And I want the remote control," she added.

"Remote control?" Omar repeated.

"Yeah, you think I'm a dumbass? I've seen the remote control in movies. A bomb ain't no good without one."

Omar felt the urge to kneel to pray, to ask for forgiveness, but evening prayers were over, and the Merciful Allah doesn't answer prayers driven by sin.

"Wait here," he whispered.

Omar retreated to his office, pushed the desk away, and unlocked the safe hidden underneath a floor tile.

He handled the bomb with care. Despite two safety mechanisms, the device remained a condensed explosion at rest. And, of course, he found the remote control.

He cradled the package like a baby and carried it to the back door. He wished upon the grave of his grandfather that upon his return, this unruly girl would be gone.

She wasn't. She waited with her unzipped backpack, opened wide like the mouth of a whale. A deal is a deal, teaches the Holy Qur'an. We must be honest in all our dealings.

The Qur'an also teaches that sin begets sin. But who needs the wisdom of the prophets to foretell the consequences awaiting a fool such as he? The blind eyes of lowly men are sufficient to envisage this tragic outcome.

"That's more like it," said Penny. She snatched the bomb and hustled away with her little child.

"Be careful!" Omar called behind her, feeling his heart fill with the poison of distress. The broken window. Now this. Punishment is swift.

He returned to the faded blue carpet that had belonged to his grandfather until the seething dusk of June 7, 1967. Omar hadn't been born then, but it is said that his grandfather had smelled the Israelis coming around the corner of his East Jerusalem home. Instinctively the old sage dropped to his knees to face Mecca for one last prayer. His final words, Omar was told, were these: *When an invading army bloodies your streets, find first your prayer carpet because it belongs not to you but to Allah.*

Prayer brought him the answer once again. Omar knew what he must do, despite the sacrifices it would require. Such is the world for the woeful such as he.

Omar quietly turned off the clinic lights and slipped out the back door. He found his black Maxima parked in the shadows and sped off toward Stanford University to gather his wife for the hasty departure ahead.

FIVE

The sting of the president's veiled threats still echoed in Shivana's ear when the rear doors sprung open. She was sure it was the members of the media here en masse to cover the announcement of the century. *Vindication at last!*

But it wasn't MSNBC. It wasn't CBS. It wasn't even the Science Channel. It was her swarthy husband, Dr. Omar Farooq, kicking up a carpet of dust as he barreled toward her on the stage, his face ashen with fright.

Shivana had the quick sense to move stage right and meet him at the stairs.

"What happened to your face?" she asked.

Omar had almost forgotten. "A shard of glass. Shivana, we have to leave."

"Leave? I'm working late tonight."

"No, I mean leave the country."

"Leave the *what?*"

"No questions, please. I am your husband, I make the decisions, and we are leaving."

President Mahoney perked up.

"Please not here. Can't you see?" Shivana pleaded.

"Something has happened. Something *big.* A day or two to wrap things up and we're off. We'll purchase tickets straight away."

"Tickets to where?"

"The West Bank or Tehran, your choice."

Shivana couldn't believe what she was hearing. All the work she had put into getting here. All the troubles of others to help her.

"But this can't be."

"Shivana, I insist!"

Shivana felt the pull of the old ways, the weight of submission, the inevitable momentum toward acquiescence. It had all been too good to be true, this life illuminated by science.

She placed a firm finger on Omar's lips.

"Omar, now listen to me. This is something to talk about, discuss. It's a big decision, huge. I'm not going anywhere, not without additional explanation. Secondly, I will not be treated in a manner inconsistent with my station in this country. And finally—"

"Shivana!" Omar halted her with a look of sincere distress. "I'm in trouble."

"*Trouble?* What kind of trouble?"

He whispered, "Big trouble. My cousin Abd Al-Ala's kind of trouble."

Shivana froze, for this was not good. "How can this be?"

"I should have told you before," Omar said. He then proceeded to whisper in Shivana's ears the details of Abd Al-Ala's bomb and how it came into his possession against his fervent will. He told her about the purple-haired girl, her angry demands, and the possibility of their life being swept away at a moment's notice by anti-terrorist forces of the United States government.

He conveniently left out any mention of Sandra Lee.

Shivana stopped to calculate the odds, consider her options. Any child in the second grade could add *one* to an existing number. She loved Omar, she did. But add one to today's totals and tomorrow's sum would equal 219 days since Tehran's heat and 1,243 days since the burqa's mass. And so Shivana Farooq, third daughter of a tent maker from Razavi Khorasan province, Shivana Farooq whose clitoris was sliced away at age eight with a rusty razor blade by a local woman with yellow fingernails. Shivana Farooq who stole an education in the village and earned a baccalaureate in the city, Shivana Farooq who had notched the rare win of gaining her freedom on the noble back of education, *that* Shivana Farooq made the quick decision to do the thing she must.

"Omar," she whispered as sweetly as she could. "I respect you as my husband, but there's no way on earth I'm leaving. May your faith sustain you."

Ethan wanted so badly to rescue Shivana from the onslaught of her husband. On this day of all days, what right did Omar have to barge in here and cause a scene? The president must have felt the same way because he nodded to the two security guards standing in the back of the auditorium.

The couple hadn't noticed the hubbub around them, until the security guards grabbed Omar by the elbows, hard. They dragged him away, shouting Shivana's name like an incantation. His heels burned lines in the carpet until he disappeared behind the swinging doors.

It had all been too good to be true, Shivana lamented. Too perfect to be of this world.

SIX

Pastor Harlen Spridgen slowed his gold Lexus LS to a stop near a shadowy young male figure squatting curbside with his hands jammed deep into his pockets. Harlen leaned over to the passenger side, buzzed down the glass, and crouched low for eye contact.

"Thanks for waiting," said Harlen.

The figure glanced left, right, then eased into the heated leather seat. A drop-dead gorgeous young man with a shock of black hair dangling over sky blue eyes, the scent of sweaty denim and leather immediately filled the sedan. Harlen almost floored it, wanting nothing more than to plant a reverent kiss on the young man's cherub lips.

Harlen pressed fast forward on his iPhone in search of some music, peppy, young, and hip. A string of corny country music tunes came through until Michael Jackson's "Thriller" kicked it up. Did kids these days listen to the King of Pop?

"I tore my jeans coming over the fence," said the young man.

"We can meet somewhere else in the future, if you'd like."

"No, this is good. Just a hop, skip and jump from my house."

Harlen placed his hands on the boy's thigh, over the new rip, seeking some leg warmth. "Cut yourself, Jimmy?" the Pastor asked.

"Whatever. Got the cash?"

Harlen was saddened the question came so quickly. He had hoped his companionship for a few minutes might be enough to keep Jimmy entertained before the urgency of the night got down to business. But he understood the teenager was young, impatient. He remembered the impatience of the young. Nice.

Harlen said, "Got a birthday coming up, don't you, Jimmy?"

"Eighteen, I can't wait."

"Me, neither," said Harlen.

Harlen flipped down the visor, and a fold of twenties slipped down. Harlen handed it to the teenager. "Here you go. As we agreed."

The boy stuffed the bills into his pocket without counting.

"Can you turn down the heat down in here?"

Harlen punched the automatic temperature control down to 68.

Gorgeous Jimmy Lean pulled a packet of folded paper from his pocket. "Here you go. One gram. Good shit."

Harlen unfolded the glossy paper, ripped from the pages of Penthouse or some such magazine. The white powder glistened like a light. "Looks good. Want a hit?"

"Nah, I got homework."

"Wow, that's very diligent of you."

"Plus, my dad is drug testing me now."

"I see."

"You're parents know anything, suspect anything?"

"You kidding? You saw them in church last week. All hallelujah."

The car was steaming up with desire. Jimmy fidgeted a little, his hands with nothing to do. He drew a peace sign in the sweaty mist collecting on the passenger side window. "Can I ask you something, preacher?"

"Shoot."

"Does your wife know you're a closet fag."

"Sandra Lee and I have our *understandings*."

"And what does Jesus think of it?"

"Jesus loves us for who we are not our temporary faults."

Jimmy chuckled. "I'll have to remember that one. And don't think you'll be screwing me when I'm eighteen either."

"Whatever you say, Jimmy."

Jimmy opened the door but stopped to turn back to the pastor. "So Jesus is okay with all your sins?"

"Jesus? He loves me. Who needs love more than sinners?"

"So you're sayin' the more you sin, the more love you get. That how it works?"

"Something like that."

Jimmy found the door handle. "And you believe that bullshit?"

"With all my heart."

"Yeah, well, enjoy the blow."

Jimmy slammed the door behind him. Harlen watched him hustle away and hop the fence with a *Westside Story* flip.

Great ass.

Harlen glanced at the little pile of cocaine, meth, crank, whatever. He rolled down his window and threw the entire packet out, unleashing the particles into the faint winds of the atmosphere. He didn't need it or want it. He had gotten his money's worth. Nor did he want to go home to Sandra Lee and her complaints about the bed sheets and his diversions, perverse as they may seem.

Isn't it ironic how powerful a force *weakness* is? If strength were a billionth as powerful as weakness, we'd all be saints. And if weakness lived up to its name, there's no telling how perfect the world might be.

Harlen possessed many sinful traits. His fingers and mind went where they shouldn't. His lust led him to the darkest recesses of shame and ignominy. But he thanked God Almighty for the thin string of strength that tethered him to the honorable side of the boy line. Didn't the Good Lord reveal in Mark 9:42: *And if anyone causes one of these little ones who believe in me to sin, it would be better for him to be thrown into the sea with a large millstone tied around his neck.*

It was a line Pastor Spridgen prayed never to cross.

SEVEN

Ethan's wife of 14 years, Naomi Weiner-Gluckstein (her maiden name rhymes with *finer,* not with the nitrate-infused sausage made from the anuses and snouts of mutilated tortured pigs and helpless farm animals, thank you), returned home after midnight from her National Abortion and Reproductive Rights Action League meeting and awoke the next morning early. There was work to be done, always was. She took a lukewarm shower to reduce her carbon footprint, toweled dried her curly red hair, flipped open her MacBook Air and synched the escort details onto her iPad to save paper.

In the kitchen, she snipped the top inch of her wheatgrass patch and hand-blended two shots for herself. She faced the east and focused on her heart chakra for a heartfelt Vinyasa salutation while the sun streamed in through the double-paned window. Plank, Chaturanga, Upward Facing Dog, Downward Facing Dog. Three times harmonically aligning her breath with her selected affirmation of the day, *I will express compassion for all living beings.*

Naomi quickly dressed and shook Ethan awake. He had snored all night while mumbling incessantly about *causality* and bosoms or bosons, or some such bullshit, his mind always in the *cloud. Space Time,* my ass, was the way Naomi felt about it. More like the *Here Now.*

Ethan struggled awake. "Naomi?"

"Who'd you expect, Gandhi? I see you used the microwave last night."

"I did."

"I thought we agreed."

"I was hungry."

"If everyone broke rules when they were hungry, the world would be in

37

chaos."

"I didn't make the rules, you did."

"For our health. Cancer-causing nitrosodiethanolamine, remember? Free radicals. Is that what you want for dinner?"

"Yes."

"Die early, see if I care. How did the announcement go?"

Ethan bolted out of bed and headed straight for his computer without saying another word.

"Be that way," Naomi said. Then she realized, a little late, as she always seemed to do, that maybe she hadn't been as compassionate as she could have been.

"Ethan? I'm sorry."

But he was face deep in his computer screen. Naomi couldn't compete with that. Never could. Naomi packed her NARAL pamphlets and squeezed the last tired out of her eyes.

On her way to East Palo Alto, Naomi listened to Amy Goodman's *Democracy Now* on KPFA, one of the few radio stations in the country not bound and gagged by corporate media thugs like the bottom-sucking assholes Murdoch and Bannon and the entire board of directors of Comcast spreading their right-wing tentacles all over cable television and the Internet. And Faux News. Don't even talk to Naomi about the devil incarnate.

Here's the deal when you get assigned as an escort: you have to be ready for odd addresses and locations that befuddle GPS systems. But even Naomi, with her uncanny ability to find her Jane, had trouble deciphering the coordinates of this destination. She drove underneath the overpass a number of times before realizing the map coordinates marked the overpass itself. She slowed to a crawl and spied a very small homeless encampment nestled beneath it.

Naomi parked the Prius (bumper stickers: *Coexist Now! If You're Not Outraged, You Haven't Been Paying Attention. If You're Against Abortion, Don't Have One. Hatred is Not a Family Value. Free Tibet! Vegetarians Taste Better. Eve was Framed*) in the shade of the overpass to reduce carbon emissions through unnecessary air conditioning later. She walked up the concrete hillside and recognized the makeshift cardboard structure as belonging to a woman. No homeless guy would attach a broken flowerpot with a plastic Geranium in front of the hanging carpet that served as a door.

A semi-trailer truck rumbled overhead. For a moment, Naomi felt sure it was an earthquake.

"Hello in there?" she called.

No answer.

"Hello?" she repeated.

Naomi looked down at her iPhone for info.

"*Penny? Penny Lean.* You in there?"

Little Emmett Jessup poked his head out. "Mamma, look. White lady!"

"Hi kid. I'm Naomi. I'm your mother's NARAL rep."

Emmett Jessup smiled without understanding a thing.

Penny jumped out with a baseball bat ready to bash heads. "You say Sheriff?"

"No, no, no. Your escort. To your appointment."

Naomi held out a 92-percent post-consumer waste cardboard cup filled with slave-free hot chocolate. She had stopped along the way (not at Starbucks, but a local coffee shop brewing fair-trade organic beans and teas), because most of her clients weren't used to getting up this early in the morning. A hot chocolate was a shot in the arm, so to speak, though Naomi naturally didn't condone vaccines, being as they were an AMA conspiracy. Had she known about the kid, she would have brought two cups.

Penny was confused. "Appointment?"

"Abortion. Saturday, nine a.m."

"Shit. What time is it now?"

"Eight-thirty."

"What day is it today?"

"Saturday."

Penny rubbed the sleep from her eyes.

"Fuck, come back next week, okay?"

Naomi checked the chart. "Says here you've cancelled twice already. It's not going to get any easier. Hot chocolate?"

Hard to pass up. Penny took a swig and handed the cup to Emmett Jessup, whose eyes widened with delight.

"What do you say, Emmett, should we go to the doctor to make mommy better?"

Emmett Jessup ignored his mother and smiled at Naomi. "White lady. White lady."

"Nice kid." Naomi smiled.

Penny asked, "What's your name again?"

"Naomi Weiner-Gluckstein."

"*Nay-oh-mee*," Penny tasted. "Rhymes with *you owe me*. That'll be easy to remember. Is this an overnight?"

"No, you'll be back in a few hours, max."

Emmett stared up at Naomi with glossy eyes and started fiddling with her wedding ring.

"Shit, I gotta get myself together," Penny said. "Wanna come in for a spell? As you can see, it ain't no palace."

Naomi weighed the risks: a schizophrenic homeless woman on meds could be tweaked out, unstable, weapons. A snot-nosed kid. And who else might be in there?

As habit goes, Naomi decided to do what she thought was right. She lifted up the corner of the tent and crawled in. "Not so bad."

The place was a bulge of blankets, a stack of spent Sterno cans, and a litter of crumpled packs of Pall Malls.

Penny fidgeted on a pair of suddenly tight jeans, then in the cramped space fell onto her butt.

Naomi had seen it before. "Second thoughts?"

"A million thoughts. But I've been doing blow, for like, every day for months now. That screws up the baby royally don't it?"

"It can cause damage or maybe not. Have you taken advantage of prenatal care?"

"Prenatal care? *You're* my prenatal care. God, I'm such an *ass-wipe fuckup*. I should shoot myself."

Naomi felt her maternal instincts kick in. "Look, if you don't feel like you're ready, take a day or two. Think about it."

Penny's jittering fingers found an overlooked cigarette in a crumpled pack, and she lit it with trembling hands. "Want one?"

"No thanks."

Naomi noticed wrist scars. "How far along are you?"

"Like I know? My guess is ten weeks, eleven, maybe more."

"There's still time to change your mind. And it's your choice alone to make."

"Well, I appreciate someone giving me a fucking choice around here."

"You can't undo it, you know that."

"It's like a ticking time bomb stitched inside me, isn't it? You ever have an abortion?"

"Me, no."

"Got kids?"

Naomi evaded the question with a non-committal shrug.

"Want 'em?"

"Someday, maybe."

"This EJ here, stands for Emmett Jessup. He's my little prince. Aren't you pumpkin?"

Emmett Jessup smiled. He jumped into Naomi's lap and wiped his runny nose on her collar.

"I wasn't on meth then, when I had him. Or Lithium. Or as whacked as I am now."

"Is there someone you can talk to? A friend, relative, clergyman?"

Penny laughed. "You're kidding, right? I like your red hair, don't see much red hair these days. EJ's got some, see?"

Penny pulled up the boy's already red hair and showed off a swirling carrot clump at the nape of his neck, sassy with curl. "See? From the day he was born, not a bit of hair elsewhere but a little red ponytail."

Naomi stood. "That's nice. So, listen, I'm going to go now. Seems like you have some thinking to do."

"No! Wait. Take a look at where I'm living. This shit hole. No way to raise a kid, let alone two."

Emmett Jessup beamed at the mention of a brother or sister.

"I can try to help you get Section 8 housing, subsidized."

"You think you could?"

"No guarantees, but I can try."

"Even if I do, the father ain't gonna do shit, the *spicwhopasshole*. He don't even know my name."

"Lots of single moms make it on their own. There are programs. I can help."

Penny buttoned up her shirt. "That's good because what are the odds of someone dumping a load of money on me?"

"You never know."

Penny stopped to look at Naomi as if for the first time. "You're kind of pretty, you know that?"

"Thank you."

"What's your last name again?"

"Weiner-Gluckstein."

"Fuck, that's a mouthful. You a Jew?"

"Yes, I am."

"Well, you're still kind of pretty, no offense."

"No offense taken."

Penny stood and tried to snap her pants. "I'm starting to show. I've done my thinking. I'm ready, let's go."

"Are you sure?"

"Hey, when I say *go*, it means pronto. Right, *Emmeroo?*"

Emmett Jessup offered a grand nod.

Penny grabbed two packs of Pall Malls and dumped them in her purse. With the other hand, she intertwined her fingers in her son's tiny five and squeezed hard.

Naomi stopped the girl at the makeshift door. "Now listen, Penny. You be sure about this because there is no turning back."

"*Sureasshit.* Let's go."

"All right, then. You got everything?" asked Naomi.

"Oops, my backpack, can't forget that."

Penny slung it on her back.

Heavymotherfuckers, those bombs.

EIGHT

Omar Farooq, grandson of the Holy Land, son of an apostate, citizen of a cravenly occupied territory, did what he always did first thing in the morning. He washed his feet, unfurled his carpet for *Salat* and fell to his knees and forehead. Sometimes prayer was enough. No mass or dimension within its space, yet prayer felt denser than the entire universe itself. If only he could make Shivana understand. Omar bent and uttered the honey words created for no reason other than to the affirm the Merciful with perfect mind, perfect heart, perfect words. *Whatever is in the heavens and whatever is in the earth declares the glory of Allah.*

But today Omar could only affirm the unworthy filth of his actions. Try as he might to beat back these mental profanities, they consumed him in the holy tent of his supplications. By the fifth round of petitions, all universal truths fell suspect in his mind's eye but one—that his weakness rendered him undeserving before the eyes of God. Sleeping with shaven apostate blondes, surrendering deadly bombs to the capricious whim of unstable teenaged girls.

And, curse upon curses, possessing a wife he loved beyond comprehension, but was unable to control, as evidenced by Shivana's last text message:

I'll come by the house in the a.m. for some clothing and to help you as much as I can. No discussion, please.

In parts of Iran, Shivana would presently be lying bloodied and dazed under a pile of stones hurled from every man worth the honor he held above all. Omar naturally abhorred such crude and severe punishment. He was,

43

after all, a learned man dedicated to healing flesh not tearing it to pieces. But there had to be some middle ground. Here in this blasphemous nation, his woman was free to proclaim her independence simply because she wished it. Where lay the justice?

And more to the point, how could he live without her? It was Shivana who encouraged him to follow his medical dreams. Shivana who became his determined study partner when the strains of medical school nearly broke him down. Shivana who encouraged him to remain in the United States to start his own practice.

Now, well before 6:00 a.m., Omar had plenty of time to phone the staff and save them the aggravation of waking, dressing, driving into work and setting up for what was already to be a short day. He would tell them, *I'm feeling horribly sick, incapacitated nearly. Please reschedule the morning appointments. So sorry.*

He bent and wept, bent and wished, bent and asked. As they do, the prayers transported Omar to a new understanding, so that as Omar recited his final homage to Allah, all praise be unto Him, the almighty ritual delivered the gift of another solution.

Until at such a time Omar could get his wife back and convince her that leave they must, he would carry on. That's what he would do. *Carrying on* often had been the only choice he had. When Israeli tanks press your nose against concrete barriers and barbwire eats your ankles, you learn to carry on. Praise be to Allah for a choice at this moment in time. Choice was a privilege of the free; at this juncture of his journey, Omar felt unworthy but for dust and chains.

Omar carried on by finding in the closet a pressed blue cotton striped shirt recently dry-cleaned. His Haggar slacks hugged his fit frame closely, and a pat of cologne rendered him civil. For his own sanity, he donned his beloved loafers; when the desert scalds the soles of one's feet, let there be loafers for the beggars and sinners. When your throat is parched from fighting for freedom, loafers. For boys about to become men, loafers. Loafers for the salt of the earth and the kings above them. And so much the better if the loafers are from Italy.

Omar scrubbed beneath his nails and flossed his teeth. Everything as usual, no coffee, but the usual indulgence of a sweetened cup of tea. Next to prayer, tea took him closest to home. He even attempted once or twice to divine the tea leaves as Shivana's mother had done. But Omar would not allow himself to entertain such foolish superstitions.

He drove along Camino Real to the clinic, past the Dunkin' Donuts and Radio Shack, the HR Block and Walgreen's, the Wendy's and Big 5 Sporting Goods. He obeyed the traffic laws and made eye contact with other drivers courteously. He listened to public radio and used his turn signals. He followed the laws of the road and the universe as practiced in this insignificant corner of the world.

Omar parked in the back. He'd be foolish to park anywhere else. His entrance, as usual, came through the steel grey door of the medical marijuana outlet.

"Good morning, Stan."

"Good morning, Dr. Farooq."

"Check's in the mail."

"Thank you."

"Thank *you*, Stan."

"Have a nice day."

"You, too."

At the clinic, the glazier was replacing the shattered front window. You know you're in the wrong business when you have a window repair company on speed dial, Omar thought. Omar exchanged niceties with his staff, good people all of them. He did not stop to notice the patients in the waiting room.

~

The clinic receptionist handed Penny a pen and a clipboard with a gazillion pieces of paper.

"Fill out completely and return them to me when you're done."

Penny looked up from the clipboard at Naomi and said, "Hey, would you do me a favor? Emmett's gotta be like starvin.' Would you take him somewhere and get him an Egg McMuffin or something? You know, away from here."

Naomi knelt down eye-level to Emmett Jessup. "Wanna get something to eat? How about bulgur wheat pancakes and Grade B maple syrup?"

Clap-clap-clap-clap!

"No animal products for us." Naomi smiled. "Okay, we'll be back soon."

"Take your time. And little EJ, you remember your mama loves you more than the whole world put together a kabillion times over."

"I love you!"

"See that?" Penny advised Naomi. "The whole caboodle turns on that boy. Don't you forget it."

Naomi took Emmett Jessup's little hand and disappeared.

Penny sighed with relief.

It took, like, twenty hours for her to fill out the socialist forms, or at least it felt that way. Questions about her abortion history, menstruation cycle, insurance carrier, sexually transmitted diseases. Next of kin. *Now there's a hypothetical.*

She handed the clipboard to the receptionist, some *dykelesbian* who said, "Penny, please come with me, we'll get you changed. You can leave your stuff in a locker."

"Locker?" Penny hugged the backpack. "Can't I just keep it with me?"

The receptionist frowned. "We usually ask patients to…"

Penny clutched the bag with her life and grit her teeth madly. "This stays with me, got it?"

"Got it."

Inside Death Room South, Penny plunked her backpack down in the corner and threw her purse on top. The paper hospital gown kept creeping up her ass crack. She hated those friggin' things. The place smelled like sex, there's no mistaking that skanky smell. Somebody did some fucking in here recently.

She plopped on the chair, found the metal stirrups with her feet, and saddled up.

A second nurse came by with a little white paper cup. "Ibuprofen. And I can give you some Ativan, for your nerves if you want it."

"Two, please."

"No problem. Water?"

"I'm good." Penny gulped down the pills. Nothing better than free drugs.

"Now, lie back and relax, unclench your fists. It's painless, almost."

"Easy for you to say."

"Now, spread a little wider for me, here comes the speculum. We'll ease it on in. Good. Now, a little swab of antiseptic for your vagina and cervix. We want things clean, clean, clean, clean in there."

Penny felt the sting.

Nurse 2 shielded the view of the syringe, but Penny could spot one of those things a million miles away.

"Here comes the local anesthesia. Might hurt for one little prick."

"Name me a prick that doesn't." Penny cackled.

Nurse 2 smiled.

Penny bit her lip in anticipation but didn't feel much.

"See?" said Nurse 2, "doesn't hurt so bad." She shined a light through the speculum. "Now, I don't think you need dilation, but just to make sure."

She stuck a *gadgetgizmo* into Penny, who felt it grab her cervix. Or maybe she was imagining things. Wouldn't be the first time. Another *gizmogadget* went in.

"There. That'll give the doctor a little extra room to work."

"What's he need, an ocean?"

"Now, I'm going to put up this curtain across your mid-section. Makes things a little easier to take, if you know what I mean."

"Got it. Danka."

"The doctor's very good at what he does, not chatty or anything, but very empathetic. When he comes in, he'll pass a thin tube through your cervix and into your uterus. Slight discomfort, maybe, but you shouldn't feel any pain. But when he suctions the tissue out from the uterus, you may feel a little cramping, sort of like menstruation. That should go away quickly. And afterward, you may feel a little nauseous or sweaty or faint. That's normal. And you'll spot for a few days. But listen closely now, if you get a fever, bleed heavily or vomit persistently — any of these symptoms — I want you to come right back in or go directly to the hospital. You hear me? It's very important."

"And what if it don't work?"

"The procedure? It's successful more than 98 percent of the time, more than that, but those are the official statistics. So don't worry about that."

Penny asked. "Then what?"

"Then what, what?" asked the nurse.

"Then what happens to the baby?"

"You mean the fetus? We check to make sure we've gotten everything we need, and you're on your way."

"Do you bury it or anything?"

"It's disposed of properly."

"Medical waste," said Penny.

"Look, hon, if you're questioning your decision, it's not too late. You wouldn't be the first to get up out of that chair. And no one will judge you."

"No, let's *go go go*. I'm ready as a whore. Can't stay crucified like this all day."

"All right then. Sit tight and relax. Doctor will be in soon."

Penny watched the nurse tidy up and vanish from the room. Penny listened for the door to shut tight. She wondered if there were any hypodermic needles in the drawers like she always did at doctors' offices, but then she realized she wouldn't be needing them no more. Tapping the vein of destiny. The last high.

She eyed her backpack.

She reached down and snatched her purse from the floor, dug into the inside pocket and felt for the bomb's remote control.

It looked like a garage door opener. Probably was a garage door opener rejiggered by the doctor himself. Ain't that the coot, she was going to blow this place with a garage door remote control come from the soulless suburbs outside. She fingered the contraption. She zeroed in on the slight protrusion of the button. She slipped it behind her back, careful to prevent premature ejaculation.

Penny Lean, with the name she can't stand, took the deepest of breaths and closed her eyes. *So many things* tripped through her head. If only they would trip one at a time instead of all at once, maybe she wouldn't be in this predicament.

And then she did what she did worst.

She waited.

~

Omar scrubbed again and in the unisex bathroom mirror found a smile. Thankfully, his first up was a routine machine vac and not a D&E. The only noticeable on the chart was a positive for Hepatitis C. Omar was impressed, most people lie on that one.

Omar scrubbed one last time in Examining Room South and snapped on his gloves. Customarily he said hello to each woman or girl and made direct eye contact. These were trying times for patients after all. A firm handshake and a warm smile went a long way toward calming apprehension. In many ways, this procedure is more intimate than sex. But, today, try as he might, Omar could not fathom the idea of idle chatter or summoning his well-intentioned fatherly concern.

He found his vinyl swivel chair and rolled across the floor to the patient. The curtain drawn across her midsection allowed Omar to shield his shame and perhaps provided the patient the same cover.

Lots of vaginal scarring, including the vestiges of a poorly executed episiotomy. A twin-horned devil tattoo on her left inner thigh countered by a haloed cherub on the right. Superior to the unshaven vaginal hairline, words in blue-green ink reading: *But For The Grace Of God Go I.*

Omar couldn't agree more.

On the other side of the medical curtain, Penny Lean leaned back and wiggled her finger on the button of destiny.

What was she...eleven or twelve years old when the first man slobbered his lips on her pussy? Thirteen when she felt the sting of dick inside her? Fourteen by the time she sucked through a neighborhood of cocks. Talk about a *lovehaterelationship.* That penis thing was a pain in the fucking ass. End it now and take an abortion killer with you. Stir it up. Start the revolution.

With a flip of a switch, Omar turned on the extractor and waited until it modulated rapidly at a casual hum. Omar placed his hands on the patient's thighs and wiggled his fingers into her labia majora. He used the semi-flexible plastic cannula wand to find the crown of the cervix. Inside comfortably, he rested his hand on the control valve.

The extractor whirred. Omar monitored.

Penny felt an agitation in her womb through the anesthesia, through the nurse's empty words. Forget what they say about feeling nothing, you don't need nerve endings turned on to feel your baby clinging for its life. You feel it up inside your heart.

Penny couldn't think of a better way to bust out of the world but with ankles riding wide apart, blood rushing to her head, and her unborn child, tiny as she might be, rushing into a plastic bottle good for two gallons of milk.

Penny found the roundness of the remote's detonation button and circled its plastic outline. A drop of salty sweat slipped into her left eye.

Nurse 2 faked a smile and said, "Now, just a little longer, hon."

Penny gripped the paper under the table and pushed her ankles into the stirrups. Like the invasion of the body snatchers. Isn't that the way it is? Feel nothing or feel everything? Somebody find her some middle ground for *chrissakes.*

"Now, we're almost done, hon."

Penny arched her back and readied her finger. When it's time, it's time. And it was time. She didn't deserve much more of chance. When you figure out that your life is one big series of screw-ups, it doesn't take an Einstein to figure things ain't gonna change much in the future.

Ten, nine, eight. Fuck me and fuck this *motherfuckinglife.*

Seven, six. People who kill babies should be killed, that's the gospel, present company included.

Five, four. Emmett will be better with the *Jewlady* and whoever she's screwing at the moment.

Three for every betrayal and cheat.

Two for every punch and blow.

And *one. One* for the one big mistake that Penny was.

Penny squeezed the trigger. The edge of her fingernail snapped off.

"One. One. One," Penny pleaded.

"That's right, breathe," said the nurse.

"One!"

"What's that hon? You saying something?"

"Fucking one!" Penny demanded.

"Talk to me, sweetie," said the nurse.

"*Damnit.*"

"Hang in, we're almost done."

"No!!"

Penny's feet pounded the stirrups. She clenched her fists. She rocked from side to side.

The nurse said, "Doctor, you better stop."

Omar waved away her concerns.

"Please, stop!" cried Penny. She kicked the instrument tray and tools went flying.

"Doctor!" the nurse demanded.

"All right, for God's sake."

Omar pulled out the wand before he should have, sloppy by his standards, but he couldn't stand it. Couldn't wait to get out.

Penny wept.

Omar flipped the switch off.

"Hon, you okay now?" asked the nurse.

Penny grit her teeth.

The nurse took her hand. "That's it, sweetie. It's done. Over."

Omar stood and wiped his brow, the roller chair spun out from under him and came to a soft stop against Penny's backpack.

Penny stifled the urge to vomit. She elbowed up her body, but the nurse gently pressed her against the chair. "Let me just clean you up, and you'll be on your way."

Penny squeezed the nurse's hand. "You don't understand."

"Oh, hon, we have counseling."

She heard the clink of an instrument into a cold metal tray, the snap of the man's gloves and the click of his shoes toward the exit.

Omar mumbled, "Cancel the rest of the day. I'm going home sick."

Penny thought she heard a slight hesitation as he walked by the backpack. The door slammed behind him.

The killing machine whirred to a stop. In the quiet, Penny pressed the button one more time. *Why doesn't anything work in my life, just tell me that God?*

"You see? After a little jitters, not so bad, right?" said the nurse.

Penny relaxed her arched back and touched her knees together for the first time in an eternity. She fingered the trigger once more.

Pieceofshit.

BOOK II

"He was a bold man that first ate an oyster."
— Jonathan Swift

NINE

In the blogosphere and textosphere, the word traveled slowly at first, no Big Bang, no instant radiation. *Slow in the blogosphere,* naturally, meaning hours rather than days/months/years as is the case with scientific journals and dissertations.

History will record one day that the earliest Theory of Everything dispatch following Ethan and Shivana's press conference emanated from one of the few bloggers present, an occasional stringer for an online astrophysics website that survived (barely) on astronomy supply banner ads and not-so-subtle porn come-ons.

The dispatch was picked up by a recent journalism grad in the Associated Press' midtown Manhattan office. He had finished sucking down a smokeless bowl of Purple Yurple in the men's bathroom before returning to the science desk (a cubicle, actually). In the fashion in which he had been trained at NYU, he penned the headline:

All for One: Scientists Discover the "Theory of Everything."

The editor used the convenient abbreviation *ToE* throughout the article, buried all the math bullshit about E_8 at the bottom, and kept the Higgs boson nonsense to a minimum. Instead, he went to the heart of the matter and supported it with a quote (condensed and rewritten liberally, per standard operating procedure):

Scientists at Stanford University's Linear Accelerator today announced the discovery of the Theory of Everything, one grand equation consolidating time and space and every law in the universe. "God's great secret revealed," said Ethan Weiner-Gluckstein, the leading Stanford physicist who announced the find.

For the record, the AP editor condensed and blasted two other stories that night: *Galileo's Tooth Found By Italian Collector* and *Robotic Spy Planes Go Green*, but these curiosities were quickly to be forgotten. And, for the record, Ethan Weiner-Gluckstein didn't say *God's great secret revealed*, but the quote was too good to pass on.

With sensitive feelers, search engine spiders picked up the term *theory of everything* and the momentum spread the message to the outer edges of the Interweb. Chatter from a hundred thousand keyboards generated random currents of thought. By midnight, the term *theory of everything* rose exponentially until it came to rest atop every major most-searched list. Bada Bing, Bada Bang, Bada Google.

CNN topped its 1:00 AM broadcast with the news, and MSNBC quickly followed. Univision trumpeted *Mundo Uno* at the top of every hour. Fox chose to ignore the development on air but deemed it worthy of a bottom-third chryon that asked: *Latest Hoax? Elite scientists say nothing distinguishes good people from bad people.*

With 12 hours to go before a print deadline, editors of *Time* magazine made the bold decision to scrap their cover story on the inevitable war between Washington and Islamabad and called in a swarm of science, religion, philosophy and culture writers to cobble together a package anchored by a top-to-bottom cover proclaiming in an urgent font at 256 points...

WE ARE ONE!

...against a Photoshop-enhanced backdrop of the Milky Way and a 20 percent screen of a bearded Old Testament God. The top-right dog ear of the cover introduced the shining faces of Ethan Weiner-Gluckstein and Shivana Farooq as *The New Faces of Relativity*. The glib material inside the weekly described the pair this way: *what better twosome to take down the tyranny of the Standard Model than an observant Jew and a brilliant Ph.D. student representing every repressed woman of the Muslim world."*

In a nondescript inner office of the Department of Physics at Stanford University, a teaching assistant spread out an assortment of print-outs of digital newspapers, blogs and social media posts from around the world in preparation for the department's debriefing. In dozens of languages, the newspapers proclaimed the announcement in the boldest of headlines. The media outlets had no choice but to use one of three poor-quality JPEGs of Ethan and Shivana snapped by one of the few correspondents in the auditorium that evening who cared to even capture a digital image, so obscure were these two spokespersons for the theory that would change everything.

Beyond requests from the scientific, religious, and university presses, Ethan and Shivana's email inboxes bulged with urgent pleas for interviews, snapshots, Tweets, phone calls, voice mail – even Morse Code for God's sake — from Al Jazeera, the Jiji News Agency, Kyodo News Service, Agence France-Presse, Deutsche Presse Agentur, British Broadcasting Corporation (BBC), the Australian Associated Press, Xinhua News Agency, ITAR-TASS, Pakistan Press International, Assyrian International News Agency, Jewish Telegraphic Agency, GlobalPost, Ihlas News and countless others. Who can price the head of rarity?

And now that CERN had mysteriously cancelled its announcement, 60 Minutes, Rachael Maddow, *The Daily Show*, Steven Colbert, and Diane Sawyer topped the list of top-shelf US outlets clamoring for interviews. Shivana, in full bloom of excitement, tallied media requests by the minute, counting 215 by the end of the first day. Triple that plus sixteen by nightfall of the second.

If Ethan Weiner-Gluckstein needed further confirmation that his world had changed forever, President Mahoney himself made the momentous effort to grace this minuscule convocation, a first in the history of the Physics Department.

El Pres squashed his Styrofoam coffee cup with excitement. "Don't you get it? Ethan, Shivana, you're famous. And, Shivana, that comment on Friday about your visa, that was just a joke."

Shivana appeared relieved beyond all measure, but Ethan's stomach churned. Why hadn't he thought this through? He had foolishly expected to make the initial announcement, gather a little easily-deflected credit and watch the spotlights sweep over the true scientists behind the advance. He wanted a thin ray of recognition, not a thousand suns. He had forgotten that the media, like electrons, take the path of least resistance.

Shivana, meanwhile, savored the media response like halvah from her homeland. Fame, even fleeting, remains the surest ticket to freedom. The religious buggers she detested might easily oppress the anonymous female, but they lacked the fortitude to confront a woman of courage.

Ethan saw it another way. "Maybe we jumped the gun in making the announcement. CERN said nothing. This is, after all, a three-sigma discovery until it's certified."

"Ethan, do me a favor, save the scientific jargon for the lab," said Mahoney. "The school is in the financial shit tank. We need money."

"But three sigma means it's not 100 percent certain that it's correct."

"What's three sigma's certainty?"

"99.73 percent. There's still margin for error."

"You're kidding me, right? You're going to clog the university's funding pipeline because there's a one in 400 chance that someone screwed up. Gimme a break."

Ethan tried another tack. "Maybe, the announcement wasn't ours to make. Maybe, we should have directed the press office to suggest the media go elsewhere for interviews."

Mahoney snorted at the sheer idiocy of the suggestion. "Like where?"

"Like CERN."

"CERN didn't have the balls to stay in this game." Mahoney shrugged.

"Then the scientists who made this discovery."

"What, like all 500 of them?"

Shivana couldn't help herself, once again. "Actually 1,386 scientists and another 12,852 students, if you count the graduate students, which I think is only fair."

"Shivana makes an excellent point. Too many faces. That's the problem with research today. Like five-year-olds playing soccer, a big dust pile around every little schnook chasing the ball. Where are the Einsteins, the Oppenheimers, the Bohrs, the Curies? The cult of personality, we've lost it. We progress by committee, one insufferable professional journal cycle to the next. No wonder the public tires of us. And then kapow! Home run. And you know what? Right now success has *two faces.* Stanford faces. Faces of clarity, innocence. I can't think of a better duo than you. People need heroes like you. They believe in people like you. They're tired of the jaded and satirical. They want real people with flaws and problems, people they can relate to. That being said, we've texted your primetime lineup to your smartphones. You leave in ninety minutes."

Shivana couldn't help herself as she scrolled on her iPad. "Actually 87 minutes and 32 seconds."

Ethan squelched a dry heave. This not being a democracy by any stretch, he felt Mahoney's decision did not merit an objection, but inside his brain, he already imagined Hebrew letters wiggling like strings of energy before his face.

The department head nodded his agreement. "It's a go, amigos."

Mahoney summed it up with a slap on the back. "Safe travels and *Go Cardinal!*"

TEN

Oprah's private jet touched down at San Mateo's private airport with nary a lick of friction. The Global Express XRS aircraft, rolled to a stop inside a cordoned tarmac on the airfield's east end, closest to the dawn. The pilot, sleek as his plane, stepped out on the air stairs for a yoga break and swanned into a Warrior II pose. Above in the kitchen, the chef warmed the meatless breakfast and chilled a Sonoma Valley Sauvignon Blanc. In the cabin, the steward clicked on electric blankets to initiate the warmth.

Shivana sped down the airport road in her banged-up red Toyota Corolla titled to her husband. Her Fitbit told her that her heart leapt from 72 to 94 beats per minute upon spotting the sleek jet in the near distance, its silver fuselage bathed in early orange sun. She estimated its distance at 725 meters. At 120 kilometers per hour, she should arrive in the parking lot in precisely 22 seconds, give or take a second or two, depending on her rate of deceleration, which she hadn't chosen yet, other than *frickin' fast.* Since childhood, Shivana had been blessed with the ability to estimate distances by sight or sound to an accuracy of three to five percent. She drove recklessly for the first time in her life and counted the meters falling between her and freedom. Now 450, now 382, now 265, now 212.

At 165 meters, Shivana's gaze snapped back with intuition to the rear view mirror and the deserted road behind her.

Free and clear.

Her deceleration began 2.9 seconds after her initial prediction, within a two percent margin of error. She would have commended herself had she the time, but better to put it in park and make a dash.

Swathed in crimson robes encrusted with gold, Shivana fumbled for her keys. She rushed to pop the trunk lid. On the strength of her determination, she yanked out (carefully, because she couldn't afford another set) matching knock-off Dior garment bags. She fobbed her car locked tight and slipped off her high heels to run to the sun.

The jet grew in perspective, rising above the horizon, a bird of paradise to behold, ready to whisk her to the world of dreams made real. The pilot waved coolly. Shivana flashed a smile. Never had man or machine appeared so delectable.

Closing in on 54 meters. Shivana's internal slide rule worked overtime as she dragged her bags along the asphalt. Forty meters quickly fell to 24.

So close. So nearly there. A stretch away.

Shivana made the foolish mistake of turning her head behind her.

She saw Omar, eyes aflame, marshaling his gleaming black Maxima to a screeching stop.

Shit.

So this is what it feels like to become a pillar of salt.

Omar jumped from the car. Shivana stumbled.

"Shivana, wait. I command you! Shivana, I ask you sweetly. Shivana, for all you know that is right and good. Shivana, do not go."

Her monitored heart rate? Who the hell cared. Her determination was immeasurable, no Fitbit could measure that. Omar had never touched her with anything but kindness, but this was not the time to take chances.

Had she been a believer, Shivana thought, a heavenly angel in despair might whisper in her ear, *not this time, benevolent sister, mercy be upon you.* But Shivana believed not in heavenly spheres but in human capacity.

She snarled and pressed her keys through her knuckles ready to strike. "Not a chance."

Omar fell prostrate. "I have no choice in the matter. Allah, the God of *your* father, needs me to protect your purity, the purity of Islam."

Shivana shrugged. "Allah needs *you?* He should be able handle it all by himself, powerful as he is."

"He exercises his power through his believers."

"Pity him the workforce."

Omar saw her grit and sunk down even further. "You think it's easy being a soldier of Allah? Ever vigilant? It's tiring. Exhausting, if one were to confess. Thank heaven for B12 and capsuled fish oil. But that's the sacrifice. We are called upon, every one of us, to sacrifice."

Shivana felt the slow burn of a dying star. No matter how deeply she yearned to be liberated from the gravity of her culture, an elemental part of her felt loyal to the old ways, the subservient state of mind as stable as radon.

But...not today.

She walked two steps toward him and wagged a finger.

"And what do you know of sacrifice? Every woman on Earth sacrifices tenfold for every man's one. And tell me, what's so sacred about sacrifice? You say we were placed here for sacrifice, but I suggest that you return to the holy Qur'an and correct your misreading. Anyone can sacrifice, it's pedestrian, commonplace."

Omar considered her words because he was, after all, a considerate man. "What then?" he inquired.

"How about *joy*? Imagine if every Muslim man brought joy to bear upon this world and abandoned the sacrifice?"

Omar had no ready answer. So he answered as he always did when he had no ready answer. "You are blind to the word of the Qur'an."

"Me blind? Obedience without understanding is a blindness, too." Shivana cared how things worked, not how they didn't. But she was glad for the discourse with her husband, as they had in college, before his piety narrowed all possibilities.

"Sacrifice is the greatest joy."

Shivana waved away such nonsense. "Sacrifice bars you from entering the chamber of the Beloved, who so longs for the gift that only *you* can offer. So I ask you, Dr. Omar Farooq, if the Beloved was waiting in your chamber, asking for a gift of joy from you...what gift would you care to offer?"

Omar contemplated Shivana's question. A surprising one at that. Never posed to him before. In fact, the proposition stunned him. His father spoke of skill and vocation. His teachers drilled him on dedication and endurance. His mother touted education and travel. His Imams preached duty and faith. He himself had spoken of the willing obligation to medicine.

But *joy*? This was a new one.

Matter, antimatter. Omar knew a thing or two about physics. The Persians invented physics centuries before Europe saw the stars for what they truly were: heavenly bodies not heavenly creatures. Could sacrifice and joy be twin sides of the same coin, one unseen when obscured by the other?

The sun lifted above the horizon for the first time that morning.

And then the epiphany came, exploding with forty times the cerebral force that had formed his Muslim faith in a blaze of insight some 12 years earlier. With telescopic clarity, he realized that the woman with the almond eyes was right — sacrifice is a form of idol worship, equally *haraam* as an image of a man on a crucifix with blood dripping down his sides or a dusty catalog of 330 million gods with eight arms and three eyes. Graven images all.

"How could I have been so wrong!" he blurted.

A window in his mind opened, and the sunshine burst through. Omar closed his eyes and traveled deeply inward to try to imagine what gift might he possess worthy of a world supreme.

What joy might he offer to the universe? For Omar the answer was easy.

"Omar, are you okay?" Shivana asked. She couldn't quite remember the last time she had seen him this...*light*.

Omar smiled. "Yes, yes I am. Better than ever."

"Because you look...."

"*Destined?*"

"Good word," said Shivana

"I am."

"Maybe you need to sit down, get a glass of water. It's early, we've all had a trying night."

Omar Farooq kissed his wife on the cheek, and with his whole heart whispered the following words, "My love, continue on, follow your dreams. Seek your happiness in whatever form you desire. I give you my blessing, full and eternal. I may be your husband, but I know I am not your journey. Who am I to deny you your journey? And every journey should be a dream in motion. And who am I to deny your dream? Who am I?"

Omar bent down and kissed Shivana's shoes. He hugged her ankles.

She wondered if her ears deceived her. Were her eyes to be believed. "Omar, are you serious, just like that?"

But, she didn't need an answer. The beneficent gaze of his visage said it all. This was the man she once knew and loved, tender, forgiving, kind.

Shivana flung her arms around her husband and kissed him on the neck, public modesty be damned. And anyway, only Oprah's pilot was watching.

"Bless you, Omar. You are a good man, and I hope you find your happiness as well."

Omar stroked Shivana's jet-black hair, shining like God's raiment. "Jazak Allah. *May God reward you.*"

Shivana kneeled slightly and kissed his hand as if he were a pasha from another time. "And peace be upon you, Omar."

She grabbed her bags and scrambled to the jet, her red robes streaming behind her like flames of confidence.

Once she vanished inside the aircraft, Omar found his carpet in the car for *fajr* prayers and removed his shoes.

His knees dropped to the stiff rug for the bizillionth time. Why did it feel like the first? With his heart pumping with unlimited potential he mouthed the opening lines of the dawn prayer. *In the name of Allah, Most Gracious, Most Merciful. Praise be to Allah, the Cherisher and Sustainer of the worlds.* He trembled in the presence of God and drew in the rare aroma of mercy. *Thee do we worship, and Thine aid we seek.* Allah so overpowered him that he felt his ego contract, dry up and blow away like cosmic dust set loose in the heavenly void. Light shined upon him and warmed him with the heat of a thousand suns. *Keep us on the right path.*

And for the first time, Omar added his own words. *In the name of Tawheed, the Divine Unity, I pledge my ever-abounding love.* He kissed the loving planet. *We are emissaries of the divine.*

~

Had Omar found cause to lift his head and open his eyes, he would have witnessed Shivana climb the twelve steps to her flight and vanish inside the plane. But he remained prostrate for a few moments after prayers, happy to breathe. Finally, he slipped on his Italian loafers and jetted away in his car at the maximum speeds allowed by law. Highway patrolmen don't take kindly to Arabs in black cars, no matter how divinely inspired at the moment.

Had Omar been more observant, he might have noticed Ethan Weiner-Gluckstein pass him on the airport road. Omar might have seen the man make a few circles in confusion before finding the aircraft in waiting. He may have deduced this was the hallowed academic mentor revered by Shivana. Omar's preoccupation prevented him from seeing Ethan grab his broken roller bag and climb into the same vessel waiting to transport Shivana to some promised land. Had Omar's eyes not been peering into the Beloved's, Omar might have noticed the aircraft's cabin doors shut tight and the wheels roll forward to the runway's end where Shivana and Ethan's journey was to begin. Had he cared to notice, he might have witnessed the steel bird take flight with the breath of God under her wings. He might have.

But his mind's eye saw only the Face, ineffable and unknowable yet familiar as his own reflection.

Ethan, for his part, was still not sure this move was wise whatsoever. After his poor showing before the shallow body of journalists at Stanford, how might it feel to stutter and stall on a stage facing 50 million daytime viewers?

In the sharp morning sun, Shivana took Ethan's hand and said, "You're afraid."

"My ticks, my stutter, my inability to—"

"This is the Theory of Everything, don't you see? All your dreams – if you choose to call them that – are in that subset, yes? They belong to you like your fingers to your hand, like you to the universe."

Ethan translated the thought into a mathematical equation that momentarily brought lucidity and ease. But then one could argue dread existed in that subset, as well. In fact, if one approached the problem logically, *everything* was in the subset before the Theory of Everything and everything in the subset after the announcement. So what exactly had changed? Nothing, nada, zilch.

That's what Ethan didn't get.

Shivana squeezed his hand with assurance. "Anyway, too late now. Strap in for the ride of your life."

Her words were an attempt to thrill, but Ethan took them literally and grew a shade paler. He donned a tepid smile so as not to dampen Shivana's soaring spirit.

In her excitement, Shivana couldn't help but turn her gaze away from Ethan and out the window. The jet accelerated down the runway and lifted smoothly above San Francisco Bay. What a beautiful curve. She gave up counting the miles between San Francisco and Chicago and all the cities in between. What numbers could measure her joy? What distance could separate her now from her destiny?

ELEVEN

Pastor Harlen Spridgen wrestled with a bad dream. Mosh pits of snakes slithered over him en route to devour his flock. He swacked the serpents away with a mighty switch of hickory like his daddy had used to correct him when he was a boy. But the snakes shouldered the blows and slinked onward, a writhing army, mission bound. Beyond, in the dream's distance, Harlen saw his church sanctuary sinister and black. Parishioners moaned in the pews beneath a pale moon. Their arms flailed skyward in unison, a stadium wave of woe. The people appeared so distant he could hardly make out their faces. They tried to signal something with their arms. The swarm of snakes rose above his ankles to his knees. The switch landed like a feather upon their backs, all his physical power forfeited. Harlen tried to scurry away, but his legs remained gripped in terror's hold.

Harlen never reached the end of the dream. He was jolted awake by his old-fashioned radio alarm clock set to an adult contemporary station. There's something to be said for interrupting bad dreams. They tap deep. Still, in the pajama dawn, the same sensation overwhelmed him now — immeasurable will power coupled with complete physical impotence. All desire but no effect.

He wiped the sweat from his chest and touched the pulse of his wrist to make sure he existed safely between his satin sheets. He listened for Sandra Lee but heard nothing except his own staggered breath. Feeling bothered and itchy, unresolved like his dream, he was trapped in an anxious purgatory of emotion. He kicked away the sheets to let the air conditioner cool his body.

He reached under the bed for his laptop and flicked it on to search for studs, but he slapped the lid closed. Not this morning, maybe later, maybe tomorrow. The taste was gone for the moment.

Instead, Harlen surfed over to Dobson's Focus on the Family website for some keywords for his next sermon. Thank God for his calling. It calmed him, centered him when the bad dreams came. He always made the attempt to craft his homily early in the week, to give him time to unearth a pithy catchphrase, a time-tested quote, an aphorism worthy of grandma's sampler to arouse the parishioners' passions – that's how you drive a sermon home. Close the deal, baby, you gotta close the deal.

But instead of Dobson's usual parenting tips and Christian bullet points for facing life's challenges, Harlen spotted this headline:

'All is One' Say Scientists

Harlen shimmied himself up to a sitting position. He clicked deeper and read an essay that echoed a call Harlen often heard in his heart but had never cared to answer. It said that science, the enemy, had irrevocably reconciled itself with the central tenant of religion -- that there was a single God, not four physical forces or a multitude of corollaries or secondary equations bursting with terms. There was a single, intelligent design after all.

Harlen shifted gears and wondered why it mattered anyway. Scientists discover this, they discover that. Preachers preach this, they preach that. Both seem to dance around the truth, never touching it. Faith demands so much of its believers. Science so little. So much suspension of disbelief on both sides.

Harlen's finger tickled the keyboard as he surfed over to his favorite guy site. He drank in their glistening bodies. Flesh may be fleeting, but at least it's real. The heat of lust warmed Harlen's nether parts, and his pressing need returned.

And wouldn't you fucking know it, who picks this moment to strut into the room?

"What are you doing?" asked Sandra Lee Spridgen.

Harlen closed the laptop lid and prepared himself for another one of his wife's high and mighty tirades.

"You've heard, I'm sure," she said softly. "One big cosmic plan that explains it all."

"I heard."

Sandra Lee sat down on the side of the bed next to her husband for the first time in a long time. "And I've been thinking."

"You thinking? That's a new one."

Sandra Lee lovingly intertwined her fingers with her husband's, like she had set out to do when they lashed hands together in marriage eight years earlier.

"All these things we possess," she began, "the Mercedes, the houses, the granite counter tops, the yacht, don't they feel trivial sometimes? Valueless?"

"Perhaps, sometimes." Harlen intentionally prevaricated in case this was a trick question.

"The electric blanket and electric warmers, the hot tubs and towel warmers, the batteries in the kitchen garbage can that lifts the lid. Our vibrators? Why are we so cold? Why do we need boxes full of double AAs to energize us? There's a reason they call them *trappings*. Because they *trap* you. Don't you feel it sometimes?"

"I do."

"Bluetooth this, infrared that, remote controls and wireless communications. Antiseptic wipes, double locks, Internet-enabled alarms, passwords, and secrets. What are we afraid of? Is there anything without cooties anymore? Material dogma, that's all it is. Material blinders that keep us from seeing what's true, what's important."

Harlen laughed.

"What's so funny?" Sandra Lee asked.

"Nothing, it's just you're the last person I expected to hear talk like this."

"Me, too."

Since hearing of the Theory of Everything, Sandra Lee wondered where had it all gone wrong? In college after watching her mother drill through a parade of Army officers, Sandra Lee vowed to love one man and one man only. Her marriage would be a partnership in Christ, in which she would jealously guard her fidelity from wedding night to four grandchildren on the retirement ranch, hopefully somewhere away from this Northern California bastion of Liberalism. Sandra Lee packaged her whole enchilada for Mr. Right. *Mr. Christian Right.* And Harlen provided the hot sauce in the second year of studies at Oral Roberts University. Man, that guy could tear the pants off Jesus with his sermons, and he was on the basketball team. And sweet. The smile of a robber. On their first date, with a seductive glint in his eye, he laid out the blueprints for the church he envisioned — a sprawling Dallas exburb compound where Christ would be worshiped in goodness and positive light. He drove her to the very plot of land behind a Walmart where it was to be built. The Walmart church fell through *but the Lord works in strange ways* as Harlen liked to say, and a school classmate oozing with Google profits offered Harlen a plot of land in Palo Alto for a ground-up church.

A few rash outings with college football players had left Sandra Lee unprepared to discern Harlen's true sexual leaning until after the honeymoon. Tragically, once you're married to a Baptist preacher, there's no divorcing, period. She was not a fussy girl, but her burning bush remained unexplored. And her mother had taught her that an unquenched fire within a woman burns only herself.

Burn, baby, burn.

She took stock of Harlen now, still a handsome man, still dedicated to Christ, and still gay as Elton John.

But he was all she had.

She rubbed Harlen's cheek, because she had no one else to talk to at this moment, and that saddened her to no end. Here she was, the wife of a lauded pastor, daughter of a warrior of valor, thin blonde with piano fingers and perfect cheekbones, yet she had no one to confide in except by default her gay husband who she couldn't bear to be around most times. But this, this Theory of Everything. She hadn't seen it coming. She had prepared herself well enough never to be blindsided again. Or so she thought. But how can you know what's on your blindside? That's why they call it a blindside after all.

"I have a question for you, Harlen."

"Shoot."

"Who do you talk to?"

"What do you mean?"

"Intimately, about your problems, demons, doubts, like everyone has."

"My parishioners, my colleagues."

"No. Not talk *at*, but talk to?"

"No one, I guess."

"Right. And who are you physically closest to? Someone, a person, a human being."

"You?"

"Exactly. And who are you emotionally farthest from, out of everyone you know?"

"You."

"Precisely. And so what keeps us together?"

Harlen shrugged his shoulders for fear a trap was about to snap.

Sandra Lee saw his confusion and whispered the answer on his neck. "*A lie.*"

"A lie?"

"And isn't that a shameful way to live a life? If you had one hour of your life left to live. No, sixty seconds of your life, and God plunked you on a mountain top to speak to the gathered, the entire family of nations, all colors and creeds, in his stead, on his behalf, with just enough time to tell the world one thing that it should know, what would you say? Sixty seconds mind you, not a lot of time for bullshit dogma. Just the truth, the real honest-to-goodness unvarnished truth, what would you say? You're the preacher, the silver-tongued devil. What words of wisdom would you offer, Harlen? The show may be short, but the stage is wide. Do you know what I mean?"

Harlen did. "Sandra Lee, let me ask *you* a question."

"Shoot."

"Where have you been?" he asked.

"Downstairs in the kitchen."

"No, I mean all my life."

"Living the lie, with you."

~

On the very next morning, the Christian day of rest, at the crack of creation's light, Harlen Spridgen sprung out of bed and donned his blue suede shoes and finest white suit, the one he had bought in Phoenix his second year of preaching. He buffed his shiny nails and snipped the shoots from his nostrils. With a full Windsor, he fitted a silk blue tie popping with pink fleur de lis. He garnished his pocket with a pink handkerchief in a fluted fold. He backed out his beloved '65 copper Mustang convertible and drove drop top in a slow procession of truth heading straight for the beaming halogen headlight of the Almighty himself.

For six days a week, Harlen lived on Chaos Street — for which he had only himself to blame — but on Sunday, Satan in his prime couldn't touch Harlen's joy of ministry, no siree, of that he was certain.

His church reflected his chest-swelling pride: Seventy-two stained glass windows, 3752 spring-bound cushioned theatre seats, four drops of velvet curtains as long as basketball courts, 112 air conditioning ducts, two 24-foot diagonal LED screens, a 7.1 surround sound system with a mixing board that would make Def Leppard weep, a full video production studio, three websites with 720,000 unique visits a month, a daily blog, a Twitter count that put him on the Twitter map, 18 *guaranteed* annual guest appearances on *The 700 Club* television program, 49 union-free, full-time equivalent employees, and for good measure, vested health and retirement benefits coupled with six weeks of vacation and sick leave on the honor system. And one very special parking spot with a golden sign that read:

Reserved for Our Good Pastor H. Spridgen

Today for the first time, Harlen drove beyond the parking spot and pulled in down below, where the parishioners park. Sometimes it's all about *the walk*.

The sprinklers didn't run on Sundays, but the lawn did gleam. Harlen smiled, shook hands, smiled and hugged, smiled and backslapped, smiled and kissed babies blue. Seemed like every one of the seven thousand souls of the blessed *Calvary Baptist Crusade for Christ the Son, Jesus, Savior of the Globe, 1st United Church* had come out this Sunday morning.

Inside, the aisle felt like the Red Sea parting for the commandment receiver as people stepped away to let the leader through. How can carpet feel so good?

At the allotted time, Harlen rose and assumed the position, his hands clutching the lectern as if he were holding the hands of God. Together, they were doing this together, Harlen told himself. Harlen Spridgen, a veteran of a thousand internal wars. Harlen Spridgen, son from no man's land in a trailer park. Harlen Spridgen, the most sincere faker in the land. *That* Harlen Spridgen always knew this moment would come in the garden of truth.

"Brothers and sisters," he started. "This won't take long."

A deep breath and he embarked. "Light is pure. When it comes from God, it is pure. Any takers on that?"

Amens from all.

"We men and women are vessels of the light, but we're all closed up in the container of our own making constructed out of the *self,* the *ego,* call it what you will. And, because we are full of shame within this container of our own making, we spend our busy lives busting tiny little holes into the sides of our vessels in search of the warmth of the brightness that once shined upon us all, the brightness that makes up who we truly are. But, they are small holes, no more than peepholes. So, why don't we shatter the container, let in *all* the light, you ask? Funny thing is, we like our container, even as it enslaves us. We like it because it feels safe, it's a known entity. Frigid shame requires no courage, just more blankets of dogma and faith. But the blankets only keep us from busting out more holes in the vessel for true warmth. Do you hear me when I say *what a heavy load, brothers, and sisters?* After a while, not one of us can move because we are smothered. No wonder we're miserable creatures in need of a Lord and Savior to rescue us."

Harlen continued, "And do you know how to make new holes? Not with a toothpick of curiosity. Not with a little drill of fanciful dreams. You make new holes with the pickax of truth, that's how. You bust walls with hammers of hope. You shatter stones with fists of fortitude. And you throw blankets aside to expose yourself as you really are. Your signature. That's it, that's all. The trick of tricks. When you shine, God shines. That's all you we to do. Reveal the light of God as it filters through our personal prism. Easy, isn't it?"

Harlen didn't stop to gauge the tenor of the congregation. No stopping now.

"And so brothers and sisters, children and grandparents, I have a hole to bust through right now with you. A personal hole. And I'm glad you're here today with me. Couldn't ask for a better group of friends. Because I *believe* in you. I love you deeply, each and every one of you. You ready? 'Cause here we go. I reveal to you today these very words, I, Harlen Spridgen, Pastor Harlen Edward Spridgen. I am a homosexual, plain as this is a church of God."

A gasp from the audience.

"Call it what you will, but I'm busting holes, children. Busting holes and I feel the light a shining. Revelation comes in many forms, none more central than the revelation we choose to make to ourselves. And I leave my fate, like Jesus before Pontius Pilate to *you* my dear friends. Send me packing, and I will be a happy man, insist that I stay and I will be a happy man. But right here, right now, I'm basking in a white blaze of light. And I

70

swear to you with Jesus as my witness, it feels mighty good. More than mighty good. *Hallelujah* good. Because I am free. Say hallelujah with me, now!"

"Hallelujah, hallelujah. Ha-le-lu-yeah!"

"And I invite you to pick up a hammer. Grab a pickax, people! Throw off your shivering blankets of falsehood. And fill your vessel to the brim. Snuggle with the One."

They were with him, praise be! The current of their love ran through Harlen as if powered by a hundred million double D batteries. He beheld a congregation standing on tipsy toes of adulation.

A swelling chant filled the auditorium. "Harlen! Harlen! Harlen! Harlen!"

Harlen stepped down from the podium. The Israelites, beholden to Moses upon entering the Promised Land, could not have provided a finer reception than these fine Christian folks of the greater Palo Alto area.

Gorgeous Jimmy's parents, Margie and Dathan Lean, slithered through the crowd until they reached Harlen. Marge pressed her hands on Harlen's cheeks like he was her son. "Fantastic talk, pastor. Love you, love your message."

"More power to you, Harlen," said Dathan. "I was against homosexuals big time, still am. But I'm on your side, and I don't know why."

They stood seven deep for the chance of warming their palms on the unbound light of Pastor Harlen. The women showered him with kisses, and the men stepped in for hugs. Those in the back lines pressed forward to feel the presence of his aura. Harlen surfed across the room feeling like a rock star, weighing a trillion tons lighter now that the closet door had been busted off its rusted hinges. Only Bev Gilliam and a few of the Pro-Life Crusade gals remained in the back of the church, unmoved and elusive.

The miracle washed over Harlen with each stroke of a loving hand. Ain't nothing ever felt better in his life. Let the caller, and the called disappear, lost in the Call.

Hunky dory, that's all he could think. Everything was hunky dory.

TWELVE

The wooden floor of the Cubberley Pavilion on Middlefield Road was newly buffed, twinkling like a sheet of ice after a Zamboni ride. A few of the women dancers wore satin dresses, and the men wore shirts open to their clavicle and tucked in their high-waisted pants. This being a Sunday evening practice, most gals wore sweats with dance sneakers, and the guys sported polo shirts and slacks.

The clothes might have been casual, but the etiquette was never dressed down. A proper bow and invitation, a curtsey of acceptance. A slight demure, a flicker of eyelashes. A willful gait, a strengthening jaw. The ritual was rooted in some deeper charm and beauty, something timeless.

Sandra Lee Spridgen could not help but buck the trend by donning a hot tangerine low-back, one-shoulder outfit with a thigh-high mini-skirt, garlanded with a sprinkle of rhinestones that twinkled like stardust even when she stood still, which she couldn't. No way she could. After all, this was her coming out party. If Harlen insisted on being so revelatory (and more power to him), so could she, and should. She tested her open-toe shoes and made sure no one noticed as she hiked up her jacquard tights. How she loved the high French stockings that brought her panty line all the way to her waist along the sides of her long legs making them appear even longer. She loved long legs. Her fingernails were filed to a smooth point and polished solid orange to match the dress. She had added little sparkling appliqués at the tips of each one. She bit them nonetheless.

Like a schoolgirl at the prom, Sandra Lee stood floor-side in anticipation of her partner's approach. She sashayed and swayed and nearly tinkled in her panties. And by golly, the moment she laid eyes on him, she did.

He wore a black pair of tails cut to the quick across his solid frame, a white bow tie across his high collar, and a pair of patent leather shoes so black they shined blue. His white gloves moved through the air as he glided toward her with patience, reverence, restraint. Omar Farooq, the Palestinian abortionist of Palo Alto, reached out his hand, his fingers making the final invitation to the pollinating blonde fitted into a flower of glorious ruffles. Sandra Lee quick-looped three times and her toes tapped out the slow two, quick two, and one slow cadence of the T-A-N-G-O as she twirled into his arms.

His thumbnail ran up her thigh and tapped her wet lips. He placed his right hand on her bare shoulder blade and traveled down to press the small of her back. Her glove alighted on his broad shoulder. The fingers of their left hands intertwined and pointed like a compass in the direction of their imminent departure. His browns met her blues in a smoldering glance before they swooped down check-to-cheek for the first foray across the floor.

The sideline couples sent in hoots and hollers because the pair sliced so nice. Why hadn't anyone noticed them before?

Sandra Lee wasted no time and surprised Omar with a double glance for a quick reverse. But he was quicker and stepped back for a dramatic corte before she could chance a lead. She roared with laughter, and the turn of her head sent them spinning into a counter rotation and another and another.

Omar smiled and doubled their speed again. She was up to the task in heels that hardly hit the floor. She reached back to loosen her hair, and her golden locks bounced to life. They chuckled in unison, twirling faster, faster. A blur of light and motion against a needless and distant backdrop.

On the five, Omar bent his arm, and Sandra Lee filled it like a reverse eclipse on a moon. Light on dark. He spun her body close. Breath feeding breath, they leapt for a final flight across the floor ending with a sultry drag to an unfathomable stop. The round began again, and the pair twisted off on a tour of every edge and corner of the floor.

As they all do, the song ended. The applause from the others was clearly meant for the startling pair, such was the synchronicity between the two dancers. And *that contrast*, dark swirl of masculine and blonde bedazzle. Luminous.

Shoulder to shoulder, Omar presented his partner to the empty judges' table, for there were none that first night. Still, he prowed and she bowed, and they both made believe. They couldn't help but check each other's eyes to be sure this was all really true, happening to them. Shivers, that's all. Everyone felt it.

No time to celebrate. Rumba!

Omar and Sandra Lee formed a box for two quick side steps and one slow step forward. A waltz followed with its majestic sweeps, and then the rising and falling twinkles of the Foxtrot, followed by the pivots, chassés, and turns of the quickstep and ending with heels beating out the rhythm of the heart of the Paseo Dobles, where there is no escaping love.

Then it all began again with the Tango, Omar and Sandra Lee's signature dance, just like couples have wedding songs and men have first cars, and girls have first kisses, universes have beginnings, beings have moments of conception. What a gift.

Omar clasped Sandra Lee's waist for the final dance of the evening. How far away were his troubles, a wayward wife, a stolen bomb, a family denied. Should the angel Gabriel himself offer Omar a drink from the divine Cup of Jamshid, he would kindly decline the elixir of immortality, such was his completeness.

And here was the kicker. It had been so close, *right here* the whole time. Directly under his feet, he thought, excuse the pun. His joy, his destiny, his gift, and Sandra Lee's as well. The two of them spinning alone on the floor of life before meeting on J-Date—there was nothing random about it. Every song that played on the PA confirmed Omar's joy, every step he took with Sandra Lee was a celebration of the divine in motion.

Omar thought for a moment of his painful past, but only for a moment. He thought it wise to bring from the past only that that is worth building upon. The remembrance of suffering creates a foundation bound to fail.

"I love you," he whispered in Sandra Lee's perfect ear.

"I love you, too." She giggled in a whirl.

It surprised no one in the greater South Bay dance community when, weeks later, Omar and Sandra Lee swept the South Bay Open Latin Dance Competition. Two weeks after that, they scored first all-around at the far more competitive San Francisco Ballroom Invitational. That win catapulted them squarely in the center of the NorCal Regional and then headlong into the upcoming Western States Finals. Getting the costumes, refining the steps, that was the busy work. Finding energy in each other's eyes, that's what brought meaning to it all.

Couldn't lose, these two.

THIRTEEN

Jimmy Lean, aka the James Dean of the neighborhood, opened the car door and climbed in. The darkness of the overpass prevented him from identifying the driver, but there was no need to see.

"Some speech today, Pastor."

Harlen smiled. "Like it?"

Jimmy shrugged. "Not bad, but I wonder how long they'll love you. They all seem pretty high on this theory stuff."

"High is the right word. The whole world is high. Everything is all right. And it will be, always will."

"I see you drank the Kool-Aid."

"Jimmy, I just wanted to say—well, I want to say a lot more—but for right now I need to say good-bye and good luck. I'll never see you again like this. Maybe in church, I hope in church, but not like this, never like this. And I pray you grow up to become a great man with a family and whatever you want. I wish my words were more profound, but I think I'm done with profound."

Jimmy twirled a packet of white powder in his fingers. "So I guess you don't want this?"

"No, thank you."

"Good blow."

"I'm sure."

In the spirit of confession Jimmy said, "You know, Pastor, I charged you double, triple of what this shit is worth. Ripped you off every time."

"I know. And Jimmy. For what it's worth, all I got to say is I'm sorry. Real sorry."

"See ya then." Jimmy opened the door.

"Jimmy, wait."

Jimmy said, "Change your mind?"

Harlen clicked on the overhead light. He handed the boy an envelope. "I want you to have this."

"Money?"

"Just a little."

"I don't need money."

"For college or something."

"My parents have gobs of it."

"Then something worthwhile, you'll find something. I insist. Now go."

Jimmy took the envelope and stuffed it into his back pocket. "What are you gonna do now?"

"You mean after I find someone my own age? Minister, keep on ministering, that's all I want to do."

"Well, then, bless you."

"You mean it?"

"I absolutely do."

"That means a lot."

Jimmy jumped out and watched the Lexus skip away. He unfolded the drug packet and let his hand fall to his side so his fingers might scatter the little less than a gram of powder onto the concrete sidewalk. His Vans sneakers disbursed the tiny pile until all that remained was a white splotch and a tiny cloud of dust. He opened the envelope and feathered the bills with his thumb.

Then Jimmy laughed. Right under the I-280 underpass with the night fog around him. Not for the money, but because for the first time in his young life, he witnessed the presence of a holy spirit radiate from someone with the courage he could never muster.

Remove the shame? Let the light shine? Really, was it that easy? Was that all there was to it? Maybe it was.

Jimmy didn't have a name for the sensation that overcame him. Funny thing, it wasn't anything like everyone always talked about, how they explained the grace of God in church. This was different, way different. He felt so awake. So alive. All he knew is that it was better than redemption and paradise and all that crap they taught in Sunday school. Way better.

Jimmy spotted the makeshift shelter underneath the overpass where the embankment angles high until it meets the underside of the vibrating freeway. A shopping cart from Andronico's Market was hitched outside like a horse in the Old West.

He climbed the hill and from a safe distance peeked inside. He saw a pair of tattooed hands warming each other over the purple light of a Sterno can.

"Penny?" he called.

No answer. "Penny."

"Who the hell?"

Penny flipped open the carpet door and switched open a switchblade with the menace of the homeless.

"Oh, it's only you." She pulled the knife back. "You scared the piss out of me."

"Sorry."

"Come on in."

Inside, Emmett Jessup stopped eating Cheerios and raced to throw his arms around his Jimmy's neck. "Uncle!"

Jimmy smiled back. "Emmett, my man, what's happening?"

Jimmy extended his hand up high, and Emmett returned with a ringing high-five.

"I ain't got much to offer," Penny said.

"Don't need anything."

Jimmy crouched over the Sterno.

"How you feeling, Penny?"

"Like shit most of the time. Like crap the rest."

Jimmy smiled. "Taking your meds?"

"Absolutely."

Jimmy shot her a glance.

"Kinda, when I remember. Don't do nothing, anyway. What, mom and dad send you?"

"They don't know I'm here."

"Like they give a shit."

"They do."

"Bull."

"Hear the news?"

"What news?" Penny asked.

"The *Theory of Everything*. It's all over the TV and shit. Wars are ending, people are getting along. It's like God landed in a spaceship."

"I got a *theory of every problem under the sun* living in this cardboard box with me."

"Things are getting better all over the place. It's unreal." Jimmy could barely hide his excitement, and then he stopped trying to.

"Babies are still hungry at night ain't they? I know this one is."

Emmett Jessup handed Jimmy two Cheerios.

"Mmm, that's good, best Cheerios I ever had," said Jimmy. "Well, not everything can change fast, I guess. It's not like a miracle or anything where you can snap your fingers, and everything gets better."

"Wouldn't that be nice."

"How's your Section 8 coming?"

"It ain't. That housing worker ain't doing shit for me."

"What would it take?"

"What do you mean?" said Penny.

"I mean for you to get your own place. How much?"

"I don't know. Two grand with the first and last month's rent and all the bullshit deposits they force down your throat."

Jimmy smiled and pulled out the envelope. "Take this."

"What?"

"A little cash."

Penny felt the envelope's weight. Her eyes widened on seeing the denomination repeated over and over again. "Hundreds."

"Fifteen thousand dollars."

"Holy fuck, where'd you get this kinda money?"

"Theory of Everything."

"You shitting me?"

"I'm telling you, *the times they are a changing.*"

"So what, money just fell into your lap?"

"Literally."

"Is this some sort a joke?"

"It's all yours."

"EJ, hear that? We're gonna get a place. Your uncle gonna get us a home. Jimmy, you're too cool, man."

"Two things," said Jimmy.

"Two things, what?"

"Two promises. You promise me you'll take your meds. Religiously."

"That's it?"

"And no drugs."

"What if I forget?

"Look, it's up to you. I'm not the police. You do it for yourself. It's your ride."

Penny fanned the bills again and held one up against the dim flame of the Sterno can to check for counterfeit. "All crisp and new. You didn't rob a bank or nothing?"

"No."

Penny stuffed the wad down her pants and capped the Sterno can. "Do mom and dad know?"

"About the money, no."

"And why are you doing this for me?"

Jimmy looked into the dilated eyes of his sister. He wished so much for her, wished he could have done so much more. "Because I love you."

"You love me?"

"I do. Because there's no one like you."

"Far out. We love you too, bro. Right EJ?"

Nod, nod, nod, nod.

Penny took a deep breath and smiled. "About that thing, what do you call it again?"

"What thing?"

"You know, theory of whatever."

"Theory of Everything."

"Yeah, *prettycoolshit.*"

FOURTEEN

Oprah was thinner in person than on TV. Television adds about 10 pounds goes the truism, and Ethan, being the scientist that he was, wondered where along the digital transmission (or analog, as had been the case in the past) continuum the 10 pounds might be added. Was it at the moment of capture in the camera's unblinking eye? In the thick confusion of cables that extend from studio underground to television sets in homes around the world? Or in the television sets themselves as they stretch the picture to achieve the arbitrary ratios designated years ago by the pioneers of film and video. Which reality was true? Perhaps it was the naked eye that *subtracted* 10 pounds from the human frame, and it was television correcting our perceptive flaw. All is relative.

That's all Ethan could think of as he fiddled in the yellow armchair on stage with nothing between him and the world's most revered television host. Beside him, Shivana twinkled like a jewel under a bank of studio lights. The notion of impending disaster had so strongly set in that Ethan felt the great calm that comes only from unquestioned inevitability. Had he been born of another religion he might have muttered at the moment *it is written.* His faith championed the school of free will, which was of little solace at the moment. That last thing Ethan wanted was the freedom to screw up royally in front of millions, including the entire faculty of Stanford and every serious physicist and enthusiast from CERN to the moon.

Naturally, Ethan rarely watched daytime television, but he did catch glimpses of Oprah and her network in the waiting room of his allergist, whom he visited every month and sometimes twice monthly during allergy season. Oprah seemed so unencumbered by human fears. Who are these people that parade every day through the public sphere with relative ease?

What genes did they possess that he didn't?

The room was cold, but the spotlights were hot. Ethan felt like a bag of fries under a heat lamp at McDonald's, not that Naomi had ever let him near that place. The make-up crew pasted foundation on his face and from the inside of his skin, he was sure it was dripping like a zombie melting in a bad movie. He wondered why no one noticed, why some assistant wasn't rushing to his aid to swab his face clean or bark out an order over the headset to postpone the show.

The audience was composed primarily of women, which comforted Ethan. On the other hand, some director in the wings wore a stern beard and black eyes and might have been a rabbi in another life, which disquieted Ethan to no end.

"One minute to go," the director shouted.

The urgency overtook Ethan like a fit of diarrhea. He felt ready to explode and considered bolting from his seat right there and then, damn the consequences. His mind returned to the debacle that was his bar mitzvah, and the scene played out again in his head, an infinite loop of shame and sorrow.

His thoughts were broken by the words: "Thirty seconds to show!"

Shivana reached over and pressed her lips against his cheek as if he and she existed alone in the studio and the audience dwelt in an alternative universe.

She whispered in her Farsi accent trimmed with gold, "I *believe* in you. Ethan."

"Fifteen to go."

The milk and honey of Shivana's sincerity and compassion bathed Ethan with a warmth and light he had never known. Had he been born of another religion he might have acknowledged the experience as *grace*. Where did his religion stand on grace? He made a mental note to find out.

"Ten, nine eight..."

This *now*, this was something special, and he took the moment to do something he rarely did. He relished it. No muse had visited him before, none dared approach. But Shivana, angelic in nature, corpus material, magical paradox. She had kissed him tenderly, innocently. Were it the last kiss offered him on this good earth, so be it.

At that moment Ethan whispered words under his breath like a secret oath uttered by the adherent of a forbidden creed. *Fear, you are banished, excommunicated. Factorless. Forsaken. Out of favor. Forgotten.* He straightened up and assumed the posture of a confidant man.

Seven, six, five..."

Shivana counted right along with the director. She loved these numbers, this American Idol countdown.

"Four," and then with silent hand signals *three, two, one.*

Oprah directed her knowing gaze to the camera with the red light pulsating. With flawless delivery, she began...

"We've got a very special show for you today. The *only* show in town, really now or forever. Our guests are Ethan Weiner-Gluckstein and Shivana Farooq, the Stanford professors who three days ago announced the news that is sweeping the nation, the world. Imagine a theory that explains *everything*. E=MC² on steroids. A proof of God for geometry lovers. The grand philosophical conundrum solved at last. A religious epiphany. It's been hailed as the Age of Aquarius, the transcendent transformation presaged by the Mayan calendar. The new age of harmony. Call it what you will, the world is a different place since these two called the shot heard 'round the universe.'"

The audience applauded with sincere excitement.

Oprah graciously turned to Ethan, who benefited from the extra ten pounds on his gaunt frame.

"Ethan, when did you know this was *the big one?*"

For a moment Ethan thought about opening his answer with *the terminus of physics postulation...* but then he caught a sliver of Shivana from the corner of his eye, and he stopped himself.

He smiled.

"You know, Oprah, sometimes in your career you know something you're working on is going to make a difference. A tsunami effect. When the existence of the Higgs boson was discovered that was big. But when E$_8$ arrived with its theoretical confirmation of the Theory of Everything, it was clear to me that science — humankind — had hit on something magnificent and significant beyond all measure."

"Significant, how so?"

"Scientifically, the theory may help us learn how to travel through time. It will help us unlock the secrets of mysterious dark energy and dark matter that together composes 96 percent of the universe. And it may teach us how to temporarily convert a person or object into an energy pattern and *beam them up* to another location."

"Shades of *Star Trek*."

"Indeed. We are on our way to fantastical breakthroughs. However, these scientific possibilities pale in comparison to the greater implication of the Theory."

"Which is?"

"Which is, we have for the first time in history pulled back the darkness from the eyes of humanity to reveal the very fabric of life. It is us. We are woven with the same atomic thread. We follow a similar pattern like stitches on a never-ending quilt. We belong together like patches fashioned by a loving hand."

He briefly paused, pushing back his shoulders. "When one of us is torn or broken, when one of us does not live up to his or her full potential, we rend that delicate fabric and weaken us all."

The audience members sighed in unison.

"You're sure the theory will hold up to the light of scientific scrutiny?"

"The best minds and most connected networks have been pouring over it since even before the announcement, and everyone seems as excited as we are at Stanford. This is it, Oprah. This is it."

From the enthusiasm of the audience applause, Ethan gleaned that he scored a hit. Unbeknownst to him, daytime television blogs were steaming up with comments about the *hot* physicist on Oprah and asking was he married and how could such a perfect specimen of intellect and good looks occur in the same guy? How lucky was *his* wife? And did he have one? And could anyone remember the last scientist celebrity? The pot-smoking Carl Sagan? Dr. Phil? *Pu-lese.*

Then Oprah turned her gaze to Shivana waiting eagerly on the edge of her chair.

"Shivana Farooq. Young, beautiful, Muslim, recently arrived from Iran. I'd like to ask you what the theory means to you, personally, not as a scientist but as a woman?"

Shivana inhaled deeply and reflected. When she was a little girl in a schoolhouse with dirt floors and an open window into which blew the bitter sands of oppression, Shivana had raised her hand often. She learned at an early age that raising her profile gave her privileges others didn't share. She would have been happy for everyone to have these privileges – an extra pencil, a book loaned from a teacher, a ride on the back of a bicycle to school on frigid mornings – but she was not in a position to arrange such possibilities for everyone. And she wished she could confer the knowledge of the secret of attaining these privileges to all, but they seemed leaden and dead to the idea. It was free for the taking. And so she practiced the art herself and perfected it along the way. In high school, she received extra tutoring help from the math instructor, invitations to special academic tournaments reserved from the country's brightest, and stellar letters of recommendations from faculty, men and woman alike. At the Isfahan University of Technology and later Tehran University, the Muslim Brotherhood gave her a pass when she donned a particularly colorful hijab. Lab partners were specially selected to buttress Shivana's weak areas, and her B+ grades were elevated to As with extra credit assignments available to no one else.

Privilege comes to those who seek it and then it is rarely revoked. That is a proven theory as well. And if some perceived her pursuit of fame as driven by vanity, then they didn't understand the dividends of the strategy.

"Me?" said Shivana. "I'm just so happy, honored and humbled to be a member of a team anchored by such brilliant people as Dr. Weiner-Gluckstein, the researchers at CERN, and part of a movement that is changing the world."

"A few years ago you were behind the veil, and now you are free. Is this a message for the women of the Muslim world?"

"How can I presume to speak for anyone but myself? I've found that I don't require a piece of cloth to establish my modesty and my dignity. I hope that I've proven one can achieve the same results by virtue of one's actions. And proper action is far easier to achieve with the shackles removed."

Audience applause, unprompted.

"Well, Shivana, in spite of your humility – or perhaps because of it – you are an inspiration to women everywhere who remain second-class citizens. If I'm correct, that's the case in the upper echelons of academia and science as well. So, you've scored a double win in our eyes."

Applause amplified.

Shivana batted her eyes demurely. If privileges were to result from this performance, she vowed to accept them with the best of intentions. All she wanted, after all, was to study and practice physics without the need to hide behind a veil, real or imagined. Was that so wrong?

After the commercial break, Oprah turned the cameras outward. "Let's go to the audience. How does the news affect you?"

A few hands shot up.

"Me," said a straight-haired blonde. "My husband is in the Army, stationed in Afghanistan, third year, and I got two little ones at home. It just makes me feel better. Like everything is going to be all right, you know what I mean? I mean, I always had faith he'd come back, but now I have no doubt. No doubt."

"Isn't he at risk?"

"Yes, of course. But...aren't we all?"

Audience applause.

Oprah found a beer-bellied gent in the back. "And you sir?"

"I forgive."

"Forgive who?"

"Forgive everyone. Anyone I know?"

"That blindly."

"Sure, why not. I mean, what the hell, what do I got against anyone else in this crazy world?"

Oprah preened at the consciousness raising. This was what it was all about.

And the television audience watching at home applauded, too. Ratings, it would later be determined, were the highest since the president of the United States himself had sat down with the host. Hulu downloads topped 44 million. Dozens of Instagram fan pages went up for each new celebrity.

At Stanford, high fives were in abundance. "Damn, that Ethan!" said Mahoney. "I swear I didn't know he had it in him."

Ethan's colleagues agreed. How could they have missed the telegenic powers of the proverbial absent-minded professor in a world of absent-minded professors? Few had respected his bumbling ways before. Now he had showed them, hadn't he? And what about that Shivana. For the first time, many saw Shivana as more than a token pretty grad student from the Middle East. Funny how beauty can be a veil, too.

"Double the number of operators on the alumni endowment phone lines. Press releases all around, update the website, alert all faculty bloggers, this is just the start," Mahoney said. "We're flying to the moon, Alice."

FIFTEEN

Naomi Weiner-Gluckstein watched Oprah with her lower jaw mopping the floor from start to finish. Ethan? Who the hell was this champion of articulation so alien to the husband she knew so intimately or thought she knew? First of all, Ethan looked a little fuller on TV, and that made him manlier. Gone were the gaunt cheeks, sunken eyes, and scarecrow frame replaced by, well, a Jewish hunk of guy. She realized now she had stopped looking at him, directly in the eyes or otherwise. She had chosen instead to gaze past him with unfocused eyes, treating him as a ghost with whom she shared a domicile. That caught her by surprise, for one. Number two, when did he learn to speak so eloquently? Really, when? Full sentences espousing broad ideas sprinkled with metaphors and spoken confidently, rather than with that usual annoying staccato hesitation, the verbal equivalent of post-nasal drip.

And the adulation from the Oprah's studio audience, for God's sake. Naomi had grown so accustomed to the contempt she held for his absent-minded ways (and his accompanying self-loathing, let's be honest), she wondered when she had stopped considering *him*? Can a lack of compassion make one so deaf and blind?

Nope, that wasn't it, this was different. He had changed. Something had changed him. His vaunted theory? Perhaps. He did love it so. Maybe he was right and here was the proof on television in full high-definition color. A new man. Or maybe it was the power of the studio lights, animating him like steroid jolt, a purely organic response to extraordinary stimuli.

And then it hit Naomi. No, it wasn't any of these. Not scientific theories or fame or any of it. It was *her*. That dark Persian beauty, Shivana *whateverhername*, who sat by Ethan's side on Oprah's set. She was beautiful, inspiring, eloquent, erudite, demure, and feminine beyond belief. Why hadn't Naomi realized this the few times she had met her at department holiday parties and astrophysics lectures? How could she have been so blind? Ethan was a man, wasn't he? Despite his disabilities, perhaps because of them, he might fall for Shivana. In fact, what man wouldn't be attracted to her *freshness*. Oh God, Naomi wondered if the two had made love. Lord knows they had had opportunity enough. All those late nights working together, the excitement of the project, the novelty of the cosmic unknown. She couldn't blame him. Their love life was non-existent or mighty close to it. Maybe she should have been more accommodating. Was it too late to start?

And while she was at it, why had they decided not to have children? Oh, yeah, that's right, Naomi's idea. *Save a thousand children or raise one.* The tilted equation she had calculated during her ovary's prime time, despite Ethan's meager objections, or perhaps it was because his objections had been so meager. Maybe if he had insisted.

But then she remembered. She had a child.

Years before she fell in love with Ethan in graduate school, before college even, as a junior at Tamalpais High School in Marin County, Naomi found herself pregnant. Well, she didn't *find herself* pregnant, that's a euphemism, and she is adamantly anti-euphemistic. You start allowing the authorities to use euphemisms and in no time at all, you have *collateral damage* instead of *civilian casualties* and *enhanced interrogation techniques* instead of *illegal torture, alt right* replacing *white supremacy,* and in no time at all *Love is Hate* and *War is Peace. 1984* all over again. Euphemism is a tool of the fascist-industrial military complex. Vigilance, people, it takes vigilance. No, Naomi *got* pregnant by a devilishly handsome Canadian bass player, Sylvester, one year her senior, who later changed his name to Hanuman (in honor of the 11th incarnation of Lord Shiva) and moved to a commune in Bolinas where he was placed in charge of lentil soup. Naomi, for all her worldly experience with high school trips to Nicaragua (paid for with countless car washes) and summers working with Habitat for Humanity, was clueless as to what to do.

Her parents, both psychotherapists, had long promoted independent thinking among their children. They framed the termination debate in terms that seemed plainly accurate at the time: *You can choose to be an impoverished unwed mother, dependent on our financial and emotional assistance forever, or you can choose to adopt or abort the fetus and continue on to college and graduate school, where you will be able to put that prodigious intellect of yours to work for the good of humanity. You want to help people, don't you?* Neither choice seemed palatable because Naomi wanted to keep the baby. Who wouldn't want to keep a baby? But her parents upped the pressure with anecdotal stories about young girls living hand-to-mouth, or so-and-so's niece who had little choice after getting pregnant but to endure daily beatings from a strung-out drug dealer. The battle escalated, and her parents' propaganda (as Naomi in hindsight understood it to be) increased exponentially the entire second trimester of pregnancy. (Naomi hadn't even known she was pregnant during the first trimester as she never was a consistent bleeder.) At the start of the third trimester, Naomi was in no mood for an abortion after seeing all those posters of cut-up fetuses, so she opted for adoption and finished the school semester with a home-schooling tutor named Wayne who smelled like scotch and Reese's Peanut Butter Cups.

Maybe her parents were right, maybe they were wrong. Maybe Naomi was right, maybe she was wrong for deferring to her parents' advice. Either way, two days before her 17th birthday, Naomi spread her legs at Marin General and gripped the bloody sheets in the greatest pain she had ever known. Maybe it was real, maybe it was psychosomatic, who cares? She *felt* it. She glanced between her knees. A little one emerged, a pink and pudgy eight-pound-two-ounce girl with a look of vital astonishment on her face. Like *what the fuck?* Naomi loved the little girl from that moment and never forgot that look because that's how she felt most of the time.

A nurse with sad eyes and a blue facemask placed the newborn on Naomi's tummy.

"My baby," cried Naomi. She kissed her child's slimy head.

Snip, snip goes the cord, and the nurse whisked the baby away out the door.

"No!" Naomi screamed. But it didn't stop anybody or anything.

Naomi never heard about nor inquired after the baby since such was the pain. Left she was to wonder the rest of her life what that child might be like, look like, smell like. Who were the lucky parents to have received this drug-free, half-Jewish baby girl? What had they named her? Most importantly, *was she anything like me?*

The deed was done but the battle with her parents, two mild-mannered and reasonable intellectuals until the pregnancy, made Naomi realize one thing: every woman deserved sovereignty over her body. Every woman deserved title to the full deed of her reproductive rights, at all times, at all ages. Why should women have to defer to anybody? *Defer.* What a shitty word. Who could rightfully claim a greater stake in the outcome of a woman's womb than the woman? Why should anyone's say trump the needs and wishes of the carrier? The ultimate subjugation with a smile. Women have been doing it for centuries, for millennia. And, sisters, it is time to stop. *Old enough to carry, old enough to decide. Period.*

Even before her teenaged vagina had time to un-dilate, Naomi made a promise to herself to labor for the underdog, the poor, the exploited. She gave birth that day, all right. To a purpose. Because nobody should feel this way. *Comfort the afflicted and afflict the comfortable.*

All her conviction only helped her to forget. The womb has a memory all its own. The heart yet another. And when they beat together, or worse, at odds, the counterpoint cannot be contained. Denial works for a time, but it is not eternal. Love is. A little red-headed squirt with a splattering of freckles across her face and a scream to scare the banshees. Who could forget that? No way, no how, mister.

What did Naomi know of her little girl? She had cherished the brief embrace she was allowed at the moment of birth. But that single touch, however profound, can't even hint at a lifetime. Naomi didn't know her daughter's name. How pitiful. Not even her name. You nurture a baby inside you for nine months, she draws from your blood and spirit, shares half your genes, and today she exists somewhere out there with a name you don't know, a life story as alien as the stranger's on the bus.

Naomi shut off the television and pondered her Petunias, dying from lack of attention. She glanced around her house, which also was dying from lack of something. The drapes sagged, the sink was filled with dirty dishes, the mail stacked in piles.

Not even her friggin' name.

Like a loyal revolutionary guard in Mao's army, Naomi had forfeited the connection with her child for a doctrine she now questioned. If all was one, then by extension she was one with the closest person in the universe to her, if you figured that flesh made of flesh is as close as you can get. Naomi felt intuitively that her girl was somewhere close by, within striking distance. If statistics on adoption were to be believed, somewhere within a 50-mile radius lived your offspring. Those were the odds or better. Naomi scoured her memory of young girls passing by at shopping malls or protest rallies, looking for the face that belonged to her and Sylvester (aka Hanuman), but she couldn't identify anyone. Perhaps Naomi hadn't been looking hard enough, just as she had stopped looking at Ethan's face all these years.

Naomi plunked herself down in the ergonomic office chair in the couple's second-bedroom office and tapped her fingers on the keyboard with a search term she had never used before: *adoption search.*

Finding someone should be easy, right? An adopted child in this day and age, with databases online that scan your eye color from photographs and know the last twelve brands of shampoo you've purchased? The internet is the oracle of our times. Somewhere within its crystal ball hid the identity of the baby that Naomi had not, until now, allowed herself to fully regret. All momentous events have lives of their own.

Plus, Naomi was a natural investigator. You couldn't be a social worker without cultivating the ability to cave your way through mounds of records in search of that certain name, address, phone number or date needed to complete some form or another.

Naomi's parents' desire for secrecy had forbidden an open adoption. Undaunted Naomi clicked onto sites dedicated to helping adoptive parents and children reunite.

DOB: easy to recall. Hospital: Marin General. Name of Mother: Naomi Jane Weiner. Name of Father: Blank, blank. Baby's Name: Blank, blank, blank.

Naomi filled in all the fields, paid the $19.95 with her American Express card and sat back in serious anticipation of *the name.* A name, something holy and mystical about a name, as if its letters contained cosmic significance. Maybe the Kabbalists are correct.

In her head, Naomi had named the girl Eddie, but odds were astronomical the girl was called Eddie today. Naomi just hoped the girl hadn't skipped from family to family, gathering names as she flew, or felt that since her adoptive parents were somehow randomly selected she had earned the liberty to change this name or that, first or last. A person is hard enough to trace without chasing a crumb trail of names along the way. Naomi prayed the young lady had held fast to the name received on presumably the second, third, or fourth day of her life, as the proud adoptive mom swaddled her in her arms and laid dreams upon her as thick as blankets.

We're sorry, but we cannot find any records to match your search.

Naomi clicked over to another site guaranteed to be the *most comprehensive people finder on the planet!* Forty-nine dollars buys a lot. She typed in all the vitals once again. Zilch, zero, Google-less.

One more try, and then another.

A few hundred bucks later and Naomi was no closer to her daughter then when she began. The internet is an amazing organ: it informs, comforts, infuses, educates, solicits, conspires, enrages, corrupts and redeems. However, not today, not for the most important search of Naomi's life.

The Weiner's family lawyer had been hired for his capacity for concealment, which apparently was superb, though he did get caught years later in some offshore money laundering scheme for which he was disbarred, lost his wife, and spent three years in a Club Fed. He was out now somewhere and greasing political campaigns with heavy Sand Hill Road money for Democrats and Republicans alike. She found his telephone number, blocked her caller ID and let it ring, ring, ring. When it went to voicemail, she dialed again because being a pain in the ass is a damn good way of getting things done.

He answered after the fifth attempt. "Who the fuck is this?"

"Uncle Bernie, it's me, Naomi."

"Naomi, who?"

"Don't play coy with me. Your goddaughter. You've got to help me. I want my daughter."

"Which one?"

"There was only one."

Naomi heard the clink of scotch glass ice during the pause.

"Your parents would kill me," said Bernie.

"They don't have to know."

"Like they're not going to find out? Secrets rise from the grave, my dear. Imagine how quickly they travel among the living."

"She's 18 now, just turned it."

"Time flies.

"I want her back."

Clink, clink. "Why now?"

"The theory."

"*That* theory is fucking everything up. You know how many calls I'm getting from long-lost clients wanting to make right crimes past? I'm changing my number, that's what I'm gonna do."

"I'm not going away, you know that, Bernie."

"You always were a pestering little shit. Well, let's see. If I remember correctly, the family was Christian. Big time holy rollers, more Southern than Sunny Cal, if you know what I mean."

"That doesn't make me happy to hear."

"Yeah, well Naomi, you should've thought of that before you fucked whoever it was you did."

"Not one to moralize, are you?"

"Who better than someone who's scraped bottom. I'll tell you what I can do. Hold on a minute."

Naomi couldn't believe it could be this easy. It didn't hurt to have inside connections when you needed them, much as she railed against them.

Bernie took his time getting back on the line. "Okay, I checked my records, have them stored in the garage. Glad it's been a couple of dry years, or everything would have flooded while I was gone. Never buy a house with a driveway that slopes toward your house. I spent a fortune on French drains, and still they get clogged with leaves."

"Bernie."

"All right, listen. I don't feel comfortable giving you the girl's name."

"But, Bernie."

"Please don't ask for the adoptive parents either."

"Well, then, you're not much help are you?"

"Instead, I can hook you up with someone who might be able to help you."

"Who?"

"There was this preacher who hung out with the adoptive parents all through every meeting, all the paperwork, all the negotiations. Young preacher, looked like a teenager to me, all pimply and stuff, little thin pencil neck poking out of his collar. But that was 18 years ago, he's grown up by now, I guess. The parents huddled around him in corners and prayed a lot.

Praise Jesus and amens. You know, like they do. I have his name. I'll give it to you, you'll talk to him, and I'm out of the picture, okay?"

"Okay."

"Good. Last name is Spridgen."

"*Pastor* Harlen Spridgen?" Naomi blurted.

"You know him?"

"Boy, do I."

SIXTEEN

93

SIXTEEN

The city of Chicago boasts 30,547 hotel rooms within a five-mile radius of McCormick Place at an average vacancy rate of 27.9 percent. Three hundred and forty-seven of these rooms are located in the signature Omni Hotel "where Oprah hosts her guests." By virtue of their appearance on the show earlier in the day, Ethan and Shivana landed two plush upper floor suites with wall-to-wall windows, bowls of fruit, standing bars, and soaking tubs set demurely behind see-through fireplaces. The suites just happened to be adjacent and there just happened to be a door connecting the two, because hotels like the Omni like to connect people, it promotes repeat business.

After you hit a home run on Oprah, after you eat a one-inch steak at Morton's (yes, Ethan ordered a piece of meat for the first time since he could remember, and though he ate less than half, he particularly enjoyed the lusty juices across his lips), after you take a ride around the city in a charming horse-drawn carriage, after all these things, you still have plenty of energy left because you just hit a home run on Oprah, and you could stay up for three days on the adrenaline rush.

So, Ethan was not surprised (and quite delighted) when he heard the *tap tap tap* of Shivana's delicate hands rapping on the adjoining interior door. He spat on his hand and slicked back his hair, puffed up his chest, and sucked in his gut – all very quickly with hopes she wouldn't change her mind before he could twist the knob on his side of the divide.

There she was, framed in the doorjamb wearing a black satin jogging suit and a string of white pearls around her neck.

"I was just thinking..." she began.

"Yes?"

"May I come in?"

"Yes, yes, of course, please."

"You won't think me immodest?"

"Not in the least bit, no, not at all."

"Just all the energy left over, you know what I mean?" she said.

"I do, I really do."

"What a day, eh?"

"Amazing. Would you like to sit down?"

Ethan waited for the ticks and accompanying OCD symptoms to kick in as they usually do during awkward or intimate situations, but surprisingly they left him alone. He took a moment to pray his demons be banished for good or for an hour or so at least. "Would you like to sit down?"

Shivana took a seat rather properly on the golden armchair with patterned burgundy brocade. Very royal. "What a day," she repeated.

Ethan smiled. He didn't know what to say. He didn't feel that he had to say anything, and wasn't that a grand relief.

"Can I confess something to you, Ethan?"

Ethan scooted up the chair. "Yes, yes, of course."

"I mean it's not a confession, something I'm rather proud of."

"Good for you. What?"

"Here I am, 25 years old, and do you know that alcohol has never touched my lips."

"I never thought of it but, of course, that makes sense."

"Not that I didn't have opportunities, particularly in college, believe me, they do drink in Muslim countries. You just don't see it. It's kept under wraps, behind closed doors. Regardless, I never partook. I had my obligations, I made my pledge willingly, and I kept it."

"That's very noble of you."

"Perhaps. But that was then. And this...this is now. It feels like all the rules have changed. Don't you feel that way now?"

"It's funny, but I do."

"I know I do, and it feels wonderful. Ethan, please tell me if I'm being inappropriate."

"Of course not. I mean you're not...being inappropriate, that is."

"I can't think of anyone I would rather have my first glass of champagne with than you."

"Me?"

"Yes, you, why are you so surprised? Don't you know what you mean to me? What do you say?"

"I'm flattered, honored."

"And please tell me if I'm being impertinent or forward."

"No, no, not at all."

Shivana smiled. Ethan smiled. A beat or two of silence came between them.

"Well?" she said.

"Oh yes, of course."

Ethan jumped at the prompt to the chilled bottle of Gloria Ferrer at the ready along with two flutes turned upside down on Lucite coasters inscribed with the Omni's logo. Though he had drunk champagne many times before, Ethan had never commandeered a bottle on his own.

She watched him eagerly because this was a new experience for her and she wanted to see how everything was done. So much catching up to do.

She leaned forward. "Is it French?"

"Yes, yes." Ethan examined the label. "French from California."

"Hmm," Shivana wondered. "I've got so much to learn."

When the world opens up, it doesn't open like an onion, but like a torrential river carving a wide swath of delight with rushing currents of surprises.

Ethan turned his back to his guest to mask his inexperience, guard against an accident. He unwrapped the foil, untwisted the cage and, like he had seen done a thousand times in movies from Bogart to Clooney, pressed his thumbs under the cork and prayed.

A sudden pop and a stream of bubbly dribbled down the bottle and onto the carpet.

"Voila!" Prayers are answered, dreams do come true in this new universe.

Shivana couldn't help but let out a belly laugh because it was just as she had imagined. Even better.

Ethan twirled on his toes like Fred Astaire. He poured a glass a little too eagerly, and the champagne overflowed over his hand and dripped like starlight onto the carpet. He laughed at his ineptitude.

Shivana laughed too, with more abandon than she ever shared in the presence of another man, even her husband at their most unguarded moments. She hadn't swilled the first swallow yet already she felt intoxicated. Life was intoxicating.

He tipped the flute and tried again, and this time succeeded in pouring with far greater aplomb. She applauded his improved performance.

"For you my dear and esteemed friend," he said, bowing.

"I thank you so very dearly," she said, curtsying from her seat.

He handed her a glass. The champagne, excited by the movement, continued to flow, running down the side of her glass, trickling over her fingers. *The sensation!*

With his newfound understanding of metaphors, Ethan seized the courage to pull a few out of thin air. "You are the opposite of the Higgs boson particle, it lasts but a nanosecond, but your beauty is eternal."

Shivana's smiling eyes emboldened Ethan. "You are like the Higgs boson particle because men of valor would readily spend billions of dollars and years of their lives just to catch a glimpse of you for a nanosecond."

Ethan understood that his ear might be a bit tinny, but his sentiments were true enough. He hoped his sincerity would make up for his lack of eloquence. Apparently, it did because Shivana's smile was as wide as a galaxy.

"To be in your orbit is to circle the sun."

Even he didn't understand that one, but it didn't seem to matter. They laughed in unison and shared the same thought. *Could life be any better?*

Holding the flute high, he toasted. "Here's to the theory. The *everything* that brought us here to this moment. Sh'hekianu."

"What?" asked Shivana.

Ethan had said it reflexively, how foolish. "Nothing, just a prayer."

"Well, I couldn't think of a better time for one. Is that it, the whole prayer?"

"No, there's more."

"Continue, please. God doesn't take kindly to abandoned prayers, I'm told."

"Well then, Sh'hekianu, v'kieamanu, v'higgianu, l'azman hazeh."

"And what does it mean?"

"Thank you, God, for creating us, sustaining us, and bringing us to this moment."

"A beautiful sentiment. I know of a similar one in Islam. Amen," said Shivana.

With that, she lifted the flute to her mouth and entered the world of spirits.

Reflexively, she spat out the champagne with a roar of laughter.

"What's so funny?" asked Ethan.

"Bubbles, so many bubbles. They tickle!"

"Welcome to champagne."

Shivana tried another sip, more slowly. "Tasty, but not extraordinary. What's all the fuss?"

"Well, it can make you tipsy, I guess."

She tried another sip. "It tastes like...a party."

He allowed himself a sip. "Never thought of it that way."

She tipped her head back and drained the glass. "Any more?"

"There's a whole bottle, maybe we should go slowly?"

She held out the glass. "Slowly? I feel like I have so much catching up to do. Who has time for slow?"

Ethan finished his glass to keep pace with Shivana and poured another round this time without spilling a drop.

"Cheers," he said.

"Cheers," she said.

In the quantum space, electrons change from one orbit to another for no apparent reason. If the electron absorbs energy, it jumps into a higher orbit. If it releases energy, it finds a slot in a lower orbit. But here is an amazing truth — the truth that had always kept Ethan a child of wonder in the world of physics — when an electron changes orbits, it doesn't seem to move through time and space to arrive at its new location. The electron exists in one orbit one moment and instantly in another orbit the next. If a quantum leap can apply to electrons and subatomic particles why couldn't it also apply to individuals, to nations, to schlumps like him?

Ethan was sure it was happening to him right now — a sudden change in status from one set of circumstances to another without time or space broached in the interlude. He tried to formulate an equation to describe the phenomenon but couldn't. He attempted to string together a few words to categorize the experience. Impossible. Maybe it was the alcohol talking or intoxication from Shivana's proximity, but the only way he could think to express it was *miraculous*.

With the clinking glasses, Ethan leaned in for a kiss. Or was it Shivana who leaned in? Who knows, who cares? Their lips pressed together, more warmth than flesh at first.

Shivana felt surprise and delight. And bubbles, bubbles, bubbles. Bubbles in her head and bubbles in her veins. Far too many to count, exploding inside her, warming her skin, which Ethan now touched with his fiery fingers that could do no wrong. Up orbit, down orbit. His orbit, her orbit. Round and round, dizzy, dizzy.

Ethan swooped in. He cradled Shivana's head and kissed her mouth with fury. They fell backward out of the chair and onto the ground where all life starts. They twisted and turned, fumbled and fawned and found their way to the bed befitting a king and queen.

And it was there, under the slippery sheets of Oprah's suite in an embrace of ecstasy, that Shivana experienced what she never thought she would, never thought she could. It began in her tailbone and climbed up her vertebrae, connection by connection, sending a quiver into her bare shoulder blades and striking the tender hairs on her neck. It rounded the crown of her head and dribbled down her forehead to tingle her tongue. It traveled through her throat, eliciting a piercing squeal as it passed by and trekked across the contours of her breasts stopping to tickle the zenith of her hardened nipples. The current merged again at her solar plexus and journeyed slowly, centimeter by centimeter, into the crevice of her belly button where it swirled with gathering force. It cascaded down her abdomen and coursed at the measured speed of lava, heating up, until its molten finger rode the hump of her pudendum, turned the corner of her vulva, found the first fold of her labia, and gently spread her open. It streamed, all of it, into the spot where her clitoris used to be, awakening the vestigial dome, triggering unfathomable pulses of pleasure through her thighs and buttocks. It demanded she arch her back in a surge of unbearable bliss that returned, again and again, to awaken her from an eternal sleep. It implored her to draw Ethan closer into her, deep inside this field of ecstasy, where he, too, could resist no more. Finally, it drifted off into the night like a visiting angel too ethereal for a world like ours.

Shivana wept with tears of gratitude for a gift she had long ago surrendered. She thanked a God she had never known for returning what she never had, for renewing her faith in a possibility long ago abandoned.

She fell asleep with Ethan inside her, or by her side, she wasn't sure. She didn't know because the ether of euphoria worked like a potion to transport her to the surreal domain of dreams, where she slipped inside a tent. Not the oppressive tent of her youth but a tent of contentment overflowing with anointing oils and fragrances of the oasis. And there she rested as though for the first time in her life.

What seemed like 10,000 years later, Shivana awoke to a sliver of sunlight. It sliced through the window like a saber. The light was piercing, brutal.

Her first thought was how on earth to stop the jackhammer pounding in her head. Next, she recognized her own nakedness. Reflex told her to cover up in shame, put up fences, begin her penance. How could something so tasty the night before feel so bad the morning after?

She glanced over at the morning Ethan, snoring gently, the curly hairs of his chest rising and falling on the pale of his skin. Somehow she didn't feel sinful, not at all. The shame receded quickly, leaving only the unfathomable headache and the returning delight of the evening before. As she ran her hand through his wavy hair, she felt love with each stroke, that's all. And impatience for sleep to release her lover from its consummate embrace so that Ethan might open his wonderful blue eyes upon her.

His eyes did open, just like that. Just like a dream come true.

He spoke with his first conscious breath. "Did you know that the probability that random events and physical laws of nature might lead to our existence here on Earth is less than 1 out of 10^{48}? That like winning the lottery every single time it's played."

"I know," said Shivana.

"I love you," said Ethan.

Shivana traced her finger down his nose. "I love you, too."

SEVENTEEN

Pastor Harlen Spridgen spent more time in the church now, not in his office but rather in the chapel itself where the sun tagged the walls with ever-shifting shades of greens and blues, and the pains and prayers of every Sunday worshipper settled in the empty seats. This was a place of God. He read scripture on the floor, in front of the pulpit, cross-legged on the lowest point on the floor, where the believers came to stand when called to bear the witness of Jesus.

When he wasn't ministering quietly by helping people solve their problems, he spent time alone reading the works of Christian contemplative writers like Thomas Merton and Thomas Keating, as well as passages from the Bhagavad Gita, the Koran, the Works of Maimonides and Lao Tzu. Deep meditation is not only a welcome refrain from worldly attachments and medial thought but also the experience of being accepted and loved by the Divine. Just as Jesus befriends the outcasts of society, so he befriends us when we embrace him in contemplative prayer. Funny how things work. Once liberated, Harlen figured his life would be filled with intimate, loving and open relationships with men his age or a bit younger. Gay freedom. But after a dalliance or two, his sexual desire had vanished, transpired. More precisely, it had transmuted into spiritual desire, as if all his sperm took a dramatic U-turn and headed not in the direction of his penis but up the tentacle of his spine. He felt the warmth of his issue roll slowly across his coccyx up his vertebrae, warming them one by one, until the slow ball of energy supported his neck, filled the cavity in the back of his skull and traveled up the rounded bone to the very crown chakra where it departed his body and continued on its journey via a luminescent thread to the limitless energy of the Godhead. Stops along the way: the sensual, the mental, the intellectual, and the divine. Intimacy with God. Genital orgasm seemed weak in comparison, like pee to a waterfall, and he wondered what all the fuss was about anymore. He relished the silence humming with vibration, now that his iPhone was switched off, and its voice-mail box filling up with the forlorn voices of would-be lovers wondering why.

He climbed Keating's Spiral Staircase, jettisoning emotional baggage along the way and making room for spiritual and creative energy. He chanted the sixteen names and thirty-two syllables of the Hare Krishna mantra ninety-six times just to taste its sweetness. *Hare Krishna Hare Krishna, Krishna Krishna Hare Hare, Hare Rama Hare Rama, Rama Rama Hare Hare.*

He touched his head to the carpet at the anja of his brow, the seat of moksha, enlightenment. He didn't do so consciously but slumped that way, as humility drained his ego and left his body momentarily flaccid.

He wept as he recalled the promise of the Lord as revealed by Mathew, Luke, and James: *For everyone who exalts himself shall be humbled, and he who humbles himself shall be exalted.* This was not proscriptive but descriptive.

He once had measured this great hall by its volume, its capacity, its capability. Big enough for a concert by Tim McGraw, important enough for a James Dobson sermon, wide enough for a chorus of a thousand praising the Lord with song. But now he noticed the particles of dust, the space between them and the softness of the quiet.

It was at a moment of communion like this that he first detected a woman walking down the aisle toward him. The insistence of her footsteps caused him to turn.

When he saw who it was, he spoke softly but firmly. "Don't I have a restraining order against you?"

"And I have one against you, so we're even," Naomi replied. "I'm not here about *that* anyway. It's something completely different."

"Fair enough," said Harlen. Who was he to judge?

"First, I want to apologize," Naomi began. "I haven't changed my position one iota, as I'm sure you haven't either, but I regret some of the words I used at times in the heat of the debate. Especially in court when I called you...well, you remember, I'm sure."

Harlen looked at his former adversary, truly looked at her, for the first time. Rosy, with fiery kindness in her eyes and the zeal of Joan of Arc.

"You have great passion. I admire you for that. Bless you for it. You are a beautiful human being," he said. "And you know, I've been thinking about you lately."

"You have?"

"Yes, with great admiration because I've come to value choice much more greatly recently. There's a Godliness in shaping our own destiny."

Naomi felt flattered, the real thing. "Thank you."

"Can I get you a Diet Coke, Sprite, something?"

"You wouldn't have an organic pomegranate spritz by chance?"

"A what?"

"Never mind."

Harlen saw Naomi wasn't sure how to start. How odd for the warrior she had proven herself to be. She cocked her head and called for words but only tears issued forth.

Harlen felt her pain. "How can I help you?"

Naomi was at a loss for words. What a strange feeling. "I'm sorry it's just that…"

Standing up to be near to her, eye to eye with her, he wrapped his arms around her, just as he had comforted ten thousand before, but never with more concern.

"Emotion is a good thing. It means a hurt is churning inside you, attempting to detach itself from your heart and fly away. You can't move a boulder without some force. What is it, my sister?"

Naomi wiped a tear on her sleeve. Harlen could see the pain was too much for her to bear and he prayed to bear some of it for her.

She withdrew. "I can't believe I'm talking to you. I gotta go."

She turned and bee-lined for the door.

"Wait," Harlen called after her. "I want to help, I want so *badly* to help."

Harlen pursued her. "Please, allow me."

Naomi tumbled to her knees in front of him. "When I was young, no more than child really, I made a decision."

Harlen kneeled down to search her eyes and found so much pain, more pain than any one human should endure.

Harlen gave her a moment or two to express the emotion. A moment is so curative, more than any prayer or medicine, often it is. He laughed at how strange life is. You're spun into orbit with people who hate you and need you, who torment you and seek your comfort. But you care for them more than you can ever measure. Who made this crazy world? Once its poles seemed so far apart, separated by an impassable expanse. Now Harlen realized that we all circle the edge of the universe in opposite directions only to find each other on the far side. Funny how the ends meet.

Naomi found her voice. "A redhead, 18 years ago."

"A boy or a girl?"

"A little girl."

Harlen stood and walked to the seat in the first-row center.

"And how can I help you?"

"You were there, helped with the adoption."

Harlen had been there. How could he not remember? His first adoption ministry, like a first kiss. "I was. I remember it well."

"Do you know her whereabouts? Do you?"

"And if I do?"

"Please, just tell her."

"Tell her what?"

"Tell her that her mother is searching. Tell her I'm sorry. Tell her a cup of coffee, that's all. And then it's up to her if she wants to see me ever again. Just once."

"And what if she wants more? Are you willing to give it? One more heartache might break her for good."

"Heartache? She had heartache? Oh, God, what have I done?"

"You did the right thing, adoption."

"I won't break her. I promise. Hand me a bible, I don't care what stripe. I'll swear on it."

"I don't know where she is. And that's the God's honest truth. I wish I did."

"But do you know her?"

"I do, and she's a lot like you."

"Really, does she still have red hair?" Naomi pleaded.

"I've seen it all colors."

Naomi closed her eyes as if to imagine. She cupped hands around his. "Will you tell her?"

Harlen saw the love and longing in her eyes. He divined a heart filled with goodness where once he imagined a heart of rancor.

He strolled to the pulpit, found the silver pen in his pocket. On the dais, he found a pack of Post-It Notes, and scribbled something, folded it in half and handed it to the sojourner with longing in her eyes.

"I'll do you one better. Why don't you tell her yourself."

"Her name!?"

Naomi gripped the paper to her heart as if by osmosis she might divine its letters. "I can't thank you enough."

"Thank me by helping her. That's all I ask. And one more thing. Forgive yourself, you've done nothing wrong, only right."

Harlen gave her a big hug. And Naomi hugged back.

"Thank you, thank you, thank you." She smiled.

"Whoda thunk?" He chuckled.

Then, as if opening a book of Psalms, Naomi Weiner-Gluckstein unfolded the pink square and beheld her grown daughter's name written in all its simple glory.

EIGHTEEN

Omar trotted up the wide steps of San Francisco City Hall, his tan loafers kicking a quick time on the granite stairs. Sandra Lee Spridgen wore a flowery yellow dress and bounced up, up, up the hall's wide steps of the building in which Harvey Milk was triumphant and killed, as someone passing by pointed out. It's actually San Francisco City *and* County Hall, which is a good thing because by California law marriage licenses are issued under the jurisdiction of the county clerk, not the city mayor.

Technically, Sandra Lee was still married to Harlen. But Harlen was thrilled with the separation, and the couple had already begun divorce proceedings with complete agreement over the division of property. *Technically,* Omar was still married to Shivana. But destiny had already written the parting and considering they had been married in Iran, somehow the legality of it all seemed in question by American authorities that, for so long, had gone to every length imaginable to de-legitimize everything Iranian. Omar and Sandra Lee wanted a record of what was an eternal union anyway, never to be unbound. After all, everything had changed. Rules weren't rules anymore. There was so much work to be done in this dawning Age of One.

It didn't hurt that a marriage license was the quickest route to a Green Card. How long had Omar prayed for a country to call his own? Citizens of the earth do not fully appreciate the pearl that is a passport, and Omar yearned for a simple string of one.

Sandra Lee's soon-to-be-ex-husband had officiated at hundreds of such events, but she had never realized the complexity of the marriage paperwork required by the state. Consider, for example, that California offers two types of marriage licenses. A *public* license, which upon execution becomes a public record, much like birth and death certificates, and is available upon request for any upright citizen caring to inquire. The state, in all its wisdom, also offers its good inhabitants a *confidential* marriage license. The consequence is the same: it marries you, but the process is a bit slier, in that only the spouses receive a copy or someone who goes through the trouble of obtaining a court order. A spousal secret with a wink from the state. A confidential license demands more from the participants. The two parties to the marriage, for example, must be at least 18 years old (whereas a minor must marry using a public license with the approval of at least one parent or legal guardian). No problem there. The couple must be living together as spouses at the time of application and must sign an affidavit on the license attesting to that fact. No problem there either as Sandra Lee and Omar had rented a 2-bedroom flat in Pacific Heights, that lucky neighborhood privileged to watch the sunset fog rush through the blood orange spires of the Golden Gate Bridge.

"What do you think?" asked Sandra Lee to her soon-to-be. "Public or private?"

"I've got nothing to hide," said Omar.

He nuzzled into her neck and whispered a stanza only she could barely hear, which made it all the more exciting.

Giggling, she turned to the county official. "Public, we'll go public."

"Fine," said the clerk. "Got witnesses?"

"Hmm. We don't."

"Well then, come back when you do."

Sandra Lee turned around. Behind her in line stood two men clasping hands, awaiting confirmation of their union.

"Would you be our witnesses?" she asked.

"We'd be delighted!" they replied.

"Never readier," Omar chimed in.

"Then sign away."

Sandra Lee danced the pen over the paperwork and chose to sign using her maiden name, Wilson. She widened her eyes in gleeful anticipation as she handed the pen to her dark and handsome Palestinian, soon to be American.

For some reason of which Sandra Lee wasn't sure, her mind wandered down memory lane to her 8th grade school year, the year of the Father-Daughter Dance. She was a gangly 14-year-old, her mouth a nettle of braces and her arms and legs too long for her breast-less torso. He was working long hours that weekend, some big War College reunion with officers who stopped by the house briefly during the weekend for slaps on the back and the chuckle of shared old times.

"Buck up, Sandy," he said. "Lots of girls don't even know their father's names. We'll go to the dance next year, I promise."

"There is no dance next year."

"Well, a trip to West Point will make up for that. How many kids get to go to West Point?"

Sandra Lee tried her best not to sulk because sulking was a punishable sin in the Wilson household. "May I be excused?"

"Yes, soldier."

"I'm *not* a soldier."

"Lip gets you to your room."

Sandra Lee stormed away without a stomp because stomping constituted a cardinal sin in the Wilson household. Lots constituted a cardinal sin in this house. She retreated to her bedroom and found the blue taffeta dress her mother and she had spotted in a store on Main Street. Sandra dabbed a smidgen of forbidden rouge and preened in prohibited pumps. A fanciful twirl in the mirror of wishful thinking. In her closet, she uncovered a green shirt with epaulets sooooo much like her daddy's uniform. She invited the shirt onto the dance floor and brightened to the step of the music playing in her head.

Da-da-da-da. Da-da-da-da-dum.

A drunk officer, a guest of her father, stumbled into the bedroom on the young daughter's fantasy.

"Whoops," he said.

Sandra Lee startled to a stop. "Can I help you?"

"My bad. I thought it was the head." His eye arrested on the beauty in blue and he stared.

"Next door on your left," Sandra Lee said.

"Thank you."

But he didn't leave. He just kept staring at the teenaged beauty. "What's wrong."

"Nothing."

"You can't fool me, I have three daughters of my own."

Sandra Lee told him about tonight's Father-Daughter Dance.

"Does your father know?"

"Know what?"

"How much you want to go."

"You'll have to ask him. Now, if you'll excuse me."

"Certainly."

Sandra Lee pressed her ear to the door, heard him use the bathroom and walk down the stairs.

Seven minutes later, Major Walter Wilson Jr. abruptly rapped on his daughter's door. Sandra Lee opened the door on her father in full evening formals from top to toe. He held out his white-gloved hand and took a slight bow.

"May I have the honor and pleasure of accompanying my lovely daughter this evening to the annual Father and Daughter Dance?"

"Absolutely!"

Not an hour later, Sandra Lee and her father entered the double doors of the school gymnasium. Sandra Lee was so proud of the best looking, sharpest, most handsome, most gracious and most charming father in the whole gym, the entire world. It was the finest night of her short life.

Thirty-three weeks later her father was killed by an RPG in a bunker within the most secure area of the rearmost base of whatever damn contested province his regiment was stationed in that day.

"Honey, what are you thinking about? You got so sullen," asked Omar.

"Just a passing thought. No worries, I love you!"

Omar touched the pen to his tongue and with a gravitas admired by all, added his name as if signing a peace treaty between Israel and Palestine.

"Congratulations," said the clerk.

"That's it?" Sandra Lee said. She felt cheated out of the pomp and circumstance that should duly accompany such a momentous occasion.

"I'm a legal officiant, but if you want someone to solemnize the marriage, like a priest or rabbi, you can take the license with you and have it returned within 90 days."

Omar cleared his throat for and prepared oath. "I would like to take this moment to thank you all and say in the witness of these two fine young men and God above, praised be his name, that you, Sandra Lee Spri— Wilson are the love I have been waiting for on earth and I will cherish every moment we have together henceforth."

Sandra blushed. She took Omar's hands in hers and gazed into his eyes.

"And I want to affirm before everyone assembled here that Omar Farooq is the man of my dreams and I know this dream will last forever."

The gay guys erupted in cheers, and the vows even elicited a smile from the county clerk.

The couple threw up their arms with joy and spontaneously began a tango across the vinyl flooring under the fluorescent lights and back again to the front of the caged window. Everyone within earshot clapped and whooped it up. With great precision and male certitude, Omar took his wife and sealed the deal with a kiss, strong and passionate. It represented only a morsel of the glory he felt inside.

The clerk gave the document her stamp of approval to make it official. "You two have a wonderful life."

Rubbing her still-flat belly and with a mysterious smile, Sandra Lee corrected but one word of the clerk's kind wish:

"Three."

NINETEEN

After Oprah, came Sixty Minutes, Ellen DeGeneres and Steven Colbert, CNN, E!, the Discovery Channel, BBC. The Al Jazeera report was broadcast in 68 countries and broke all records for video on demand on the network's internet site. From Marrakech to Jakarta and all points in between, university women flooded the streets in spontaneous celebration. In Dubai and Tehran, women tore off Niqābs covering their faces and threw them into pyres of liberation. That's what they called them in Arabic, Farsi, and Bangla—*pyres of liberation* dedicated to the university woman from Tehran who had the audacity to single-handedly make it to the big time. The universal big time. If she could do it, any woman could. In days and weeks, hundreds of thousands of veils came off, revealing beautiful, intelligent faces of women feeling the public sun on their cheeks for the first time. It was like someone painted the dusty desert hills with the green from the very Garden of Eden. With cell phones in hand, roving celebrants videotaped the acts of liberation and Youtubed and Instagramed the videos around the world.

Babies born into every corner of the new world were given the name Shivana. Not so much the name *Ethan*. In East Jerusalem, a gate opened, and both sides swore never to close them again, and new pipes were laid to share fresh water among neighbors.

Somewhere off the coast of Japan, they let the dolphins swim away.

The reports of the New Age of Harmony seemed untrue because they felt so unbelievable. Who could dream this up? God maybe. May this was God's dream. At first, it was certainly Shivana's dream — a whirlwind tour of New York with eight, ten, twelve interviews a day. Who wouldn't love the attention? But Shivana could see that Ethan was feeling fatigued as his newfound facility with phrases was slipping. Shivana herself started feeling sick by the third day, and by day five she was vomiting in every women's bathroom in midtown Manhattan.

Shivana remembered back to her village, the last time she had felt so sick. One of her cousins had kicked her in the midsection, hard and without reason. Shivana vomited, and through the night grew weak and yellow. She dreamed her hair was on fire and awoke the next morning in shivers and cold to the touch. Her mother blamed it on bad melon seeds the girl had most probably eaten or water drawn from the wrong well, but the symptoms persisted. On the second day, her mother consulted the village spiritual leader, a stern and wise imam who helped all the villagers make important decisions. He prayed over Shivana and issued his injunction.

"It will pass. Keep her home and feed her goat's milk with honey to soothe the digestive tract. In two days it will pass."

Shivana felt worse the following day. She grew confused and lightheaded, had trouble focusing her eyes. Everyone who checked her wrist felt a weak pulse. The milk and honey seemed not to help at all.

At dawn, the whites of Shivana's eyes were growing yellow. Worried sick, Shivana's mother wrapped her daughter in a blanket and secretly paid a princely sum for a taxi with instruction to head for the city. Lucky she did, for Shivana was suffering from a ruptured spleen. Her belly had filled with blood.

"Another few hours and she would have been dead," said the doctor after the emergency surgery. "You came just in time."

Funny how Shivana had forgotten this episode in her life. Not the spleen (who could forget the sensation of almost dying and believing milk and honey might save you) but her mother's quiet heroism. The uneducated woman had only been once or twice out of her small village, yet in the dark of the night she made a unilateral decision to spend a month's income, incur the wrath of her husband and imam, and provoke a beating or two, three or four if her intuition had proved to be wrong. She put her trust in a doctor. A doctor. Shivana could not remember anyone in her family seeing a doctor before, but her mother knew, perhaps only as a mother can, that her daughter required medical attention quickly. And she had been right. How could Shivana ever thank her mother? Had Shivana thanked her enough? Had Shivana thanked her at all?

As the jet touched down at San Mateo airport, Shivana looked out the window onto the tarmac overflowing with hundreds of people (how were they able to arrange such a gathering in this era of extreme airport security?) waving pom-poms and bearing signs that read: *ONE Great Team. Go, Shivana, Go. Atta Boy, Ethan!*

Ethan leaned over from the aisle seat. "Well, look at that." He was genuinely surprised and happy. "Are you ready?"

"I'll be right back," said Shivana. She stifled her vomit and raced down the aisle.

"But we're deplaning," Ethan said, calling after her.

"I'll be just a —." She had to gag herself on the last word.

At another time, Shivana would have reveled in the compact, yet luxurious, design of the aircraft's lavatory. She didn't have the inclination at the moment to smell the soaps or see what was offered by way of free toiletry. Instead, she reached into her own purse and pulled out a pregnancy test purchased in a Manhattan drugstore in the rush to JFK. She positioned herself to catch a stream of urine at the ascribed area on the test strip and waited the short time before the test returned the results. She buried the box and all the accouterment deep into the garbage bin, fixed herself up and stepped out to the chivalrous Ethan.

"Are you okay?" he asked.

"I'll be all right."

Ethan escorted her out of the place. At the top of the air stairs, they waved like arriving dignitaries, like homecoming king and queen, stars in the latest Hollywood blockbuster.

The crowd went ballistic on seeing the two celebrities. Ethan raised his fist in victory. The local news channels were in full force with satellite trucks and shoulder-mounted cameras. At the bottom of the stairs, a Stanford grad student originally from Shanghai stepped up with a dozen red roses for Ethan and a dozen white ones for Shivana, who smiled and did her best not to gag all over them.

Ethan whispered to Shivana "You look a bit green. Are you sure you're okay?"

As they walked the red carpet, Shivana whispered, "I'm pregnant."

Ethan stumbled. "Are you positive?"

"Three sigma."

They reached the landing, and Shivana smiled as she double-kissed Mahoney. The accuracy was actually greater because Shivana hadn't told anyone at the time, but somewhere in between an interview at MSNBC and *The Wall Street Journal*, she had slipped into a CVS and picked up two pregnancy tests, the first of which she had administered in the pharmacy's bathroom. A big blue + in the little circle confirmed her intuition, and she instantly began counting months and days to the birthday. At first, she thought the test must be wrong. However, she was a scientist after all and understood that metrics were rarely wrong; it's the people who read them that misinterpret results. She was incapable of getting pregnant, barren, wasn't she? Three years of trying with Omar, 38 ovulation cycles proved it. There was, however, no misinterpreting these results. She counted back the days and realized she had indeed been ovulating during the night of champagne with Ethan. It had slipped her mind with all the excitement. What's the use of counting if you don't count when it's most crucial?

Ideally, Shivana would have preferred to wait, to spend time with Ethan, get to know him before thinking about babies. But since when is life scriptable? If a baby was destined to come now, so be it. Baby names flashed through Shivana's head and despite her illness, excitement coursed through her body.

Ethan ventured the obvious question. "Would it be mine?"

"Six Sigma."

Ethan faced the crowd. "No more questions, please!"

"We haven't asked one yet," snapped a reporter.

Ethan led Shivana to the waiting limo and helped her inside. He zipped the mirrored window shut. How quickly they all become paparazzi. Or was it a matter of perception? Now all the adulation and approval meant zip, zero, mere cosmic background radiation to the little universe forming inside Shivana's womb.

Safe within the cocoon of the smooth limo, Shivana rested her head on Ethan's lap and fell asleep, dreaming of that bumpy taxi ride long ago on the road to a distant doctor with her head resting on the lap of a mother she never fully appreciated, until now.

Ethan thought of that hangman's noose that he was so close to stringing up over the wood beam inside his parent's garage back when he was thirteen before his mother stopped him with love. Did she know about the rope below the bed or was it pure love that guided her kindness? What did it matter? How lucky he was then. How lucky he was now.

TWENTY

How cool are vinyl windows? They glide so effortlessly on their pearly white tracks. No peeling paint. No cracks to let in the howling wind. No prison bars. Penny couldn't help but work the windows in her new 2nd floor apartment overlooking the Bayshore Freeway and its steady rush of cars and trucks. And two locks on the front door to keep the pervs away, shiny new, like trinkets. How cool was that?

How cool was this total package? Two bedrooms, new wall-to-wall carpeting, a small bedroom balcony big enough for two chairs, and if you cricked your neck just right you could catch a glimpse of the San Francisco Bay, sort of. The Oasis Apartments on 13th Street. Not bad, not bad at all.

"Which room you want?" Penny asked Emmett Jessup.

"I like 'em both."

"And I like you. Tell you what. I'll take the one with the balcony so I can smoke outside and no monsters can come and get you, okay?"

"Okay."

"Check this out." Penny laid flat on her back on the brand-new carpet. She flapped her arms and legs against the carpet's nap. "Come on, Em, get down here and make carpet angels with me!"

Emmett Jessup flapped out an angel, erased it with his arms and legs, and made another one.

"Cool apartment, huh?" said Penny. "Beats a cardboard box."

"Me like."

Penny hugged her boy and rolled on the floor with him.

"Paradise, EJ. We've landed in paradise."

She would be good this time, she promised herself. She would deserve it *this* time. No more meth, junk, coke, pot, all that crap. Out the window. No more asshole boyfriends and pimps coming around with their attitudes and demands, whipping out their dicks whenever they goddamned felt like it. And cigarettes would go after that. But one thing at a time because you can't do too much or you're bound to fail.

"And we're going to go to the park every day, and you can swing all you want and play on the slide. They got a sandbox there I bet and those little elephants on springs that you ride. I like those. I bet you'll make a lot of friends."

Penny ran the numbers again in her head. It cost her $2800 and change to move in. After groceries and some new shoes and socks for EJ, she had over ten grand left. Ten frickin' grand! She felt like Michael Gates or whatever that Microsoft guy's name was. She patted her back jeans pocket where she kept her new bank debit card. So cool she thought to have money like that all wrapped up in a plastic card. She figured she'd make do with thrift store beds and furniture. No need to spend big time on shit like that when rich people around here put expensive stuff out on their curbs for the garbage men to pick up. She'd do things smart this time. This time would be different.

"And mommy's going to stay on her meds, promise, promise, promise. No more wacko episodes. Just you wait and see."

Penny tried the vinyl window one more time because that was the most fun thing to do in the empty apartment and because she wasn't sure what else to do now even though her head was filling with ideas. You don't trust your ideas too much when you're crazy because you can't separate the good ones from the bad ones. They all seem good, and they all seem suspect, and you don't know what's real until the consequences rear their ugly heads afterward, and that's a scary thought.

She heard a knock on the door.

Christ. For sure someone was coming to take it all away. *It's all a mistake,* they would say. *That money belonged to someone else, and you've got to give it all back. You don't deserve a place like this. We got someone better for apartment 2F. Here's a new cardboard box for you.*

Fuck the bad thoughts. That's what Penny wanted to think the most. But it wasn't easy to fuck the bad thoughts. The bad thoughts lived.

Back in junior high, when the voices started telling her things she ought to do, her parents didn't understand at first. They accused her of smoking pot and drinking, running around with boys and lying about it. Why else would she make up shit about someone telling her to pee in the corner of her room, or forcing her to slice her thigh with 101 razor cuts, or demanding she twist the neck off Willy, her pet rat? She knew she was crazy after that, but no one believed her. They called her reckless and callous and narcissistic and criminal. She didn't know what half the words meant, but she didn't feel like any of them. Nothing is scarier than having no control of your mind. Like a fast car without brakes.

Late one night, her father came to visit Penny in her bedroom. He sat on the corner of her bed. Penny pressed her knees together. He looked so evil in the shadows of the bedroom. He moved closer, and she felt his breath on him, and she saw the graying hairs in his flaring nostrils.

He kissed her on the cheek. It made her skin crawl. She wished they hadn't taken away the knife she used to keep under her pillow.

He drew closer and said, "Penny, I believe you. I believe you hear voices in your head. I'm sorry for not believing you for so long. I'm so sorry."

Penny felt so good at that moment. "You do?"

"Yes, and I'm sorry. Your mother and I are sorry."

All it takes sometimes is for someone to believe you. It doesn't change one damn detail about your miserable life, but it makes it all better somehow. You're not alone anymore. Someone's on your side. "Thank you."

"That's why your mother and I have decided to send you away, to a place where they can help you, with doctors and professionals."

"A place, where?"

"Up in Napa. A hospital with people who understand you, who know how to help."

No! The word screamed in Penny's head. "I want to stay here with you."

"We leave tomorrow. Your mother will help you gather your things. It's for the best. Your psychiatrist agrees, and we made sure you'll have every comfort."

Penny pulled the pillow tight in between her legs.

"We'll visit. I promise. We'll pray for you, every day to Jesus Christ Our Lord, I promise you that. And if we all pray hard enough, maybe he'll help you through this evilness."

He kissed her on the forehead and walked out the door, locking it behind her.

Penny ripped through every drawer, looking for a razor blade, pills to take, a knife to bury deep in her heart, but they had been in her room, the fuckers, and taken it all away. Everything, the assholes.

Why adopt me then send me away?

Her impulse said *run*. Run from these fucked up *Jesusfreak* parents who pray for righteousness then abandon their young. *Fuckinghypocrites*. They couldn't stop her if she ran, they wouldn't find her. She'd run and keep running because she wasn't going to some retard home. No way, no how they were going to lock her up and shock her into dullness or jam her full of pills until she turned zombie-like.

Penny wrote a note to her little brother. *Hey Jimmy, I love you, pal, and I'll never forget you. You're the best brother in the world. Be good, do good, don't let them screw you up, too. And never forget your sister. You're the only one in the world I got. Love, Sis.*

She climbed out of bed and slipped on her jeans and boots. She found a warm jacket, some stashed dollar bills, and a crushed half-pack of smokes. They left the smokes behind.

She rushed toward the window.

It was locked. Worse than locked. Nailed shut. Nailed with big fat 16-penny nails. How ironic was that?

They had locked her in, locked her like a stray in a kennel so they could take her to the pound in the morning.

Well, *fuck them.*

Penny wrapped the jacket around her forearm and shattered the pane with her elbow. Shattered glass flew and smashed to the ground below. Penny pushed the remaining shards away and slipped out the window into a new life.

Back in the reality of her spanking new apartment, someone kept rapping at the front door to take it all away. Penny eyed the squeaky-clean vinyl window. No 16 penny nails holding it shut here, just a free ride to the street below. She opened the slider wider, just in case. Love that escape breeze.

"You stay here, son. I'll get the door. Any problem, you lock yourself in the bedroom, you here?"

Emmett Jessup beelined it to the white and bright front door and nestled himself under the belly of his mother.

Penny looked through the peephole. She relaxed a little bit when she saw it wasn't KJ or T Dogg or some other peep toting a bag of tricks.

Penny opened the door the chain length on the lady. "What, the abortion didn't work?"

"No, no, not at all, may I come in?"

Emmett peeked through the crack. "White lady!"

"I brought you these." Naomi lifted two bags of groceries.

"Why? What for?"

"Penny, we've got to talk."

"Talk right through this chain. I don't owe you no money, no way no how."

"No, please, just give me a moment. I have something to tell you, please just let me in."

The woman had been fair so far, so Penny went against her intuition and unchained the door.

"Thank you," said Naomi.

"Now, what? We're making angels here."

"I've been doing a little bit of research. I talked to your pastor."

"Pastor Spridgen? Because he's a queer, you know that."

"It doesn't matter what he is. What matters is that... and I know this will sound hard to believe—"

"I got HIV?"

"No, no, no. I don't know. It's not about that either."

"Cause with my Hep C, I can't afford nothing more. Fuck, I knew all this was too good to be true."

"Penny listen! Listen to me. *I am your mother*. Your birth mother. And *you* Penny...*you are my daughter*."

Hang out with junkies and prostitutes, you see and hear pretty much everything. But this took the cake with the cherry on top.

"You're my what?"

"Your mother. I was the mixed-up teenaged girl who gave you up 18 years ago. I was young and foolish. I was 16 for God's sake and felt like I didn't have any choice. I am so sorry, and I love you so much, and I just want to get to know you, to see who you are. And most of all I want to help. I want to help you so bad."

Naomi leaned down to Emmett Jessup. "And, young man, that makes me your grandma."

Emmett Jessup gazed upon. "Grandma!!"

Penny's heart fluttered like a coke whore. She looked at the *Jewlady* like for the first time, really looked. "What your name again?"

Naomi smiled. "Naomi. Naomi Weiner-Gluckstein."

"Well, Naomi Weiner-Gluckstein, get the hell out of my house!"

"Please, let's talk—"

"You hear me? Get out."

Penny shoved Naomi to the door, and the grocery bags ripped open. Bananas, vitamins, yogurt and more spilled to the floor and rolled to all ends.

"And don't never come back."

Penny slammed the door shut and slumped down against the inside. Her fat ass broke open a yogurt container, and it spilled all over the brand-new carpet. "Fuck."

"Strawberry," said Emmett Jessup with a touch of his finger.

Penny just let the tears flow, what the hell.

Emmett sat on her lap and licked the yogurt off his fingers. "Me want grandma."

"You ain't getting one," said Penny.

Penny once yearned for a real mother so bad. That was back then. Back then she was young and stupid. Really stupid. She prayed to Jesus because for whatever stupid reason she still sort of believed that if she prayed hard enough, the thing she prayed for would come true. Like God cared or something.

"Emmett, listen up. There are no tooth fairies, no Easter bunnies. No Santa Claus."

"No Santa Claus?"

"A big joke on kids, ha, ha. No band of angels. No Jesus. No Mary. And all that crap you heard about salvation in Church? A fucking joke."

And there damn well ain't no birth mothers caring enough to come around a second time to drag a girl named Penny out of the gutter. So Penny had stopped praying, stopped believing, and her heart grew wide and empty like this very apartment, only dirty and cold, instead of new and bright.

"What God given right did that lady have to come back, now that things are turning up in spades? Where'd she buy the balls to fuck up our little peace of mind?"

Emmett Jessup wondered what his mother meant.

Penny wanted a line of blow so bad she could taste it. She searched the spilled groceries hoping maybe the Jewlady bought a jar of Clorox. Hadn't Penny stepped in a ton of that shit?

Fuck, not the spiral. Not again.

"*Fuckthatladyfuckthatladyfuckthatlady* to hell and back. You hear?"

"I love you, mama."

"I love you too, sweetie."

Then again, Penny thought. To have a mother, a real mother. A flesh and blood mother. One that couldn't deny you because you shared blood. And that red hair, just like Emmett's little lock in the back, the one you can't see until you lift his curls. Just like Penny's was before she dyed in black and blonde, and purple and green. In fact, he had her eyes, those sloping eyes that look sad until they laughed and lit up the world. And when exactly was the proper moment for a birth mother to show up in your life? Was there ever a right time?

"It would always be a shocker, right?"

"What, mama?"

A sudden shock. A mother wouldn't abandon her child twice, right? Right? Not a lady like that one who helped her at the abortion clinic and all.

Somebody tell me what to do, Penny whispered in her mind. *Please God, send me somebody telling me what to do."*

Emmett Jessup reached up, curled a twirl of Penny's hair in his fingers, and whispered in her ear. "Mama go."

Penny opened her eyes. She jumped up. She wiped the strawberry yogurt off her ass.

She unlocked the locks, top, and bottom both. She unzipped the chain. She raced down the stairs. She looked to the left. She looked to the right.

"Fuck, I lost her."

But then Penny brightened. She saw the front of a *hippiecar* pulling out from a parallel parking spot.

Penny bolted down the road, leaving Emmett Jessup behind. She flailed her arms like a burning woman.

"Hey, mama! Come back, mama."

The *hippiecar* drove away.

"Please, mama, please."

The car picked up speed.

Penny dropped to her knees.

"No, please, no."

She did something she hadn't in a long time. Eons.

"Please, Jesus, please. I'm asking you now like I ain't asked for nothing before. Please bring her back, just please bring her back. That's all I ask. For

121

me. It's Penny."

The red brake lights lit up.

"Mama?"

The white back-up lights switched on.

"Mama!"

The car zigzagged backward, almost hitting the parked cars lining the street.

"Mama, don't hit me!"

Penny jumped out of the way.

The car slammed to a stop in the middle of the block.

Naomi didn't take the time to close the car door behind her. She raced to Penny on the street. She embraced her in one big motion.

"My baby."

They sobbed. Holding each other tight so the other would not slip away. Not again, not ever. No way, no how.

Penny thought she smelled the scent of freckles. She felt home.

Emmett Jessup popped his head out the window and waved.

A honk came for Naomi to move to her car. Penny squeezed her mother tighter. Even tighter still. Light and darkness came to her kiss.

Naomi sighed. "Now we are one."

Penny liked that. She liked that a lot.

Beep, beep.

"I'm so sorry for everything." Naomi sobbed.

"Forget it, it was nothing."

Honk, honk!

Mother and daughter threw the driver dirty-looks.

"We've got so much to do, to talk about," said Naomi.

"I can't wait," said Penny.

The driver stuck his head out the window. "Hey, ladies, get a room!"

Mother and daughter flipped him a bird in unison. That *motherfucker* could wait. Nothing was gonna break up this mother and child reunion.

TWENTY-ONE

Everyone worldwide marveled at the speed of change, a whirl of momentum traveling faster than human consciousness had ever witnessed, could ever have imagined.

At the Vatican, Monsignor Jacque Carabi, fourth in charge of public relations in the Incoming Future Treatises Department, had first read the story in English. Even though it wasn't his first language, he quickly understood its significance. He couldn't help but wonder what underling had occupied his position in 1664 to help Pope Alexander VII craft his Index Librorum Prohibitorum forbidding the works of Galileo and Copernicus that advanced the heliocentric theory. Vatican operations were more modern now, but not by much. Carabi hastily arranged for the story's translation into Italian, Spanish, Filipino, Portuguese, French, and Russian and emailed the development to the 64 archbishops sitting on the seven governing boards and councils that oversaw his department. Within 72 hours, several suggestions for a response returned. The quick reaction suggested a favorable response, and Monsignor Carabi was proud he had accelerated the Vatican reflection on this matter from a usual 90 days to just less than 72 hours.

Imams teaching in the tents of Morocco to the jengkis of Indonesia reminded the worshipful that Islam was founded as the religion of Abraham, Moses, Jesus, and Mohammed and had long proclaimed the unity of all things. And even the radical Islamists who preached violent jihad in the Iraqi and Syrian valleys of terror retreated to their caves to make sense of the revelation and see how the Holy Qur'an might instruct them to respond.

The Chief Sephardic and Ashkenazi Rabbis of Jerusalem released a joint response some fourteen pages long citing sources from the obvious

Talmudic tracts to the most obscure texts of Rashi, Maimonides and the Kabbalah that boiled down to *we told you so*.

In the political realm, the United States and Pakistan seized on the opportunity to secretly rush their most senior diplomats to Prague to consider a negotiated settlement. The basement of the White House collectively sighed over the potential de-escalation of tensions.

Meanwhile, leaders in Islamabad quickly welcomed the military step back. As it was, the country existed in a pressure cooker. Name a sovereign leader in his or her right mind who would care to share borders with this foursome: Iran, Afghanistan, India, and China? No thanks, but these were the four tigers Pakistan dealt with every day. Look south to the choppy Arabian Sea and north to the jagged edge of K2 piercing the snow driven Himalayas. Where else on the globe did the battle between opposing forces rage so fiercely as in Pakistan?

On the world stage, Great Britain and Argentina surprised the family of nations by declaring the immediate commencement of negotiations over the final status of the Falkland Islands, the first such interchange since the resumption of diplomatic relations in 1992. The presidents of Greece and Turkey announced bilateral talks to completely unify Cypress. Japan promised discussion on reparations for China. A significant number of remaining Columbian rebels climbed down from the jungles and surrendered their guns. More than a smattering of White Supremacists in Idaho unlocked their bunker doors. Governments in Jerusalem and Ramallah agreed to draft the terms of reference required to permit the resumption of Israeli-Palestinian negotiations based on the Geneva sub-protocols necessary for the recommencement of the next step of negotiations within the parameters agreed to by the two parties two peace talks earlier, minus subparagraph B6.

War still raged and intolerance and cruelty pressed on. But people around the world for the first time felt the pain and misery of the tens of millions of children slaving from dark to dark on the dank dirt floors of third-world factories, and they cried for the millions of young girls chained to the degradation of the brothel. Miners still rarely saw sunlight and the elderly and infirmed remained cloistered in their shuttered apartments. Light was coming, all were assured. Light was on its way.

Television and magazine commentators rushed to explain the marvel. How could a simple pronouncement of an esoteric, complex mathematical equation coupled with the results of a fleeting subterranean experiment (lasting no more than a femtosecond or two) produce such a profound effect on societies the world over? Some said it was the butterfly effect in action, a few good deeds multiplied rapidly, exponentially, until the world fluttered with good deeds. Perhaps we had been at the tipping point already, several commentators postulated. On the precipice of the next consciousness, and the ToE was the straw that broke the camel's back. That's just the thing, the commentators noted, nothing seemed hackneyed anymore. It was all new and amazing although nothing had changed. Did we not intuitively know it all along, that we are one? Are there not one, not two, but three monotheistic religions built on this very premise? Is it not our intrinsic nature to comprehend subconsciously, at least, that we are all bits of rock extracted from the same mountain? All shattered pieces of the first fiery explosion? A collective toenail of God? What more proof do we need? And why was the scientific proof more persuasive than the numinous truth that lay underneath?

A few respected Humanistic prognosticators and others from the liberal wings of religions and spiritual practices suggested the true Age of Aquarius was blossoming, perhaps a few decades later than the Broadway play had foretold, but what are decades when estimating astronomical time? Perhaps the Aquarian Age had prompted the discovery of ToE. A cadre of religiously-tinged pundits on the Right took to the airwaves to assure the world that ToE was the beginning of the Messianic Age, the second coming, a biblical revelation coming to fruition, high time for the Anti-Christ and the four horsemen. These pronouncements did not resonate beyond a small, dedicated audience. Stock in dogma fell in the minds of all but the feeble. Bishops and tyrants were left to reason why.

Requests for comedies overwhelmed the distribution services of Netflix and Hulu. Disneyland and Disneyworld considered reducing hours as a cost-saving measure, as the masses, it appeared, no longer needed doses of forced gaiety offered at outrageous prices to satisfy their longing for joy.

The sun had not stood still as it might have for Joshua but for tens of millions of people from the wealthy to the impoverished, it *felt* as if an unseen and undiscovered celestial body, fixed in one position for thousands of years, had begun a slow tilt on its axis back – or forward – to a time of greater mercy, justice and equanimity. More than one armchair philosopher wondered this: if a change of a mere degree over a few days could initiate this reasoned season of congruity, how might the planet transform once the phenomenon had ample time to work its gravity on the viscous fluid of human consciousness? Strange and wonderful still to be seen.

How many times in how many households in how many languages in how many nations in how many religions was Micah 4 (or an Eastern counterpart with similar thematic optimism) dusted off and read out loud?

They will hammer their swords into plowshares and their spears into pruning hooks.

Nation will no longer fight against nation, nor train for war anymore.

Everyone will live in peace and prosperity, enjoying their own grapevines and fig trees, for there will be nothing to fear.

Deep in the Brazil rainforest, chainsaws were powered down by the thousands. Eighteen thousand chickens in a socialist collective deep inside Albania were spared death. In Dhaka, Bangladesh, the Liberation War vets of 1971 gathered over chai to collectively forgive the Pakistanis for the brutal murder of the intellectuals. In Beirut, it was said that fig trees offered a rare third harvest, an occurrence not seen since biblical days.

In the streets of all the nations, smiles returned. Handshakes dusted off centuries of animosity. Overdue embraces closed a trillion miles of gaps between estranged friends. Legal and illegal drugs sales dropped precipitously as did sales of alcohol, following a short surge in champagne purchases. Official records were not kept, but government officials reported that marijuana sales remained constant and may have even seen a slight rise. People found it less necessary to self-medicate and a greater desire to accentuate.

The number of people foreswearing the consumption of meat skyrocketed. After all, if we are one, we share the suffering of all the turkeys, pigs, cows and chickens cramped in dark cages on beds of their own excrement kept alive long enough only to witness the slaughter of their offspring in a sea of blood. Domestic abuse calls dropped to the lowest levels in 40 years to the amazement of local law enforcement officials everywhere. In the more affluent countries, calls to marriage counselors soared as couples sought to heal the festering wounds of their marriages and repair broken bonds between parents and children. In poorer countries, a smattering of landlords were reported to have rescinded onerous rents from tenants and even offered grace for past due debt. Within a few days time, the conversations on street corners from Lima to Seoul centered around the fog lifting from the peoples of the world and a rare light sparkling in so many homes. Humanity 2.0.

In prison, a good number of inmates discovered the freedom within, thereby transcending the tyranny of cells without leaving them. At universities, students thirsted for knowledge like beer, and they cracked books in search of more wonderment. Poets celebrated with freshly twisted verse, musicians explored long-forgotten intervals, and artists found new colors to tease.

People asked *what did you do last night?* And in a thousand dialects and a million incarnations, the answer came: *I luxuriated in joy and harmony.*

In the first of many strange paradoxes noted by the perceptive, joy was deeper now, yet also closer to the surface. Social philosophers hailed the dawn of Quantum Consciousness, in which everyone tapped into the collective consciousness of all humanity. The network had gone organic. Harmony on steroids.

~

Back in Palo Alto, California, Jimmy Lean rode his bicycle up Page Mill Road almost to Skyline Boulevard, a long hard climb. Each time he turned and glanced below, he witnessed the house lights grow more distant in the valley until they shined liked a canopy of stars turned upside down. He saw the wide dark of Stanford University and the long straight track where they tested things at the speed of light and faster. The world was upside down sometimes. Who's to say what direction things should turn? You got to flip it around sometimes, reverse the poles, turn black into white and quiet into roar.

Down on the sparkling clean streets of Palo Alto below, Omar and Sandra Lee popped a bottle of Moet Chandon and toasted an impending new passport and sure wins at every dance competition they entered. They sat on a frayed carpet of prayers and dreamed of names for a baby boy entering the world at its most glorious moment.

Across town, Ethan and Shivana painted a spare bedroom (what used to be Naomi's office) and wondered out loud what other mysteries of physics yearned to be discovered and how these might affect humankind in ways as unimaginable and magical as the golden Theory of Everything.

Every morning in his walk-in closet, Harlen selected expensive suits to donate to the Salvation Army, which he followed by dressing in sackcloth. He emptied his former media room of all the whiz-bang electronic gadgetry and turned it into a meditation room for breathing.

Naomi grabbed a few things from her home and moved into the little Oasis Apartment on 13th Street overlooking the Bayshore Freeway. Emmett Jessup, with a smile on his face, fell asleep every night snuggled between mother and grandmother. Naomi and Penny caught up on stolen years over endless cups of coffee and read *Goodnight Moon* to Emmett Jessup whenever he wanted to hear it, which was at least ten times each day. Penny on one side, Naomi on the other, each woman reaching across him to hold each other's arms.

And a hundred thousand stories like that, all happier than the next, unfolded somewhere on the surface of a green-blue planet under a swirling blanket of clouds in a solar system spinning effortlessly inside a galaxy that breathed outward toward the next galaxy and beyond. Always in the middle, never in the center. Somewhere, somebody, *lots* of people, were telling the truth about who they were. Secrets, no more. Shame banished. Jimmy liked that.

And who knew how the fish in the sea were feeling? The worms and bees, had they heard the news or had they possessed always the knowledge. The roots of flowers and trees drinking deep from underground streams, what did the hidden currents think anyway? Maybe they were moved too, swept away, as might be the aliens on Planet B346a4, or wherever, and all the dots in all the universes where life chooses to exist. Surely it was possible because all things were possible now.

Jimmy rested his head on his bright blue bike and gazed up at the stars. Damn it if he didn't feel like the body and blood of Christ himself making real God's intention. Jimmy wondered out loud about the meaning of the word *universe*. Universe. *One song*. Pretty cool, thinking of that.

BOOK III:

"Nothing is exactly as it seems, nor is it otherwise."
—Alan Watts

TWENTY-TWO

The same stars that shone down on Jimmy Lean in Palo Alto, California, also shed their light on a minor character far, far away, one Stefan 'the Snipper' Snodgrass, so named for cutting strings and strings of unnecessary code from computer programs designed for everything from iPad apps to Stuxnet-like viruses.

Stefan did not consider himself liberal or conservative, Communist or capitalist. He preferred neither golf nor tennis, dogs over cats, ketchup more than mustard. He was simply an odds-maker fixing the odds. He didn't care much for the Theory of Everything, not because he was opposed to such highfalutin ideas but because the metaphysical aspect did not affect him materially. Stefan Snodgrass did not concern himself with things that didn't affect him directly or materially, and he was not ashamed to admit it. In fact, he was proud of his delusion-less existence, it promoted clarity in a world reigned by fable and volatile emotions. Look at wars, violence, madness—all rooted in emotions, innuendo, superstition, all of them. The world would be a better place (though far less profitable) if everyone thought like Stephan Snodgrass, so thought Stephan Snodgrass.

So when Stefan set out to deconstruct the E_8 solution, he did so by applying 147 algorithms and proprietary models, which generated results large enough to fill up terabytes of storage. He first saw the error in the E_8 solution with one eye on his computer monitor and one on his big screen TV broadcasting a Sunday afternoon cricket match.

Stefan called to order a Domino's pizza with salami and sausage and a liter of Diet Coke and then sat down to write the first of many blog posts on his findings. The first one he entitled: *Findings on a Potential Inconsistency in the E_8 Postulation with Wide Enough Potentiality to Refute the Theory* *of Everything.*

The thread traveled the same viral routes as the original Stanford ToE announcement, starting with obscure science, astrophysics, and math blogs and then among a few conspiratorial *flat earth* societies. By sheer coincidence, the same AP editor was on duty in New York as during the initial ToE announcement. He was just returning to his windowless office after jamming on a smokeless bowl of Blackberry Kush in the men's bathroom when he picked up the Anti-ToE thread. Ensuring enough room for equivocation, should it be wrong, he tapped out the following headline and hit the send button: *Obscure Scientist Disputes the Theory of Everything.*

The AP report began:

DURBAN, South Africa — *A Ph.D. candidate from Oxford University and full-time sports odds maker has posted what he says is proof of an error in the now-famous E_8 equation that lies at the root of the Theory of Everything.*

For the record, the editor condensed and blasted two other stories that night: *Researchers Can't Explain It: The Great Pacific Garbage Patch is Shrinking* and *The Haves and the Haves: Gap Between Rich and Poor Begins to Shrink.* But these curiosities were quickly to be forgotten.

The top media outlets brushed off Snodgrass' conclusion as the findings of an amateur, but the math could not be ignored. Once alerted, corporate computer guys around the world were able to replicate the E_8 error with ease. Academicians picked the conversation and ran the numbers from here to CERN.

Preliminary reports were not good. The Theory of One might be *The Theory of 99.99999999999999* or *The Theory of Almost One* or your choice of any other number for that matter. It was, simply, not the integer *one.*

Fox News was the first to break the story wide open in the U.S. with Al Jazeera leading the international charge. That no one but Stefan Snodgrass was able to detect the error for all these weeks was a mystery to many. To be accurate, history will record that Snodgrass was not the first to find the error. Others had begun discovering the anomaly as well, from Reykjavík to Colombo. But the spotlight found Stefan Snodgrass first, and the first spotlight wins. The anti-findings naturally lit up the blogs on every math, science and spirituality portal. Snodgrass' reputation was tailor-made for the math portals, which were collectively in awe of the rogue whiz archetype toiling away in some faraway cabin or his mother's bedroom, solving the great mathematical perplexities without the aid of supercomputers or teams of colleagues and assistants.

On second look, the mainstream media resisted reporting the Anti-Theory story (#*atoe* in Twitterese) because it seemed so catastrophic. The positive energy flowing from ToE was the story of the decade, of the century for that matter (even though the majority of the century had yet to unfold), and to lead with its refutation in a world that still shot the messenger would be a ratings disaster. Trained journalists worth their credentials immediately applied a healthy dose of professional skepticism to the findings of a shady bookie living on Dominos pizza on a houseboat off the coast of South Africa.

And imagine if the Anti-Theory turned out to be incorrect, requiring an apology and correction? Career ending.

The anti-simmer persisted, but the tide began to change when CERN confirmed that Snodgrass's numbers were indeed correct, which is why, it now reported, it had cancelled its announcement which had initially been scheduled for the day after the preemptory Stanford announcement. With CERN on board, the media outlets had no choice but to devote larger and larger chunks of time dissecting, debating, and explaining the Anti-Theory claims.

Editors at *Time* magazine once again made the bold decision to replace its cover story on *The Return of the Bees* at the last moment with a package anchored by a top-to-bottom cover proclaiming in the now-familiar 256-point font of urgency...

ONE NO MORE!

...against a Photoshop-enhanced backdrop of a column of tanks kicking up dust in some undisclosed desert, presumably a battleground in the Middle East. The top right cover flap referenced Ethan and Shivana (now instantly recognizable by their first names alone like Sonny and Cher) as "Charlatans of Science?" The material inside the weekly described the pair this way: *the darling twosome of science that took down the Standard*

Model may now find themselves accused of what may be the most audacious hoax in scientific history.

Snodgrass followed the tracks laid by Ethan and Shivana, changing polarity wherever his name appeared. He accepted an invitation to appear on the Christiane Amanpour show. Christiane played a three-minute compilation of all the great minds in science agreeing with Stefan.

As the Anti-Theory began its triumph march, the people of the world walked the stations of grief, beginning with a hard stop at denial. Impossible, won't have it. Not true. Stone the bastard. *You can have my theory when you pry it from my cold dead fingers.*

They burned an effigy of Snodgrass in Sweden of all places. The voodoo practitioners in Haiti worked their magic to no avail.

The Vatican was *carefully reviewing the claims,* said Monsignor Jacque Carabi, now second in charge of public relations in the Incoming Future Treatises Department. Imams across the Muslim world rejected the Anti-Theory outright and banned its discussion. Saudi Arabia shut down the Internet itself for a time to cut off the mouth of blasphemy. In Jerusalem, a trio of rabbi's said that nothing had been changed by the ToE and nothing by the Anti-Theory because that's the way it had always been and will always be.

Denial was followed by anger. Demonstrators crowded the streets of Rome and Seattle, Montreal and Mumbai. But where to go, whom to protest against? There was no Anti-Theory government office to angrily storm, no shrine to desecrate. Letters to the editor denounced the Anti-Theorists as reactionaries, rabble-rousers, atheists, religionists, conservatives, and liberals. The problem was that the unidentifiable Anti-Theorist was everybody and nobody all at once, the opposition wasn't people, but an idea, an anti-idea. It was a conspiracy, people proclaimed, promulgated by the Communists, the MAGA hats, the Islamo-Facists, the Jews. A monk in the holy city of Angkor Wat, Cambodia lit himself on fire in protest of the Anti-Theory, while soccer moms in Ann Arbor held a bake sale to support efforts to debunk it. The ToE itself was an obscure enough concept, with not one in 1,000 people qualified to understand the math. But largely it was difficult to sustain any sort of viable opposition to the Anti-Theory. Might as well stage a protest against chill winds from the northwest.

In a very Kübler-Rossian manner, the initial anger was followed by bargaining. *Can't we just continue to believe, even if it's not true?* How many religions, after all, required little more from their adherents than faith in an immutable dogma. Couldn't everyone just believe? Because even if the Anti-Theory defrocked the ToE, it didn't mean that another Theory of Everything might not be proven sometime in the future. It was a possibility still, just as it had been before Ethan and Shivana's announcement. The problem was that people found it hard to have faith in probabilities. No one prays to Jesus because he *might* have been the savior or reveres Muhammad because *there's a good chance* he is the seal of the prophets.

The bargaining took strange shapes. How about we believe the ToE for one month more? After all, everything is so good. If not one month more, how about Tuesdays and Thursdays, or maybe Friday nights? It'd be like just like Happy Hour for the soul. These ideas suffocated under the weight of their own folly. And bargaining was followed by a massive global endorphin shutdown. Gardens went untended, cars unwashed, ice cream uneaten. Lovers met and just held each other. Sales of confetti, banners, and balloons plummeted. Three students in Vancouver clasped hands and jumped from a tall building. What was the purpose of pursuing joy now that it came in such small increments compared to what had been so recently available? Like a meth addict cut off. Shut off the light, and the dark appears darker than before the light was ever turned on. Such is the law of perception.

Depression was followed by acceptance, begrudging acceptance, like a totalitarian regime to be endured but not resisted because resistance was futile. Neighbors reworked downed fences, women covered up their faces, and the moribund arms trade again showed signs of life. The steel and rubber assembly lines of slaughterhouses that had been shut down just weeks before, presumably for good, were oiled up and powered on again. Trucks backed up to unload herds of cows, sheep, pigs, and chickens. The phones rang off the hook in the offices of divorce attorneys, and corner beggars were hard pressed to find souls generous enough to drop coins in coffee cups. Indiscriminate shots were fired across borders. Homeland security alerts escalated from blue to yellow to orange. Young men with guns garnered respect once more. The world was again as it was, as if a carefree summer was over and the storm clouds presaged a severe winter ahead. The waves of all these stages traveled not in succession but in concurrence gathering speed with each pass, fanning flames, sending sparks upon contact. A superstorm. A spiritual polar vortex.

Not everyone was unhappy with the developments. A portion of the population was relieved, elated even, that this nonsense of *true oneness* and *transpersonal consciousness* was over and done with for good. It smacked of the New World Order. There were vital material and financial interests to protect and serve. The new jovial, tidal wave of ToE reciprocity and the atmosphere of camaraderie and cheer had been a major hindrance for a select business class. It's tough to exploit differences when people care only to help their neighbors. You can't divide and conquer with propaganda when the people collectively adhere to a simple, uncopyrightable tenet. You can't ignore the disparities among people and celebrate the rich when we are all brothers and sisters on spaceship earth. Hippie garbage all of it, and for them Stefan Snodgrass was hailed as the hero who ushered in the return to reason. He was labeled as the *Demystifier,* the *Boomerang,* and the *Exposer* depending on the continent on which he was being described (though the latter term did not translate well in English-speaking countries).

Even some in the New Age movement felt relief with the announcement of Stefan's Anti-Theory. Theirs had been an intimate camp of like-minded human beings of a higher understanding. With ToE came a flood of red-blooded meat eaters running rampant over their well-tended philosophies and conventions. Like a private beach that gets a superlative write-up in a trendy travel magazine, ToE had become a crowded overnight sensation. Suddenly the place had been trashed with spiritual litter from people who didn't deserve the real estate. Clumsy in their approach and sophomoric in their participation, the nouveau riche of consciousness was not a pretty bunch, what with their beer bellies and snot-nosed kids. The sooner they returned to their suburbs and ranches, their condos and villas, the better. Enlightened philosophies are so much safer when not meddled with from the outside.

No dark is darker than the darkness after light.

TWENTY-THREE

Ethan took a bite of his fifth Dunkin' Donut, a powdery affair that turned his stomach. It also resembled the predicament he was in. A big hole in the center of a collapsing universe.

"I don't understand," Ethan said. "We reviewed the calculations repeatedly. Every department on campus did, along with every reputable institution in the world, the entire global physics community."

Shivana nodded in agreement, but the president of Stanford University wasn't having it. "Did you get the stamp of approval from the Numerical and Astrophysical Council?"

"We received provisional approval, but the council doesn't meet on voting matters again until the upcoming annual plenum."

"*Provisional* approval? You went forward with *provisional*?" Mahoney spoke the work like a curse. "No wonder CERN pulled their announcement. They let us take the fall, the bastards."

Ethan felt unsure of many things at the moment, but he knew without a doubt, he was a feeble political match for the master of the domain. "Three Sigma. You instructed us to move ahead."

"I did not, and I dare you to find an email that states otherwise. This is serious stuff, Ethan, serious. The university's prestige is on the line. Tens of millions in endowments withdrawn. My inbox is flooded. Stanford's name is all over this mess."

Shivana said, "Please sir, allow us to run the numbers one more time."

"For what, the zillionth time? Remember, you're nothing but a grad student and an F1 immigrant at that. The only thing you deserve is a one-way ticket back."

"But—"

"But nothing! And absolutely, positively no more talking to the press. You've made fools of yourself and a mockery of this institution. Have you seen the columns in *The New York Times* and *Wall Street Journal?* Scathing. The parodies on YouTube, for chrissakes, dragging the Cardinal through the mud. How'd I ever let you talk me into that media blitz?"

Shivana could stand the stoning no more. "You demanded we make the announcement. You sent us on those trips!"

"With confidence that you got this stuff right. From now on, you go into isolation, the two of you, and I mean officially. Do you understand me?"

"Yes, sir," said Ethan.

"Yes, sir," said Shivana.

Thank God it was a Friday afternoon, the rabbit hole of media releases. Everyone inside the Stanford administrative office hoped the drama would die a quick death, or at least the spotlight would shine elsewhere henceforth. The university issued the following press release at 4:57 pm:

For Immediate Release

Palo Alto, Calif. – It is with regret that the office of the President of Stanford University finds it necessary to issue a correction concerning the E$_8$ breakthrough, which, along with the Higgs boson confirmation, had recently promulgated with great fanfare and optimism a purported Theory of Everything. Upon further and more detailed review, contrary to the first observation there is no basis at this time for a unified field theory or so-called unity theory. Scientists, including those at Stanford, will continue their valiant search for such a noble truth. We are sorry for any unintended consequences as a result of the initial announcement. Ethan Weiner-Gluckstein, Ph.D., and graduate student Shivana Farooq have been placed on paid administrative leave until further notice pending a full and impartial investigation by this institution.

For more information, please contact the Public Relations Office via email or the phone number below.

Ethan and Shivana's next few days were bombarded with a media shower of telephone calls. Ethan's voice mailbox filled up and stopped taking messages. His email inbox overflowed with tens of thousands of messages. He tried answering the queries because he had been taught it was polite to answer correspondence. It became a futile task; for every one-sentence apology, he found time to craft, 100 new emails arrived.

The full-throated venom of the nastier messages startled Ethan and ran the gamut from *You fuckin' Jew asshole, you ruined my life* to *eat cosmic shit and die, loser*. Those in the academic and scientific fields understood that Ethan and Shivana were spokespersons for an alliance that included tens of thousands but still, they resented the twosome's hubristic choice of making the announcement themselves and spared them little sympathy. *That's what you get for trying to be somebody. Hope you like the fame, asshole*. A few of the messages were just plain wacky. *Come visit my Centurion Station, and we will bedazzle the universe with ferocious fire dust smoked in a vaporizer of time and fill my fuzz box with eternal damnation so that I may see the glorious light of orgasmic whirl*. Ethan unplugged the telephone and shut down the fax (though only one person thought to send a fax, a grad student from the Ukraine). He shuttered the blinds so as not to see the camera crews camped outside his home and let the newspapers pile up. He was elated when his ISP blocked all further incoming messages because his account had reached some unspecified limit for personal emails on the server.

Celebrity renders one bare and raw as if the flesh has been torn from your body and your organs leaked out for all to see. The man who had desperately craved clarity in arriving messages more than any soul alive now pushed them back as far too clear, ravenous even, and Ethan felt like a worm.

Post-announcement emails to Shivana were more lurid, and they frightened her with their bluntness and cruelty. *You little brown terrorist bitch, I hope you implode and die* to *My syphilitic cock wants to empty a bucket of cum inside your Iranus*. Shivana mourned over her prideful mistakes but could not fathom what she had done to deserve this treatment. Though she understood these types of messages represented only a very small fraction of humanity, they distressed her, because as long as a small fraction of humanity thought like this, then in truth, all humanity did.

For the masses, the people working regular jobs and worrying more about the next rent payment, Ethan and Shivana had been transformed in an instant from the faces of a dream gifted to the reminder of a dream denied. Social commentators on television reported that the middle and lower classes understood scandal and tragedy best when it could be personified. Ethan and Shivana were the faces of their disappointment.

Out of curiosity, Ethan peeked at an email with a subject line that read: *Ethan, Please Help Me!*

Ethan, you don't know me, but my life changed when you announced the theory of everything. It was like all my problems that had plagued me for eons vanished one by one. I never had a sincere, honest boyfriend, and then I met someone. My skin was covered with eczema, and then it disappeared. I had been sexually abused as a child by my father, and he apologized...and I forgave him. I had been terribly frightened of leaving the house, scared to cross bridges and tunnels, but then I was able to travel freely. I was allergic to strawberries, my favorite food, and then I had a strawberry shake for the first time. Then the other announcement came. The Anti-theory announcement and I couldn't believe it at first. My boyfriend left me for a woman 20 years his junior. The eczema crawled all over my body again, even worse. I'm shuttered in the house, and my father pounded on the door drunk. If this is the way it's going to be, I can't take it anymore. I'm sorry to have burdened you like this, but if I don't get help soon, I'm going to end it all. I have no choice. Please respond soon. Sorry, Sonia Jimenez, Pueblo, CO.

Ethan looked at the time/date stamp and saw the email was 36 hours old. He looked up her number and called, but the call went into voice mail. He Googled her name and city, and a short AP article came up as the first listing. *Suspected Suicide for Pueblo Woman.*

After Ethan confirmed the name, he couldn't stomach to read the details but caught wind of a few snippets: *hanging in garage* and *recluse who lived alone.* He thought about crying but wasn't quite sure how to tap his emotions to get tears flowing. He damned his condition one more time.

On the second Sabbath following the Anti-Theory announcement, Ethan braved a few hours out of the house disguised in a Rastafarian wig and sunglasses to see what changes the Anti-Theory had wrought. People strolled along, drove in their cars, bought things, just like before, but it seemed to him the Pacific fog had rolled in perpetually clouding every interaction and mood. On the third Sabbath, Ethan found a bottle of scotch in a back cabinet that Naomi had somehow missed (or maybe she was a closet alcoholic, wouldn't that be a turn?) and took to drinking. Once past the smell, Ethan found the courage to down a shot and choked back the urge to vomit. He got a headache on the right side of his brain that lasted two days until he cured it with another shot and another. He ended up vomiting so hard his testicles ached.

On the fourth Sabbath, Ethan sat in a bathrobe learning the finer trickeries of the remote control and wondering who were these people on television. Every time a news clip or mention of ToE or Anti-ToE came on, Ethan lunged to change the channel.

He grew horrified when he flicked the remote and found some late-night show host grinning into the camera.

"Ladies and gentleman, tonight's top ten list... *Top Ten Reasons Why You Don't Want to be Ethan Weiner-Gluckstein Right Now*:

Number 10. Your name.

Number 9. Your other name.

Number 8. Who's gonna believe you ever again?

Number 7. Try to pick up a girl in a bar, just try.

Number 6. Your mother isn't proud of you anymore.

Number 5. You've been offered a new faculty position....as a kindergarten teacher.

Number 4. You've got nothing left to prove.

Number 3. Congratulations, they just renewed your fifteen minutes of fame.

Number 2. That Arabic chick? She's come to her senses and found an Arabic guy.

Number 1. One is the loneliest number.

"We'll be right back!" Cut to commercial. Cut Ethan to pieces.

Ethan shouted at the television. *"In a mathematically perfect universe, we would be less than dead. We would never exist. So there!"*

The outburst didn't help to lessen the pain.

On the fifth Sabbath, Ethan decided to take up cigarettes. He wore dark shades and a hoodie for the walk to the corner store. He stood stunned at the counter to learn that a pack of smokes eats up the better part of a $10 bill. He slapped his money down popped a cigarette in his mouth. He took a tentative inhale and coughed like a Stage 4 emphysemic. He spent the next three days trying to gargle the taste out of his mouth, and that little jolt of nicotine placed his nervous system on an unmanned carnival ride. He donned his disguise once again and stepped out to offer the 19 remaining cigarettes to a homeless woman he met on the street. Naomi would never have approved of providing the indigent with addictive substances, but Ethan hated the thought of throwing something away that might be of value to someone else.

On the late afternoon of the sixth Sabbath in the nondescript inner offices of the Department of Physics at Stanford University, President Mahoney held the floor.

"Ethan and Shivana, I'm sorry, but the decision came from above. The board has made its recommendation, along with 24 of 32 department chiefs. Nothing personal. I admire your courage beyond belief. I hope you realize how hard I fought on your behalf. Extremely hard. But the board is the board, and if you're ever president of a major university complex, you'll understand. The administration wants to thank you formally for your service, and I hope you'll work out a sufficient termination package with Human Resources. I, of course, cannot provide HR with any instructions in this regard. Against regs. But I can ask *you* to please be aware that lawsuits only hinder our ability to continue the fundamental scientific research that all of us scientists cherish so dearly."

Mahoney shook Ethan's hand. "Sorry Ethan, double sorry because of your *condition*. You're the most honest man I know. You'll learn."

The Prez double kissed Shivana and double-kissed her again. "For you, I'm truly sorry. You were a bright one with a future, but this too shall pass, give it ten years or so."

With that, he left, just like that. Came, changed their world and departed. His iPhone surely filled with pressing commitments, Skype appointments, benefactor lunches, recruitment, recruitment, recruitment.

Ethan relived the entire nightmarish experience and tried once again to see where he had gone wrong. Deep in his heart, his philosophical heart, he felt the world was One, capital "O." How could it not be? He thought of Koestler's Holon, an entity that is itself a whole but also a part of a whole. Subatomic particles are their own agents, and yet they combine to make atoms. An atom lives a life of its own but is also the building block of the molecule. A molecule needs no further definition than itself, yet is an intrinsic part of a cell. Cells form organisms, organisms live in ecosystems, and on and on. Holons all of them for eternity in either direction. Surely underneath the quantum particle, science will one day find more galaxies to explore. Beyond our universe already there is talk of other universes, multi-verses. Could you make an organism without a cell? Certainly not. Could you fashion a cell without a molecule? Not a chance. Could you construct a molecule without atoms? No way. Up and down the line we all are our own beings made up of smaller but no less consequential Holons. We belong to something larger than ourselves, and that something belongs to something larger still. Not only do we reside in the cosmos, but the cosmos resides in us. This Ethan knew in his heart.

This was his God.

Ethan hugged Shivana, careful not to squeeze her swelling belly. "At least we have each other."

"I hope so," said Shivana.

"What does that mean?"

Shivana gave him a nervous smile. "Let's go home."

She felt she had let them down, all of them. Every robed woman in every dusty town with no route out but on a cart of death. *You see?* The men will say. *Give a woman liberation, and she destroys the world.* Wrap the burqa tighter, get home before dark, prepare the meal and take to the bed. Pull the girls out of school and return their menstruation to the dark. They surely cursed her now, these women who for a foolish moment believed that she might be the savior to lighten their burdens. A dark star, she was now. A curse.

When they returned home, Shivana quickly retired to the cloister of the bedroom, leaving Ethan perplexed. They had stopped talking to each other, laughing together, making love.

After a while, Ethan could stand it no longer. He rifled through kitchen drawers and cabinets for a pair of items he longed for. He searched the garage through dusty cardboard boxes with *Ethan's Stuff* scribbled on the sides in Naomi's hurried handwriting. Not there. He rummaged through the house, racing the fading evening light. On a lark, he opened a plastic box Naomi had left behind in her former office marked *Thrift Store*.

He found just one of the pair. He clawed deeper and found the second. Together again. Each Shabbat candleholder held a half-burned candle, a vestige of the last observed Sabbath of splendor. When was that exactly, he wondered? Before his marriage, maybe in honor of his father's passing? His memory wasn't working well now. The alacrity that had graced him those glory months of the ToE had faded. Instead of seeing far with his mind's eye, he could see only that which was close by, apparent, obvious. Nearsightedness of the brain was the best way he could describe it, but even

142

that description didn't make sense to him anymore, and the fact that a self-authored description no longer made sense just added to the confusion and doubt that had returned to haunt him.

He brought the candles inside and placed them on the kitchen table. Ritual, he thought, help those who don't understand or at least help them feel better for not understanding. As a boy, he had anticipated Shabbat all week long, relished its arrival and marveled at its ritual objects. The tall white candles of stored potentiality. A golden fractal of Challah hidden mysteriously under a lace cover. The silver cup, polished brightly each week and brimming with wine.

Ethan found a Bic lighter. Now, there was a miracle—finding an item like that that in a house long ago purged of toxins, chemicals, and fun. He didn't know how Shivana would feel about it, but he didn't care. He needed this for himself.

As he did when he was as a little boy, Ethan looked out the window to see if he had beaten the first appearance of a star. But tonight the heavens were obscured by clouds that hung low and gray. He could race to his computer to find the exact time of sunset, but that didn't matter anyway. The sun was setting. He felt the darkness coming.

Before he could coax a flame from the rusty lighter, Shivana stepped in, her hair covered with a dark blue swath of silk. He had never seen her before wrapped up so, with her wild mane of floating hair hidden in a tight wrap. Framed in the hijab, her face became stern and somber. She looked five years older. He saw for the first time thin wrinkles around the edges of her eyes.

The first sight of his beloved dressed so reminded him of his mother, who each Friday night lovingly draped a shawl around her visage to better capture the glow of the Shabbat candles. Here he was, sparking the divine flame of one religion and Shivana wore a shawl of another. Crossing paths again, those religions.

"Why?" he asked.

"A reminder."

"Of what?"

"My shame."

"It wasn't our mistake," he said.

"Not that. My vanity."

"We all have it."

"I invited mine. I allowed it to seduce me. I welcomed the

143

consummation with my free will and permission. I whored myself." She tugged tightly on the silk dupatta constricting her face. "It's easier than having to remind myself."

Throughout her life, Shivana had experienced modesty as a capricious punishment meted out by the tyrannical and dogmatic. Now she understood it to be a virtue best nurtured from within. A silk scarf around one's head was a constant reminder of restraint, particularly for someone like her, susceptible to flights of fancy, closer in composition to the stars than to the earth.

She stood by Ethan's side. In silence, he touched the flame to the first wick.

"Praised be the light, able to give of itself without reducing itself."

She watched the glow take root and lost herself in the graceful movement of the tiny flame, like a fingertip pointing to God.

She wrapped her arm in his.

Ethan handed her the lighter. "Would you like to?"

Shivana took the lighter from his hand. She lit the second candle, and as soon as it glowed, Ethan closed his eyes. He rocked back and forth and recited from the very depths of his heart the words indelibly inscribed within: *Baruch ata Adonoi Alhenu Melech Ha Olam, Blessed are you King of the Universe.*

Two small flames before two small flames. Ethan raised the cup of wine. "Praise be the fruit of the vine and all the colorful, tasty and unnecessary beauties on earth that make life pleasant."

He took a small sip and gave the cup to Shivana so that she might sip if she cared to.

She did.

Ethan lifted the linen napkin to reveal the challah. "And praised be the bread of the earth that sustains us. My father used to say *sustain* is the finest miracle of all...that the world was created not just once, but it is recreated at every moment. There is not one creation but a continual creation. Blessed art thou, the God who sustains us and brings us to this day."

"I feel better," said Shivana.

"So do I."

"Have you thought about a name?" asked Shivana.

They did have one reason to hope. One shining, unassailable miracle on which to rest all hope for the future.

144

"Not really?" Ethan said.

"How about Kalil, like the great poet. It means friend."

"I like it, but what about a name that crosses boundaries."

"Like what?"

"Gabriel, the angel through whom God revealed the Qur'an to Mohammed. That Gabriel."

Ethan knew him well, that Gabriel. The heavenly angel who under divine orders gathered up the clay needed to fashion Adam. Gabriel who took pity on Adam and Eve after the first couple's expulsion from paradise and taught them to sow and cultivate grain so that they might learn to tend themselves. Gabriel who interceded at the moment when Abraham brought down the sword on his son Isaac bound on an altar. Gabriel who saved Lot from the dusty destruction of Sodom.

"How we need a Gabriel now."

"And if it's a girl, Gabrielle."

"Gabrielle."

Shivana held Ethan's hand. "God willing."

Funny, Ethan had never heard her use this expression before. "God's willing," he added.

A knock on the door shattered the Shabbat silence.

Ethan expected a news reporter following up on a story already beaten to a pulp, or a graduate student stopping by with a basket of fruit. A few have been nice that way.

Ethan peeked out the peephole. His face turned Ashkenazi white.

Shivana said, "Who is it?"

"*Him.*"

"Oh, God."

"What should I do?"

Before she could answer the question, Omar's voice boomed from the other side. "I know she's in there."

With little hesitation, Ethan did something he had never done before in his life, not consciously.

"She's not here." The words stung Ethan's tongue the moment they left his mouth. Does not one lie lead to another, one sin to another? Hadn't decades of studying Torah taught him nothing else?

Listening in the wings, Shivana's body filled with the urge to flee. And, by God, if she didn't feel little Gabriel or Gabrielle give a swift kick to the inside of her gut.

She could slip out the back door, but she knew better than to attempt to fool or delay Omar. He was if nothing else relentless. One must be to be pious. He would find her, if not today then tomorrow or the day after, but he would find her.

She whispered in Ethan's ear. "Open the door."

TWENTY-FOUR

Omar trembled in his shoes. "Please, I must speak with her."

Had Omar been in a chattier mood he would have explained how he had suffered a flood of days of progressive hell since the Anti-Theory.

Shivana stepped into the foyer. "Hello, Omar."

"Shivana, it's time to come home."

"And what about your dance career and your blonde?"

"An injury and a mistake."

It was true. In the first week following the Anti-ToE, Omar had sprained his ankle, later diagnosed as a ligament tear, which took him out of practice. This meant that the dynamic dance duo of Sandra Lee Wilson and Omar Farooq had little choice but to withdraw from the Western States Finals (this after buying non-refundable airline tickets to Colorado Springs), with faint hopes for recovery for the following year's season.

In the second week, a trio of teens in a pickup truck waving a Confederate flag heaved a trash can onto Omar's lawn and in red spray paint scrawled *Towell Head* (sic) on the side of the house along with a crude attempt at a swastika that ended up backward. He could never determine if the insult was directed at him or Shivana, but it mattered little. A line had been crossed, and a chapter of fear opened. Sandra Lee totally freaked out at the cross burning on the lawn, never having been on the receiving side of such hatred. She called an army investigator and used all her inside sources to find out who the hell it was. But how can you finger three kids in a pickup truck? Randomness has its advantages.

In the third week, Sandra Lee paced like a caged lioness in Omar's cramped condo, her eye wandering back to the hills of her station. While Omar attempted to placate her, two alarming developments worried him.

First, his gazelle tongue now bleated like a goat. *Your eyes of glass make me desire to drink your liquid.* That's not what he meant, but that's the way it came out. *Each moment with you leaves me wanting for pork.* What he meant to confess was that the forbidden for him was attractive, but who could take such a phrase as anything but an insult. He knew that the moment you have to issue an apology to a woman, it is already too late.

Second, Sandra Lee's skin grew cold. Two to three degrees Fahrenheit colder, verified by thermometer. She took to wrapping herself in blankets and wearing two pairs of socks. Her nose turned Rudolf red. When Omar tried to touch her, she shuddered like a POW. He attempted to seduce her with language as he always had. *Not having you makes me as crazy as a deformed child with no mother.*

"Shut up, you bleeping fish," she responded

Week four marked the couple's return to the dance floor, but Sandra Lee stepped out every five minutes to vomit from the pregnancy, and when they finally caught a rhythm, Omar fell backward and sprained an ankle while attempting the simplest of Paso Dobles spins.

The flub sent Sandra Lee sliding on her ass halfway across the floor. "You jerk!" she blurted from the seat of her pants.

She stood up and huffed toward the exit. What hurt Omar the most was that Sandra Lee didn't turn back to see if he was injured, a common courtesy, he thought. Obviously not for her. Omar clutched his pained ankle as they exchanged vile words in the parking lot like crude commoners. They spat on the ground in front of each other.

Very next day, with Omar flat on his back from his premature return to the dance floor, Sandra Lee entered the bedroom carrying two valises, not the twenty with which she had arrived packing immeasurable passion.

"It's over," she said.

"But my darling, how have I offended you?"

Sandra Lee sighed and for the first time in weeks showed a modicum of emotion. "Who are we fooling? We come from different worlds, our only attraction is our difference. We played a game like children without regard for the inevitable punishment."

"We have our dancing, our love. We both are tender and romantic under a tough shell."

"I feel like I'm living in a hotel, a low-rent one at that."

"And what of our child?"

"Good question."

Omar protested and pleaded. He begged and berated, but it was of no use.

Sandra Lee flung her suitcases into the trunk of the Mercedes, muttered something about an annulment, and shifted into low gear. She floored her return to the land of hillside homes where gardeners are the only outsiders allowed on the grounds.

Omar called her, he emailed, he texted, he sent bouquets of flowers, boxes of chocolates. He spent hours summoning his inner Rumi to create poems more beautiful than language itself, but nothing inspired a response.

As a result, week five brought with it a mental depression so severe that Omar couldn't bear the thought of returning to the clinic, despite a spike in appointments. All that ToE ecstasy had resulted in a rash of pregnancies, and all the Anti-ToE despair, a rash of abortion appointments. If nothing more, the tumultuous events of the past months had succeeded in putting humanity on the same cycle, like a house full of menstruating women.

Omar considered surrendering his medical practice altogether. He retained cash sufficient to last him months, years even. With the recent spike in abortion demand, he might be able to sell the practice at a princely sum. A rare and temporary opportunity to cash in on a once-in-a-lifetime circumstance. But money was not the issue, nor his business. Few understand what it's like to live two lives, sandwiched between two worlds, loving and detesting elements of both. It's enough to drive someone crazy. Someone like Omar.

That very morning, Omar flung himself and his magic praying carpet to the floor in unison, not caring to follow the prescribed procedures for prayer. It felt so good just to weep into the carpet of his grandfather. Was this not prayer enough? What had possessed him to abandon the tenets of his faith in the first place? A theory does not alter that which is eternally true. An American blonde is no substitute for a wife. And a floor is best utilized to praise Allah not to initiate flights of fancy that end two minutes hence in tepid applause. How foolish he had been.

Allah, Allah, always Allah and nothing but Allah.

As he touched his forehead to the ground, it dawned on him with such clarity, the sins of his ways. Not only had he abandoned his faith, but he had turned his back on his true wife, violating the most holy oath of matrimony, disgracing his family and hers. Sure, she had run from him, but he had not chased her. She was a child and he the adult. He had not fulfilled his duty as a husband to instruct her morally. In Arabic, the word was *Muruwah*, which translates loosely as manliness, but this translation neglects a far more honorable significance. Like knighthood or the code of the samurai, Muruwah requires courage in battle, patience in struggle, endurance in suffering and above all dedication to the tribe. Muruwah requires one to obey his chief and defend the honor of his family.

Now with each refreshing kiss to the floor, Omar vowed to return to the ways of Muruwah, to fully comply with the laws and dictates of a faith that had survived nearly 1500 years on its merits alone, praise be to Allah. Islam literally means to submit, to surrender, and Omar pledged to walk the road of redemption starting with his spousal duties.

First stop, home of another man defiling his wife. What blasphemies we are capable of when we veer from the path of righteousness? That Allah forgives is the surest sign of his rightful dominion.

Plus, he missed Shivana terribly. He longed for her precious smile, her bright eyes beaming with curiosity, her gentle ways. He ached for her couscous and tabouli, her creamy mahalabiya pudding as sweet as the first draw of mother's milk. More so, he missed her advice when he faced business problems or issues with his staff. She quickly raced to the core of the issue and found there the seed of a solution that Omar had overlooked. He appreciated how she understood his moodiness and saw through his thick skull. She laughed at his silly jokes, funny or not. And, oh, how he missed the comfort of speaking his native tongue, for she spoke Arabic brilliantly — far better than his staccato Farsi.

He realized he had been at times intemperate with her, disrespectful. Why had he not appreciated her more for who she was, not blinded by her gender, her station in the imaginary hierarchy? Ideology gives its practitioners justification for irrational behavior, and he was guilty. Had he a whip he would flog himself with the vengeance deserved.

As he stood on the doorstep of Ethan's home, Omar did not wish for confrontation, but there was only one acceptable outcome. He tried to look at Shivana with compassion for truly he was the sinner here.

"It is time for you to come home," he repeated.

Shivana had never had the opportunity to compare the two men side by side. Ethan, surprisingly, was taller, but he habitually rounded his shoulders in a continual attempt to shrink himself. Omar was broader in the chest and more menacing or maybe she was projecting.

"This is my home now. I am never returning to the burqa."

"Shivana, I am asking you to return to your true home, your true religion. I love you and need you."

"You're talking foolishly now because you cannot get what you want."

"That is not true. Well, it is true but can you deny that we belong together, we belong to a culture? Think of your mother. Think of your father."

"I think of them all the time."

"Have you talked to them?"

"No, not since all...this."

"They are saddened, beyond comprehension. They face ridicule merely walking down the street," Omar said. "They are spat upon, and your family name is cursed below the minarets of prayer. Their daughter has become a plague on their house, and they cry every night for you to return to the way."

"I am sorry to hear that. It pains me. Truly."

"The world is larger than our selfishness permits us to see. Your sister, Jala?"

"What about my sister Jala?"

"Her betrothed called off the marriage. Who can blame him? Why marry into a shamed family when girls more beautiful and with larger dowries go unmarried? She sits at home in the shadows, destined to be unwed and barren. Yet she will not blame you, will not say an unkind word toward you."

"I love Jala."

"Your brother, Mohammed, has been thrown out of the university. He begs now in the coffee houses for menial jobs. When he's lucky, he earns a few tomans by dusting the steps of the mosque or polishing the shoes of travelers who don't know he is a relation of yours. His feet have become raw and his brow heavy and wrinkled like a man 20 years his senior. Yet to his own detriment he defends you at every turn."

"I love Mohammed."

"Your mother has drowned herself in Sufi song and poetry to forget the pain of your betrayal. From dawn to dusk, and dusk to dawn she prays over trinkets, incense, candles and other defilements for you to come home. Yet in the center of her altar sits a photo of you, as if you were the mother of Mohammed. If she were a man, she would never leave the mosque."

"I love my mother."

"And your father. Remember the strong man that he was? The lion? Now he weeps like a child, an orphan with no parents to feed him a glass of milk. Pillar of the community? Once he was, now he has crumbled like a column of salt. He hides in the dusty corners of his own home where he should be king. Once was king. Now he's a pauper. Lower than a pauper, a leper shunned and exiled by friends and acquaintances he once so loved and who loved him."

"I love my father."

All of Omar's accusations were correct. Shivana knew these things and had ignored them. Humility is the act of acknowledging the truth. Wasn't that the humility that gave strength to Moses and Gandhi? She had been prideful in her disregard for the well-being of her family.

"And I, Shivana, I know I have done wrong. I have been stiff-necked and strict. I have wronged you. I have sinned. I have blasphemed. I allowed my vanity to rule. I am the greatest transgressor of all."

It was that word *vanity* that shot a dart through Shivana's heart.

In her moments of quiet reflection, Shivana, the countess of count, counted the true desires of her life and tallied but two.

The first was to be free of anonymity, to be something other than a shapeless female blob beneath a shapeless cloth tent. A shapeless form existing in a shapeless void. Desiring recognition shouldn't be such a crime, Shivana thought. Then, perhaps it should.

Second, she wanted to be a student of Descartes, applying methodical doubt to all knowledge that was susceptible to deception. This included knowledge codified and warranted by false authority, the senses, and reason, emotion, theories — all of it, a Google full. She revered the empirical because it could not be manipulated by the ideological. Perhaps it is vanity to think that all can be discovered, settled, understood with empirical inquiry. Maybe it takes more to truly understand the cosmos than a computer full of algorithms and a whiteboard on which to write them. Perhaps empirical thought is limited, and whole worlds exist beyond them that cannot be measured by the tools of science and the mind. Maybe she had been as dogmatic in her views as the religionists who accept all on faith and reject science as the work of man.

Such were Shivana's two sins. Look at the misery they had brought her and the wretchedness it had delivered her loved ones. Shame and self-abhorrence were her companions now, the twin penalties of desire.

Ethan saw Shivana equivocate. He stepped in and took a wide gulp. No one in the world could love and worship her as did he. Omar might not be a match for him physically, but Ethan would gladly risk it all, bet it all, lose it all to keep her by his side.

"Shivana is with me now. We are devoted to each other. I care for her, understand her. I treat her as my equal, more than my equal, not my chattel. She deserves to be treated like a queen, not a servant."

Omar stepped even closer. "If you know anything of devotion, why then are you not by your own wife's side? Did you not swear to her your devotion for life?"

Omar had a point, but Ethan didn't care to argue. "My previous marriage is none of your concern, and I will have to ask you to leave now."

Ethan couldn't believe his own audacity. It felt so strange and new. Then again, he had never fought for something he wanted. Never wanted something worth fighting for.

Omar felt the challenge and did what most every man does when challenged: he puffed his chest and stepped up toe-to-toe. At close range, Omar caught the scent of his betrothed on Ethan, which made his blood boil as if cooked by the desert sun. Had he been a violent man, Omar might have struck a blow to slay this distant cousin of his.

"I will not have some infidel address me so."

Shivana stepped in. "Omar, you should be ashamed."

Ethan's blood boiled too because a man is a man after all. He pushed a stiff finger into Omar's chest. "This is the woman I honor and revere. I will not allow you or anyone to smother her soul again. I will fight to the death, so be it. If you think I'm bluffing, try me."

"She's mine!" came Omar's retort.

The two men circled each other like desperate wolves.

"Stop it!" Shivana demanded. "Both of you!"

She refereed them to neutral corners. "Do you think I'm a ball in your play yard? Look at you two, arguing like schoolboys. Do I not have a say in this? I make the decision here. Not *you,* she scolded Omar. Not *you,* she admonished Ethan. Neither of you."

The men fluttered back.

Shivana waited until her breathing slowed.

She stroked Omar's coarse stubble. "Omar, you are a good man. And when young and unsaddled with obligations, you made me laugh. I thanked

153

Allah for joining us together. In your heart, I know there is an altar of goodness within you."

Shivana pecked Ethan on the cheek. "You, my Ethan, are the kindest man I ever met. You have showered me unconditionally with love and it has healed me like a salve on a wound open for a lifetime. I'm always in your debt and will treasure the gift of your love forever."

Ethan smiled at the win. Could it possibly be that the world had not fully crashed after all? Maybe there truly is an element not found on the Periodical Table that Ethan could now identify as *grace,* lighter than hydrogen. He had already isolated one called *love,* and another *intimacy,* and still one more, *peace,* back when ToE ruled. They had since disappeared, but once upon a time they *existed.* Ethan had the proof. He had experienced them, if only for a few nanoseconds longer than the life of the elusive boson particle.

Shivana pulled down her hijab tight so that she might be closer to the one she loved. "Ethan," she continued. "I love you, but I do not deserve you."

"W-w-what?" Ethan stuttered.

"Not with this litany of sins I've committed before man and God."

"I don't deserve *you,*" Ethan retorted. "We don't deserve each other. The equation cancels out, don't you see? That's the beauty of it."

"I understand. You are right, but I am so wrong. Plus, there are powers out of our control."

"Powers, what powers?"

"The power of a vow."

She turned her gaze on Omar. Had she not sworn to him her fidelity? What right did she have to break her vow?

"What would the world be if we broke our vows as we pleased? I must start with myself if I want the world to heal. And my vow to Omar precedes you."

"How about your vow to true love?"

"You are correct again. Always correct. But my true love, my first love belongs to Jala and Mohammed. It belongs to my mother and my father. I cannot ignore my family — and with them comes allegiance to my village, my country, my culture, my religion. In a way, you are both correct, the choice is not mine after all."

Shivana bowed before Ethan, in deference, in respect, but not in devotion. Not in loyalty. Devotion and loyalty belonged to neither man.

They belonged to the empirical truth, and as Shivana now had to accede, the moral truth, as well.

She implored with her teary eyes to Ethan her great regret, but he was not understanding. There was nothing more she could do. The quicker the cut, the better.

"Wait here, Omar. Let me get my belongings. But I'm telling you, things will be different. No more subjugation, no more six steps behind. Agreed?"

"Agreed."

"Never again a burqa. And if I wear a hijab it is of my own volition."

"But—"

"But nothing. These are my terms."

"Accepted."

"Okay then." Shivana had won the battle. Did she want to win the battle? It would have been so much easier if Omar had been intransigent, but for better or worse he wasn't. She turned and headed toward the bedroom.

"Shivana!" Ethan yelped. "What about the baby?"

Shivana stopped on her second step.

"Baby?" Omar said.

Shivana faced Omar squarely in the eye. Not how she had hoped to introduce the subject, but better now than later, she figured. Get it all on the table. "Yes, a baby. Ethan's child."

"How far along?" asked Omar.

"Nine weeks."

"First trimester," Omar calculated.

She knew what he was thinking. Had he become so cold as to curse the arrival of an angel? Such were the times now, thought Shivana. Perhaps it was the end of times, as the prophets harkened.

"Please hurry with your things. We'll talk later."

Shivana searched Ethan's eyes. "I am so sorry."

She disappeared to gather her belongings.

Ethan's chest deflated, emptied of its hope. His bowels filled with toxic disappointment. It was for the better. Who was he fooling? What could he expect? Would Shivana truly remain interested in him after the thrill was gone? Would she truly care to grow old with him? She would grow impatient with his perpetual obsessive compulsion. She would tire of a man locked within the borders of a small, finite world of his own making. If this whole miserable experience had taught him one lesson, it was that dreams get dashed, expectations remain unmet, and one's rare triumphs have a very short half-life. Yes, grace, love, and intimacy may exist, but at what benefit if their brevity only serves to remind us of their inability to endure. Shooting stars streak across the sky and dim before your heart has a chance to beat but once.

Truly, who was he kidding about being a father? What healthy, normal child would want an absent-minded dad, head always in the spheres above? Better to spare the child the shame now before he grows up and is forced to explain to his friends why his father is so quirky and absurd. *Dad, how can you be so stupid? Go away, you're embarrassing me.*

Omar placed a comforting hand on Ethan's shoulder. He understood the pain of losing a beloved. We are all brothers in sorrow. Allah is merciful and so must we all be.

"I am sorry," Omar lamented. "I know you must be a good man for Shivana to love you so. She does not love easily, so when she does, it is with all her heart."

His words did little to console the inconsolable.

Shivana returned with two bags and the little brown teddy bear that she and Ethan had purchased, a first token to remind themselves that the baby was really truly real and happening to them.

She stuffed the bear into the zipper pocket of her garment bag, the same one she had taken to Chicago and New York on their triumphant media tour. How long ago it seemed. Time is measured by what passes in the heart, not by the ticks of a clock.

"I'm ready."

"Shivana," said Ethan.

"Yes?" she pivoted.

"Are you sure?"

"I am."

"I will let you go, not because every fiber of my being tells me to act otherwise, but because you tell me this is what you want."

"It is."

"I ask only to let our child know, sometime in the future, when the time is right, that I love him. That his father loves him."

Shivana wiped a tear away for she knew this would never come to pass. Two tears, one for the loss of Ethan and one for the future destined for her. Her kismet.

It *is* written, she thought. How foolish had she been to think otherwise.

Omar fired up the Maxima and thanked Allah with 10,000 times the fervor he had mustered in the past. He had his wife back, and now they would begin anew, from the very start, as if they were toddlers in school learning their Alif Ba as scribbles on the dusty blackboard, the first utterance of the Good Name.

"Omar," said Shivana.

"Yes, my beloved."

"I feel so ashamed."

"Me, too," said Omar. "Me, too."

TWENTY-FIVE

Ethan Weiner-Gluckstein closed the door on Shivana and Omar.

He pressed his ear to catch the last hint of her voice. He should have tape-recorded her laughter so that it might delight him long after her departure. He thought he heard Omar mention the '*A*'word as they walked away. He heard Shivana softly sobbing.

Ethan returned to the kitchen and positioned himself at the kitchen bar. He laid his head on the granite, cold as a gravestone. He picked up a red shiny apple from a bowl of fruit Shivana had lovingly arranged. He took a crisp bite. Her absence filled the room. For the first time, he fully understood the property of vacuums. He witnessed the powerful effects of corrosion firsthand. The mystery of exploding stars eluded him no more. Those electrons that jump orbits at will? There is a corollary that Ethan had forgotten until now. You can't predict when a quantum leap will occur, not precisely. Just as quickly as an electron leaps, it may tumble back down. Damn chaos theory. Damn it all.

He found a pad and pencil and began scribbling a note. But who to leave it for? His parents were dead. No brothers or sisters — that was another deficit to be added to that column on the right. Dynamic macros in the spreadsheet of life, that's what Ethan needed in order to update that column as quickly as the deficit entries accumulated there.

He opened his computer and typed two words in Google: *Suicide methods.*

Top Ten:
1 Bleeding (i.e. wrist cutting)
2 Drowning

3 Suffocation
4 Electrocution
5 Jumping from height
6 Firearms
7 Hanging
8 Vehicular impact
9 Poisoning
10 Immolation

Faced with such an uninviting list, Ethan couldn't help but surf over to *The New York Times* to see if the ToE and Anti-Theory had fallen off the front page. Thank God yes, replaced by a bold headline that read:

Pakistan Crisis Reaching Boiling Point

Members of Congress on the left and right called for aggressive measures to combat the growing menace in the region. The President responded by saying the administration was *considering all measures to respond to the belligerent provocations of the Pakistani government.* Pentagon brass burrowed into their bunkers to update war plans. *War, war, war* went the chant in English and Urdu.

Ethan didn't give a shit.

He would be gone in an hour, laughing from the beyond. He concerned himself with his sorrows, no one else's. He searched around the house to find what was at hand and what would be the least painful. He locked tight all the windows. He swung shut the kitchen door to prevent drafts.

Without a prayer upon his lips, Ethan Weiner-Gluckstein, the son of a scholar, a physicist of great promise, a little quirky and slow on the uptake, twisted the stove's burner knobs, all of them, quickly bypassing the pilot lights. He welcomed the hiss in four-part harmony. Make the pain stop, his only desire. No, one more wish, for consciousness to cease. If life was the price, so be it. Nothing comes of nothing.

The distinctive odor of mercaptan filled the air. Ethan climbed a kitchen stool, thought again, and found a spot on the floor propped up against the refrigerator so as not to fall from the stool and potentially bleed all over the kitchen. He did not want to make a mess for whoever might find him.

He thought about finding rags to use as diapers because he remembers that one releases both the sphincter ani externus and sphincter urethrae upon death, releasing the contents of the bladder and intestines. But the dwindling modicum of pride remaining within him didn't want anyone finding him bundled up in a soiled homemade diaper. Suicide was demeaning enough.

He waited to feel the spirit leave his body. Prayed for the God of Sustain to take a Shabbat absence and leave him to his cowardly devices. That's the way he looked at it. That's the way he felt. *Give me that satisfaction at least.*

He took a deep breath of the natural gas and another. Anxiety gone, peculiarity gone, desperation gone.

It should always feel like this. Light, airy, unconcerned, sluggish, slow. A world of ether and fog, careless confusion. He loved this, death filling his nostrils. Death was his lover now, his Shabbat bride.

Ethan closed his eyes and filled his lungs once more. Peace at last.

The last conscious thought he entertained was *sefirot.* It glowed inside his brain like phosphorus unbound.

Sefirot, as in the grand Kabbalistic diagram representing the 10-step divine vessels through which creation unfolds. Sefirot, as in the way God continuously creates both the physical realm and the chain of higher metaphysical realms. Sefirot, the careful balance of life that needs to be constantly tweaked by humans in order to amplify God's presence on earth. *That* sefirot. And for the first time, Ethan understood it. This great mystery.

How do you say *Eureka* in Hebrew?

Ethan willed himself to stand. Woozy from the gas, he fell over and scraped his chin on the edge of the kitchen island.

He dragged himself to the stove and turned the knobs to *off.* He crawled on the floor because he remembered that's where oxygen settles during a fire.

This wasn't a fire, and in his fog, he couldn't remember if natural gas was heavier or lighter than oxygen. He clawed his way to the dining room. He caught a pure breath of fresh air.

Sefirot.

The illumination came to him in a flash. Like a prophet's vision or a genius' stroke of insight. Why it came at this moment, who knew? Had the gas acted as some sort of catalyst that freed his mind from the clutter to truly see? Or had an unseen angel intervened surreptitiously on his behalf?

Ethan opened a window and stuck his head out for air.

He tried to focus on the Italian Cedars that separated his property from the Prasad's yard, but there, looming in the space between the houses, Ethan beheld energy arranged in the mysterious emanation of the sefirot, comprehensible to him for the first time.

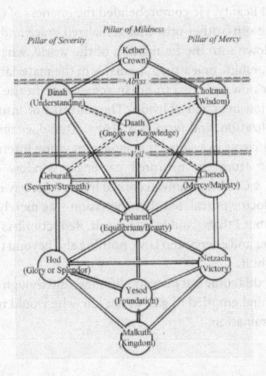

It looked like a snippet of DNA or the midsection of a construction crane, or the chakras of the human body, highlighted by bulbous orbs of quasar light. Ethan not only saw it, he understood it. On the top of the structure in the middle, sat the Crown, glowing with a color beyond the spectrum of color, the color of nothingness, pure light, translucent as it acted as a bridge between the unknowable world above and the world below. The will of God just before manifested in the material world.

On the left, Ethan saw the column with the orb of the female palace of Understanding balanced on the right by male Wisdom. He understood these to be the first separation of divine energy into masculine and feminine, yin, yang, the first duality. With the crown, these formed the major triad of the universe.

And below them, an orb of Justice balanced by the orb of Mercy. He understood that if justice is not tempered and balanced by love and mercy, the world will see hard punishment. And if love and mercy are not tempered and balanced by justice, anarchy will reign. When balanced correctly, the four orbs: Understanding, Wisdom, Justice, and Mercy give birth to both Knowledge and Beauty. He comprehended the oneness of the blueprint.

Below these orbs, other orbs that actualized grace and sincerity in the world spilled down into the foundation of the world, where the male and female forces combine on earth, in humans, in the material plane.

It was clear now, revealed to Ethan somewhere in the hazy penumbra between consciousness and oblivion. The universe of infinite emanation, creation, actualization, and formation. How often does one see the entire design of the universe in a singular magnificent vision interrupted only by a sharp reflection from the mirrored passenger window of the Prasad's Chrysler Town & Country minivan parked in the driveway next door?

Later the doctor postulated that the vision was merely the result of a lack of oxygen, but Ethan wouldn't believe it. Reductionists say the world is made of particles and energy and laws, nothing else beyond the realm. Ethan no longer bought it.

Visions like this come but once in a lifetime, and though its clarity began to fade as his mind emptied of gas, Ethan knew he would never forget this moment of illumination.

TWENTY-SIX

Harlen Spridgen slipped into the warm water of the bubble bath. He held the Penthouse magazine high above the marble Jacuzzi tub to keep it from getting wet and soapy.

This was it. The moment of truth. The point of no return. He flipped open the centerfold on a glossy female hottie, air-brushed to the max, breasts as orbital as small planets, vagina as mysterious as dark matter. He sunk his hand below the sudsy water line to feel for a pulse. Not much.

Behavioral Modification 101. If he wasn't gonna be gay anymore, by golly, he was going to be straight, because a life of closed-eye masturbation wasn't going to cut it, plain and simple. He flipped forward a few pages to a new spread of a petite boyish woman, small breasts, undefined hips, pixie hair. Hey, whatever works. He got it working. It thrilled him so much the pages slipped into the water, and the magazine became all wet.

"Shit."

Just then he heard a car sounding vaguely familiar zip into the driveway. Was it a pro-life splinter group coming to drive home their anti-gay message? They're getting bold, those pesky protestors. Rattled, Harlen's erection imploded.

The automatic garage door rolled open. The familiar jangle of keys answered the mystery. Then, strangely, it sprang back to full blossom.

For the first time in his life, Harlen was happy to hear his wife arrive home, or Omar's wife, or whoever she was until the lawyers sorted it all out. A night of firsts. He chucked aside the soggy magazine. The Internet was far more effective anyway. Unlimited possibilities, no unsightly creases.

The weeks following the anti-Theory announcement had not been good to Pastor Spridgen. The first week brought an unmistakable undercurrent of dissension in the pews. Harlen detected it first as a collective resistance to responsive readings, a tide heading out instead of in. When the flock did answer his calls, the good people of his church did so in a resentful mumble, a nanosecond later than usual.

Harlen was accustomed to preaching to a packed house and had forgotten the bright red of the plush seats. But on the second Sunday, the place was half-empty, and the seats stared back at him like angry denials. Even his sermon, a sure-fire rousing denunciation of abortion and the breakdown of the traditional family, brought only scattered applause and amens. A good percentage of parishioners apparently had come for what they hoped would be a rousing denunciation of Harlen's earlier pronouncement. The disappointed streamed out of the hall during the service.

Harlen was certain things couldn't get worse, but upon completion of the third Sunday service following the anti-Theory, he was bodily confronted by a few of the more committed members of the church's Pro-Life Crusade. Bev Gilliam punched the air with a sign that read *God Hates Fags*. Cindy Zusin had hand-painted one that read *Mourn for Your Sins Sinner* and Tammy Felix's held aloft a suggestion to *Butt F**k Somewhere Else*. The group sneered as Harlen walked by.

He knew them all so well and their sins, too.

He wanted to say, *people in glass houses shouldn't throw stones,* but instead, he smiled and intoned, "I love you all. And I understand your pain."

That's what Jesus would do, or Gandhi. Unconditional love, non-violent behavior. His message obviously wasn't resonating because the usually understanding Virginia Ratcliff walked up to him and spat in his eye. "Loser."

Bev Gilliam added, "Get ready for God to drop-kick you to hell."

Harlen spotted Margie Lean, Jimmy's mom, in the way back carrying a poster that read, *God Hates America Because of Scum Like You.*

"Marge, it's me, Pastor Spridgen."

"I'm sorry," she informed the Pastor, "but you've got one foot in hell."

The ladies pestered him until he had safely locked himself in his car and was driving away. One of the gals threw a raw egg in his direction but missed. He kept an eye on their hatred through the rearview mirror. They'd never see past his God-given sexuality to the Christian heart within.

For a moment (only a moment), he empathized with all those abortion providers he had picketed in the past, including the handsome and debonair Dr. Omar Farooq across town, who had married Sandra Lee even before their divorce. The theory made everything messy. Who in the heck was going to clean up the wreck now? Like a hurricane on the coast. It's so much better to put your faith into a belief that can't be discredited. That way they can't take it away from you no matter what evidence is presented.

Still, thanks to his charisma and preaching chops, Harlen felt lucky to retain a core of one or two hundred parishioners who had the decency to stand by him. God bless them for choosing to see him as a man of God, not a man of men.

Sometime during week four, Harlen received a visit from two taciturn Church elders. One hailed from Riverside, California and the second directly from Church headquarters in Dallas. They looked like G-men in their double-breasted suits and shiny shoes. They invited Harlen out to Denny's for a Grand Slam breakfast.

"Look, Harlen," the Riverside elder said, "everyone got thrown by the Theory of Everything. Everyone suffered from the irrational exuberance. I bought a mountain bike. *Mistakes were made.* And while we don't condone your decision or lifestyle whatsoever, we understand your desire to come out of the closet. But that was then, and this is now. The party's over. It's fix-it time. A deserved return to the normalcy of before. Please pass the maple syrup."

The Dallas elder said, "If you ask me, I think it's a socialist conspiracy. *For they prophesy a lie to you in order to remove you far from your land, and I will drive you out and you will perish,* Jeremiah 27:10."

The Riverside elder poured the syrup all over his pancakes and bacon until his plate runneth over.

"To give it to you straight, there is no place in the ministry for a queer. Your options are to step down from the pulpit immediately and continue being whatever you want to be, or taking a leave of absence for six months with no contact with parishioners. On your probation, you will undergo gay conversion therapy. Right here in the Bay Area, the Reverend Kyle Myles runs a wonderful chapter for this type of therapy. He's worked miracles with people like you. Sky high conversion rates. He does dykes, too."

This did little to reassure Harlen.

"We will follow your progress, and if we deem you sincere in your efforts and the modification a success, then you will be given a chance to state your case for reinstatement before the board. Meanwhile, you will lead one Sunday service more, this coming Sunday, during which you are to renounce homosexuality in no uncertain terms as repugnant, sinful and ungodly. Play it well, my friend."

The Dallas elder added, "*Then will I also confess unto thee that thine own right hand can save thee*, Job 40:14."

With no appetite, Harlen played with his runny eggs. "When do you need a decision?"

"Right now."

Harlen had never felt so pure, so free as during the weeks after coming out of the closet. He had underestimated the healing power of transparency, a rock 'em sock 'em antidote to shame and guilt. How wonderful the world might be if everyone lived without guilt and shame. But then, he had lived for a short period without guilt and shame and look where it got him? In trouble with the Lord. Damn that Snodgrass guy who brought guilt and shame back into the New Eden. And what was wrong with being gay, anyway? God made him this way. Try as he might (and Lord knows he had tried), he couldn't shed his desires. It's as if they shared DNA with his blue eyes and that little dimple on his right cheek. Surely one of Jesus' disciples was gay, statistically speaking, one in twelve. Perhaps the Old Testament Joseph, the dreamer? Sold into slavery by his macho brothers and able to withstand the advances of Potiphar's gorgeous and predatory wife? Coat of many colors? Come on, gay all the way.

"Well, what's your decision?" asked the pastor from Riverside.

Harlen half-remembered the famous line of Henry of Navarre, *Paris is well worth a mass.* The nobleman had said this before his quick conversion to Catholicism that allowed him to take the throne of France as Henry IV. Of course, later he was assassinated by a religious fanatic, but that's not the point.

On Sunday morning of the fifth week, with the elders in the first-row center, and Jimmy Lean a few rows back, Harlen Spridgen assumed the pulpit in the church he felt he had built by hand and uttered the following pronouncement:

My dear brothers and sisters. Evil comes in many forms. We've seen evil in the faces of the liberals, the socialists and the abortionists. And I am here today to report firsthand the face of evil in one place more — in the bedrooms of the homosexuals where sodomy and hedonism are practiced without regard to the laws of decency or the will of God. I have witnessed this inequity because a weakness in me allowed it too near. The Devil in me allowed me to partake in the abomination of the flesh. The Bible is clear in its abhorrence of homosexuality. It leaves no room for interpretation. Yet in my irrational exuberance, I lost my way. I sinned mightily. I became everything I detest. Now I realize my error, I understand the foolishness of my ways, and I desire more than anything a return to the fundamental Christian way and to set foot once more on the path of righteousness. This is my dream. And my prayer is for your forgiveness. I beseech your forgiveness as good Christians who are blessed with the ever-loving capacity to forgive above all other faiths. Thankfully, I have been shown the wickedness of my ways. Thankfully, the kind and generous elders of the church have brought wisdom's ways to me and set me on redemption's path. Won't you help me, too? Won't you stand by Jesus and be my guide as I return from inequity to goodness, from transgression to righteousness? I ask for your blessing as I stand before you in this consecrated hall and renounce my homosexuality. I look forward to counseling. With help, your support, and Good Jesus' guidance, I will regain my proper sexuality. I will fight off Satan. I will return to the fold of heterosexual marriage, as ordained by God above. And as Jesus as my witness, I will return to this pulpit a healed man.

Harlen watched the parishioners as they surveyed the room for Sandra Lee. Not in attendance, no surprise. There was another scandal right there. Everybody knew, having seen the wedding section of the *Mercury News*, that she had run off with that Arab from the abortion clinic, and without a divorce, no less. Scandal heaped on scandal. "A" for adultery (and Arab), "B" for bigamy, "C" for crime, "D" for done for, "E" for egregious, and "F" for finished.

The assemblage was not sure how to react. Harlen beamed the smile that had won him converts the world over.

Please, he prayed silently to Jesus, *take away my gayness, this time I mean it.*

The awkward silence was broken by a single clap from far back in the crowd. Harlen scanned the tops of heads until he saw Penny Lean in the way back, standing now and clapping mightily. Harlen recognized her purple hair, no missing it.

"Thank you," he whispered.

Then someone closer to the middle of the pack began to clap. Then two people simultaneously from either side of the room.

Harlen smiled because he had been here before, winning them over one person at a time. It didn't take long for the place to burst into affectionate applause. People stood on their seats, some of them did.

Thank God Almighty, for the forgiveness of Jesus.

Spontaneously, just like on television, the parishioners walked up the three steps to the dais and placed their hands in prayer on Harlen. *Praise the Lords* and *hallelujahs* aplenty. Harlen closed his eyes and soaked it in. This was his community. This was his life. Without it – without them - he would dry up and wither away.

The next morning, Harlen shaved extra close, picked out a polo shirt color that wasn't too gay, and set his GPS to take him to the Reverend Myles and his miraculous Palo Alto Center for Reparative Therapy. Harlen arrived 15 minutes early because he was jazzed to give it a go for Jesus. He was happy to sit in his car and listen to the Spanish Evangelical radio. He didn't understand a word, but the meaning came through nonetheless.

Inside the innocuous office, Harlen greeted his superior with a rousing handshake.

"Harlen, I've heard so much about your gifted ministry. Welcome, welcome. I am so honored to be working with you. Come in and let's get started."

They strolled into the red brick medical center.

"I was gay myself once," Reverend Myles offered in a whisper.

"I didn't know that."

"Yes. And I still feel the attraction sometimes. I'm telling you only so you know I've walked the walk and talked the talk. I'm not one of those fire and brimstone preachers. You know what else? I believe being gay is a sexual orientation, not a lifestyle choice."

"That's refreshing."

"Furthermore, I firmly believe God doesn't hate you for being gay like those ridiculous preachers and protesters would have you believe. They do more to harm the work we do here than anybody or anything else. They drive people away with fear. Assholes. Pardon my French, but that attitude drives me up a friggin' wall. I say let's look to scripture, shall we?"

The men adjourned to Reverend Myles' office, smartly outfitted with two leather couches beneath matching abstract paintings of red and yellow. Reverend Myles opened his well-worn Bible to Leviticus 18:22 and handed it to Harlen.

"Read that for me, will you?"

"*When one man lies with another as a woman it is an abomination before the Lord,*" read Harlen.

"Pretty clear, isn't it?"

Harlen nodded in agreement. "God hates us."

"Ah, but look again. What is an abomination to the Lord? Not you, not me, not gay people everywhere. *It* is the abomination. God loves you, he's just not so crazy about the act. God knows the sins of all of us, and he loves us still. That is the redemptive message of Jesus, even for gays. Instead of sending hellfire and brimstone, He sends us a savior to pay the price of our foolish sins. It's what you've been preaching all along, but you didn't think it applied to you. Well, it *does* apply to you, big time, more so than anyone, because God loves the sinners best."

Harlen felt inspired. "But what about my feelings, my desires?"

Reverend Myles was ready with his answer. "You're smart, I can tell. Once we peel away the layers of shame, what we do here is a little reprogramming. Once we put God squarely in the middle of your life, we try to take your sexual feelings, now directed toward men and redirect them toward friendship, brotherhood. Then we redirect the concept of friendship to women and *then* connect women to your desires. It's sort of like a relay race in which each runner alone can't finish the race, but with each other's help the team finds the finish line."

Harlen got it. He knew he did because, on any another occasion, he would have been attracted to Reverend Myles and attempted a pick-up, but this morning he saw Reverend Myles as a mentor and friend. He saw the light, and what thrilled him the most was the twin vision of faith and reason pointing him in the direction of his neglected heterosexuality.

"I think it's going to work!" Harlen exclaimed. He felt it in his blood, his once gay blood.

"You bet it is. See you next week?"

Harlen strolled down the street and slipped into a Safeway to test his theory. In the produce department, right near the green beans and yellow squash, he sidled up to a hunk in a sweaty t-shirt and tight jeans. Nary a pull. Then he shuffled toward a female sweetheart in halter-top and tight jeans and *come-fuck-me* high heels. He sniffed the babe and felt a little tingle down below. How could he have missed the attraction all these years?

He desperately wanted to try out his new heterosexuality, quickly, while it was still fresh, while it still worked. But he wasn't about to seek out a prostitute and risk a run-in with police, or worse, a pimp. He felt clueless working a line at a straight pick-up bar. So he picked up a Penthouse at a convenience store on his way home and ran a warm bath.

Just at the moment he settled in under the soapy bubbled, voila, the garage door chugged open, harkening the return of Sandra Lee Spridgen Wilson Farooq.

Destiny? A gift from God? Here was someone he could love. Had loved. Someone with whom he could explore male/female intimacy in a way they had never tried despite having shared the most intimate of human relationships. Someone safe and clean (at least he hoped after relations with Omar).

If, of course, she was game.

It didn't take long for Sandra Lee to find Harlen in the master bathroom. She sat down on the closed toilet seat and sighed.

"What's the matter?" Harlen asked.

"Men."

"Men or a man?"

"Well, in this case, you're right, a single man. Do you have time to talk?"

Harlen slipped the Penthouse magazine to the floor and frothed up the bubbles with his knees. "All the time in the world."

"First, I heard about what happened at church. Assholes. I'm sorry, and I hope you get it back. You built it, and you deserve it. They shouldn't have the right to take it away."

"Thank you, I'm working on it. Now tell me about you."

Sandra Lee edged up on the seat and rested her chin on her clenched fists. "Everything was just perfect after the announcement. Our dancing? You should have seen us together! We had real possibilities, real potential to storm the nationals. Most fun I had in my life, really. I lie awake recreating every dance in my head. Now *he* was a dancer."

"So what happened?"

"Is that a Penthouse?"

Harlen nodded, but Sandra Lee didn't seem to comprehend the ramifications.

"The injuries to his ankle I could live with. I could even live with never dancing competitively again. But after the Anti-Theory announcement, it got bad, Harlen. First, he started shouting at me as if I were the cause of all his worries and concerns. Then he began ordering me around. Not even asking, but barking like a dog. *Fix me dinner. Wash my clothes. Don't talk back.* Did he think I was some Arabic wife or something? You know me....*complacent* and *subservient* aren't two words you'd use to describe me, am I right?"

Harlen looked at her in a new way, as a sexual object. She wasn't half bad, her figure intact, and when she talked emotionally, kind of cute.

Sandra Lee continued, "I called him on it, but he just grew angrier and continued to insult me, calling me *pork* and a *deformed child*, even in Arabic sometimes, as if I understand that blasphemous language. He grew cold and stopped kissing or touching me, like I was a pariah. I hadn't changed one bit from when he first met me. If anything, I lost a couple of pounds from all the dance work. Oh, but I loved him still and wanted so much for it to work. When he started calling her name in his sleep, one can forgive only so much. *Shivana, Shivana.* I elbowed him every time. He'd grumble something, fall back asleep, and start all over again. How is a woman supposed to live with that?"

"You got me."

"Do you know how much time it takes to pray five times a day? Oh, my gosh, how do they get anything done over there? On your knees, stand up, mumble mumble, on your knees, stand up. It's like yoga class for extremists. And just when it's thankfully over, there's enough time only for hummus and pita, and it starts all over again. Thank God I was born a Christian, it's so much easier. Sunday church, maybe Wednesday nights, a few quick Our Fathers before meals. Thank Jesus. Then, all the dietary restrictions. I thought only the Jews did it. He won't eat bacon, finicky on shellfish, and everything has to be prepared a certain way, in a particular fashion. Animals have to be slaughtered in the name of Allah. How the hell can you know what the butcher is yelling when he zaps the animal with a stun gun? If a drop of blood shows up on the plate, he won't touch it. No MSG. Show me in the Koran where it mentions monosodium glutamate, will you? God forbid if I happened to say something forbidden, he wouldn't touch me for a day. During my period he called me unclean and took his pillow to another room. In hindsight, it's easier being married to a gay man, I'll give you that

Harlen. I really came to appreciate you during this episode of my life."

"I'm straight now."

"Yeah, and I'm Melania Trump. Listen, I've been thinking."

Sandra Lee shimmied up to the edge of the toilet seat. "Do you want me to wash your hair?"

"You've never offered that before."

"Things are different now." She grabbed the shampoo, squirted a small amount on his head and began rubbing indifferently. "You know, you and I, what we had wasn't *that* terrible."

"You hated every minute of it."

"Granted, I hated you. Well, not you personally, I take that back. Your failure as a man. Our lifestyle, all *this* wasn't bad at all. That's the other thing. How do people live in those cramped condos with Formica countertops listening to neighbors humping on the other side of the walls? What kind of life is that?"

"I think my hair is clean." Harlen submerged his head to rinse off the shampoo.

"Conditioner?"

"Please."

Sandra Lee massaged the cream in gently.

Harlen said, "So you want to move back in, is that what you're saying?"

Sandra Lee felt it was good to be back home, right in some way. He might be gay, but he belonged to her tribe, and she took comfort in that. She paused and lowered her voice. "Hear me out, Harlen. I'll admit, I was part of the problem. You know I always had high expectations. Always expecting you'd change, be different, be attracted to me. I know that's not going to happen now. I've grown up. This whole *Theory* this, *Anti-Theory* that, it's made me reassess my thinking, matured me. I was wrong, selfish, and juvenile. And I believe I can change."

She smiled.

She did have a certain glow, a *joie de vivre*. No wonder other men were constantly attracted to her.

"I also know the political pickle you're in right now, Harlen. You need the respectability and veneer of marriage. Desperately. Who else are you going to find so quickly, someone who knows your secrets and is willing to keep them that way?"

Harlen sighed. "Your name, I'm afraid, is dirt at church."

Sandra Lee worked the conditioner in harder. "That is a problem, but fixable. You fixed the homo question with one tearful *mea culpa*, didn't you? Or maybe not, but you are on your way. Plus, everyone did something screwy during the false time of oneness. Agnes Bryant ran off with her Filipino gardener. Jill Dupre opened a medical marijuana clinic, and Bill Belink, did you hear what he did? He converted to Judaism and had a *bar mitzvah*, for God's sake. They've all repented and come back. It's fashionable to repent. A trend. Ellen should do a show. Plus, the crowd loves repentance, it makes a good story. I can do it in a heartbeat, and they loved me there, they always loved me.

God and country. We could have it all back again, Harlen. Everything. I could help you. The empire will be ours again."

"We lost more than half the congregation over this. It took years to compile that email list."

"They'll be back. My God, the nearest Evangelical church is in Gilroy. Nobody likes to drive to Gilroy. It smells like garlic, and the restaurants suck, believe me, I know."

Harlen slipped under the water. His hair never felt so clean. When he surfaced, he said, "And what about your marriage to Omar? You're double married."

"Big mistake and I'm sorry about that. But I've begun annulment proceedings. You didn't seem to mind at the time. And we split amicably, didn't we?"

"The money isn't there anymore."

"I'll be more frugal, I promise. I did it in college, remember?"

She had been a beauty in college, bright and determined. He saw a little of that young lady in her now. Tara would be hers at the end of the war. "Are you sure you're not going back to him?"

"Please. Absolutely positive. Harlen, don't you see? We *need* each other. We laughed, didn't we? So it'll be a marriage of arrangement, big deal. Think of all the legendary arranged marriages from Buckingham Palace to Hollywood. We're royalty, think of it that way. My only stipulation is none of your boyfriends come over, but if it's all computer-based chatting and surfing, I don't see why not. We'll buy you new sheets, and I'll take another room anyway."

"I don't want an arranged marriage," said Harlen.

"You don't?"

"No. I want the real thing. I want you."

"What's that supposed to mean?"

Harlen winked and drew a wry smile. "Sex and intimacy."

"With who?"

"With you. I've changed, Sandy. I'm not gay anymore. It's women I want. It's you I want."

Sandra Lee stood, mouth agape. "You're off your rocker."

"I'm converted, I swear to God I am. You're turning me on right now. Look."

Harlen pointed to a hint of a hard-on, not very impressive, but something to work with.

He told her all about Reverend Myles and the good work being done at the conversion ministry, and how it all made sense to him now and how the heterosexual light had been turned on in his head. So simple.

"Wow, well this is a surprise." She pondered the new equation. "It sounds great in theory but have you tried it out, I mean in reality?"

"That's why I'm glad you're coming home. That's why I'm glad you're here. It's the Lord setting things right, praise be Jesus."

Harlen unbuttoned a few of her blouse buttons and fondled her breasts.

Sandra Lee squealed. "Oh my God, you are serious."

"I would love nothing more than to try out the theory with you. Something I should have done a long time ago."

Sandra Lee wasn't quite sure how to respond. At the least, she was intrigued to see if he could do it because her women's intuition told her it wasn't possible. And she was flattered because he wanted her. That was never a bad thing. But then she thought of Omar and how she wished things had turned out differently. Nothing could compare to her fuel-injected spine the moment she slowed her dark blue Mercedes into a parking lot to meet the princely dark one. You simply can't explain the sensation of being the recipient of martyrdom intensity in the sack. So self-righteously wicked, just like on TV but without the machinegun fire or bits of flesh flying from suicide bombs. Maybe Omar was just going through a backlash phase. Maybe he would soon realize what he had lost and come back to her on his knees. That's where Sandra Lee wanted him, begging on his knees. Maybe he would, but until that moment she wanted her old life back, the safe life.

"I'll get some candles," she said.

She disappeared into the walk-in closet leaving Harlen alone. He toweled off and ventured into the bedroom to slip under the sheets while she did whatever it was women do before they have sex.

Sandra Lee returned moments later, wearing a drop dead gorgeous see-through negligee that barely covered her privates and thigh-high fishnets in matching black.

"Well, what do you think?" She twirled around for Harlen to inspect.

"Beautiful," he said. His penis shrank.

Sandra Lee sidled next to Harlen and caressed his chest. She fondled him down there. He felt lifeless and cold.

"It's all so new to me," he said. "It may take some time."

"Naturally." Sandra Lee smiled and raised her I-know-exactly-what-to-do eyebrows. She disappeared under the covers like a submarine, and Harlen felt her lips around his penis. *God please*, he prayed. Please let it be real and fixed. He prayed hard and true.

He felt something, a stirring, a thickening as she yanked and tugged down there, working harder than anyone should have to. He stroked her blonde hair. It was so soft and long, and he felt the round of her shoulders and the mild upstroke of her collarbone. A little more progress down there, but nothing major, nothing like sleeping with Jeff or Dave or Rocky. He imagined their bodies, their hard cocks and he felt the sudden rise. He dreamed that it was Marcus under the covers, big black Marcus with a tattoo of a dragon on his forearm working his genitals rather than Sandra Lee. He felt himself grow bigger. He fantasized about Demitri and Luke and the way they laughed and the ripple of their hard bodies toned solid by hours in the gym. It's okay, Dr. Myles had explained. *Expect sexual confusion at the start* he said. Go with it, Harlen thought. If that's what it takes this time around.

Next romp he would jettison the images in his head, and it would be about Sandra Lee, all Sandra who aroused him. He felt his erection slackening again, so he conjured up a vision of Frank, the Italian with muscles bulging under his armless tee shirt. He remembered the way Alejandro's armpits smelled like a sultry Havana night and how his Cuban accent made everything sound so exotic.

Sandra Lee resurfaced, gasping for air.

"You *are* straight!" she exclaimed.

She proceeded to straddle him like a horse. In the process of her gymnastics, Harlen caught sight of her bare hairless vagina with nothing there (where was the penis and dangling balls?).

She rubbed her breasts in his face. "Oh, baby, fuck me, fuck me!"

With all the commotion, the demands, Harlen lost his train of thought. Gone were the visions of Jeff, Dave and Mark. No more Jerry and Luke. Good-bye Frank and Alejandro. All that remained was Sandra Lee and her aerobic gyrations.

It took but a few seconds for him to go flat, flaccid, kaput.

"What's the matter?" she asked.

"Nothing, it's just so new."

"I have just the thing," said Sandra Lee. "This will do it."

She crawled up his body. She snuggled her vagina on top of his face. She writhed like a banshee.

Harlen squirmed. The Brazilian with its microscopic new growth. The viscosity. The lack of definition. The odorous tang. It was all too much for Harlen. Too sudden.

He tried to tell Sandra Lee, but his words were muffled in the fleshy folds of her labia. He tried to come up for air, but she pressed down on his face like a murderer. He tried to tap out, but apparently, she took it as a signal of encouragement.

She wrangled harder, riding a bull in the ring. She grabbed a shock of his hair to hold on.

He had no choice. He flung her off with a brisk sweep of his arm. She fell to the floor right on her ass.

"What the matter?"

Harlen sucked in a deep breath. He wiped his nose with the sheet. He leaned over the side of the bed. He gagged once to hold it back but he couldn't. He let it fly — a throat-full of vomit, right there on the $32-a-square-foot carpet. The backsplash bounced onto the edge of the $1600 comforter.

"Oh, shit," said Sandra Lee.

Harlen slipped all the way to the floor until his cheek lay in his own retch. But it was way better than trapped underneath the saddle of womanhood. He lay there to catch his breath, to still his dizzy mind.

Sandra Lee jumped from the bed and raced away.

Harlen lay there a bit longer because he so deserved the punishment for his self-delusion. How could he have ever imagined he could go through with it? You can't have faith in a lie, not when reality is so ready and willing to press the question.

At least it was over, the charade. Now it was back to the old charade. We fool ourselves, or we fool others, as habit goes.

"Harlen?"

Harlen looked up on Sandra Lee, returned in a bathrobe.

"You still here?" he muttered.

"Of course, I'm still here. I'm your wife." She helped him to his feet and toweled the vomit from his cheeks and mouth.

Harlen helped himself to a sitting position. "I'm so sorry, sorry about the carpet."

"Screw the carpet, 'bout time we ripped it up."

"Sorry about the comforter."

"That's what dry cleaners are for."

"You're not angry?"

"Harlen. I know who you are. What you are. Apparently better than you. Come on, let's clean you up."

Harlen felt too weak to get up, and instead, he crawled onto Sandra Lee's lap and laid there.

She stroked his hair. "It's gonna be okay, Harlen. You'll never have to go through that again."

Harlen found himself whimpering like a little boy. "But you'll stay with me?"

"I will, I promise."

"Thank you. Thank you so much."

Now, this was love, Harlen thought. Devotion, true devotion.

Why hadn't he appreciated her before? Why hadn't he noticed how she stood by her man, crazy and fucked up as he was. She had shouldered disappointments and stuck in there with him. The things he put her through. No healthy person should have to be subjected to the antics of a frustrated gay man, except maybe another frustrated gay man. Yet she endured like Jesus would have done. *Be kind to your spouse because he or she may be Jesus.* How many times had he preached that? And now was the first time he applied it to himself.

Sandra Lee stroked his hair and let a moment of silence go by to calm his nerves. "Now, there is one complication," she said demurely.

"What's that?"

Sandra Lee wasn't sure how to say it, so she said it like she said everything she didn't know how to say, with a whispery voice meant to please and tease.

"I'm pregnant."

Harlen rolled over and spewed another pint of vomit onto the carpet.

"There, there. Nothing to worry about. I've got it all figured out."

TWENTY-SEVEN

The way Jimmy Lean explained it later to the police was like this: He was laying in bed sexting a friend when he heard a light tap on his window, like a pebble. He thought it was a piece of debris stirred up by the wind, so he ignored it. Moments later a second pebble, maybe even a rock, thwacked the window and nearly shattered it. He tapped off his iPhone and peeked out the window for a look.

Curbside below, his big sister Penny gave him the finger and smiled. She carried a backpack, and her hair was a normal color, maybe with just a tinge of red, or maybe the false glare of the streetlamp was changing its hue.

Jimmy quietly walked down the stairs and snuck out the front door. He trotted to the secret spot in the neighborhood green belt where the two always met when something was up.

He found Penny shivering cold even in the fogless night. The gentle wind tracked from the east bringing hot breezes from the Central Valley.

Penny lit a Marlboro Light. "I can't take it anymore."

"Take what?"

"*Her.* The way she smothers Emmett and me. She fixes our lunches, does our laundry, reads Shel Silverstein poems every night like it's the gospel according to Luke, emails me self-help articles, texts me like twelve times a day, recycles every last little piece of tin foil, makes us floss, won't set foot in a 7-Eleven, does all our laundry with this organic soap that smells like crap and doesn't even get stuff clean."

"Sounds like a mother."

"Yeah, just what the hell I don't need in my life right now. I mean, at first, it was kinda cool. Her cooking ratatouille and quinoa. Can you say that, *keen-wha?*"

"Keen-wha," Jimmy repeated.

"Taking us to movies with subtitles that you got to read because sure as shit nothing happens on the screen but people talking and smoking cigarettes, and then she don't let you smoke cigarettes outside the theater, *hypocriticalbitch*. After a while, all you want to do is chill, watch MTV, smoke a fat one, and down a juicy burger with bacon, know what I mean? Emmett digs her, but he doesn't know better. He misses his gummy bears and Hostess Twinkies and shit like that, but when I try to buy 'em, she nearly cuts off my hands."

Penny took a deep drag of her cigarette. "Anyway, sorry to unload. How's mom and dad?"

Jimmy twisted a shoulder. "For a while after ToE they got cool, I mean really cool. Mom wore a sari one day, like the women in India. She took a course in Indian cooking, making dishes with names like Panek Paneer and Kofta, big piles of mush. Dad took a philosophy class at the college."

"No fucking way."

"No shit. And he peeled the bumper sticker off, the one that said *Gun Control Means Using Both Hands!* I wouldn't have believed it if I didn't see it with my own eyes. Here's the kicker, he ate the food mom made, the spinach, too. But then when the anti-Theory hit, man, rebound city. Back to the same old, *the Bible tells us this,* and *you can't be thinking that.* He tried to hit me again, but I got too strong on him. Or he got weak."

Penny started fidgeting, rubbing her neck.

Jimmy Lean knew the answer but asked anyway. "So what's up?"

Penny picked up a stick and made a circle in the dirt, then mussed up the drawing with her fingers.

"Dude, I'm taking my meds and all, like I promised you, I swear. But I'm *frickin dying* here for a line."

"Line of what?"

"Coke, meth, junk. I don't give a shit. Just something to unwind these ropes is all. Just once. I've been good, real good, honest I have."

Jimmy understood the desire to get high, explore an alternate reality, visit someplace else, take the weight off. It shouldn't be a crime. So what if you're not 100 percent alert all the time, that's what vacations are all about. Anyway, it's on vacation that you get your best ideas.

Jimmy knew that Penny's mental vacations were horror stories, like camping in Iraq with the bombs flying overhead or watching the floods in

New Orleans from Poverty Row.

"Can't or won't? Cause you know I can handle my shit," Penny said.

"No I don't. In fact, I know how shit sets you off."

Penny twitched with impatience. "I ain't looking to go back forever. *Just one time.* It's been like months, and I've been fucking dying, you wouldn't believe it. Ever since that ToE crap or anti-ToE crap — I don't know what's up or down anymore and I don't give a flyin' fuck — I just want to get high. I got money. If it ain't you, it's somebody else. Some pimp in East Palo Alto. I'd rather get it from you."

Jimmy studied her face. "You're not telling me everything."

"That's it, I swear."

"Penny. It's me, Jimbo." He knew her well.

And she knew him well. She had changed his diapers, read him ghost stories, offered him his first joint, handed him his first condom, protected him from their father's backhand as best as she could. And he had reciprocated, pounding on her bedroom door when their father dragged Penny inside and locked the door, so father and daughter could *pray.*

Penny sighed. "Well, that's the way Naomi was *during* ToE. Afterward that Snodgrass asshole, she did a 360, pretty much like everyone else. At first, she tried to do all the same stuff and to be there for us. Then she got to spending time on the Internet and getting outraged over shit. You know...dolphins and migrant workers, oil spills and secret campaign donations. Ugh, and if I hear the words *global warming* again, I'll puke. So she started making phones calls and writing emails to Congressmen and advocates or activists — *whateverthefuckyoucallthem.* Then she said, *it's not enough to just write and donate money.* She said it like it was *my* fault. Like the whole world was totally fucked up because Penny Lean was wasting her life away. So she left us alone, first for hours at a time to go to meetings and rallies and coffee with those smelly liberal types at anywhere but Starbucks. Then she stopped coming home or came home whenever the hell she felt like it. I mean, for me, I don't give a shit what she does, but no one treats my EJ like that."

Penny wiped away a tear. Or not.

"Anyway, after that I missed a rent check, and then Arnie – you know my boyfriend from a couple of years ago, not EJ's daddy but the tall guy with glasses and the Dos Equis tattoo on his stomach — he needed to borrow some cash, and the motherfucker swore he'd bring it back in 48 hours with a twelve pack. That's what he said, *two days and twelve cold ones.*"

"How much?"

"Lots."

"Lots like how?"

"Lots, like all of it or nearly all of it."

"Where is he?"

"Who the fuck knows. Blew out of town, I'm sure. All I got is a fridge full of Naomi's foo-foo food. Thankfully they can't kick me out for like 90 days. I got a hundred spot that ain't gonna do us no good in the long run. I just need a break from every fucking thing."

After a silence, Penny began again. "Okay, I'll tell you, but only 'cause it's you. One night, a couple of weeks ago, it was late, she was out doing some protesting shit. I was half asleep. I heard someone come in so I wrapped my hand around Emmett's mouth to keep him from breathing because he snores, so the killer wouldn't hear us. Then I heard her voice, Naomi's. *Penny, you awake?* she said. I didn't answer because I was thinking now *she* wants to kill us. She's come to kill my Emmett Jessup. I froze. I pressed my hand across Emmett's face harder. I didn't want her hearing us. EJ struggled because he wasn't getting any air, but I didn't care because I wasn't gonna let anyone take the life of my son, especially her. I knew it was a delusion even when it was happening, that's the thing. I identified it, just like my therapist told me to do. She pressed her ear against the door. *Penny, is everything okay?* she said. It was a trick, I knew it, so I squeezed EJ harder. He kicked me, but I held him tight. She wasn't gonna kill him. I sleep with a knife under my pillow just like most people. I pulled it out ready to pounce on her fuckin' ass if she so much as tried to lay a hand on my kid. The doorknob twisted open. It reminded me so much of dad when he would come it late at night. I thought it was *him.* I thought, *oh, no!* He was using Naomi's voice or holding her hostage so that he could come in on the sly and touch me all over again. Was I whacked or what, but that's what I thought. I said to myself, *no fucking way I'm going to let him do to EJ what he done to me. No fucking way.*

"I slipped the knife under Emmett's neck because nobody was going hurt my kid, 'specially not dad. If EJ was going to die, I'd do it myself. I know it sounds crazy, and it *is* crazy, man. It's fucking insane. Emmett turned blue, and he struggled his little ass off because I was smothering him so hard, but I wasn't gonna let dad get anywhere near my boy. Emmett bit my hand, hard.

Look at these teeth marks. Proof I ain't lying."

Penny shoved her hand out for evidence.

"Then what happened?"

"Then what happened is Naomi came in and said *Good night, my loves.* That's what she said. Just like that. And then I realized it wasn't dad. That nobody was trying to kill us. It was just Naomi saying good night. It was all in my head. Snap, like that. All in my fucked-up head. Everything. EJ sucked in a big gulp of air. I slid the knife under the bed before anybody could see. She blew a kiss, closed the door and that was it. Scared the fuck out of me. See how crazy I am?"

"You're not crazy."

"Then what am I?"

"Wounded."

"All I know is I need to check out for a little while because my mind's set to explode. Please, Jimmy, don't make me beg."

Jimmy reached into his pocket and pulled out a packet. "Here you go."

Penny unfolded it and smelled the pile of cinnamon powder. It glistened even in the dim light of the moon. "Man, Jimmy, you're my knight in shining armor."

She offered Jimmy four crumpled twenty-dollar bills, two fives, a one, and the rest in change, mostly quarters.

"I don't want your money. Just promise me one thing."

"What?"

"You don't snort it all at once. This shit's pretty close to uncut."

"On my word, Jimbo. You know me."

"That's the problem."

Penny pecked Jimmy on the cheek. "I love you. You're the best. As for mom and dad...tell them *to fuck off and the train they rode in on.*"

Jimmy watched Penny lumber away. On his way home he stopped at the south wall of the 280 underpass and pulled out a couple of cans of spray paint. It didn't take him long to alter a recent tag that went up after the ToE charge. Just squeeze in the letter "d" at the beginning is all.

God is dOne.

That's the way Jimmy felt. Over, kaput, nada. Bye-bye Big Guy.

He felt sad because there was a moment there, back when they first announced the Theory of Everything, a real moment, when Jimmy thought the world was a poem in motion, and each of us a brilliant line in a piece that rhymes. He felt vindicated for being right like all the world saw for the first time what he always knew, what he perceived in his mind's eye. He didn't need any theories. How could it be any other way? And it made him happy, elated, ecstatic to have seven billion people on his side.

It was back then, with the theory on, with his mother doling out Aloo Gobi over steaming basmati rice, and his father citing Kant's categorical imperative (*act as if your actions will become universal law*), that Jimmy decided the time had arrived to spill the beans.

He waited a few days to tell them, to make sure this wasn't all a dream, a big cosmic joke, but the news about the world healing came in from all over. He asked his parents to join him on the front porch of the house. He sat them down on the wicker chairs his mother had just painted *a shade of lavender as lovely as love.* Those were her words.

"What is it, son?" his father asked with newfound compassion and clarity.

His mother topped off his ice tea and smiled.

It was just as he had imagined it might be when he dreamed about the confession all these years.

Jimmy sighed and readied himself for the announcement. He remembered back to his first time, just to make sure he was sure about all this before changing his world. He was fifteen years old, and Leonard Kraminsky had invited him over for a PlayStation sesh in his house up in some subdivision where all the houses are painted the same bland shade of tan and topped with fake Spanish tile roofs. Leonard's parents worked at Apple or Intel or Facebook or one of those companies, seventy-hour weeks, leaving two empty daytime spots in the garage where the BMWs slept at night. Jimmy came in through the open garage and looked for oil spots on the floor where cars ought to be. There were none. Bicycles up on pullies. Laundry folded and pressed. Cat food in plastic containers. Smashed 7-Up cans in a tidy box labeled "cans." Inside the house the counters were crumbless and a bowl of fruit looked plastic. As instructed, Jimmy took off his shoes. He felt the carpet pile tickle the soles of his socked feet. Leonard blasted through the kitchen with little regard for the neatness so highly regarded by his parents. He flung open cabinets and the refrigerator and dug deep before coming up with a liter of Sprite and a bag of Nacho Doritos.

"Does your mother hide this shit, too?" he asked.

They migrated into the family room with its massive flat screen and leather sofas with nary a dent of an ass.

"What do you want to play?" Leonard asked.

"What do you got?"

"Everything."

They suited up for a round of *Call of Duty*.

After about 15 minutes of play, Leonard asked, "Had enough?"

"Sure," said Jimmy.

Leonard leaned forward and kissed Jimmy on the lips, straight on, no hemming and hawing, no shame.

Jimmy drew back.

"You okay?"

"I don't know," Jimmy wondered out loud.

"Because I thought you were, you know, gay."

"I am, or at least I think I am."

"Cause you act gay."

"How's that?"

"Receptive."

And that's the way Jimmy felt. Receptive in a world that frowned on receptivity and championed the sure, the dominant, the senders.

Jimmy kissed Leonard back because he wanted to. They fumbled on the squeaky couch until sufficiently hot and then moved to Leonard's bedroom painted blue with a Prince poster above the bed. Jimmy thought it should feel wrong and dirty, but it didn't. Leonard guided Jimmy's hand below, and they laid there holding each other's penises. They played with them like joysticks and laughed, but mostly they snuggled with each other, not much else.

"I like your scent," Jimmy said.

"I like yours, too."

That was the first time, and there were others but not many, just enough to confirm the attraction. No denying something like an attraction. It comes from way, way deep.

Now Jimmy faced his smiling parents sipping ice teas with sprigs of homegrown mint and rocking gently on lavender chairs. He was sure there was only one way to announce it. Straight on, like Leonard had kissed him.

"Ma, dad, I think I'm gay. No, I *know* I'm gay, and that's the way it is."

Nobody knew except Leonard, not even the boys Jimmy had crushes on because Jimmy kept it out of school. Penny, she knew.

"Well, son," began his father. "It's not my first choice, but as long as you're happy and good to the people you love, I guess it's okay. Seems silly to try to make you into something you're not. That would cause all sorts of problems."

His mother smiled. "We'll accept anyone you love as a child of ours, dear."

Jimmy nearly shit in his pants at the ease of it all after years of cooped up fear and fighting the truth like a tiger. If ever there was a sure sign of the next coming of Christ here it was. Mom and dad onboard. This easy? Couldn't be.

It wasn't.

Anti-ToE brought the cruel antidote and what's that they say about the medicine being worse than the disease? Once the world tilted back, Jimmy's parents turned on him fierce and brought down the fire and brimstone, big time. *Gay isn't happening in this house,* said his dad, and *Shame on you, you keep being gay and I swear you'll regret the day you were born. I already have,* said his mom, like they forgot what they had said on those lavender chairs like they were living in a dream. Maybe they were.

Jimmy didn't tell Penny that their parents changed their tune in a heartbeat. She didn't need more ammunition. He didn't mention that his father looked at him like a piece of shit and his mother mumbled prayers of forgiveness for bearing a gay son.

He felt even worse for giving Penny the dope. Too late.

Jimmy saw the lights of a car coming. Thinking it might be a cop, he ditched the spray cans and frantically scraped the wet paint from his fingernails.

The car approached, and Jimmy saw it wasn't a cop but a customer.

Jimmy tapped his pocket and felt a few packets left, good shit. He approached the car and got in.

A corny country tune played on the radio.

"Long time," said Pastor Spridgen.

"Yeah."

"Lot of water under the bridge."

"You can say that again. You buying?"

"I don't think so, not today."

"So, what then?"

Harlen Spridgen smiled. "So, how old are you now?"

"Eighteen last week."

Harlen smiled. "Lucky me."

"I thought you turned straight, Pastor."

"In theory."

"Those theories are killing us."

"Amen. You ready?"

Jimmy wasn't interested in the pastor, wasn't attracted to the man. He was a perv, when you think about it, ass chasing Jimmy and probably a shitload of other underage boys while preaching the Gospel no less. Fucking hypocrite. On the other hand, the world was falling apart and who knew what was what anymore. Jimmy felt terrible for giving Penny drugs, for selling drugs, for spray painting shit all over the place, for being gay or feeling bad about being gay or not feeling bad about being gay. It was all so frickin' confusing. The world sucked big time, Jimmy was sure of that.

Jimmy waited a moment to give his answer to the preacher, though he wasn't sure why he waited — just so used to playing it too close to his chest, is all. In a cold world you take affection anyway it comes.

"Yeah, let's go."

TWENTY-EIGHT

Penny Lee had a ritual for when she copped a fresh load all for herself. First, turn up the heat in the house. She fuckin' freezes to death when she gets high. Second, lock them doors up tight because you don't want no skank strolling in just when you laid out a gorgeous pile ready to go. No line sharing around here. Third, make sure Emmett Jessup is asleep, fast asleep. Benadryl, double dose, because he don't need to see his mommy like that. Fourth, shuffle *The Doors* because nothing sounds as good as Jim Morrison singing *The End* when you're riding the sky.

Penny used her extra clean fingernails to meticulously unfold the Penthouse origami — two, four, six, folds, until the sheet revealed the belly of a voluptuous, airbrushed Latina beauty, her vagina obscured by an ample heap of magic dust.

She inspected her syringe, used only a couple of times before, all by herself. She might be an intravenous drug user, but no fucking way was she going to poke herself to an HIV infection like some junkheads do. She prided herself on that.

Penny placed the unfolded square paper on the table and tipped in a Buck knife to carve out a portion of the powder. She tapped a little less than a third into the kitchen teaspoon.

Whatthefuck, she thought. And she dumped the rest in. If she was going to get high one time, make it one hell of a time. It was all about the initial rush anyway. After that, nothing but the long, slow, hard claw back up from the bottom.

With the needle, she extracted a measure of water from a glass and squirted the liquid into the spoon until it brimmed.

The heroin dissolved slowly but not fully. She flicked open a Zippo lighter, fired it up and caressed the underside of the spoon with the flame. In seconds the magic dust bubbled to a boil and dissolved into a puddle of dull brown liquid. Poof, just like that.

Penny sat the spoon on the table, squeezed off a pinch of the cotton ball and dropped it in. She kissed the cotton with the needle tip and pulled back on the plunger. In a moment the spoon was empty, and the cotton had collapsed into a saturated clump the size of a grain of rice. But the syringe, that American Beauty. The syringe was full of cloudy liquid.

She pointed the needle skyward and pressed until a little spritz told her all the air bubbles were gone. Embolism, she was hip to that bummer, too. Hell if she was going to die from an air bubble blowing up her brain.

Lockedandloaded. Penny always thought the needle looked like a miniature rocket ship ready for takeoff. Or maybe a church spire.

Penny cocked an ear for Emmett Jessup. Fuck, she knew this was wrong. She glanced at a photo of him that Naomi had shot at Half Moon Bay. What a cute kid. Her son deserves better than a mother who sticks needles in her arms. He deserves gold, and she was shit. Worse than shit. Shit's shit. And this shit in the needle is the only thing that takes the pain away. Ain't that the shits.

No, she told herself, not this time. This frigging time she was going to be strong and get rid of the junk. Jimmy didn't take no money, right? So it's like she got it for free. No loss to her. Jimmy wouldn't care, he'd be glad.

She grabbed the syringe and headed to the toilet. Piss it down the tube before it had a chance to fuck her up.

She stood over the toilet. She aimed the needle downward. *Squeeze away.*

She tried to push the plunger. She did, really.

But it ain't that easy squirting good junk away. Nobody on the light side understands what it's like to be so close to a fix. There's an attraction that can't be broken. Penny damn well knew why people worshipped the needle like a cult goddess — not the drug inside her — but the needle itself, the thin steely bitch, so fucking precise and cold, so fucking potent. You have to love her even if you hate her fuckin' guts. Penny wondered why the hell everyone wasn't a junkie.

Penny shut the bathroom door and found a nylon stocking to tie off her arm. She pumped her fists a few times to persuade the veins to come out. River blue. With her left hand, she pressed the needle against a freckle on her white skin. It sat there for a moment.

She took a deep breath and plunged the needle in. One push, like a dick going the distance. A flourish of blood in the chamber signaled she had hit pay dirt. She panicked at the invasion. She wanted it off her, out of her. But the impulse was weak, and it faded quickly.

She pulled back on the plunger until a whirl of blood backwashed into the chamber. The blood diluted into the murky brown of the drug.

Houston, we have contact.

She waited a second, holding back the orgasm.

Oh, fuck, Emmett what have I done. What am I about to do.

With these cries on her lips, she depressed the plunger, praying not to drive the needle clear through the vein wasting a perfectly good hit.

The brown liquid disappeared into her arm.

She felt nothing for a moment, relieved the load was pure crap. Happy all this was one big disappointment. She was used to disappointments. Could handle them.

Then she felt the rush. No...more than a rush, a woosh, a gallop. The horsemen of the Apocalypse, all of them, trampling her senses to the floor and releasing her spirit for the swift ride up the devil's personal stairway to heaven.

In her mind's eye, Penny surveyed the new terrain. Time took longer, and her arms and legs weighed more. Her head hit the toilet bowl, or at least she thought it did. She didn't know, wasn't sure.

She licked the tile floor. She felt woozy and gray.

A trickle of blood traveled by her and kept going.

Five minutes, five hours. You can't tell time at a time like this.

And then the pleasure drained. Quick as it came, a riptide pulling away. A tsunami going out. Hazy as fuck.

She searched for the high. Her lips begged its return. She promised her soul in exchange for a comeback. No way, no how. *Nosuchluck.* She drowned in a sludge of confusion and nausea. She felt brown, the brown of the dose of fluid ripping up her veins. She became *that* color, runny, rancid, repulsive.

She climbed up the toilet. No mind, no volition, just vomit. A whole gut worth. And more until there was nothing left but the vapid piety of dry heaves. She collapsed once more and littered the cold floor, sniffing the urine, searching for who the fuck she was, how she came to creation.

And then the fade, the long dark fade to where? Where did it lead? Penny never found out as she entered that netherworld between life and death.

Her eye cracked open, and she saw the needle dangling from her arm. She tried to get it out, but you needed hands for that.

You needed will.

~

Darkness. Awake. Quiet. Fear.

Mama.

Look under bed for monsters.

Mama? Grandma?

Have to pee. Find mama first.

Walk, walk, walk. Stairs, stairs stairs. Mama here? No. Mama here? No. Bathroom door. Shut.

Mama. Me need pee pee.

No mama. Kitchen, no mama. Look out window, no mama.

Car. Mama car here. Grandma nice, give mama car.

Mama?

Back door, porch, fence, tracks. *Mama? Mama?*

Turn knob. Bathroom door. Not opening, blocked. *Harder push. Harder push.* Open little. *Peek inside.*

"Mama! Mama get up."

Mama, bleeding. Mama blue.

"Mama open. Mama get up." *Mama vomit. Mama, needle. Mama needle arm.*

"Mama!"

Go, go. Run, run. Out front door. Outside.

"Mama, my mama!"

Nobody here, nobody come. *Look one way.* Wall. *Look other way.* Road,

cars, people. *Walk to people. Walk to road.*
HONK!
Walk faster.
SHOONNK!
Cry. Run.
BLONK!!!
Home, go home.
SCREECH.
"Mama!"

TWENTY-NINE

In times of crisis, Omar's thoughts often drifted to the crowded cinderblock two-bedroom home he shared with his mother, father, two sisters, a brother, and his grandfather. Funny how, as a child, a happy home makes the whole world appear happy, carefree, even if occupiers prowl the streets outside and the threat of violence hangs like a song. As a boy, if he had a soccer ball, he was in heaven. If the little neighbor girl next door twinkled at him, the world was a miracle. If he curled up in his mother's lap, no worry could find him.

And yes, it was no surprise that with his mind engaged in vanished moments, Omar, driving home from work, didn't see the wandering boy step off the curb and into the street. Perhaps that's why it took Omar an extra split second to register the calamity ahead. Perhaps that's why, when he locked eyes with the stumbling child, Omar felt the innocence of all childhood in jeopardy. Perhaps that's why Allah, praised be his name, sought fit to stop the Maxima inches from the boy's nose.

Omar jumped from the vehicle. He raced around to the boy. "Are you okay, hurt? Let me look at you."

A tear and a quivering lip.

Omar hugged the boy tightly as if he were his own. He thanked God above for the boy's well-being as well as for the providence that averted a tragedy. He was reminded again that grace does not need time to work its magic.

A quick prayer of thanks and Omar's thoughts turned to the pragmatic. *Where is the boy's parents, he could have been killed! I could have killed him.*

"Where is your mother, son?"

The boy pointed inside.

193

"Is she home?"

"Mama dead."

"What is your name?"

"Emmett Jessup."

"Have we met before?"

Emmett Jessup shrugged.

"Here come with me." Omar led the boy to the safety of the curb. "You say your mother is inside?"

"Dead," said the boy.

Omar knocked on the door. Hard, harder. He twisted the knob. Locked. He peeped into the window, but the curtain was drawn shut.

Omar thought about depositing the boy right there on the stoop with a stern warning not to move and driving away. After all, Omar hadn't hit the boy, just came close. No harm done. And if the boy's mother was dead or hurt, he would be considered a suspect if he should call the police. Just what he did not need.

The boy appeared so helpless, and this wasn't the best of neighborhoods, and Omar remembered being that age once in a hostile territory and so thankful for the kindness of strangers, Israelis among them at times. *How do I know this boy? I know this boy.*

"Hello, 9-1-1? I'm with a boy, maybe two or three or four-years-old. Yes, and he says he's locked out of his home, and his mother is inside in some sort of trouble, unconscious or dead. No, I don't know his mother, I just got here. Drove up and saw the little boy crying on a stoop...Street? 13th Street, I believe...My name? Why do you need my name?...Okay, okay. Omar Farooq. Dr. Omar Farooq... Of course, I won't leave the little boy until an officer arrives. He's scared, this little boy. I hope his mother is all right."

Omar squeezed the little boy's hand. It felt reassuring, pleasant to have a little creature look up to him, rely on him. He remembered taking his father's hand in a similar fashion and strolling in springtime along the littered roads of the refugee camp beneath the high wall of jangled barbed wire, playing word games and talking about the good times ahead. *One day, perhaps in your lifetime, you will enjoy the Golden Era when mankind wages war no more and all are brothers and sisters in the Friend's Court,* his father had said. Omar thought him a foolish and quixotic, that man. But it did feel so good and right holding the little boy's hand here in a strange land.

It distressed Omar not to be able to place this freckled cherub face with his shock of red hair.

Holy shit! The parking lot, behind the clinic. Sandra Lee's brake lights. Crazy teenaged mother. Purple hair. *Blackmail.*

Omar dropped the boy's hand and dashed for his car. A conspiracy, a Zionist frame job. He had to get out of here fast.

Damn it, he had given his name. They had his cell phone number. His entire life lay a Google search away.

A police car growled up the street. Omar froze, fear spiking his spine like a tap gone wrong. He backpedaled and smiled at the boy. "See how nice I've been to you?"

The car squealed to a stop. An officer stepped out and looked up and down the street and then on Omar and his young companion.

Omar summoned a face of fatherly concern and applied liberally.

Be cautious, be very cautious.

"So, can you tell me what's happening here?" said the officer.

"Yes, officer, I found the boy wandering the street. Officer Gomez, is it? A random turn took me down this street on my way home from work, honest. I thought it was my civic duty to stop. More than civic, my Hippocratic duty. You see, I'm a doctor...yes, that's right...my office is just off El Camino, a few blocks from here at most."

"That right? May I see some identification, please."

"But I have nothing to do with this situation."

"Then you have nothing to worry about."

Omar handed over his driver's license.

She jotted down his contact info and handed him back his license.

"Am I free to go?"

"Not quite yet."

She squatted down eye level to Emmett. "What's up kid? Can you tell me?"

"Mama, bathroom floor. Mama blood. Mama blue."

"This guy, you know him?"

"Yes," shrugged Emmett.

"No, he doesn't," Omar pleaded. "Perhaps we met once, in passing, by chance."

Omar felt the policewoman's stare crawl all over him like a desert spider.

More police cars arrived. Officers made phone calls. Omar started breathing heavily. He flashed on Israeli nightsticks chasing him wildly down narrow paths.

"Please, Officer Gomez, my wife awaits."

"It won't take long until we get it sorted out. And we always do."

An officer knocked gently on the front door. No answer. He knocked more forcefully, still no answer.

Omar squirmed.

"So you know this kid or not?"

"Perhaps his mother came by the clinic once. Maybe I saw the boy there."

"So, you didn't tell me the truth."

"I wasn't sure, I swear to you. I see so many children."

"Pediatrician?"

"Ob-Gyn."

Several officers huddled while another retrieved a one-man battering ram from the trunk of his car. One heave and the door splintered open. That's how fast they can enter your space. That's how fast they can change your life.

Radios crackled, officers scrambled. Omar heard an officer call for an ambulance.

"You say you were never inside?"

"Just passing by, swear to Al-. Swear to God."

"But you went to the front door."

"Yes, naturally, to see if the boy's mother was home."

"Did you knock?"

"Politely, yes."

"Did you touch the doorknob."

Had he tried the door? He thought not, but he couldn't remember. What if they found a print? That would be the second lie.

"I honestly do not recall."

Within moments the ambulance arrived. EMTs unfolded a stretcher and disappeared into the house.

Officers knocked on neighbors' doors. They stared at Omar as they talked. Glared.

A social worker swooped in on Emmett Jessup with bended knee and a teddy bear. "Hi. My name is Ling. This is for you."

Emmett Jessup pushed away the bear and glanced toward the house. "Mama?"

"We'll take care of your mother. We have the best people in the world."

She took the little boy's hand and started walking to a brown car.

"Where are you going to take him?" Omar said.

"Somewhere safe for now. Come little buddy."

The child waved to Omar as he walked away. Omar waved back.

More hushed conversation from the police officers, more glances toward Omar.

The social worker's car drove away down the street.

Omar stood alone, the sole object of attention. The carnival clown in a circus of accusers. This is the injustice piled upon the pious. How quickly he had forgotten the burden of purity.

The stretcher emerged from the front door loaded with Penny, her face obscured by a breathing apparatus, a blue hospital blanket covering her still body. Two EMTs flanked her side. They loaded her into the ambulance.

Lights, siren.

A plain-clothes detective broke away from the pack and approached Omar. "Were you with her today?"

"As I told the kind Officer Gomez, I finished up at work at my clinic and was merely driving by. You can check with my assistants, my patients. Just driving by."

"Pretty big coincidence."

"Life is full of them."

The detective returned to the pack, and the whispering continued.

Omar felt naked, guilty, convicted, sentenced. He damned this country and its hatred of foreigners, Muslims. He understood for a moment the sentiments of those wanting to blow it up.

The moments slowly ticked. Omar wiped the sweat from his bush of his eyebrows. Two officers returned. "Okay, doctor, you can go now."

"I can?"

"Yes, unless you have something more to tell us."

"Me? No nothing. Thank you. Thank you."

"Thanks for your help."

Maybe this wasn't such a bad country after all. Omar turned to leave. "The boy's mother. Will she be okay?"

"Can't say."

"And the boy?"

"He's in good hands."

The neighbors began to disband. A few police cars rushed from the scene on their way to other crimes, common as they were these days.

Omar rolled away realizing he had never learned the mother's name. Oh well, he would learn her name tomorrow. It was easy enough to scan the newspapers or search the Web to find out what had happened here at the apartment around the corner from the abortion clinic.

While driving away he wondered why on earth he had taken this route today, one he rarely took. Oh yes, it was talk of war on the radio between Pakistan and America. Pakistan threatened to close the US embassy and arrest 122 employees as spies. The US government retaliated by freezing certain Pakistani assets, sending the nuclear-powered USS Ronald Reagan super-carrier into Gulf waters, increasing the domestic threat level to red and instructing all non-essential US citizens to leave Pakistan within 48 hours. And then the blessed thoughts of home. Omar had missed his usual turn and came down this secondary lane instead.

Who or what directed the traffic of our lives? The hand of Allah, that is who.

And Allah, praised be his name, had led Omar down this very street for a purpose of the grandest proportions. Any qualms Omar may have felt concerning the reason for his wrong turn vanished now in the face of these fortuitous circumstances. *What an opportunity!*

Omar pulled over and hatched his plan.

Did not the Qur'an observe that *the Night of Destiny is worth one thousand months?*

~

Omar waited a good three hours before returning to the scene of the incident. He drove by, slung low in the driver's seat to ensure that the last police car had departed. He parked two blocks down and slipped around the back of the house.

He tiptoed up the back porch stairs and jiggled the door. Locked tight. He noticed a window cracked open just a bit, not even enough for a fly to slip in. But the window slid with ease on its quiet rails, and Omar hoisted himself up and let himself in.

That easy.

Omar waited for his eyes to adjust to the darkened room. He began his search with a single question — where would a floundering drug addict with silly tattoos and purple hair hide a bomb in a place like this? He didn't wait for a cryptic email or coded message to assure him the bomb was here. These things are transmitted among the channels that connect the righteous. Virtuous intuition. Over 25,000 kneels on the carpet gets you prepared for moments like this, it strings the wires for the knowledge that need not be spoken.

He stepped deeper inside and hastily looked around the apartment, surprisingly new and clean. He remembered well that backpack, a shoddy, sagging affair. But he didn't see it anywhere, not in plain view.

A rustle at the front door startled Omar. It was followed by an insistent key trying the lock. He froze in place, thankful for his loafers softening the sound of his criminal presence. He stopped his breath.

The front door whooshed open.

The police? Thieves? It couldn't possibly be the girl back from the hospital already, not in the shape she left in. No more confrontations with that unbalanced woman, please.

He found a shadow and drew himself in. He dug his fingernails into his thighs to keep them from trembling.

He wished he had a weapon on him. Why hadn't he brought a weapon?

Maybe they would just go away. Maybe Omar could slither out the window unseen, undetected.

A voice called out, a female voice. "Penny?"

Why had he come? And then he remembered, *destiny*, that's right, *destiny*.

And that's when he saw it, tucked poorly behind the couch, so close he could smell it.

THIRTY

Naomi Weiner-Gluckstein had returned to the Oasis Apartments on 13th Street and parked her Prius under a palm tree. A few neighbors cast strange looks as she entered the house. She sniffed the air to catch a scent of mischief.

She threw down her bamboo bag on the living room chair and plopped down beside it.

Was that a noise in the back bedroom?

"Penny?" Naomi felt too exhausted to check, too defeated having come from six straight hours of phone banking. Three hours calling Alaska households in an attempt to drum up opposition to a new northern gas pipeline disrupting caribou migration routes. Most Alaskans hung up on her, and those courteous enough to engage wondered why New Yorkers always saw fit to butt into Alaska's business. She explained she wasn't a New Yorker. The irate folks at the other end of the line barked, *you're all New Yorkers.* The next three hours she called residents of New York City in hopes of convincing them not to oppose a renovation of the United Nations that would result in a 27 percent reduction in parking spaces throughout the rectangle bounded by 41st Street and 49th Street and 3rd Avenue and the East River. In New York, if you're not a New Yorker, you don't count. *Screw you* was a good summation of the response she received from the residents there.

She helped herself to a glass of Alexander Valley Zinfandel. So what if she had started drinking again and toking a pinch of weed every other night. The Anti-Theory was the shits. Everybody was feeling it.

She felt a breeze drifting from the hallway. "Penny, you sleeping?"

Naomi wondered when everything had become a chore again.

Everything a battle with Penny. It wasn't like that during ToE. No, after that first ecstatic reunion, the two paired up like girlfriends. They made red velvet cake and roller-skated in Golden Gate Park on Sundays. They talked dick size and dolls. Caught matinees and tanned in the park. Love birds, this mother and child reunion.

And Emmett Jessup, bless his heart. A saint, a blessing that kid. All joy, all love. Eternal happiness delivered to Naomi, a bigger load than she could have ever imagined.

Wouldn't you know it, then came the Anti-Theory. Poof goes contentment, Adios peace of mind.

Considering Penny's mental illness, Naomi should not have been surprised, but who could have foretold the ferocity of the fall? Penny got into the habit of slamming bedroom doors, accused everyone of every deceit large and small, drew Emmett Jessup and Naomi into her fits of rage. She yelled, demanded, scorned, accused, rejected, nullified, brutalized and incited. And that was before noon. The afternoons consisted of tearing down, ripping apart, abusing and ignoring.

Naomi countered by removing Emmett from the toxic environment whenever possible — an hour's respite here and there for the boy and a little quiet time to inculcate some progressive values. But blessed child that he was, he didn't seem to mind his mother's tirades, preferring to snuggle by her side as she flicked ashes of Pall Malls into an empty Diet Coke can.

And don't talk about the cigarettes. That's a world war happening every night.

Penny became jealous and insisted Emmett Jessup be with her at all times. She grabbed his wrist and dragged him to Mervyn's Lounge and other nefarious bars and clubs that still stank of cigarettes, even though cigarettes had been banned decades ago from indoor spaces in California.

Naomi, believing it best, offered every convenience and assistance. She bought Penny a used car, paid for insurance, catered to her every need. Naomi utilized techniques she had learned at a weekend seminar on Non-Violent Communication. It seemed so easy during the seminar. Naomi listened and affirmed, as the program suggested. But one little criticism and Penny would explode with craven anger like a Dybbuk. Naomi had no choice but to stay out of the house for longer and longer periods of time. Yet she longed to be back with Emmett Jessup and Penny.

Penny, on the other hand, seemed fine with Naomi's absence, more than fine. She reveled in it. That was to be expected, Naomi figured. Who was she kidding? You can't turn a lifetime around in seven weeks. Bi-polar disorder doesn't disappear because of the confirmation of an obscure scientific theory. And miracles only happen in Hollywood and crazy religions. No parting of the waters on this choppy bay. Just two boats adrift. East-West, up-down, going-coming.

Naomi opened her eyes on the thought that the deteriorated situation might be partially her own doing. She was fiery herself. Obstinate, stiff-necked, intransigent, you name it. *Fuckshit,* they were cut from the same unholy cloth, mother and daughter.

The house was cold.

Naomi stilled to listen.

"Penny, you in there?"

A flash of light, then dark. She quieted her feet and cocked an ear.

"Pen?"

A breathing unrecognized, a scour of must.

Naomi straightened her spine. Tiptoed toward Penny's bedroom door. A soft hand on the knob, a quick turn inside.

She froze on an Arab in a suit.

"What the—?"

The intruding Omar flashed the whites of his eyes. He danced one foot out the window with Penny's backpack gripped tightly.

"Hey, you get back here!"

Omar snagged his loafer on the edge of the mini-blinds. The shoe flicked like a football into Naomi's face.

"You *motherfucker,"* said Naomi, as she dove onto his coattails.

He karate-chopped her arm. On the rebound, Naomi hooked one strap of Penny's backpack. She pulled with all her might.

The burglar Omar tumbled on top of her.

"You don't understand," he said.

Naomi socked him a good one in the eye. She yanked on the strap with all her might.

"I know you," she said.

On that identification, Omar let the backpack free in the tug of war. It catapulted Naomi to the back wall.

With the flash of a bedeviling eye, he bounded out the window.

"Coward!" God, he looked familiar, the musty Muslim, but from where?

Naomi stuck her head out the window. "And never come back!"

She returned to the living room to phone the police. But first, she poured herself another glass of Zin to calm her nerves.

On the kitchen counter, where the telephone should be if anybody had landlines anymore, Naomi spied a slightly dog-eared business card left behind by Sergeant Roberta Gomez of the Palo Alto Police Department.

~

Naomi almost crashed twice on her wild ride en route to the Kaiser Permanente Hospital. The ER was clammy and filled with noise and chatter. In the hall, a Mexican family wept over an ancient grandmother on her way to the other side. Two men with what looked like gunshot wounds leaned against each other like soldiers of war. A father barked at his daughter in Vietnamese.

Naomi found Penny unconscious, sunken in a bed, smothered by machines, cloaked behind a curtain. Rushing to Penny's side, Naomi collided with a nurse. Naomi asked her, "My baby! My baby! Is she gonna be all right?"

"She's stabilizing, but it's too early to tell."

"God, forgive me."

Naomi stroked Penny's arm just below the IV line. Penny's arms were bruised, and blue veins ran through them like rivers of death. Her head was wrapped in a bandage, and her eyes were sunken as if decay had already started.

"Hon, it's me, mom. Well, not mom, like I've-been-a-good-one mom. But one of your two moms who loves you so. I'm sorry for all that I've done and the pain that I've caused."

The patient did not stir. Naomi checked the blood pressure monitor, 60 over 45. Her oxygen intake was at 92 percent, heart rate 53. Not good signs.

"We were happy, weren't we? We had it right for a few days. Wasn't it the best?"

The patient quickened.

"I mean, you are the only one I love totally, you are perfect. In need of no fixing. How strange is that? Something that doesn't need fixing. I'm so sorry for all my wrongdoings."

The patient startled awake.

"Penny, my Penelope, you're alive!"

The patient coughed and sputtered, and then weakly uttered, "Fuck you."

"What?"

"FUCK YOU!"

"How can you tell me that? I'm your mother."

"FUUUCKYOOOOU!?"

"Yeah, well, then fuck you, too."

"Get the hell out of here...or..."

"Or what?"

"...or come with me to the clinic."

"The clinic? What clinic?"

A nurse popped a head in. "What's going on in here?"

Penny tried to respond but coughed up blood instead. She pumped her fist to speed whatever was coming through the IV into her vein.

Naomi grinned. Penny grinned. They didn't need a nurse right now butting into their business. Naomi whispered to her daughter, "And what do you mean telling me *fuck you?*

"I'm pregnant."

"Pregnant? But how? The abortion."

"He didn't get it all. Any of it for that matter."

"You're joking, right?"

"Ask the doctor. He'll show you pictures. It's a girl, and right now she's got more smack in her than a Mexican mule."

"Holy shit."

"Holy shit is right."

Penny laid back on the pillow and wheezed herself a breath. "Why me, Lord?"

"What are you going to do?"

"That motherfucker is gonna finish the job."

"But that's your daughter you're carrying. My granddaughter."

"You didn't seem to care when you didn't know who she was. Hot chocolate, remember?"

"So much has passed, changed. Think of Emmett, he prays every night for a brother or sister."

"Not one retarded from all the drugs I've done. This baby is stir-fried chicken."

"You don't know for sure."

"Helluva good chance, don't you think?"

"I'll be there for you, no matter what."

"I've heard that line before."

"I promise."

All of a sudden Penny's demeanor changed. Gone was the bristle and brimstone replace by the pout of a little girl in trouble. "You really promise? 'Cause I could use someone so bad," she said softly.

Naomi couldn't help but respond in kind because she knew exactly how Penny felt. "I will be there, I swear I promise."

They touched foreheads for a quiet moment. Nice.

"Thanks, mom."

"*Mom?* You never called me mom before."

"First time for everything."

"Let's get you fixed up and out of here. I hate hospitals. And then we'll talk about all the options."

Penny crimped her eyebrows and flipped an informal finger to her mother. "My mind's made up and you ain't gonna change it."

So much for blossoming vulnerability.

Naomi could protest until her face turned pink, but then she'd risk never seeing Emmett Jessup and Penny again. They were her life now. No living without them anymore. No, better to stay close to Penny's side, where Naomi could convince, persuade, cajole, and bribe her if need be, like Naomi's parents had done. Just like that.

Naomi adjusted the pillow behind the thick skull of her daughter.

"Anything you say, sweetie."

THIRTY-ONE

Seven weeks, Sandra Lee counted, since she last set foot in the church. And she chose to wear red because when you want to shrink, that's the time to stand out. Her mother taught her that. And so red it was. A red tight-waisted jacket over a slim-fitting knee-high skirt. Red pumps with spiky heels and red nylons so sheer a raindrop could slide down them without bursting. A hat of red and a shade of lipstick seven times redder. The weak prey on the weaker not the strong. Her mother taught her that, too.

As Sandra Lee strutted in, half the crowd smiled, half didn't. Sandra Lee recognized the smilers. Those who couldn't afford to throw stones because of their ToE sins, like Robyn Roistacher who joined a samba group, and Fred Willander who gave up his NRA membership. The non-smilers were with sin as well but still felt it their moral duty to throw first. She tried offering a smile to Cindy Zusin, Bev Gilliam and the smattering of others from the leadership team of the Pro-Life Crusade. They grimaced with righteousness. Margie and Dathan Lean sneered and turned away. Turncoats.

Sandra Lee squinted to get a good glimpse of the replacement preacher. New and squeaky-clean that preacher boy, pressed fresh and right out of the box, and occupying the altar that rightfully belonged to Harlen. She was sure the yearling applied wax to his bulging forehead before the show to shine even brighter. She knew all the tricks of the pulpit trade. Plus, he wore a wedding ring, damn it.

See *that?* He needs a teleprompter, the greenhorn. Harlen doesn't need one, that's how smooth her husband is.

The preacher cleared his throat (bad start, makes the audience doubt your conviction), and he began…

"Now, before we praise the Lord Jesus, let me take a moment to address the Pakistani crisis. We are a peaceful nation with enmity toward none. But threaten our citizens, and you awaken the sleeping giant. Raise oil prices willy nilly, and we invoke our moral imperative to protect our corporate interests. Continue your reign of hegemony over the moderate peoples within your borders, and you give us no choice but to overthrow your tyranny and replace it with a freedom-loving democracy. It's time we take down once and for all the Satanic Saracen horde of hateful Arab Muslim Sand-Nazi Terrorist Infidels. As for the Muslims here on our own blessed soil, it's time we send them packing back to the oil pits from whence they came before they sully our nation with their Islamist fascist conspiracies of evil. It's time we send them back to the caves of their grandfathers to pray in the dark of their damnation. It's time we send them back to their goats and madrasas. I will say the Word of the Lord is clear on this. Open your books to Hosia 13:16. *The people of Samaria must bear their guilt, because they have rebelled against their God. They will fall by the sword, their little ones will be dashed to the ground, their pregnant women ripped open.* Am I right, honest, God-fearing Christians?"

Amens by the scores.

"So close your eyes, brothers and sisters. Find someone's hand to hold onto, because heaven knows we need each other at a time like this – the end times – and accept Jesus into your heart as we join in our singular Christian prayer. Dear Jesus, give us the strength for our crusade to crush these infidels once and for all. Provide our leaders with the will to use whatever means necessary to reduce the Muslim extremists to rubble if need be. Fill our nation's coffers with the moral and fiscal capital necessary to finish this job once and for all. In your name, Jesus, we pray. Amen."

What crap, Sandra Lee thought. On the nose, as they say. But the parishioners were buying it. Fools. Sheep. If Harlen were up there, he would have finessed the message. He would have made people feel right and inevitable, not angry and vengeful.

As the applause died down, it was replaced by the grumble of a small commotion at the back of the auditorium.

Lo and behold, looky here.

Sandra Lee's ex-gay (and now gay again) preacher-husband strolled up the aisle, wearing a Cheshire Cat grin and a grey pinstripe suit that broadened his shoulders and trimmed his waist. An orange shirt and deep green silk tie for effect. What a thankful sight. He had returned to take his church back. Go Harlen! Lord knows he deserved it. Lord knows she needed it. And if anyone could pull it off, it was Harlen the Magician. All the good clergy are illusionists, and they must be, considering the material they have to work with. Look at him. Now, there's a pro. There's a preacher. There's a man. And what was so wrong living a lie, didn't everyone do it?

Harlen tipped his imaginary cap as he strutted past Preacher Riverside and Preacher Dallas in the front row.

He bounded the carpeted steps by threes.

"Excuse me." He bumped Preacher Clean out of the way and took the podium as if Jesus himself had ordained him.

"Ladies and gentleman, brothers and sisters, esteemed elders. I apologize for the interruption. I know war is imminent, shared sacrifice and all, but we've heard it before, haven't we? I have something to confess to you, and it can't wait. Something deep and personal that won't take but a minute. I am here to report to you that, per my instructions, I attended gay reparative therapy with an open heart full of enthusiasm. I listened to the counselor and prayed on his council. I reconnected with my beautiful wife, sitting presently in the audience in dazzling red. *Hello there, honey.* And despite the efforts on my part, on very best efforts on the part of Reverend Myles, and on the sensually touching efforts of the scented beauty below, I'll say it now, I'll say it again, I'll say it in front of you, and I'll say it in front of my Maker: I am gay. I am as the birds, brothers and sisters, the colorful ones. And none of us, not even the Man upstairs, can change that. If the news offends you, I am sorry. If it means you want this boring, indolent pastor to replace me with his sermon ripped right off the Internet then be my guest. But know that I love you all and am always available to minister to you should you want the council of a man not afraid of his own secrets."

What? What the fuck was he doing? Sandra Lee thoughts. What about the arrangement, the retaking of their church, all the plans they had meticulously laid? Could he say anything worse at a time like this?

"And to my lovely wife. It was all my fault, our failed marriage. I see that now. I wish you and the baby well."

A gasp through the crowd, the word *baby* whispered like a curse.

"I'll always be available as Uncle Harlen, if you don't mind a gay man in his or her life. So farewell my dear friends and remember, the Lord works through you not on you. Cheers and *adios amigos.*"

Everyone knew whose baby it was. Of all the ToE indiscretions, Sandra

Lee's slipping and sliding with an Arab abortion doctor topped the cherry on the biggest cake of shame. You can forgive a sinner, but forgive a traitor? Never in a million blessed Sundays.

"*Whore!*" "*Harlot!*" "*Slut!*" Not words for church and Sandra Lee couldn't believe the simple human desire to love and be loved by another human being could be met with such hostility, in church, no less. Where was Jesus when you needed him?

Pastor Clean slicked down his hair with a bit of saliva and elbowed Harlen away to reclaim the podium.

Sandra tried a smile to salvage what dignity she had left, but the vexed eyes of the faithful made her redder still.

~

Twelve blocks away and later that afternoon, Omar Farooq keyed open the clinic door and cut through the darkness. He switched on the television. The Al Jazeera announcer spoke in urgent pulses. *Pakistan shutters border with India. Israel calls up its reserves. Gulf states batten down for war. Iran ready to assist all Muslim brethren. NATO Ministers convene in Brussels. Hamas vows to shower Tel Aviv with rockets. North Korea offers nukes in exchange for bread. ISIS on the prowl once more.*

So this was how it was going to end.

Omar peeked out the window and saw them. Gone were their anti-abortion signs. Now the seething throng of Americans carried signs scrawled with slogans like *Terrorists Go Home! Islam is Bad! Throw Out the Dirty Rotten Towel Heads.* Church quite obviously had been a feast of brotherly love this morning.

Abortion provider was defensible in a court of law. For his defense, Omar could rely on an established cadre of supporters, colleagues, the American Medical Association, (bless the power to lobby). But as a lone Muslim in an angry Christian world, no rational claim could be argued with success before a jury drunk on the prospect of war. He vowed to work fast today. One irate, angry client, in and out, and then back to the safety of his anonymous condo.

Omar couldn't believe his eyes when he spied the midnight blue of a familiar Mercedes Benz pull right into the parking lot, not even around back. His eyes popped further when his worst fears were realized, and Sandra Lee emerged like a starlet from the tinted automobile in a dress redder than hell. She ambled past the Pro-Life group as if they were hawking roadside cherries.

"Trollop!!" yelled Bev Gilliam.

"Turncoat!!" shouted Cindy Zusin.

Sandra Lee must have gone truly mad, for Omar watched her smile and wave at the ladies as she strolled up to the clinic's front door. He cracked it open and pleaded, "Are you insane? What are you doing here?"

"What are *you* doing here?"

"Emergency appointment."

"Make it two," Sandra Lee delivered the news.

Omar led his second wife (annulment pending) inside and shuttered the blinds.

She was as beautiful as he remembered. He could not contain a spontaneous emission of affection. "It's good to see you."

"And you, too."

"Remember the Tango in Durango?"

She smiled. "How can I forget? And the Foxtrot in Phoenix?"

"The finest of our career."

"We did move well together."

"Yes, we did."

Omar didn't object when Sandra Lee placed her hand on his shoulder. "One for old times?" she said.

"One."

Omar marked the count. "Three, two, one, and..."

The two launched right into a Tango across the commercial carpet of the clinic. They cheek-to-cheeked on the swoop and turn.

She spun away with a smile. "I'm out of breath, it's been a while."

Omar flopped next to her on the waiting room couch, his foot still tapping to the beat he missed so much. He leaned in her to smell her hair. "I miss it. I miss you," he said.

"I miss you, too."

Truth be told, Sandra Lee missed the dance more than the intimacy, more than the sex, more than anything. She slid toward him and nestled against his chest.

"Do you think? Is there a chance? Could we be wrong to be apart?"

Omar traced the curve of her eyebrow. He feathered his fingers between hers. Then he pulled away. He could not allow himself to entertain such thoughts, not because they weren't attractive, but because he knew where they led, away from his faith and into a valley of iniquity. He was back on the path, the straight and narrow. Deviation from faith had delivered all that had gone wrong in his life. It was that simple.

He spoke gently because he did not want to cause more harm. "As they say, the bird and the fish can marry, but where will they live? Those people out there, on your side of the fence and mine, they will never let us live together."

"Those people are harmless. It's us who determines what we do."

"I live by laws, not of my making."

"You interpret laws as you see fit."

"I am so sorry."

"For real?"

"For real."

Sandra Lee Spridgen (née Wilson), the girl who people never believed got her heart crushed got her heart crushed all the time. Nothing ironic or tragic about it, just a universal truth, thought Sandra Lee. *Love breaks your heart.* And when your heart breaks, it hardens, like a cooling diamond. Just the way it is, if you ask Sandra Lee.

Seeing no alternative, Sandra Lee saw no reason to mince words. "Okay then, I want an abortion."

Omar shook his head. "Sorry, but that is out of the question."

Sandra Lee couldn't believe her ears. "First of all, I don't need your permission for anything. And second, you think this is easy for me? I abhor abortion. I truly do. I'm not a fawning believer when I say I believe it to be morally wrong. I have precious few values, maybe, but the sanctity of life is one of them."

"Please understand, my wife Shivana was never able to conceive – my child at least. This will be my first."

"What am I, your handmaiden? This is *our* kid."

"Yes, of course, my apologies. You are correct. And I promise to be its financial caretaker through college, every penny."

"A child is more than a checkbook entry, I'll have you know."

"On moral grounds then, I beseech you."

"Beseech all you want. I've made up my mind. I want *you* to do it."

"What?"

"You made this mess, you clean it up. Half your mess, anyway. I'm mature enough to admit my share."

"Impossible. I'll refer you to any one of several excellent practitioners. But I cannot and will not perform a procedure on you, on my own progeny."

Sandra Lee pulled out her cell phone and held it aloft like a weapon. "See this? I'm calling my friend at Homeland Security and telling him you're a terrorist."

Omar stumbled back a few feet. Did she know about the bomb? She couldn't possibly.

"That's preposterous."

"Who cares? With all the crap happening in Pakistan, he will investigate. He lost a son in Afghanistan and loves to feed that chip on his shoulder."

"You wouldn't."

"Try me. And then I'll call my reporter friend at the *Mercury News,* and she'll do an entire exposé on you, and you will be ruined. We still have a free press in this country, thank God."

"Do all women in this country receive training in blackmail?"

Omar thought about his limited options. He could call her bluff. Calling bluffs works nine times out of ten. Sandra Lee was many things but a bluffer she was not. He could kill her in the next five minutes. Just one tiny flaw. Half the congregation of the local Bible Belt church was standing on the hot pavement outside having just witnessed a gay preacher's pregnant adulterous wife walk into a clinic run by a Palestinian bigamist and potential suicide bomber. Not the ideal environment for furtive murder. Nor did he have the stomach for murder.

Plus, he loved her. And who was he kidding?

Omar's options fell to one. Again. He wondered if his limited options led to radical ideas or radical ideas limited one's options.

"All right, then."

Omar led Sandra Lee to Examining Room North. "Undress and get in the stirrups. I'll be back in a moment with what we need."

Sandra Lee began to disrobe. Her pumps, nylons, skirt, jacket, the red came off, and with each article she stripped away, a shred of dignity went with it. She reviewed the events that led to this moment of willingly readying herself for an act she counted as one of the few cardinal sins before the court of the Lord.

A dance. How could a dance cause such a curse? Maybe the holy rollers were right. Sin is everywhere and to be avoided at all costs because it leads to this — the decision to wrench an innocent baby out of a guilty womb. She removed her panties and let them slip onto the floor.

If only she had someone to talk to, someone who could help her know what to do, counsel her with wisdom.

And then she thought of that very person.

Naked and cold, she found her cell phone and punched the speed dial entry for the only person on earth who knew her, and perhaps even loved her, the person who understood her better than anyone, maybe even herself.

And God bless his gay soul. Harlen answered on the first ring.

THIRTY-TWO

Shivana Farooq circled Ethan's house twice before parking half a block away.

She hustled quickly to the home she had inhabited such a short time ago (but oh, how long ago it seemed). To be anonymous, she tightened her hijab over her face, just in case any reporters lurked nearby.

Never one for regrets, Shivana had one to address, as big as the deserts in Iran.

She knocked on Ethan's door.

"Who is it?" he asked.

She gave the password. "Shalom, salaam."

Ethan opened the door but did not attempt to hug her or even smile for that matter. Shivana took it as a sign of acceptance for her decision, respect for another man's wife because Ethan was a gentleman to a fault and would never presume to touch her or share an intimacy after all that had occurred.

"May I come in for a moment?"

"Did Omar give you permission to be here?"

"I am here without his knowledge."

"Why have you come?"

Shivana pulled free her hijab and let out her mane of jet-black hair.

"Ethan, you know I've always prided myself on my counting, my measurements, but I'm afraid I've made one tremendous miscalculation. I need to make good. With all the numbers and equations, I want to believe still in a purposeful universe, one in which it matters what we do, with whom and to whom."

"And so?"

"When Omar persuaded me to return to him by invoking loyalty to my family, he was smart and correct to do so. I would never want to be the agent of misfortune for my mother, my father, and my siblings. However, I failed to include one critical factor in my equation, Ethan. That's twice in a span of seven weeks I've calculated incorrectly. I once thought myself invincible.

"What factor did you omit?"

"Our child, Ethan. Our little girl. It *is* a girl, the doctors tell me. Gabrielle. Whatever damage I inflict on myself or you, or the society, I could never live with myself for bringing up a girl in a culture I abhor. I cannot subject her to the tyranny of the burqa. I cannot in good conscience be her conduit into a world I've tried so desperately to escape. But I respect you, Ethan, more than you'll ever know, and I cannot make *this* decision without you."

Ethan wasn't quite sure what she was suggesting. His head remained in a haze after sitting uncomfortably in a lotus position all morning (as he had for many mornings) in a vain attempt to recapture that glorious Kabbalistic vision that had followed his suicide attempt. All he was sure of now, after hours of meditation, was that natural gas provided a level of spiritual lucidity that clear-headedness did not. What he would give for the gift of sober understanding?

Even Shivana's request seemed vague and unclear. Ethan answered as he felt she would like.

"Do what you feel is right," he mumbled.

This was not what Shivana had hoped to hear. She wanted Ethan to take her in her arms. To madly kiss her. She wanted him to draw her up onto his white horse and order his steed to gallop away so they could be together forever. She wanted him to give her no option but to ride off together into the intellectual sunset, the world be damned. Let the dictators and terrorists do as they must. For the first time, Shivana wanted to be *taken*.

She waited a moment more. "Are you sure?"

"You know, I've been thinking..."

"Yes?" Shivana perked up.

"...about the Theory of Everything. We were all wrong. Not just us, you and me, but all reductionist scientists. We were wrong to think we could utilize advanced mathematics, multi-dimensional spaces, and quantum experiments to produce a single equation that accounted for all the laws of the universe. Even if we had succeeded, at best it would not be a theory of everything but just a theory of every *physical* thing. There's a lot more to the universe than quantum events, force fields, and vibrating strings. Even if we had produced a valid theory? So what? What does that explain? Just the particular characteristics of *our* universe. What of the multiple other universes that exist? Would our Theory of Everything be valid in a universe in which, say, gravity is just slightly stronger? The quantum strong force a fraction weaker? Where $E=MC^2$ might be recalculated as $E=MC^3$?"

Despite her pressing need, Shivana couldn't help but get caught up by the intrigue of the philosophical questioning. "If gravity were stronger, then stars would burn through their nuclear fuel in a heartbeat rather than billions of years. If the strong force were weaker, the stars could never have come into formation."

Ethan grew animated, as he always did when contemplating this subject. "But in those other universes, maybe another kind of intelligence exists. Not recognizable to us, perhaps, but recognizable to the sentient beings born out of the same intelligence. There can never be a mechanistic Theory of Everything because it would have to account for every variation of every law and every law yet to be discovered."

"So what does that make us?" asked Shivana. "Freaks of nature? Accidents? I don't buy it. There must be some equation that can encompass all the possibilities in motion, all modes of existence."

Ethan grew excited. "Imagine a prism. On one side is the pure white light, on the other, the light is refracted into the gamut of spectral colors. However hard we might attempt to quantify, measure or unify the physical characteristics of red, orange, yellow, green, cyan, blue, violet, we can never explain what's on the other side of the prism — the white light and what other characteristics it might have. We know, for example, that light contains infrared and ultraviolet wavelengths beyond the color spectrum— light we can't see."

"So you're asking what else does that pure white light contain?"

"Exactly, the Kabbalah calls it the Ein Sof, the pure empyrean state without any distinction or differentiation. The Hindus call it Brahman. The Buddhists call the pure state nirvana, and the Christians call it the Godhead. We are phantasmagoria projected on the wall of reality. What I'm saying is that you can't decipher the mind of God by looking at matter."

"It's not up to science to decipher the mind of God."

"It is, *if* we are looking for a Theory of Everything. The theory must include the consciousness that creates matter."

"But matter creates consciousness. It is because we possess a brain that we have the consciousness that allows us to think, comprehend, question, to ask *who am I?* It is the organic grey matter of our brain charged with 20 watts of energy that creates consciousness."

"But what if it's the other way around — what if it's consciousness that creates matter. A river of matter, and a flow of consciousness. Can you have a river without flow?"

Shivana's mother with her Sufi leanings used to refer with reverence and wonder to what she called *dhat,* the pure essence of Allah before it was shattered into endless forms of *sifat,* the manifestations of creation. Back then, when Shivana was a presumptuous little girl with her eyes on the West, she considered such talk foolish and superstitious. Now she was beginning to understand the wisdom of the teaching.

She cried because of the beauty of the thought and in admiration of Ethan's strange mind that so few understood. But mostly she cried because such metaphysical musings were of little use to her now.

The eternal rules of the universe — or the multi-verses as the case may be — did nothing to solve her current very temporal predicament. Her troubles were ruled not by the hidden splendor of dhat but by the petty laws of man. And how small they were. A thousand laws needed to rule a single thin shade of a single color of the spectrum of light. To think of all the cultures and religions, creeds and beliefs that expend so much energy creating laws to govern their narrow shade of color instead of seeking to understand the laws that govern all colors and all light.

"I love you, Ethan. I always will."

"And I love you Shivana, with all my eternal heart."

Ethan wanted desperately to give her a gentle kiss on the cheek, but he did not want to offend her or give her cause for guilt or shame. Shivana wanted so desperately to give Ethan a gentle kiss on the cheek, but she did not, for fear of hurting him once more. Neither did she turn back to glance upon him as she left. She had made that mistake once.

Ethan did indulge himself by stretching his neck to follow her as she hurried down the sidewalk.

He tried to return to contemplating the mysteries of the Ein Sof, but his mind was bothered. What had he missed during his encounter with Shivana?

Precisely 18 minutes later Ethan realized the specifics of Shivana's request. What a clod! She hadn't come for his approval but for his denial. How stupid could he be?

"No!" he screamed.

He raced to his car, cursing himself for having his head stuck in the limitless while the love of his life had stood so finitely in front of him asking him to help her answer the most basic question of existence.

THIRTY-THREE

Omar put on a white coat and scrubbed his fingernails mightily, but nothing could cleanse the sickening feeling inside. He considered running, escaping. How much of a head start could he gain before Sandra Lee realized he had fled? And how damning might it look should he be picked up by Federal authorities on the way to San Francisco Airport with a one-way ticket to Karachi or San Diego for that matter.

The television drumbeat showed video clips of columns of armies marching in the streets of distant cities, masses of angry people waving signs of hatred, leaders of countries at podiums explaining why they have no choice.

Suddenly, a knock at the door. More than a knock, a thumping. More than a thumping, a drumbeat of indignation.

Omar hesitated, knowing perfectly well who it was, having received the scornful phone call earlier in the day. In this business, hell has no wrath like a woman forced to return.

Omar swung open on the inevitable.

"You motherfucker," said the tattooed teenager. "Fix me now."

Next to her stood an equally indignant middle-aged woman with red curly hair, eerily familiar. She said, "You touch her doctor, and I'll sue your ass from here to eternity."

In between the dueling women, holding the hands of both, was a little boy clutching a familiar backpack. *That* little boy.

"Hi!" said Emmett.

"Hi," said Omar.

The feisty girl nodded toward that damnable backpack Omar knew so well and had come to abhor. An entire universe of ramifications appeared to him in a vision of fear. The little boy, the crazed teenager, the angry woman, the apartment, the bomb. He knew them all so intimately, and now they had assembled in his office — with his ex-wife/lover waiting in the other room.

Strangely, he didn't recognize the girl as a patient. "You were never a patient here."

"The fuck I wasn't. You wouldn't look at my goddamned face, remember? You went home sick. And before that—."

"—Wait...vaginal scarring, vestiges of a poorly performed episiotomy?"

"That's me."

"A devil tattoo on your left inner thigh and another above your pubic line that reads..."

"*But For The Grace Of God Go I,*" she answered for him.

"Holy shit," said Omar.

'Holy shit, is right," said Penny.

A random universe? Not a chance, thought Omar. Not a fucking chance.

Sandra Lee, hearing the ruckus, emerged from the examining room, half-dressed and still buttoning herself up.

"What the hell is going on?"

Penny wondered, "You two screwing in here again? Is that all you do?"

Sandra Lee thought to respond but couldn't decide which alternative answer was preferable: *no, we're not having sex, I'm here for an abortion,* or *yes, we are having sex again, that's all we do.*

Sandra Lee knew Penny, but the redheaded stranger was unfamiliar. "Hi, I'm Sandra Lee. Who are you?"

"I'm Penny's mother."

Sandra Lee scrunched her face. She turned to Penny, "But I thought your mother was Margie."

"*Adopted* mother. This is my *real* mother."

Naomi studied Omar up and down. "God, you look so familiar. Sierra Club?"

Omar tried a smile. "No, I cherish the environment but have no time to serve such a worthy organization."

"I know!" said Naomi.

Omar melted with fear.

"National Organization of Concerned Arabic Men."

"Not quite."

"I'll get it sooner or later, I swear. I never forget a face."

Omar prayed she was wrong. He asked Penny. "Obviously I am terribly sorry the original procedure was not successful. How about we consult today and then we'll set up an appointment for first thing tomorrow morning?"

Penny had just about had it with bullshit excuses. She did everything everyone asked of her, but when she depended on others, did they come through? Hell no. Like this *dorkhead* doctor. It's tiring, you know, having no one to depend on but yourself. No time to sleep, no one watching your back. The river is wide, and the water is cold. And when you don't got a boat, you're up the creek without a paddle, or something like that, whatever they say.

"Do it now, or I'll blow this place to smithereens," Penny nodded to the backpack that Emmett Jessup cradled in his arm like a kitten.

No one seemed to take the threat seriously, except Omar who did so in frightened silence.

He said, "Well, I do have another patient waiting. And naturally, no nurses today, so forgive me if things move along a little slowly."

Penny said, "Who is the second patient?" It didn't take her long to figure it out. "You?" Penny pointed to Sandra Lee. "*Ohmyfuckinggod,* you reap what you sow, literally. How hilarious is that."

Emmett Jessup swung the backpack in wild circles. Penny said, "Put that down, honey. You might hurt yourself."

Naomi's eyes looked down to Omar's expensive Italian loafers.

"Hey, wait a minute! *Now* I know you. You're the guy in the apartment."

"Shhhh!" said Omar. "Please."

"Holy shit."

"Please, don't. You don't understand. And then he switched to French because she looked like a cultured lady and it was all he could think to do to stop the disaster in the making. "Si vous restez tranquille, je ferai ce que vous demandez."

Emmett smiled up at the doctor. "Mister?"

"Yes?"

"My mommy's alive."

"I can see that."

~

Shivana had been to her husband's clinic only once. Truly. On the day of the opening reception. She brought helium-filled balloons and a cardboard box of steaming Starbuck's decaf. She made small talk with the nurses and office assistants and at Omar's request tuned her iPod to inoffensive music. She never thought much about his work, positively or negatively. His chosen field, that's all. A street sweeper and an astronaut make the same decision. A physicist, too. Now as she parked out back by the garbage dumpster and hustled like a criminal to the thick metal door that led to the labyrinth behind the marijuana clinic, she considered this place in a new light. What once was innocuous had become noxious. What once was a source of steady income was morphing into the graveyard of dreams.

She rang the bell and waited. When no one answered, she rang again. Two minutes later, Omar arrived.

"Shivana, what are you doing here?"

"We have to talk."

"Please, Shivana, this is not a good time. I have patients."

"No. We have to talk now. I need your services. Your professional services."

Omar shut the door in her face, but Shivana slipped her foot in the jam, reverting so quickly to her old rebellious ways.

Omar insisted, "You'll have to go somewhere else."

"I will leave you if you don't. And patients? What patients come on a Sunday?"

"None of your business."

This whole subservient wife thing was getting old. Shivana pushed him aside and started toward the clinic. "I don't care what you say, I will not take no for an answer."

"Okay, I will relent," Omar said with a gentle push back. "But let's do this tomorrow, that's all I ask."

"Why are you so defensive? Who is in there?"

"Patient privacy rights."

"Sandra Lee's rights? Is she in there?"

"She is, but it's not what you think."

Shivana busted through Omar's outstretched arms and marched along the corridor toward the clinic.

When it was clear Shivana was not to be stopped, Omar added, "she's pregnant. Just like you."

Shivana turned to face Omar with all the anger of the elders. "From conception to termination, a full-service provider. Is that your new motto?"

"You're being disrespectful."

"Let's go. I want to meet this woman."

In the clinic, Omar stepped up to make the introduction he had hoped would never materialize. "Sandra Lee, may I introduce you to Shivana. And Shivana, please meet Sandra Lee."

Sandra Lee stepped up and offered her hand. "You're much prettier than he described."

"How did he describe me?"

"Dark."

"He never described you to me, but now I understand the attraction."

The bluebird eyes of Sandra Lee and the walnut eyes of Shivana simultaneously bore down on Omar.

For the green-eyed Naomi, this had been all about Penny and Emmett Jessup. But the moment Shivana walked into the room, Naomi knew who she was, having met her a few times and having seen her on television *ad infinitum.*

Naomi turned to Shivana. "Do you know who I am?"

Shivana studied the woman and felt that she should, but she couldn't place the face. "I beg your pardon, I can't say I do."

"I'm Naomi Weiner-Gluckstein. Don't tell me you're pregnant, too?"

"Ethan didn't tell you?" said Shivana.

"It's his?" asked Naomi, sort of proud that Ethan's sperm could swim.

"Are you suggesting I sleep around?"

"No, not at all."

"Whose child are you carrying?" asked Shivana.

Naomi was thrown by the question but realized it wasn't out of the question since she had presented herself in an abortion clinic. "It's not me who's pregnant. Penny is."

Everyone did the quick math, four women, three pregnancies.

Emmett Jessup found the kids' corner and raced a plastic fire truck around the carpet track. "Fire, fire, fire!"

"And that's my boy," said Penny.

Omar used the momentary lull to peer out the window. The anti-abortion/anti-terrorist/anti-immigrant crusade had grown appreciably larger in the short time since the afternoon activities began. A taco truck was doing a brisk business in the parking lot selling *asada burritos, tamales*, and *horchata* over ice. They hate their immigrants but love that immigrant food.

Suddenly, two cars raced up from opposite directions. One a gold Lexus sedan and the other a miserable green Kia.

The vehicles came within mere inches of each other as they rushed to park directly in front of the clinic. In handicapped spaces, no less. Big tickets coming for these two.

The drivers, both middle-aged men, jumped from their vehicles and bumped into each other at the clinic door, both in a major hurry.

"Hi, who are you?" Harlen asked.

"Ethan Weiner-Gluckstein."

"And who are you?" Ethan said.

"Harlen Spridgen, Pastor Harlen Spridgen. Nice to meet you."

"Nice to meet you, too," Ethan panted. To get here, he had run three red traffic lights and made two rights on red at intersections clearly designated *No Right On Red*, which was the first time in his life he had knowingly disobeyed traffic ordinances. A police officer lurking behind a billboard on Middlefield Road spotted him. Ethan sped away like a common criminal, but the policeman chose not to follow. Emboldened, Ethan stepped on it.

During the drive, he berated himself for being such a stupid asshole. He cursed time's one-way direction. He hoped it wasn't too late to stop Shivana from going through with the procedure. And if she had already, he vowed to wrap himself in a prayer shawl and light himself on fire.

Harlen, meanwhile, had raced over to the clinic for a second chance to step up to the idea of having a baby. He wished he had been more empathetic at the moment Sandra Lee told him she was pregnant, but the timing was poor, to say the least; it took several hours for Harlen to recover any semblance of equilibrium after the vaginal ambush. So when Sandra Lee called him earlier in near tears, from an abortion clinic no less, Harlen was thrilled to hurry over, eager to assist. Any chance to minister is a good one.

The chanters with signs in the parking lot shouted with conviction as the two men stood in front of the clinic.

"Pornographers!"

"Degenerates!"

"Homosexuals!"

"Jesus loves you," Harlen tossed back.

"Not my Jesus!" returned in an echo.

Ethan and Harlen rapped on the clinic door in unison.

Omar opened the door, having quickly grown accustomed to surprise visits. "Come on in, everyone else is here."

Penny forced her foot in the jam and called out to the angry protesters outside, "fuck all of you in *pavementland*."

She thought she saw her parents in the back somewhere and wished they gave a shit. She wished so many things.

Omar slammed the door shut.

Inside, Ethan saw both Shivana and Naomi in the same flash of light. For the life of him, he couldn't figure out what set of circumstances might lead to his wife and his former lover standing shoulder to shoulder in a place like this.

Omar locked the door tight.

"What are you doing here?" Ethan asked Naomi.

"What are *you* doing here?" Penny asked Harlen.

"What are *you* doing here?" Harlen asked Penny.

"You're asking me?" said Naomi. "Why didn't you tell me you got her pregnant?"

"Are you telling me you care? And what are *you* doing here?"

"I'm with Penny," Naomi replied.

"Party," said Emmett Jessup.

This was getting confusing.

Shivana walked to the window. "Shhh! Listen."

The crowd outside chanted, *Stop the Doc! Stop the Doc! Stop the Doc!*

Penny hated that crap and opened the door to share her feelings. "Hey, *Santaheads*. I got a bomb in here. If you know what's good for you, you'll shut the fuck up and take a walk."

~

Jimmy Lean believed in fate, coincidences, destiny. He had read about the Akashic field where all information about the universe, past, present, and future resides in a big cosmic hard drive and everyone and everything is connected in unusual ways, miraculously impossible to comprehend. A big Facebook in the sky. But even Jimmy Lean thought it a mighty coincidence beyond all reaches of probability that he should be riding his bicycle to the medical marijuana clinic just at the *exact moment* his sister should pop her head out the abortion clinic door and scream something about a bomb. If Jimmy could trust his eyes, he swore he saw Pastor Harlen Spridgen in the shadows behind her. And that was his unmistakable Lexus illegally parked. He was gonna get a ticket for that.

"Jimmy!" Penny yelled. "Get the hell over here, bro."

Jimmy locked up his bike and ran over. "What the hell is going on?"

"Jimbo, you got a joint, because I could really use one about now."

Someone from the crowd lofted a plastic Coke bottle at the building. The cap broke free and the bottle spun on the ground propelled by escaping carbonation. The protesters cheered.

Jimmy sidestepped the soda bomb. Penny waved him closer. "Don't look now," she whispered, "but mom and dad are out there somewhere."

Jimmy scanned the crowd but couldn't make out his parents faces in the angry mob.

Penny yanked Jimmy. Jimmy's probability quotient stretched even further when he saw the preacher and the preacher's wife.

The chant outside morphed into *Kill the Doc! Kill the Doc! Kill the Doc.*

In the parking lot, Bev Gilliam, known to many for her uncanny ability to overhear gossip and innuendo, spoken or otherwise, caught the word *bomb*, even if no one else did. She immediately understood the grave threat facing Sandra Lee (despite her bigamous criminality), Pastor Spridgen (despite his immoral sexual lifestyle choice) and the other white Christian citizens inside the building. And wasn't there a child in there as well? A suicide bombing waiting to happen.

Bev Gilliam, being the patriot she was, dialed 911. Afraid of being overheard by foreign spies, she told the dispatcher with reasoned calm, "There's a Muslim with a bomb at the abortion clinic holding Americans hostage. Come quick, or we're all gonna die."

THIRTY-FOUR

On the flat screen inside the clinic, an Al Jazeera's graphic proclaimed in the boldest letters *Preparing for War*. The program cut to an interview with a Muslim cleric declaring (with English subtitles) that Pakistan "had no choice but to prepare for war and the sacrifices necessary to ensure the preservation of Islam."

Sandra Lee couldn't stand the fake news and clicked over to Fox News for the real story. The lower-third ticker-tape crawl read *Preparing for War* in the boldest of letters.

The announcer said, "The President is scheduled to speak shortly to prepare the country for war and the sacrifices necessary to vanquish our enemies."

Much better, thought Sandra Lee.

Emmett Jessup sidled up to his Uncle Jimmy and interlaced his fingers with Jimmy's.

Jimmy asked Penny. "You pregnant again?"

"No way, same baby. *This* guy screwed it up." She pointed in no uncertain terms to Omar, his teeth still chattering from Penny's bomb pronouncement, which no one seemed to take seriously.

"Well, you got a joint or don't you?" asked Penny.

"I don't."

The camera cut to two desk-bound anchors backed by a translucent map zooming in and out over an oceanic section off the coast of Pakistan *where the provocation occurred*. There are moments one never forgets — JFK assassinated, World Trade Towers collapse. Would this be one of them?

"The Pentagon and White House are now confirming earlier unconfirmed reports that a Pakistani Navy battleship fired on the aircraft carrier USS Ronald Reagan in international waters in the Arabian Sea, near the Pakistani port city of Gwadar. At least seventeen seamen were injured in the ensuing blaze. Three US Super Hornet fighter jets destroyed the Pakistani warship. The search is on for enemy combatant survivors. The Pakistani Prime Minister is blaming the United States, claiming that the Reagan strayed into Pakistani territorial waters and ignored numerous directives to return to neutral seas.

"We're waiting now for the President who will be speaking from the Oval Office. Sources say she will invoke the War Powers Act, giving her the constitutional power to retaliate against any person, organization, or state suspected of involvement in terrorist attacks on the United States."

"It's war," said Harlen.

"What else is new?" Penny said.

The crowd outside grew edgier as the news spread via smart phones. The chant transformed into "USA! USA! USA! USA!"

Inside the clinic, Sandra Lee peeked through the shades and was the first to see a police car squeal to a stop outside, lights twirling in a blue-light special. Another police car high-tailed it into the parking lot, trailed by three more official cars, blacker than black. A red fire truck pulled up the rear, and within 60 seconds, a dozen more vehicles squeezed in and officers set up a haphazard barricade.

"Oh shit," said Omar.

The uniformed officers pushed back the crowd and strung yellow police tape across the length of 15 stores. Officers in helmets wielding hi-tech weaponry and Kevlar vests found sniper positions and took aim. Men in black suits emerged from the black cars wearing black shades and speaking softly into their cuffs.

A media chopper and then another thundered overhead.

On the clinic's flat screen inside, the anchor said, "We are going to break away briefly from the Pakistan crisis to focus on a story rapidly developing in Palo Alto, California, home to Stanford University. It's a potential terrorist bombing at a strip mall."

Camera crews arrived and erected satellite poles that reached to the sky. The smartphones faced their video eyes toward the clinic to *netwitness* the terrorist showdown. The footage could be worth some something if shit were to happen here.

Omar, Shivana, Ethan, Naomi, Sandra Lee, Penny, Harlen, Jimmy, and even Emmett Jessup crowded the window to view the activity first hand.

"Check it out," said Harlen. "The cavalry. What's going on?"

Omar said, "She's got a bomb, that's what."

The phone rang.

Omar ran to the desk to pick it up. "Good afternoon. Redwood El Camino Clinic. Sorry, but we are closed...Yes...I am Dr. Omar Farooq...Yes, I am the proprietor...Yes, there is a bomb in here...Yes, I will walk out with my hands up."

So this was it. This is how it was going to end. Not with a bang, but with a whimper. Omar felt relief. Relief he would not have to witness the sinewy results. Relief that the agony of the unsure would be replaced by the certitude of solitary confinement in Gitmo. That's how relieved he was, preferring the stone-cold certainty of 23-hour walls to the prevarications of the free mind. And maybe, just maybe, the authorities would show a little leniency should he exit quickly and exhibit not a hint of resistance. Submit, he knew the action well.

"I'm sorry for all the hurt I caused," Omar announced to the assembled.

"Not so fast," said Penny. She held up the bomb's remote control like a stone ready to be thrown. "I got *this*. I got a bomb."

She faced Omar and in the most serious tone imaginable assured him, "and this time I got fresh batteries."

Penny was ready to have it her way. For too long she had been walked all over, pressed into the pavement, yelled at by her father, boyfriends, teachers, social workers, landlords, dealers. Too many two-bit rip off artists fishing through her pockets. Too many uninvited fingers up her twat. This time she was gonna call the shots. Step back people, Penny was raising the ante. "You and I, Doctor Death, we got a little business to attend to before you even think of walkin' out the door."

"But the police are waiting. Federal officials."

"I don't give a rat's ass if Christ almighty is out there announcing the rapture."

With an astonished look on her face, Sandra Lee said, "Bomb, what bomb?"

Penny explained, "When I saw you screwing this guy a few weeks back in the parking lot back here, I took an educated guess and blackmailed this guy for a bomb. And he gave it up in like two seconds. Surprised the heck out of me that he even had one."

Sandra Lee turned to Omar. "You did that for me?"

"I did."

"That's so wonderful."

"And I'd do it again." But Omar didn't have time to profess his undying love or explain that the bomb had not been his in the first place but his cousin's. He turned to Penny Lee and said, "In fact, I'll do as you ask if you just let Sandra Lee go free."

"What about me?" said Shivana, feeling again like the second wife with Omar, even when she was the one and only. Second fiddle, if not fourth or fifth, such was the fate of a Muslim woman. The last plate of food with the scraps left over, the last in line for affection, a life of thanklessness endured under oppression's thumb.

Omar corrected himself. "Sandra Lee and Shivana. My two wives."

Penny didn't need long to think it over. "Deal."

With the quick negotiating going on, Naomi realized that it would take more than the power of her persuasion to prevent the abortion. She had had enough of feeling alone, unconnected. And now that she had found her family, she was going to fight for it with the same ferocity with which she fought against a world of plastic water bottles and pirate whaling on the high seas.

"Nobody leaves!" Naomi pronounced. "Nobody is aborting my grandchild."

"You can't be serious," said an astounded Ethan.

Naomi pulled out a snubbed-nosed revolver and drew a bead on everyone. "Try me."

Sandra Lee was astounded to see at a handgun in the hands of a Prius owner.

"You're a liberal, you can't have a gun."

"Hell, I can't. This is America," said Naomi proudly. "Plus it's licensed, and I went through a mental health screening, so there."

Ring, ring, ring.

Omar held the telephone receiver to his ear with great trepidation. "Yes, officer, I did promise to come out, and I *want* to come out, but I can't...Why? Because I'm being held, hostage... By whom? A Jewish woman with red hair who doesn't want me to perform an abortion and a tattooed teenager with purple hair who does want to have an abortion. Yes, it's complicated...Yes, everyone is free to leave....Well, they *were* free to leave when there was only a bomb before the red-headed woman pulled out her gun and told everyone to stay put and stop the abortion...I know, it is confusing. I'm confused."

Omar returned the receiver to its cradle.

On television, the station cut away from the scene directly outside the clinic to the Oval Office in the White House, where the President of the United States sat behind the wide mahogany desk flanked by a gazillion American flags. She wore a blue suit with her hair pulled back. Serious business.

"My fellow Americans, this nation has faced grave challenges in the past, from conflicts in Vietnam, Iraq, and Afghanistan to terrorist bombings here on our sacred soil. While we have always pursued peace, and chosen peace whenever possible, we have never ignored our responsibility to protect freedom, diplomatically and militarily when called upon to do so. We are being called to do so now in this dark hour. In response to the untenable provocation by the Pakistani regime, I have instructed the Joint Chiefs of Staff to initiate plans for preemptive defense, effectively immediately. We cannot say and will not say when a strike will happen. To the Pakistani people, please understand that the American people hold no ill will against you. We seek peace above all. But we will not hesitate to defend our people, our borders, or servicemen and women anywhere in the world, at any moment by any means. Thank you and be well."

Following the President's address, Fox News shifted to a split screen. On the left, a repeating series of images: cars lining up outside of the Pentagon; shoppers stocking up on groceries and water at Walmart, members of Congress hurrying to meetings, large crowds delighting in an American flag burning on the streets of Islamabad.

On the right side of the television screen, the image was more static but far more local: a slow pan of the abortion clinic and a phalanx of law officers armed to the teeth in the parking lot where not ten minutes earlier Bev Gilliam and her coterie ruled.

Omar faced his clinic mates and threw up his hands. "So what are we doing here?"

Penny held up the backpack. "Okay, look. Give me that abortion and everyone can leave. That's my final offer."

Penny figured it this way. With her legs strung up in the chair and all those medical devices sticking out of her vagina, she wouldn't be in any shape to stop anyone from leaving anyway. Might as well let them go now and save the headache. "I got you, doc. One hostage is as good as a million in my book."

Emmett Jessup tugged on Jimmy's hand. At first, Jimmy wasn't sure why the boy was so insistent, but then it dawned on him.

"Penny wait," Jimmy said. "Why don't you ask Emmett Jessup if he wants a brother or sister."

Emmett Jessup smiled.

"Because this baby is fucked. I messed it up with the drugs *you* gave me. I'm not raising a retard. I don't give a shit what the rest of you do. Except you, doc, you're coming with me."

Omar tried to fashion a quick response, but his attention was drawn to the television. The split screen was gone, replaced by a full-face photo of Omar himself (snapped during a sub-committee meeting at the most recent plenary session of the National Abortion Federation).

Said the announcer, "we now have confirmation of the potential terrorist at the abortion clinic. He is Palestinian, Omar Farooq. Our sources tell us he has confessed to police that he has a bomb and is holding an undetermined number of people hostage, including a young child, according to eyewitnesses."

"That's not true!" Omar shouted at the screen.

The blonde anchor with the low-cut blouse and a practiced look of concern reported, "We don't know at this time if this incident is tied to or has been prompted in any way by the presidential announcement of war with Pakistan. We do know that local, state and federal police, as well as Homeland Security and the FBI, have surrounded the building and negotiations have begun. We do not know anything about the bomb, if there is a bomb, and what potential destructive force it may hold."

The group looked at Omar with new eyes. All except Penny Lean, who didn't give a shit what the TV said.

Penny bent down to Emmett Jessup and planted a kiss on his forehead. She wiped a tear away from his cheek and tried to push his lips into a smile, but it wouldn't stay. "You know your mama always knows what to do? Well, this time, she doesn't, honey. She screwed up a lot. And don't do drugs, okay? You just remember I love you and always have."

Penny faced Omar. "Doc, you got sixty seconds to make up your mind, or this bomb goes off. Got it? Sixty, fifty-nine, fifty-eight."

Behind her veil, Shivana was deeply moved by Penny's words to her little boy. Shivana saw in Penny for the first time, not an angry, ignorant, petulant angst-ridden American teenager, but as a woman struggling in a world stacked against women and double-stacked against single mothers. "Penny, we are sisters. I pray for you to come into the proverbial tent with me where we will confide. I know your pain because I have lived it. I know your desire because I feel it."

"I have no idea what the fuck *proverbial* means, and I'm not going into any tent made of that shit. Forty-four, forty-three, forty-two."

God have mercy on my soul, thought Omar. He calculated his options. He could perform the abortion pronto as Penny requested, but then he risked a bullet from Naomi, the crazy Jewess. Or he could do nothing and prompt Penny to set off the bomb, which might harm all the assembled.

Omar wondered most when this crooked spin might come to rest. And then he realized. He himself had set the spin in motion — accepting the bomb, swinging with Sandra Lee, abandoning Shivana, corrupting the word of Mohammad to mean something other than peace and mercy. He was responsible for tilting the spin, and he was the only one who could right the topsy-turvy.

Shivana had been wrong, or at least partially wrong when declaring it all about *gift*. It is about *sacrifice*, or partially about sacrifice. They do flip the same coin. And Omar felt ready to sacrifice, for the first time truly, perhaps. Not for creed or carpet but for the humans he loved most, Shivana and Sandra Lee and the two little ones they carried.

On that sentiment, rode in an option Omar had yet to consider, but first, he had some business to attend to.

"Thirty-eight, thirty-seven, thirty-six," Penny counted down.

"Shivana, my lovely crown of a wife, please keep your baby, and live the life you want with whomever you choose. Just speak to your child kindly of me, that's all I ask so that she might imagine with sweetness the man who brought you to womanhood."

"Thirty, twenty-nine, twenty-eight."

Omar continued, "And Sandra Lee, keep in your heart an image of us dancing. Striding with you completed my life, sacrilegious as that might be to say."

"Twenty-one, twenty, nineteen."

"And Ethan, please take care of Shivana and continue to be the kind man that I know you are, kind and wise. The world needs more of you."

"Twelve, eleven, ten..."

"And Jimmy, I don't know who you are and what you are doing here, but you look like a nice young man so please take care and think twice about drugs. Try other paths to happiness. Yoga and wheat grass come to mind. And Emmett, your name means *truth*, just so you know."

Penny: Four, three, two...

That said, Omar Farooq, son of an apostate, grandson of a believer, follower of Islam and student of medicine, lunged toward the little boy and grabbed the backpack before Penny could startle with a protest, let alone react.

Omar dashed madly into Examining Room North. He locked the door behind him so Penny couldn't follow him. He fell to his knees in the far corner by the extractor. Panting like a desert refugee, he hugged the bomb on his belly.

He remembered that as the Israelis attacked, his grandfather bent to pray. On bended knees, a single bullet entered his brain. Maybe it was a Palestinian bullet, maybe an Israeli, but it matters not. He was murdered on his palms in prayer. Who deserves to be butchered upon their knees?

If someone were to be the victim of this implement of death, it would be he. God's merciful hand rolls us out into Rumi's sea and leaves us to swim in the direction of our choosing. This bomb he now hugged? Maybe not Omar's creation, but his responsibility. One must take responsibility for our actions. And now Omar was doing just that, and if his legacy were to be strung together by the plastic and wires of the bomb intended for death and destruction, so be it.

What a strange loop in which we live.

Suddenly the fear slipped away, and peace overcame him. Complete surrender. He slipped to his knees for the 24,517th time and for the first time he got it. He understood. Ritual may kneel you on a rug of devotion, but righteousness surrounds you with a blanket of peace.

THIRTY-FIVE

In the waiting room, Emmett Jessup tugged at his mommy's sleeve. When she didn't respond, he balled up his fist and punched her in the thigh.

Penny turned impatiently. "Not now. Mommy's under a lot of pressure."

She wished for another way, she did, but she was in a shitload of trouble. They would never let her have her baby now after this whole bomb episode, even if it was the Arab's fault. They never would allow her to keep Emmett Jessup.

It always landed on her, fault. Took a big fat dump right on her head. And so better end it right here and hurt nobody else. That's the least she could do on this earth. Keep the damage to a minimum, wow, what a life goal, huh?

The bomb wasn't in the backpack, anyway. That was just to fool them all.

The bricks of death were strapped tightly in a nylon vest with a shitload of pockets under her floppy orange sweatshirt, duck taped right up against her would-be fucked up baby. Right there, about four inches beneath her heart that Jesus never saved and right atop her aching liver with its degenerating cells. She showed everyone so they could see. There wasn't gonna be no salvation for Penny, not in this life. So go out with a big bang, what the fuck. Let 'em splash her picture on the front page as the chick who took out an abortion clinic and saved all those babies. When you got no hope, no power, no future, you blow shit up. Who wouldn't?

Penny's only regret was leaving Emmett Jessup. It was a mighty big one, a whole heart's worth. But she'd be no good as a mother in prison. Wasn't much of one outside. That Naomi Weiner-Gluckstein lady would take care of him better anyways. She wasn't so bad after all, that lady, even if she had fucked up Penny's whole life. Everyone makes small mistakes. Her little angel deserved someone better. Someone sane and sober, two things Penny was never gonna be.

With her finger poised and her eyes locked on the hostages, Penny Lean, adopted daughter of a father molester and a mother denier, doer of drugs and sometimes tricks, backtracked toward Examining Room North at the far end of the clinic.

Harlen jumped on the impulse to minister, to salve the wounds of a pained young lady, because *this* is what Jesus would do.

He cried out, "Penny, please don't. Jesus loves you." He felt his words hollow and untrue, and so he tried again. "I love you."

Penny startled. "For what?"

"For it all."

He reached out his hand, eyes locked on hers. He summoned all his practice as a preacher of faith to deliver his message of hope.

Penny dismissed the preacher's notion with a wave of her hand. "I believe in paradise, Pastor, I really do. There's just no way I'm ever gonna get there."

"Funny you should say that because I've sort of changed my position on that. I no longer believe our lives should be dedicated to getting to paradise. Jesus wants us to dedicate our lives to bringing paradise to earth. Help each other. That's all we can do in the end."

Penny rolled her eyes. "*Now* you tell me."

Harlen got down on his proposal knee. "I dedicate myself here and now in front of all these witnesses and God almighty that I'll do everything in my power to help you, henceforth, so help me Jesus. Come on, sister, let's find you a plot of paradise right here on earth."

Penny let out the chuckle. "You don't get it, pops. I live in a hell inside my mind."

With those words, Penny continued to Examining Room North.

Naomi, her hand heavy with the pistol, found Harlen's hurried homily quite moving. He had phrased it so lucidly, with elegance. A way with words, that man, even if a tad Pollyannaish. Maybe Pastor Spridgen wasn't such a bastard after all.

Furthermore, the dawning irony was that Naomi had come to believe in that very same paradise of which he spoke—even while training a .38 loaded revolver on her only offspring. Resistance begets resistance. It's love and understanding we need. Positive reinforcement, sympathy, empathy, kindness, forgiveness. These words crossed Naomi's lips in a stutter, like the first words of a foreign language. Through the long years, Naomi had often wondered when she might reach the limit of her ardor. Well, she had her answer. *Right now.*

So Naomi Weiner-Gluckstein, the grandmother with a mane of untamable red hair, the only daughter of devout secularists with a vestige Holocaust mentality, the abortion rights crusader and champion of countless worthy causes (and wouldn't there always be worthy causes) slipped the safety on and slid the handgun into the back pocket of her fair-trade blue jeans. It was the first time in a long time she could remember changing her position, standing down. Retreating. But it didn't feel that way, it felt like flying away.

"Penelope," said Naomi, "you are a flower waiting to bloom. Please believe that the frosty spring is lifting and the summer of your existence is near."

Penny wrinkled her nose with puzzlement. "You never talked to me like that before, so I'm figuring you're putting me on."

"I'm not, please believe me."

"Either way, too late."

Naomi had learned one question from her parents, one that stayed with her forever. She asked it now. "But why?"

Penny didn't need time to think. She just shrugged and said, "Hardwired. What can I do?"

Penny continued her forced march backward toward the examining room. With her eyes, she pushed Emmett Jessup toward Naomi.

Emmett Jessup wasn't happy. "Mama, don't go. Me love you."

Penny couldn't help but hesitate.

"I know my little man. Mama loves you. Never forget that. *Never.* When you're older, get a tattoo that says *Mama* on it, okay? With a big heart with a crack down the middle, 'cause that's how I feel."

She opened the door to Examining Room North and planted one foot inside.

"Wait," said Ethan. "Stop right there."

"Who the hell are you, anyway? I never figured that one out," Penny asked.

"Me? I'm Naomi's husband, Ethan. There has got to be a solution to this."

"Talk fast."

Ethan did everything he could to pull it all together, to regain the lucidity he had enjoyed during ToE, but this time to save lives. "Okay here's what we know. We are all here in this room, every one of us. Look at the connections, each of us connected to each other in some crazy, totally irrational way. Can this circle of connections be random, what are the odds? My wife, your brother, the preacher, Sandra Lee, Shivana, Emmett Jessup, Jimmy, all of us here, and you. A circle of interactions so tightly wound that if we existed in the quantum world, we would be a tightly packed molecule."

"What is this, science class?"

"And if this isn't a coincidence then what? What if it's our synchrodestiny? There must be purpose for our intertwining. If there is purpose, then who are we to destroy any of it, most of all ourselves?"

"What have you been smokin'," Penny said.

"What if, like the preacher says, our purpose is simply to take care of each other? All of us, everyone here. The universe could be trying to make that easy by bringing us together in tight little bundles that give us the opportunity to do so. Did you know that most of the mass of any object is not contained in its particles, but in the intense energy it takes to keep the object in one piece? All of us here, together, form a single entity bound by that mass. Round and round we go, our little molecule in this cell of a city, in the body earth, traveling through the eternal cosmos."

Penny looked to the crowd to confirm her suspicion. "Dropping acid."

"Why do we desperately seek certainty when God lives in the mystery, through the mystery? If the universe cares so much to take the time to put us all together, shouldn't that be a sign, even if we don't understand it, for us to at least try?"

Ethan thought about the E_8 and the nanoparticles he had spent his life chasing. What was the purpose of it all? To find the truth? What was the value of a truth that lasted no more than a million millionth of a second or existed in theory alone? Truth should last forever. Truth takes form in the flesh and blood of the sentient. It's revealed in the beauty and workings of an intelligent universe made manifest.

"We are truth in the flesh," Ethan said with triumphant emphasis.

Penny scratched her head with the remote. Everyone backed away a step, fearing she might press that button while trying to figure out what the hell Ethan was talking about. She nodded slowly. "You make sense in some strange way I can't figure out."

Ethan smiled. "Good. Then why don't you put down the remote? Let's work this out."

Penny considered the offer. Working it out made sense for the scientist, maybe all of them. But then she remembered, "You got no clue about the dark side, Professor."

"We all do. We're comprised of light and dark, each one of us, just like you. We couldn't exist as just light or dark. It is the dance between the two that allows for our very existence."

"Maybe you're right." She sighed. "Maybe this is all wrong."

Ethan smiled at this rare triumph, and for a moment he thought his recent misfortunes were worth it all, for this. "So let's work together. All of us."

Penny said, "But you got me thinking, what if our purpose is to *die* together? Maybe that's the strange coincidence that brought us all here. If light and dark live together then dark's gotta win sometimes, too, ain't that right?"

Ethan paused to consider Penny's well-reasoned response because logically she was correct. Dark did indeed reign supreme sometimes, as both physics and history testify. Hadn't it won with him?

"You have a point," Ethan stipulated, "but we also have been blessed with the capacity to change everything. We can't change the past, but we can forgive ourselves and begin again, right now, at this moment. If God recreates the world at every moment, why can't we? And if we can change the future, doesn't that trump the existence of evil and give us all a little of the power of God?"

Penny wasn't buying it. "I got bad in my bones, twisted DNA. Sorry, professor, this evil ain't going nowhere."

With that, Penny blew a kiss to Emmett Jessup. She checked inside Examining Room South where Dr. Omar Farooq cowered over a backpack he thought contained a bomb – and continued to the far side of the clinic and Examining Room North, where she could be alone with the explosives hugging her like a rapist.

She slumped on the examining chair and prayed for this *motherfuckingremote* to work. A tinge of regret worked its way up her legs, but she pushed it out hard.

This wasn't nothing like she dreamed it would be back when her suburban bed overflowed with cuddly dolls and fluffy pillows. Back when heaven was as sure as shit and hell was a grainy, far away abstraction, like a birth mother. Somewhere along the way, heaven rode off with Santa, leaving nothing but visions of hell dancing in her head. If at this very moment someone would open the examining room door to give Penny a shred of evidence that she might be freed from the guilt she carried, then *here, take this remote, I'm flying out of here like a bird.* But she knew this death hall well. She had been here previously, even before her last dismal attempt at blowing this joint to bits. Here, carrying the love child of her very own father. Here, laying that child to rest, Jesus save his soul. There was no atoning for that sin. The worst part was having to act so hard just to keep from melting.

Abandoned in the waiting room, Ethan, Naomi, Harlen, Sandra Lee, and Jimmy looked at each other with unbelieving eyes.

"What do we do now?" asked Sandra Lee.

The answer dawned collectively.

Naomi grabbed Emmett Jessup's hand so tight the boy flew off the ground like Peter Pan on the way to Neverland. With her free hand, she grabbed the pistol falling out of her pocket.

Sandra Lee and Harlen rushed out of the clinic together in a clutch, just as they danced down the wedding aisle. Shivana pushed Ethan out in front of her and gained nanoseconds as she fled. Jimmy brought up the rear and scanned the waiting room to ensure everyone was out.

One by one, they emerged squarely into the gun sights of the waiting armies of local, state and federal agencies and a few private military contractors to boot. All steely-eyed and barricaded behind parked cars. Men with helmets and Rambo weapons, camouflage outfits and shields.

Even in the afternoon sun, the clinic hostages met with spotlights enough to blind them. Sandra Lee cupped her hands to her mouth and shouted, "Don't shoot! We're Americans!"

Just in case they didn't get it, Sandra Lee threw her hands in the air, as did everyone else. Except Naomi. She had promised herself she would never surrender to *the Man*, whatever the circumstances.

Being a novice handgun owner, Naomi didn't realize she was still brandishing a loaded handgun.

"Drop the weapon and down on your knees!" came the bullhorn shout.

"What?"

"Drop the weapon now!"

Naomi heard the rustle of rifles and steel of machine guns. She glanced at the pistol in her hand and down at Emmett locked in her grasp like a kidnap victim.

"Oh, sorry," she said. "This isn't what it seems."

She placed the .38 on the ground. "My bad."

"Now release the boy!"

"The boy? No way. He's my grandson."

The rifles trained higher.

Ethan called out, "Naomi, please!"

She drew Emmett Jessup tighter because you don't find someone after searching all your life and then let them go at the first sign of resistance.

"Over my dead body," she said.

Ethan cupped his hands and shouted, "Naomi, don't make a mistake that you'll regret the rest of your life."

The words stung Naomi because she understood the double meaning, even if Ethan didn't. The fact that Ethan could so clearly see the pending consequences made Naomi think twice.

An officer stepped up with a semi-automatic weapon that looked mighty powerful and accurate. He aimed it so close to Naomi's nose she could smell the cold metal.

"Lady, this is your last chance."

Emmett Jessup quizzically looked up.

Naomi bit her lip. "Let's try to help your mom, okay?"

But before she could relent, a team of officers bore down on her. One thug knocked her to the ground and planted a knee in the small of her back.

A female officer swooped in and snatched Emmett Jessup.

"Grandma!" he shouted, his little arm outstretched. "No leave me!"

The officer smothered Emmett Jessup's face in her chest. She hustled him toward a black car with windows of tinted black. They locked him inside the blackness, but they couldn't keep him from pressing his face against the glass to watch his grandma's face squished against the pavement while bits of gravel punctured her cheek.

On went the handcuffs, tight. The knee came off, and Naomi was able to catch her breath. She cried for Emmett Jessup, but she couldn't see the boy anywhere.

"Fascist pigs," she spit.

A few paces away Ethan pleaded with an officer. "Please, there's no time.

The bomb."

A police voice thundered, "The Palestinian's bomb?"

"I don't know whose bomb. But he's the one who's gonna die. He tried to save us."

"Who? The terrorist?"

"He's *not* a terrorist. He's a doctor. Doctor Omar Farooq. A good man."

Sandra Lee had to chime in. "He has the heart of a lion."

Shivana added, "Actually, he is a big coward, couldn't hurt a fly. That's why you have to help him!"

Inside Examining Room South, Omar entertained second thoughts. He cocked an ear and heard nothing but silence in the waiting room while he was in here alone like some schmuck willing to lose his own life in order to save others. Why hadn't she hit the trigger yet? Why was he considering martyrdom anyway? He considered opening the window and throwing the bomb outside, or leaving the bomb in the examining room and crawling out himself. He rejected both ideas. If he threw the bomb and it hurt someone, he'd be guilty of murder by Western eyes. If he crawled out the window, he'd be accused of escaping like a dog with his tail between his legs by Eastern eyes. It wasn't his innocence he was protecting, but the reputation of the child inside of Sandra Lee and the one within Shivana, should the two women decide to keep them. He even entertained the hope that if he martyred himself here, perhaps it might inspire his two lovers to keep their progeny. Since he was making wishes, perhaps Sandra Lee's child might carry his name. A long shot, but aren't we all seeking redemption on Desperation Street.

What the hell was Penny waiting for anyway? God, Omar hoped she got the remote working. All she had to do was reverse the batteries and switch the bomb on.

Oh, shit, she had mentioned the batteries earlier, but she didn't mention the switch.

Omar unzipped the backpack to find the answer.

Only problem was, *there was no bomb in the backpack.* Not at all. Just a few bricks and a stack of $20 bills with a note attached that read:

Penny, thanks for the loan and sorry for the late payback. Life's a bitch. I owe you one. Your partner in crazy – Arnie.

If Omar didn't have the bomb, then –

And that's when the bomb blew. At 3:16 p.m. to be precise, designed or otherwise.

Shards of glass punctured Sandra Lee's white skin. The concussion knocked Ethan down. His head slammed against the pavement. A gash above his eye drew blood that ran down his forehead and into his eyes.

Shivana's palms shredded open as she skidded along the asphalt. A flying chunk of concrete hit Jimmy square in the chest and nailed him against the police car.

The blast shattered storefront windows five deep. Naomi felt a sliver of glass puncture her ribs. Harlen sat dazed with a ringing in his ear that turned off his thoughts.

The ground roiled like an earthquake. Hunks of shopping center concrete rained down on everyone. Echoes returned again and again and then softened to a background hum.

In the explosion's dust, Shivana and Sandra Lee found each other.

"Omar" they cried in unison.

Shivana immediately mourned his life and the life they shared. She flashed on the time when they were lab students together at the Tehran University, and they laughed until they cried over the silliness of the West and the foolishness of the East. She remembered fondly how he returned to her dusty village to ask for her hand in marriage and stood up to speak on behalf of her brother when the members of the local Sharia committee deemed his women's clothing store offensive. She recalled his tender and brilliant medical care after her niece's leg turned gangrenous following a malicious push from the back of a motorcycle because her ankle showed in the wind. How many nights had Omar stayed up with Shivana helping her study for her physics courses despite the baffling mathematics? How sweet were the rare times they laid in bed on some Sunday afternoon watching old Iranian movies from the 1950s? "Oh, Omar," she wept.

Sandra Lee mourned the brief time she had shared with Omar. It was but a scant few seconds of a lifetime, and she hadn't appreciated him nearly enough. She reminisced about the sweaty afternoon dance practices. Always with a smile, that man, and a kind instruction. She blushed upon the vision of his hardened naked body, his loins on fire and a singular purpose informing his sparkling eyes. She remembered how handy he was around the house, very good with plumbing and carpentry chores, a characteristic she had never known in a man, and boy did it come in handy. Most of all she remembered the magic of being in his arms, the thrill of release from his twirl, the surprise of the return to his embrace and hot breath upon her cheek. His chest was firm like an immovable ballast, heaving with desire. "Oh, Omar," she wept.

Shivana and Sandra Lee's grieving ended promptly when a sooty, coughing, staggering, stumbling Omar emerged from the clinic, a refugee from near death.

His fine shirt was in tatters, and he walked with a limp thanks to the loss of one of his beloved Italian loafers.

He fell to his knees, partly from the lingering loss of equilibrium and partly to thank God for saving him. Had it not been for the distance between the two examining rooms and the steel-reinforced walls, it may not have been so.

Law enforcement officers came from every direction, some with clubs, some with fists, some with canisters of gas aiming for his face. They gang tackled him, pulled his hair, yanked his feet, throttled his neck, cuffed his hands.

"He's innocent," Sandra Lee shouted.

"He tried to save us," Shivana said.

"He's a hero," Harlen insisted.

The officers drew Omar to his feet. He had just enough breath left to utter a single phrase. "Save her." And one more short breath to add, "I am innocent."

"You have the right to remain silent..."

Ethan tried to interven, but he was manhandled to a waiting car.

Sandra Lee used her smile and a healthy dose of white privilege to disarm an officer and made a dash for Omar.

"Don't say a word!" she yelled as she ran. "They *will* use it against you."

Immediately she was clothes-lined by a uniformed officer and landed on the pavement hard.

Naomi and Jimmy Lean found each other because they both locked eyes on the smoldering clinic with a shared hope.

"Penny." Naomi cried for the daughter off her rocker who was so hard to love, and that's why Naomi loved her. Naomi had finally found someone who shared the same crazy and thereby presented the best reason to heal herself.

"Penny," Jimmy whispered because his sister of secrets was his flesh and blood even if they had been adopted. Their kinship came from growing up under the same roof, enduring the same punishments, resisting the same tyranny. Jimmy banked on Penny's hardcore because from it he drew the strength to persevere. And for the record, she never hurt anyone. Never. Not a hair on anyone's head, even though she had license to, what with the way people heaped abuse after abuse on her. Fuck them all. It's easy to be kind when kindness raises you, but saints arise from the ranks of the tortured.

Dathan Lean in the back of the crowd heard the name and called to his son yonder. "Penny?"

"Penny's inside." Jimmy wept.

Dathan wished for the earth to swallow him up for he knew his own failings were much to blame for the tragedy unfolding before him now. Had he only been able to curb his appetites. Margie Lean cried in her hands. She had not done enough to rescue her daughter when rescuing was still within the realm of possibility. She had stood by and done nothing when the crimes were committed. For this, she grieved the most.

Naomi and Jimmy watched as the bomb squad entered the building. Their lumbering outfits made them look like astronauts walking the moon. The fire department sent a ladder lurching into the sky to douse the smoldering roof.

Jimmy and Naomi surveyed the settling dust hoping beyond all hope that Penny might appear. They prayed for her as they were hustled away by the authorities for triage, security debriefing, trauma counseling. They waited for word as the nameless and faceless medical workers wrapped blankets around them and doctors peered into their eyes with tiny flashlights. No miracles. No Penny found. Not this time. Not in this universe.

Not on this spin.

BOOK IV

"Everything that can happen does."
— Postulate of quantum mechanics

THIRTY-SIX

27 Years Later

Who needs churches, synagogues or mosques when you have the crashing waves of the Pacific Ocean? Is not the beach God's true sanctuary? Love her only instruction? That's the way Gabrielle Peni Farooq felt about the sparkling ocean. Underneath her flowing saffron wedding sari, Gabrielle squished her toes in the moist sand of Half Moon Bay and laughed because everyone should laugh on their wedding day.

Her parents felt a little differently about the sandy venue. Her mother, the gracefully aging Shivana, had wanted the wedding ceremony to take place in a Wine Country vineyard in Sonoma County, more specifically a Champagne vineyard. That's only because, during a mother and daughter tell-all, Shivana slipped the bubbly story of Chicago and the orgasmic conception inspired by a bottle (or two) of Gloria Ferrer.

"I hadn't visited Chicago before, haven't visited since. But, my dear delight, the Night of Destiny is worth one thousand months," Shivana Farooq told her daughter.

Gabrielle's adoptive father, Omar (who, by no coincidence, had been married to Shivana at the time of Gabrielle's birth) wanted the ceremony to be held somewhere more official.

"Why not a mosque, and if not, then at least officiated by an Imam?" Omar said.

Gabrielle loved her father. From his lips, she had learned the verses of the Qur'an, love songs from Persia, the aspirations of the world's great philosophers, enough to keep Gabrielle up at night with unbounded wonder. She understood his position, a man from a fractured homeland with an iron faith trying to succeed in a foreign country, making some big mistakes along the way, and ultimately suffering the pain of Penny's tragic death a few months before Gabrielle's birth.

As it went, the Palo Alto abortion clinic bombing story lost traction once the authorities assured the public and press that the culprit wasn't an Islamoterrorist (which overnight had become a non-hyphenated word), just a good old red-blooded American psycho-abortion terrorist who ended up being the only fatality. This was apparently a far less interesting sort of bombing, and so the story only survived three days on the inside pages of the local *San Francisco Chronicle* and *San Jose Mercury News*, and the major media outlets drifted away after 24 hours. Fox ditched the story after midnight of the bombing choosing to aim their broadband artillery at the near-cataclysmic events in Pakistan.

Three years later, after a six-week trial, the jury returned from their sequestered conference room to render a verdict on Omar. "Not guilty!" the foreman announced on count one: Conspiracy to Conduct Terrorism.

Omar's defense attorneys had demonstrated clear volition on the part of the victim, attested to by each of *Clinic Seven*, as they were called. And the witnesses (except the toddler Emmett Jessup) passionately testified with exacting detail to Omar's heroic attempts to save them all at his very own dear expense.

"Guilty!" the foreman continued on count two: Possessing an Explosive Device, for which Omar was sentenced to a two-year suspended sentence and stripped of his medical license.

Young Gabrielle grew up hearing about the crime, witnessing Omar often lost in thought, invoking the name of Penny on his carpet of remorse. As for his lost medical license, Omar had grown tired of being the maligned abortion doctor in town. Paranoia is far more endurable when imagined.

"I'm selling the clinic," Omar announced one day.

"And what are you going to do?" asked Shivana.

He did a little shuffle and announced, "*Omar's Dance Studio.* I found a vacant space on El Camino Real. Perfetto."

Omar was lucky enough to ride a wave of renewed interest in ballroom dancing. Seven years into the venture he brought on a partner and renamed the enterprise *Dance Along with Omar and Sandra Lee.* Eventually, Omar became a judge on a televised ballroom dance competition program and his notoriety helped him gain Senatorial support for US citizenship. He brought his ailing father to Palo Alto where father and son patched up their embittered relationship and the patriarch lived the last years of his life in comfort under the care of a passel of Jewish and Indian doctors, praise be to Allah.

"You see how great America is?" Omar said.

He was indeed grateful and proud to be an American. He had changed, evolved — emerged, he might say, but never for one day did he feel anything but a stranger in a strange land. He yearned for a country that existed far away, over an ocean and back in time. He could never return, not like it was, not like he had been. And he mourned for the loss for the country in the aching way that only expatriates and fugitives can understand. The loss kept him quietly, secretly, in mourning despite the success and comforts that surrounded him.

On the point of a mosque for the wedding venue, Gabrielle had to gently stand her ground. "I love you dad, but a mosque just isn't my thing," she explained with a kiss.

It was not an aversion to the religion, quite the contrary. She loved all things Islam and, in particular, Sufi poetry, for which she gained her Masters of Arts from the Abbasi School of Islamic Studies at Stanford. After not making any living whatsoever with a Sufi poetry degree, Gabrielle spent time at the Weizmann Institute of Science, earning a Ph.D. in her second love, ultra-theoretical physics. She stayed in Rehovot, Israel with her birth father's relatives, an eccentric but luminous bunch. The confluence of Gabrielle's two chosen disciplines (along with a year-long trip around the world to study the humor of God) spawned her very unusual thesis *God is Laughing: The Ecstasy of Super String Theory,* which won her a Fresnel Prize for most outstanding thesis and spurred a three-book series, now the curriculum for graduate-level courses in over 1,500 universities (though her favorite work was teaching poetry to inner-city and suburban school children alike).

Her mosque objection was also made with deference and respect to her birth father, Ethan Weiner-Gluckstein. Gabrielle had spent quite literally every Friday night with the gentle, brilliant man and his fiery redheaded wife celebrating Shabbat with two candles, a glass of wine, and a fractal of honey bread. They shared stories from the Torah, ramblings about the intersection of Kabbalah and quantum physics, and hours upon hours of discussing Tikkun Olam, and the best ways to repair the world.

By the time of Gabrielle's birth, Ethan had recovered enough from the public humiliation of the ToE debacle to return to work. Despite a kind and sincere invitation (from El Presidente of Stanford himself) for Ethan to resume his tenured position, Ethan decided on an untenured post at San Francisco State University. He spent his time working with students rather than neutrinos and gravitational waves, but he never gave up his quest for a Theory of Everything. Nights and weekends, coffee breaks and holidays, he devoted his time reworking the E_8 equation this way and that. He even resorted to ingesting psychedelics in an attempt to find fertile creative ground in which to plant his ideas. No luck (though he did spend one blissful day rollerblading in Dolores Park).

Ethan felt he owed the world something, starting with an apology. If only people would listen. He tried desperately to get on television shows and submitted articles to popular science journals. Rejection upon rejection. Producers and editors urged him to move on, but he couldn't. He started a blog, but nobody read it.

For Ethan, the elusive theory was his only road to redemption. His stubbornness brought him ridicule and derision.

"Difficult things take a long time, impossible things a little longer," said Naomi.

Above her freckled breast, Naomi had emblazoned a tattoo of a fractured heart and the single word *Penny,* scripted in a font stolen right from the abs of Latino gang homies. When she wore low-cut blouses, the tattoo endeared her to the Spanish-speaking parents who cared enough to enroll their kids in the charter elementary school Naomi had opened in East Palo Alto. Within several years, she had won numerous awards and commendations for a graduation rate that was 52 percent higher than nearby schools with similar socio-economic profiles. *Penny Elementary* was golden, and educators from around the country came in to study its success. Naomi still occasionally marched at protest rallies around the Bay Area but mostly for nostalgia's sake. There was too much work to be done to squander valuable time subsumed in a mass of like-minded people filming themselves. Not that there wasn't still plenty wrong with the world.

"It's a never-ending battle against the powers that be and their imposed greed-based hierarchies that cause the great imbalances in the world."

The righteous shtick hadn't changed, but now she laughed at herself quite often. And she gave up on all that organic crap. Except for fresh vegetables and no high-fructose corn syrup. LOCALLY grown only, *por favor.* And of course no meat, but that goes without saying. "If it can run away, let it."

Deep down, Naomi spent an inordinate amount of time reliving the brief few months she had spent with Penny and remembering how her daughter had brought her so much happiness. Like peas in a pod, they were, better yet, two matchsticks in a tinderbox. But what fun they had. Like all survivors of suicides, Naomi ran the scenarios through her head that might have prevented Penny's tragic end. If she had just kept the child when she was young, if she had recognized the signs of mental illness just a little earlier. Naomi had been so blinded by her causes, her beliefs, she hadn't seen the needs of the one person who needed her the most, the one problem that needed her truest attention, purest intention. Forget the Happy Meals, let's work on being happy. Sometimes at night, Naomi pulled out the final pack of Pall Malls that Penny had hidden in the house. Four stale cigarettes left in the pocket-crushed pack. That's right, cigarettes, because the smell and crunch of tobacco reminded Naomi of Penny. Penny found. Not Penny lost.

Closer to home, Gabrielle's birth mother, Shivana, had held her head high upon her return to Stanford following the ToE retraction. She earned her Ph.D. in nuclear fusion, first in her class, with baby Gabrielle breastfeeding while mother studied thermal power production and the properties of deuterium until delirious. Shivana's post-grad research on aneutronic fusion, the Z-pinch phenomenon, and, most importantly, her contributions to the mechanics of inertial confinement fusion implosions helped launch the nuclear fusion industry.

The promise of nuclear fusion for humanity was nothing short of miraculous as Shivana tirelessly explained. "Fusion is an unlimited energy source requiring mere drops of ocean water, costing nothing and leaving nothing to clean up afterward. It allows humankind to unshackle itself from the heavy chains of the extraction, distribution, and consumption of fossil fuels. A cup of water to shutter the coal mines, a bucket to save the rain forests, a barrel to save the oceans, two barrels to reverse global warming."

When Big Oil bought all the patents just to shelve them, Shivana earned her law degree and worked on the team that took the monopoly to the United States Supreme Court.

Big Oil won 5-4 . They always did, but things would change one day. Shivana was sure because they already had.

"Look at me if you need proof. A tentmaker's daughter arguing a case before the United States Supreme Court in hopes of saving the discovery of the millennium."

A smattering of hubris had returned, but, hey, when you're good, you're good.

With the permission of the Iranian government, Shivana had visited her home village, where the tribal elders hailed her as a returning hero, a Saladin of science. She wept at the feet of her mother and kissed the grave of her father. She blessed the heads of the children belonging to her brother and sister. She spoke words never forgotten but never uttered since her departure west.

Upon returning to America, she began a non-profit organization to put a halt to female genital mutilation, once and for all. Some things cannot be allowed to stand.

Through it all, Shivana taught the growing Gabrielle three languages, chemical classification, and nuclear numbers, as well as how to count. She taught her daughter how to count things like lucky stars and happy coincidences, the joys of learning, everyone, and the many reasons to be a strong and confident woman. And she taught her daughter that not everything that can be counted counts, and not everything that counts can be counted. And Gabrielle understood.

In between all the busy work, Shivana longed for Ethan's incomparable mind and his rare tenderness. Her pining remained unrequited. So much had conspired against them through the years — religion, society, family, and the angry anti-ToE tide that had swept them apart and marooned them on distant islands. Thankfully she had learned to love her husband again, and it was easy, Omar being the kind and caring man that he was. Shivana thanked heaven for having not one, but two fathers for her daughter. Both loved Gabrielle so. For this, Shivana was eternally grateful. But how she missed exploring mathematical and theoretical ideas with Ethan. And the gaze of his trusting eyes, she missed that, too. Life brings love, love brings loss, loss brings longing. Still, she felt something was karmically right about her loss of Ethan, a mortgage on the house they never were allowed to build.

As for the music at the wedding?

"No brainer!" Gabrielle announced with her infectious enthusiasm. "My favorite accordion player in the whole wide world."

The now grown-up Emmett Jessup Weiner-Gluckstein Lean had

garnered the nickname *the Irish Rastafarian* thanks to ropes of red dreads spilling down to the small of his back. The dreads wrapped him like a shawl; he had refused to cut his hair from the day his mother died. He screamed like a banshee when approached with scissors. By age five, Ethan and Naomi had given up trying, and the topic was hardly brought up through his teen years. Both parents honored Emmett Jessup's commitment, though Naomi had no choice but to become Palo Alto's lice eradication expert in residence (petroleum jelly, vinegar, dish detergent, and plastic wrap).

For Emmett Jessup, if not an accordion, a ukulele. If not a ukulele, a flute. And if no flute, then knees, a butter knife and the flippity-floppity of bare knuckles with the flash of a gold ring. Spin the eyes, whoopty-do, set 'em up, get them home.

His adopted father's eccentricities somehow gave Emmett Jessup full reign to roam and nurture his silly muse, as all silly muses should be. Yesterday a gymnast, circus performer, henna artist, barefoot peddler of jokes. Today a juggler, magician, lover, goodwill ambassador, and muffler mechanic. He vibed at every Burning Man since age twelve and celebrated his bar mitzvah with a dozen Glow Sticks circling his neck.

Emmett Jessup chose not to tattoo himself with his mother's name, her final request. She sang to him often from her residence in the cosmos, with a smoky, gravelly voice. Her songs came at the most unexpected moments, like when he sobbed on a curb flattened by the *weight* as he remembered his mother calling it. Or inviting the autumn breeze to slip inside his jacket. Or suffering a bellyache of hunger because his mind wouldn't let him eat. At moments like these, sometimes in his left ear, sometimes the right, and sometimes in *simplyholycrapping* quadraphonic stereo, his departed Mamma Mia raising her holy voice and howled a belly whopper of a tune that only he could hear.

Emmett Jessup did take to wearing a lucky penny around his neck on a piano wire. More and more lately, he touched it whenever the unmentionable darkness descended.

"Mama!" he'd cry when her songs faded away, but it didn't bring her back.

Now on the beach under the halo, at the wedding of a girl and a boy he had known from before they were born, he fiddled on the accordion while the last guests arrived. A spritzy tune that hobnobbed around D major, the penny warm against his throat and the strains of his mother's voice returning.

Gabrielle had envisioned a wedding of one big circle in the round with dancing and singing.

And here it was.

The groom's birth parents wanted something a bit more traditional. So to satisfy Sandra Lee Spridgen (née Wilson) and Omar, the engaged couple invited bridesmaids and groomsmen and agreed on a long red carpet sprinkled with white roses.

If Gabrielle had selfishly followed her heart, the wedding would have been one big sandpit of delight. But she was following her heart by considering the wishes of those she loved. She felt the winner for winning either way.

She giggled at the thought. And her laughter, as habit goes, brought a smile to her one, her only, her treasured beloved.

Seth Penn Spridgen could be a poster child for natural selection, Gabrielle thought (as did most of the co-ed class at Berkeley). Seth had inherited his father's raven hair, dark skin, and love of study. From his mother came his sapphire eyes, fine nose, and *joie de vivre*. He shared a name with the third son of Adam and Eve, the son not involved in Homicide #1. From an early age, it was clear Seth had been blessed with athleticism of rare caliber. He had bicycled across America at age 15, scaled K2 at 18. High school letters in swimming, soccer, badminton, and football. Played quarterback for Cal Berkeley as a freshman and all three years following. Heisman finalist. Track coach for the Regional Special Olympics and Coach of the Year twice running. And a fine shooting guard if your pick-up basketball team ever needed one on the streets of Oakland.

His smile? Countless starry-eyed girls with acoustic guitars waxed poetic over his milky crescent moon. Naturally, he had grown up in a dance studio which made him wicked good on the floor. Orgasmic good. Somehow the gods conspired to give him an operatic voice, not a dramatic tenor but the passionate lyrical timbre of a *tenor de grazia*. Irresistible.

But it was Seth's love of the practical application of polymers and the integration of non-toxic regenerating organic materials that inspired him to create a biodegradable shoe that could be manufactured locally, just about anywhere for pennies with inert, recycled materials. Over 2.3 billion shoes later, *the J-Shoe* resulted in an 81 percent reduction in the reported cases of fatal foot diseases caused primarily by bare footedness. Over 2.6 million human lives saved and 1.3 million foot amputations avoided, according to the most recent study by the National Association of Podiatrists, Committee on the Shoeless, Subcommittee on Solutions.

Seth felt blessed with an abundance of natural abilities. Even more so because he had not, for some strange reason, inherited the capacity to fear. This simple twist of genes had allowed him to accomplish everything, anything he desired.

"Don't ask why, just enjoy," said his beautiful mother, Sandra Lee had taught him in between nursery rhymes.

Seth had figured out at an early age that his mother — his *over-the-top mother* —possessed the rarest of traits: a heart grew late in life. Music, flowers, and sweet perfumes filled the house, and she hosted musicians in passing to spend evenings in her salon of delight. Why not celebrate when presented with the shared surprises friends and strangers might bring? She loved life from inside the sphere of a champagne bubble and what was wrong with that? And the kids growing up? Seth's friends from school remember Sandra Lee as the mom who fed them. She never smoked pot with them nor raised a toast of ale, but she delivered wood-fired pizzas and bags of tortilla chips, Tropicana and pots of Lipton tea, quesadillas and Pop Tarts, ice pops and Band-Aids. She hunted for lost cell phones and gave hugs following spats with parents who didn't seem to understand.

When Sandra Lee felt that her belly was growing flabby and her arms were a melting mess, she returned to the dance floor — not to compete but to lose weight and pass on to others the steps that mimicked life in a way that she didn't fully understand, but didn't care, because it was all a glorious movement, so there! Cha, Cha, Cha.

Her chosen partner? Why naturally, the syncopatic Omar, alas not her lover anymore, but a thrilling dancer, the noble father of her Seth, and as it turns out, an excellent dance teacher. Plus, anyone who had a hand in creating blessed Seth was blessed by the Maker himself. Sandra Lee adored her gay husband at home, deeply, but was it wrong to fantasize about those few slutty months she had spent with Omar and the explosive sex they had? If Omar wasn't now such a royal prince of fidelity, she would be screwing him still (with Harlen's permission, no less). But Omar wouldn't have it, and Sandra Lee had to make do with a gaggle of vibrators and pleasure toys. What she would give for an Arabian Night on his hairy chest.

Omar might not have had the honor of living with his son, but he gave

Seth his life, whatever was left over after raising Gabrielle, the other wedded-to-be here. Omar was glad he had stuck around. Good move, not blowing himself up. He felt sick and awful about what happened to Penny, truly, but as a few American friends explained to him, it's not the bullet that kills, right? It's the trigger finger or the finger of the *triggerer*, if there is such a word, and if there isn't there should be. Second Amendment and all. Now that Omar was a naturalized citizen he got the concept, but it did little to assuage his guilt. And so he did what Allah asked him, truly asked him, and transfigured his pent-up hatred into channels of goodness. What better goodness was there than children? Two he was blessed with, a son and a daughter, a Christian and a Jew, or thereabouts. They didn't define themselves, so why should he? And by extension, why should Omar define himself in the many narrow terms he had once applied to himself. He had forgotten half of them by now, windstorms of yesterday. Better to be a footbridge on the path of humanity than a wall of *narrowtivity*, if there is such as word, and if there isn't there should be.

The residual hatred and resentment? Omar danced it away because hadn't Allah created sweet music? Hadn't he compelled people to dance by placing music in their hearts? Omar could not think of better reasons.

Omar and Seth, birth father and son, found sanctuary in the simple things like walks along the beach, one-on-one basketball games, chess. Omar was Seth's biggest booster and hadn't missed a game except during those three weeks in junior high when Omar finally made his *hajj* to Mecca, praise merciful Allah, with a stop in Tel Aviv for the annual meeting of the International Association of Dance Studios. What a city, Tel Aviv. The falafel shops, amazing!

Seth's adopted father, Harlen, was all right, as well. How many people can claim to have started the first *Gay Evangelical Universal Eclectic Dialectic Church of the Triangular Redemption*. He had attracted 4,567 followers and counting, including a large minority of whom were straight and just dug the chill groove. Harlen had discovered you can help people so much more when they don't hate you, and you don't have to hate them for hating you. Plus, humanity had sort of unknotted its underpants when it came to being gay. And for the bigoted holdouts, Harlen strove to impart the lesson he had learned along the way, that it's futile to attempt to balance power from the outside. Change comes from within. His church had no pews. It was a virtual congregation conducted over videoconferencing, albeit with face-to-face Jubilees held quarterly in the most wonderful of places like Golden Gate Park, Petaluma, and Treasure Island.

Harlen's blessed life included laughing along with Sandra Lee and her revolving entourage. And cooking together, how the couple loved to cook together. Deserts especially, the creamier, the better, in one big tornado of activity that left them all a mess and laughing in a cloud of flour. Friendship is so underrated in marriage.

Of course, there were the occasional salacious weekends with Pierre, a ball bearing salesman from Fresno, who for some reason made Harlen feel, all at the same time, safe and wild.

Harlen stayed with Sandra Lee, not for convenience or appearance, that was long over, but because they enjoyed each other's company (and if it hadn't been for her stubborn courage following the anti-ToE fallout, they would have lost it all). He just wished he could satisfy her as a heterosexual male, not because he had the desire, far from it (and he was long done with that reparative nonsense), but because she deserved to be intimately loved. He gave her a wink and his blessing (not that she needed permission) to go find what she needed. She chose not to. Much to Harlen's surprise it was wasn't about sex for Sandra Lee, it was about love — and the man she loved happened to be unavailable. Unrequited love. Harlen was wiser now than then, when he had married her knowing full well at the time that he was queer. That was a selfish move, very un-Christ-like and Harlen found it hard to forgive himself for the sin of deception.

Harlen was not officiating at today's union. That non-coincidental pleasure belonged to Jimmy Lean, though the title *clergy* was inappropriate as Jimmy disavowed all titles of leadership.

"Those who practice love have neither religion nor caste, neither title nor ownership," Jimmy often said.

Jimmy preferred to be called a *Celebrant*, because his calling called him to celebrate life in a *multo realidade dimensão*, as his Goan guru had taught him. After his sister's death and after marijuana became legal in all 50 states, Jimmy spent two-and-a-half years traveling India and Bangladesh as a Sannyasin, a traveling ascetic, that is, until a rickshaw accident landed him in a nearby ashram with a laughing guru who practiced the ecstatic, not the ascetic. So much more fun.

As a result of his spiritual explorations, Jimmy did not believe in celibacy. He took a wife and a husband, at the same time, and the three shared a profound and sacred intimacy. It wasn't polyamory. And bigamy had such negative connotations. And ménage à trois sounded so sexual. And so Jimmy, Roberto, and Enid described their relationship as *triangulamory,* if there is such as word, and if there isn't, there should be.

Jimmy named his community *The Ancient Secret of the Flower of Life,* and his *inspirations* (not sermons, thank you) explored the wonders of sacred geometry and sound harmonics and the connectivity of all things, despite the continued absence of a theory to prove such a thing. He also became well versed in the teachings of the long-vanished Sethians and their radical reinterpretation of the Genesis and the very nature of God.

Speaking of the Theory of One, the world remained a splintered mess, Gabrielle was sad to report. What else could be expected? It has always been this way and always would be. Way back when, just before she was born, the military dribble with Pakistan almost cost the world a nuclear war, but it didn't. The reduction in tensions was followed by new flare-ups with Venezuela, Turkmenistan, Belize, Norway, a small island in Indonesia soon to be consumed by the tides of global warming, and a non-identified Internet address somewhere on the Indian Ocean with a killer virus that shut down Facebook along with half the governments of the world. A skirmish between Lebanon and Syria prompted bookies to post 7 to 2 odds on full-scale conventional war and 22 to 3 odds on a limited nuclear engagement with more than one million dead. But the underdogs won when saner heads prevailed. Now that the state of Palestine was flourishing, the oddsmakers upped Israel's survivability quotient from 99.997 percent to 99.998 percent.

Vibrations intersecting, vibrations phasing vibrations. Overtones galore. "The world is in constant cacophony, pick your own music and play on," Gabrielle repeatedly proclaimed.

Some people thought it strange that Seth and Gabrielle might choose to wed each other considering their complex and inexplicable confabulation of fathers, mothers, aunts, uncles, faiths, lovers and angels. They conjointly recognized the blessings of the rich array of constellations in their sky. They shared no blood, just occasional vacations in Tahoe and Cabo, a co-ed soccer league until the age of 12, and carpools to the ice rink where briefly they were skating partners until Gabrielle's studies took her one way and Seth's pitching arm another. They often wondered if their parents kept them at a distance to keep them fresh. If so, Seth and Gabrielle were in on the joke. No matter, destiny needs bodies through which to work and bodies gravitate to destiny's call. Such a deal. Gabrielle felt the connection from the time they were children. Seth swears it was earlier. Once, when they were both six, as playmates, they scurried under a blanket tent, and Gabrielle kissed Seth on the cheek.

"You're going to marry me," Gabrielle said.

"I know."

THIRTY-SEVEN

Celebrant Jimmy Lean cleared his throat and tuned a cosmic transmission with his very active third eye. He wore a ceremonial beaded Miwok breastplate over leather leggings to honor the spirit of the original inhabitants of the California coast. Spirituality is a two-way street. The clouds parted slightly, and the wind took a breather. A trio of seagulls swooped in and alighted at the feet of the beloved.

Jimmy spread his arms and with a pregnant pause created a moment of suspense. For the skill of his advanced stagecraft, he tipped his cap to Pastor Harlen, an able teacher by example. All those hours in the church pews paid off now.

Pastor Harlen admired Jimmy Lean's spiritual leadership. The boy, now a man, always had a glimmer in his eye that shined on high. It is through generations that humankind advances. The young can do what the old never dreamed of.

Jimmy Lean winked at Harlen and addressed the gathered.

"Brothers and sisters, gather around and grasp the hand of the local manifestation of universal energy standing next to you."

Seth took Gabrielle's hand and kissed it. Shivana and Omar intertwined fingers. Ethan and Naomi stood shoulder to shoulder. Sandra Lee and Harlen threw arms around each other and tapped toes in time.

"Take a moment to allow the glow of Shakti male and female energy bathe your lower chakras, your inner organs. Tickle your pancreas. Love your liver."

Seth and Gabrielle closed their eyes and smiled to their internal organs, spreading warmth from thyroid to lungs, kidney to colon.

"Don't forget to breathe. Deep into your solar plexus. Fill your vessel with life-sustaining oxygen. Let the life force reach and revive every cell and fiber within you, children of the Good Name."

Friends of Seth and Gabrielle from school and work, from the neighborhood and the virtual worlds, collectively shared a rib-expanding inhalation of the cool sea air sweetened with a tinge of salt.

"Now let's all of us locate the one thousand petals emanating from our Sahasrara chakra atop the crowns of our heads, everyone. Immerse yourself in the infinite delight. Free yourself from yourself."

Shivana's mother, who had miraculously survived old age despite an army of ailments, had flown all the way from the deserts of Iran to be here on this momentous day, moved by intuition and the inspiration of a first-class plane ticket with a single stop in London. She did not understand English but felt little need to. Witnessing the happiness on the faces of her daughter and granddaughter were language enough.

Ethan squirmed because he had to pee so badly, a public urge he hadn't felt in quite some time. Joy will do that to a man. And then, at that very moment, He penetrated the E_8 enigma. That's right, after 27 years, the solution arrived to him on the crest of an ocean wave crashing with timpani persuasion during this magnificent display of betrothal. He got it!

Why now? Who could say? But without question, Ethan was sure he had received the answer delivered in a packet of pure contentment. He saw the Kabbalistic Sefirot twirling within the E_8 geometric pattern, fitting effortlessly, like a key opening the door of life. Joy pays so many dividends. No natural gas needed!

A mystical symbol from old partnering with a geometric pattern of modern complexity illuminating an anti-anti-correction to Stephen Snodgrass's anti-correction. How perfect. Ethan made a mental note to confirm with Snodgrass, the South African odds maker who had debunked the original ToE, but then Ethan remembered Snodgrass had committed suicide with a gunshot to the brain, the surest way to kill oneself. A predictable method for an oddsmaker.

Nevertheless, Ethan felt fully confident he could now present an amended ToE equation and thereby prove to the world (truly this time) the basis for a mathematically sound, buttoned-up tight, and complete Theory of Everything.

His urge to urinate instantly vanished. The Theory of Everything. Ethan couldn't believe the epiphany. What a stroke of luck.

Ethan gazed upon his daughter, a radiant beauty in her wedding sari. How proud he was of her. He looked at his soon-to-be son-in-law, a shining avatar of goodness. He wondered whether it might be best to forget the ToE revelation altogether, ignore it, return it to its mysterious source from whence it came because, as he saw it, the world was pretty much perfect as it is.

Not a chance.

Jimmy Lean raised his palms upward.

"Now everyone, close your eyes, and on the count of three, shoot out a golden thread at warp speed through your top chakra and reconnect with the non-local universal intelligence as you know it — because you have been connected to the source since before you were born and before then, too. We just forget sometimes. Ready? One. Two. Three!"

The wedding guests radiated golden threads at warp speed, and everyone felt warmer.

"Yeah, that's it! Now we are a bundle of vibrational mass approaching a photon in strength. Now we are one big energy field traveling on a sleeper wave of love. Now we are all threading the needle of God. Trippy, eh?"

The 200-odd folks shouted with spontaneous praise.

To be precise, 206 guests according to Shivana's count. Nerves made her count. How could she not count— her daughter was getting married!

Jimmy Lean loved moments like these, but then again he loved most moments. "Now let's raise our hands and shower these two lovers with our heart-generated goodwill."

Sandra Lee Spridgen and Shivana Farooq, sisters in some inexplicable way, blended tears on cheeks pressed together, warmth to warmth.

Pastor Harlen Spridgen and Naomi Weiner-Gluckstein, enemies long ago, stared into the streams of love that were each other's melting eyes.

Omar knelt on the carpet of sand, weeping with joy.

Emmett Jessup rested his right hand on the accordion's keys and his left hand on its buttons to form a G major chord because his heart already quivered with the triad's positive brilliance.

Gabrielle giggled with elation. Seth puffed his chest like Vishnu boasting another vanquished enemy of earthly harmony.

The lovers drew close under the sheltering chuppah constructed with the Shabbat tablecloth of Ethan's grandmother. Their bare feet faced each other's on the prayer carpet of Omar's grandfather. Between them, nothing but a pool of unlimited potential.

Celebrant Jimmy Lean faced the two columns of light.

"Gabrielle and Seth, what a day. What a blessed day. How blessed are we to share in it. How blessed do I feel to be the one chosen to celebrate this confluence of two remarkable rivers of God. How blessed are you, Seth and Gabrielle, to stand beneath this chuppah of grace on a carpet of magic at the threshold of a combined life. Like the crashing waves yonder, remember to remain unique, but never forget — you arise from the ocean of the Friend. And Seth, do you have a message for your bride."

Seth, from the inscription carved on his heart, began. "I give you two rings, Gabrielle. The first to symbolize our devotion to each other and the second ring to symbolize our devotion to the world. With these two rings, I promise all my heart, all my soul, and all my devotion to you and the world, because in Gandhi's words *he who wants to be friends with God must remain alone or make the whole world his friend.* And I love you much too much to be alone, so I chose to befriend the whole world and all who dwell in it."

Seth slipped one ring onto Gabrielle's slender finger, and then he slipped on the other.

Gabrielle clasped Seth's hand.

"Seth, it's funny to say, but I feel like I've loved you since before time and before space. In this life, this incarnation, you've made me so happy and taught me so much, how can I thank you? I will try to return the blessing by reflecting the light of your love back to you and to all those I meet, friend and stranger equally. I will extend the example of your goodness wherever I go. I will treat each and every sentient being as a manifestation of you. In the words of Rumi, *in your light, I learn how to love. In your beauty, how to make poems. You dance inside my chest where no one sees you, but sometimes I do, and that sight becomes the Art.* I, as well, give you two rings, one to circle our union and the second to confirm our union with every living being from here to eternity. For who am I to share my love with you and you only? It is because of you, my love that I desire all and nothing. My only prayer is that my capacity to love will grow every single day."

Jimmy Lean cupped the hands of the two beautiful beloved in his.

"With the ocean and earth as my witness, along with all who are gathered here — I pronounce you Seth Spridgen and Gabrielle Farooq, partners in matrimony. The glass, please?"

Emmett Jessup placed a wine glass wrapped in a napkin underneath Seth's foot.

"Together?" whispered Gabrielle.

"Together," affirmed Seth.

Gabrielle placed her foot on top of Seth's. On a silent count of three, they shattered the glass on the floor.

"May the marriage last as long as the glass remains broken."

"Mazel Tov!" cried the voices. "Mubarak!" "Congratulations!"

"So kiss!" said Jimmy.

Seth moved to sweep up his bride, but Gabrielle was faster and planted a big fat lusty smooch on Seth's succulent lips. They embraced with such a passion that everyone in the crowd felt envious of not having someone envelop them so.

Seth and Gabrielle skipped down the aisle, showered with birdseed and vibrations of love. They twirled and leapt, fired up the sky with their happiness, and returned the Friend's love like it was the easiest thing to do.

That's when it hit Gabrielle.

She noticed first her quickening breath. Her temperature suddenly rose a degree or three. Hormones swept over her, an ocean of milk. Deep within her abdomen, she sensed the development on the right side, she was sure. A tiny tickle, an infinitesimal pinch. A woman in tune knows these things.

Gabrielle kicked up her heels, brightened her black eyes. She squeezed Seth's hand. Hard.

And when Seth saw her cheeky radiance. He got the message loud and clear. How could he not? New life is that exciting. He kissed Gabrielle's nose in delight.

Gabrielle and Seth scampered to the ocean's edge to touch the salt water for the first time as a couple unified in purpose, emissaries of divine light.

They did not stop to wonder what bright delight might be ticking inside her. No mystery here. They long ago had learned to divine the cues of a universe enthusiastic to share its intentions. They understood that the circuit was to be completed, the loop closed, the time had come. The Blessed One would be arriving in mere months on a chariot of pure love, destined to change the world forever.

ABOUT THE AUTHOR

NOTE FROM THE AUTHOR

Word-of-mouth is crucial for any author to succeed. If you enjoyed *Cosmic Fever*, please leave a review online—anywhere you are able. Even if it's just a sentence or two. It would make all the difference and would be very much appreciated.

Thanks!
Eric

ABOUT THE AUTHOR

Eric J. Adams is an award-winning novelist, screenwriter and film producer. He's the author of the mystery/thriller novels "Birdland" (available on Amazon) and "Plot Twist." Alongside executive producer Harold Ramis, Eric co-wrote and produced the feature film "Archie's Final Project," a Crystal Bear winner at the Berlin International Film Festival. His film "Supremacy" stars Academy Award winner Mahershala Ali and Danny Glover. Eric lives in Northern California and teaches the art of writing worldwide.

Thank you so much for reading one of our **Dark Humor** novels.

If you enjoyed our book, please check out our
recommended title for your next great read!

Managed Care by Joe Barrett

"Witty, occasionally crass, and an unqualified delight." *–KIRKUS REVIEWS*